INTRIGUE

Seek thrills. Solve crimes. Justice served.

Big Sky Deception
B.J. Daniels

Whispering Winds Widows
Debra Webb

MILLS & BOON

BIG SKY DECEPTION
© 2024 by Barbara Heinlen
Philippine Copyright 2024
Australian Copyright 2024
New Zealand Copyright 2024

First Published 2024
First Australian Paperback Edition 2024
ISBN 978 1 038 90553 6

WHISPERING WIND WIDOWS
© 2024 by Debra Webb
Philippine Copyright 2024
Australian Copyright 2024
New Zealand Copyright 2024

First Published 2024
First Australian Paperback Edition 2024
ISBN 978 1 038 90553 6

MIX
Paper | Supporting
responsible forestry
FSC® C001695

Published by
Harlequin Mills & Boon
An imprint of Harlequin Enterprises (Australia) Pty Limited
(ABN 47 001 180 918), a subsidiary of HarperCollins
Publishers Australia Pty Limited
(ABN 36 009 913 517)
Level 19, 201 Elizabeth Street
SYDNEY NSW 2000 AUSTRALIA

Cover art used by arrangement with Harlequin Books S.A.. All rights reserved.

Printed and bound in Australia by McPherson's Printing Group

Big Sky Deception

B.J. Daniels

MILLS & BOON

B.J. Daniels is a *New York Times* and *USA TODAY* bestselling author. She wrote her first book after a career as an award-winning newspaper journalist and author of thirty-seven published short stories. She lives in Montana with her husband, Parker, and three springer spaniels. When not writing, she quilts, boats and plays tennis. Contact her at bjdaniels.com, on Facebook or on Twitter @bjdanielsauthor.

Visit the Author Profile page
at millsandboon.com.au.

DEDICATION

This book is dedicated to Barb Otteson—a wonderful neighbour and talented quilter friend who has brightened so many of my days! For years, we hardly saw each other in the neighbourhood because I was blocks away at my office writing books. So glad for the mini quilt retreats where we have gotten to know each other and shared stories—and always laughter.
This one is for you, neighbour!

CAST OF CHARACTERS

Molly Lockhart—She grew up believing her father preferred his dummy over her. On news of her father's murder, she went to Fortune Creek, Montana, to find Rowdy and destroy the dummy.

Sheriff Brandt Parker—The young law officer thought all he had was a murder to solve—and a ventriloquist's dummy to find. But it turned out that he and Molly had another mystery to solve—while trying not to fall in love.

Clay Wheaton—What was the ventriloquist doing lying murdered in a small-town Montana hotel? And why were so many people interested in his missing dummy, Rowdy the Rodeo Cowboy?

Georgia Eden—The insurance saleswoman has her own reasons for wanting Rowdy the Rodeo Cowboy found.

Jessica Woods—The parapsychologist/ghost hunter wants to check out the claim that Rowdy the Rodeo Cowboy was heard singing—after his ventriloquist was murdered.

Cecil Crandell—He did what he felt was best for his family—including sending away his son all those years ago.

Irma Crandell—Her regret—along with her anger—have been building for years. She can never forget what happened to her son, Seth—nor can she keep on pretending that she's forgiven.

Chapter One

Clay Wheaton flinched as he heard the heavy tread of footfalls ascending the fire escape stairs of the old Fortune Creek Hotel. His visitor moved slowly, purposefully, the climb to the fourth and top floor sounding like a death march.

His killer was coming.

He had no idea who he would come face-to-face with when he opened the door in a few minutes. But this had been a long time coming. Though it wasn't something a man looked forward to even at his advanced age.

He glanced over at Rowdy lying lifeless on the bed where he'd left him earlier. The sight of his lifelong companion nearly broke his heart. He rose and went to him, his hand moving almost of its own accord to slip into the back under the Western outfit for the controls.

Instantly, Rowdy came to life. His animated eyes flew open, his head turned, his mouth gaping as he looked around. "We could make a run for it," Rowdy said in the cowboy voice it had taken years to perfect. "It wouldn't be the first time we've had to vamoose. You do the running part. I'll do the singing part."

The dummy broke into an old Western classic and quickly stopped. "Or maybe not," Clay said as the lumbering footfalls ended at the top of the stairs and the exit door creaked open.

"Sorry, my old friend," Clay said in his own voice. "You need to go into your case. You don't want to see this."

"No," Rowdy cried. "We go down together like an old horse who can't quite make it home in a blizzard with his faithful rider. This can't be the end of the trail for us."

The footsteps stopped outside his hotel room door, followed swiftly by a single knock. "Sorry," Clay whispered, his voice breaking as he removed his hand, folded the dummy in half and lowered him gently into the special case with Rowdy's name and brand on it.

Rowdy the Rodeo Cowboy. The two of them had traveled the world, singing and joking, and sharing years and years together. Rowdy had become his best friend, his entire life after leaving too many burning bridges behind them. "Sorry, old friend," he whispered unable to look into Rowdy's carved wooden face, the paint faded, but the eyes still bright and lifelike. He closed the case with trembling fingers.

This knock was much louder. He heard the door handle rattle. He'd been running for years, but now his reckoning was at hand. He pushed the case under the bed, straightened the bed cover over it and went to open the door.

Behind him he would have sworn he heard Rowdy moving in his case as if trying to get out, as if trying to save him. Old hotels and the noises they made? Or just his imagination?

Too late for regrets, he opened the door to his killer.

"MOLLY LOCKHART?" The voice on the phone was male, ringing with authority.

"Yes?" she said distractedly as she pulled her keyboard toward her, unconsciously lining it up with the edge of her desk as she continued to type. She had a report due before the meeting today at Henson and Powers, the financial institution where she worked as an analyst. She wouldn't have taken the call, but her assistant had said the caller was a lawman, the matter urgent, and had put it through.

"My name's Sheriff Brandt Parker from Fortune Creek, Montana. I found your name as the person to call. Do you know Clay Wheaton?"

Her fingers froze over the keys. "I'm sorry, what did you say? Just the last part please." She really didn't have time for this—whatever it was.

"Your name was found in the man's hotel room as the person to call."

"The person to call about what?"

The sheriff cleared his throat. "Do you know Clay Wheaton?"

"Yes." She said it with just enough vacillation that she heard the lawman cough. "He's my...father."

"Oh, I'm so sorry. I'm afraid I have bad news. Mr. Wheaton is dead." Another pause, then, "He's been murdered."

"Murdered?" she repeated. She'd known that she'd be getting a call one day that he had died. Given her father's age it was inevitable. He was close to sixty-five. But *murdered*? She couldn't imagine why anyone would want to murder him unless they'd seen his act.

"I hate to give you this kind of news over the phone," the sheriff said. "Is there someone there with you?"

"I'm fine, Sheriff," she said, realizing it was true. Her father had made his choice years ago when he'd left her and her mother to travel the world with—quite literally—a dummy. There was only one thing she wanted to know. "Where is Rowdy?"

The lawman sounded taken aback. "I beg your pardon?"

"My father's dummy. You do know Clay Wheaton is... was a ventriloquist, right?"

"Yes, his dummy. It wasn't found in his hotel room. I'm afraid it's missing."

"Missing?" She sighed heavily. "What did you say your name was again?"

"Sheriff Brandt Parker."

"And you are where?"

"Fortune Creek, Montana. I'm going to need to know who else I should notify."

"There is no one else. Just find Rowdy. I'm on my way there."

BRANDT HUNG UP and looked at the dispatcher. The sixty-something Helen Graves was looking at him, one eyebrow tilted at the ceiling in question. "Okay," he said. "That was the strangest reaction I've ever had when telling someone that their father's been murdered."

"Maybe she's in shock."

"I don't think so. She wants me to find the dummy—not the killer—but the *dummy*."

"Why?"

"I have no idea, but she's on her way here. I'll try the other number Clay Wheaton left." The deceased had left only two names and numbers on hotel stationery atop the bureau next to his bed with a note that said, *In case of emergency.* He put through the call, which turned out to be an insurance agency. "I'm calling for Georgia Eden."

"I'll connect you to the claims department."

"Georgia Eden," a young woman answered cheerfully with a slight southern accent.

Brandt introduced himself. "I'm calling on behalf of Clay Wheaton."

"What does he want now?" she asked impatiently.

"Are you a relative of his?"

"Good heavens, no. He's my client. What is this about? You said you're a sheriff? Is he in some kind of trouble?"

"He was murdered."

"Murdered?" He heard her sit up in her squeaky chair, her tone suddenly worried. "Where's Rowdy?"

What was it with this dummy? "I...don't know."

"Rowdy would have been with him. Clay never let him out of his sight. He took Rowdy everywhere with him. I doubt he went to the toilet without him. Are you telling me Rowdy is missing?"

Brandt ran a hand down over his face. He had to ask. "What is it with this dummy?"

"I beg your pardon?"

"I thought you might be more interested in your client's murder than his...doll."

Her words came out like thrown bricks. "That...*doll* as you call it, is insured for a very large amount of money."

"You're kidding."

"I would not kid about something like that since I'm the one who wrote the policy," Georgia said. "Where are you calling from?" He told her. "This could cost me more than my job if Rowdy isn't found. I'll be on the next plane."

"We don't have an airport," he said quickly.

She groaned. "Where is Fortune Creek, Montana?"

"In the middle of nowhere, actually at the end of a road in the mountains at the most northwest corner of the state," he said. "The closest airport is Kalispell. You'd have to rent a car from there."

"Great."

"If there is anything else I can do—"

"Just find that dummy."

"You mean that doll."

"Yes," she said sarcastically. "Find Rowdy, *please*. Otherwise…I'm dead."

Brandt hung up, shaking his head as he stood and reached for his Stetson. "Helen, if anyone comes looking for me, I'll be over at the hotel looking for a ventriloquist's dummy." She frowned in confusion. "Apparently, that's all anyone cares about. Meanwhile, I have a murder to solve."

As he headed out the door for the walk across the street to the hotel, he couldn't help being disturbed by the reactions he'd gotten to Clay Wheaton's death. He thought about the note the dead man had left and the only two numbers on it.

Had he suspected he might be murdered? Or traveling alone—except for his dummy—had he always left such a note just in case? After all, at sixty-two, he was no spring chicken, his grandmother would have said.

Whatever the victim's thinking, how was it that both women had cared more about the dummy than the man behind it?

Maybe worse, both women were headed this way.

Chapter Two

The sheriff walked up the steps of the historic Fortune Creek Hotel onto the full-length porch across the front. It was a beautiful late March day in Montana. But while spring-like and sunny today, it would change in a heartbeat and start snowing again. He took in the all-wood edifice that had been built in the 1930s by a wealthy easterner who'd wanted a hunting lodge for his many friends. Since then, it had changed little structurally. A tall rather skinny building, it rose to four floors with only four large rooms per floor.

While the building had sat empty for a few years after changing owners several times, a local man had bought it and was now remodeling the rooms, starting on the fourth floor. Ash Hammond was determined to keep it open year-round—no easy feat in a town as small as Fortune Creek.

"'Morning, Ash," Brandt said as he pushed through the large front door. The former football star nodded from behind the reception desk. "Sorry about the inconvenience."

Ash, his own age of thirty-four, waved off the apology. "Just another day in small-town Montana." A good-looking dark-haired cowboy, Ash had left after high school to play college football as a quarterback at the University of Montana. He'd gone on to the NFL, playing for a few years before returning to town to buy the hotel. No one had been more surprised by that than Brandt who'd rodeoed at Montana State University before going into law enforcement.

Brandt had returned home after working in several large cities as a cop. He'd quickly tired of the rat race, missing the peace and quiet of Fortune Creek. He figured Ash had felt the same way. Leaving had made sense at the time. Coming back had made more sense. He'd come home to escape it all, but murder seemed to be the one thing he hadn't been able to get away from.

"Any idea who did it?" Ash asked quietly even though the lobby was empty.

The sheriff shook his head. Murder here was as rare as hen's teeth, which was another of his grandmother's sayings. "Anything you can tell me about Mr. Wheaton?"

"He checked in three days go, paying in cash for a week." Ash shrugged. "Only thing odd was the doll he had sitting on his arm. It talked more than he did."

"So you met Rowdy?"

"Was that its name? Kitty said when she went up to clean his room, she'd heard two voices inside, but hadn't seen another person when she'd knocked and Wheaton had opened his door. Looked him up on the internet this morning. Seems he used to be a pretty famous ventriloquist. Played Vegas."

"So what was he doing in Fortune Creek?"

Again Ash shrugged.

Brandt thought of the two women he'd notified of the death earlier by phone. "Do you know what he did the three days he was here?" The sheriff had heard everyone in town talking about the man and his dummy, but he'd never seen the guy until he'd died.

"He didn't go out much," Ash was saying. "Hardly left his room. Didn't let Kitty in to clean it. I hardly ever saw him, but the few times I did he always had the dummy with him. Alice said he came down to the café a couple of times. He usually had his meals delivered. She said he had the dummy with him, and the dummy did his ordering for him. She thought he couldn't talk."

Brandt shook his head. "But the dummy definitely wasn't around when you found his body."

Ash shook his head. "I only stepped into the room to check for vitals, then I called you. I left the room, closed the door and didn't leave until you arrived, so no one could have taken it when I was there. Think the killer took it with him?"

"Looks that way. Did anyone visit him during those three days?"

"Not that I know of," Ash said. "At least they didn't come through the lobby. But they could have used the fire escape exit."

"Isn't that kept locked?"

"It's exit only, but when I came up to check Wheaton, I saw that someone had propped the door open with a book."

"A book?" the sheriff asked in surprise.

"An old paperback. *East of Eden*. Read that in school, don't you remember?"

Brandt ignored the question and asked one of his own. "Did you remove the book?"

Ash shook his head. "Like I said, I opened Clay Wheaton's door, stepped in to check on him and called you. When I looked at the exit door again while I was waiting for you, it was closed and the book was gone."

"So it's possible the killer was still in the hotel and exited when you were busy in Wheaton's room," he said. Had the killer brought the book to prop the door open, which would indicate the killer had used the fire escape before? Brandt thought of the books on the shelves down the hall from Clay

Wheaton's room. "Do you know if the book could have come from the fourth-floor lounge area bookcase?"

"Could be. Guests are encouraged to take a book and leave a book, so I never know what's there."

The sheriff frowned in thought for a moment. If the book had come from down the hall, then the killer hadn't used it to prop the door open—his accomplice had. "Who are your other guests?" He'd seen a sedan parked out front. Nothing went unnoticed in Fortune Creek.

"An older couple. Toby and Irene Thompson from North Carolina."

He made a mental note to ask them about the book, before returning his questioning to the dummy. "The killer could have taken the puppet or hidden it in the hotel planning to come back for it. What time does Kitty come in to clean the rooms?"

"Should be along soon. You want her to help look?"

Brandt nodded. "For the dummy and the book. Tell her not to touch either if she finds them."

"She just has 402 to clean until you release 401 once your investigation is done, so I'll tell her." Fortune Creek didn't get a lot of tourists except in the summer. Things would pick up come Memorial Day then die off again after Labor Day—except when ranch hands came into town to kick up their boots. Often they'd stay at the hotel until they sobered up. Unfortunately, what happened in Fortune Creek, seldom stayed in Fortune Creek.

Brandt thanked his friend and headed up the stairs. He found his deputy interviewing the only other hotel guests from last night—the elderly couple who'd been in the room closest to Clay Wheaton's.

"Here's the sheriff now," Deputy Jaden Montgomery said and motioned Brandt over. "These people have some information for you, Sheriff. They were in the room next to the exit and just across from Wheaton's."

"Why don't we go down the hall to the lounge," the sheriff suggested. The four rooms were divided by a small sitting area. Once they were all seated in the alcove, deep in the overstuffed chairs, he pulled out his notebook and pen and took down their names.

Toby and Irene Thompson were a cherub-cute couple, chubby pink cheeked, bright eyed and quite animated. They wore matching T-shirts. His read, She's My Sweet Potato and hers, I Yam.

"You saw something last night?" the sheriff asked hoping they did have some information that would help with the case.

"Not saw," said Toby. *"Heard."*

Irene nodded, eyes widening.

Toby continued, with Irene adding her two cents after him, giving Brandt the impression that they always finished each other's sentences. "We heard a loud thud."

"Like a body hitting the floor."

"Then nothing."

"We'd gone to bed," Irene said.

"I was already asleep. Doesn't take much to knock me out."

"I was reading, just dozing off when I heard singing." She shivered and hugged herself.

"Irene woke me up."

"The singing was chilling, so sad sounding."

"Melancholy," Toby agreed.

"Then this morning we found out that he'd been…" She lowered her voice. *"A ventriloquist."*

"It finally made sense, the other sounds we'd heard like there were two people over there in that room."

"Which was odd because we knew there was only an elderly gentleman," she said.

Brandt chuckled to himself—the couple, who he suspected were about the same age or older than Wheaton, referring to the deceased as an elderly gentleman. *Do we ever see ourselves as we really are?* he wondered. Doubtful, he thought and reined in his thoughts.

Toby was saying, "We'd seen him a couple of times."

"Only when the housekeeper knocked on his door," she said, nodding.

"Did you see anyone go into his room other than the housekeeper?" the sheriff asked.

"He never let her in, just took his towels and thanked her," Irene said. "Seemed like a nice enough man."

"Did you hear anyone on the fire escape last night?"

Toby shook his head.

"He uses a CPAP to prevent snoring so wouldn't have heard anything. But I heard someone coming up the stairs and then a knock at the ventriloquist's door. The door opened— the person went in. But, before you ask, I didn't see any of the men who came up the fire escape stairs."

"There were more than one? Two?" She nodded, but didn't look sure. "There could have been three people."

Brandt rubbed his neck, wondering if he should take any of this seriously. "You could tell by the sound of their footfalls on the metal fire escape they were male? How can you be sure none were female?"

Irene again didn't look quite as sure now. "I heard one person coming up the stairs. The second person was following the first but not closely. I'd say the first was definitely a male, heavy footfalls. The second…" She considered. "Maybe a male who was sneaking up, same when he left much later after the first one. Either he came back or someone else did, both quietly. That exit door makes a kind of swishing sound when anyone enters or leaves."

"Wait," the sheriff said. "Let me get this straight. You heard two people for sure? Close to the same time? Like they were together? But possibly a third?" She nodded. He thought of the book still propping the door open when Ash had come up to check on Clay Wheaton. "Did you hear the door close both times?" She shook her head. "The last time someone left by way of the fire escape stairs, was it before the hotel owner came up to check on Mr. Wheaton or after?"

"After," Irene said empathically.

That could explain why the book was in the door when Ash came upstairs, but gone after he found Clay Wheaton dead. "Did either of you use the fire escape stairs?" They both shook their heads in unison. "Did you ever see a book that was used to keep the exit door from closing and locking from the outside?" Another no.

"Irene probably didn't hear the door close behind the last one because of the dummy singing," Toby suggested.

She shook her head. "The singing was much later after the thud we heard and after I heard the first person leave by way of the fire exit. I heard the second one go, and then I heard someone come up the stairs. Then the singing started. I'm not sure I heard the person leave after that."

Brandt's head had begun to ache as he tried to make sense of what the woman might—or might not—have heard. Flawed recall was a problem.

Irene heard one individual come up the fire escape, then another one, quieter. Both went back down the same way, the second one later than the first. Then who had come back up and why? Did that mean that one of the suspects had been hiding in the hotel? Had that person used the book to prop open the exit door so the killer could enter? But who had removed it while the deputy was in Clay Wheaton's room?

The sheriff had too many questions and few answers at this point. He had to nail down times, if possible. "Okay, about what time did you hear the thud?"

"Nine twenty-one."

He glanced up from his notebook. "How can you be that precise, Mr. Thompson?"

"Toby, please. I set the alarm on my phone and noticed the time."

"He is very precise," Irene said.

"I was an engineer."

"He built bridges, had to be precise. I quilt so I also have to be precise."

"Okay, what time did the singing start?" Brandt asked, fighting to keep a straight face since these two were a kick.

"Much later." Irene made a face.

"Nine fifty-two," Toby said. "I looked at my watch."

Brandt looked at Irene. "That was after the two of the visitors had left by way of the fire escape stairs? That's when the singing began?"

She nodded. "It was…haunting. Almost childlike."

"We knew we were never going to get any sleep with that singing."

"So Toby, you called down to the desk," Brandt said. That's when Ash had gone up to Clay Wheaton's room and found the man dead. "You're sure of the time?"

They both nodded, their expressions emphatic.

"Did you hear anyone come or go from the room during that time?" he asked.

"After the thud," Irene said. "Nothing until the singing started."

"Which is why we thought he was all right," Toby said.

"Neither of you went into Mr. Wheaton's room?" he asked. Both shook their heads. "Did either of you see his dummy, the doll he used for his act?" More adamant shakes of the heads.

Ash had stayed outside Wheaton's room until Brandt arrived with the coroner so no one had entered or left the room. "I appreciate your time and your help," he told the two witnesses, although he had no idea what to make of what they'd told him. They appeared to be very credible. So how did he explain what they'd thought they'd heard?

"Do you have the time of death?" Toby asked.

"Not yet." But Clay Wheaton had been wearing a smart watch. When he'd hit the floor, at 9:21 p.m., the watch had asked if he'd fallen. He hadn't responded. The watch, programmed to call for help, did so after asking a second time if he was okay and getting no answer. The 911 operator had called Brandt at 9:25 p.m. to notify him.

He'd then called the hotel, talked to Ash, who called upstairs at 9:30 p.m. A man answered the phone. Ash asked if everything was all right. The male guest indicated it was. Ash had said it had sounded as if the elderly male guest had been sleeping because his voice was different. It wasn't until he'd gotten the call from Toby Thompson about the singing disturbing their sleep that he went up to the room and found Clay Wheaton dead.

The times checked out. So how was it possible the couple had heard the dummy start singing at 9:52 p.m.—twenty-two minutes *after* the ventriloquist died? Someone had answered the phone in Clay Wheaton's room at 9:30 p.m. but it couldn't have been him. The singing started at 9:52 p.m. Brandt didn't have an answer for that.

He started to close his notebook when Toby said, "I went online this morning."

"After hearing that the gentleman was a ventriloquist," Irene said.

"We watched one of his shows." They both fell silent for a moment.

"It was the doll singing that we heard," Irene whispered and hugged herself.

"No doubt about it," Toby said.

"After he died, his puppet sang as if…in mourning." Irene's eyes filled.

"I'm sure there is a logical explanation," the sheriff said. The Thompsons seemed to be anxiously waiting for him to supply it. He closed his notebook. "The investigation into his death is only just beginning."

"Murder," Irene said.

"Yes," Brandt said and looked to where his deputy was standing, looking sheepish. There was no keeping a lid on any of this. The murder was more interesting because of what the victim did for a living. Add what these two swore they'd heard… "Thank you for your time. I hope this didn't spoil your visit here in Fortune Creek."

As he walked back down the hall, he noticed that the Thompsons' bags were packed. He wondered if they'd cut their visit short because of the murder. He hoped not. Ash could use all the guests he could get if he hoped to keep the hotel doors open.

Deputy Jaden Montgomery watched the sheriff coming down the hall toward him, wondering what Brandt had made of the old couple's story. It had given him chills. Then again everything about this old hotel did that to him—not that he was about to admit it to Brandt.

But the case? He was fascinated by all of it. Murder was so rare here that when he'd become a deputy, he'd never thought he'd get a chance to be part of this kind of investigation. Add in a ventriloquist and a missing dummy; he couldn't have been more intrigued.

As they ducked under the crime scene tape and closed the door of room 401 behind them, the sheriff looked around the room and asked, "Still no sign of the dummy?"

Jaden shook his head. "I thoroughly searched the room after the crime techs out of Kalispell gave me the all-clear." The sheriff had called for a state forensics team last night. The techs had arrived before the sun came up. "The dummy's not here. Thought it might be in the man's suitcase, but I only found clothing."

There was a large stain on the carpet near the bed and a battered valise by the door, but otherwise, the room looked unoccupied. He watched the sheriff pull on gloves and check the closet and bureau drawers. Empty, just as Jaden had found. Clay Wheaton must have either packed to leave the next morning or he'd never unpacked.

The sheriff swore under his breath. "Unless the killer took the time to hide the dummy in the hotel..." That seemed improbable given what the Thompsons had told them. They would have heard the person going up and down the hall— let alone if they had used the elevator. It was more probable that the killer took the dummy with him when he left by way of the fire escape stairs.

"Could have been a woman," Jaden said. "Shot the way he was, a woman could have pulled the trigger. Would have had to have had a suppressor on the gun though. Don't see a lot of those."

The sheriff looked at him and smiled. "Seems you've given this some thought." He nodded. "Nothing looks out of place to you?"

"You bagged the note the man had left with the two names

and numbers he'd left to call. But the pen he'd used and the rest of the hotel stationery are missing and I can't find Wheaton's keys for his pickup parked out back either—not counting the missing dummy."

"You're sure the crime techs didn't find them?"

"They wondered about the missing objects as well."

The sheriff's cell phone rang. Jaden stepped away, but he'd overheard the gist of the conversation right up to the curse that left Brandt's lips as he hung up. He guessed the news hadn't been good.

"We've got time of death," Brandt said.

Jaden had arrived at the crime scene right behind Brandt. He'd seen the body. He didn't need the coroner to tell him that the deceased had died brutally and no doubt quickly. A bullet to the back of the skull and into the brain would do that.

"9:21 p.m.," the sheriff said and shook his head. "Clay Wheaton had been unresponsive at 9:21 p.m. Coroner said he would have died instantly because of the angle of the gunshot. Yet someone answered the phone at 9:30 p.m. in this room and it wasn't Clay Wheaton."

Jaden glanced around the room. "Had to be the killer, but why stay so long in the room?" He felt Brandt's gaze on him. "Unless the killer was looking for the dummy and then the dummy started singing and he didn't know how to shut it up." He could feel the sheriff's gaze on him. "Clay Wheaton was the one who threw his voice *not* the dummy."

Jaden had to grin. "Then how is it possible that the couple across the hall heard the dummy singing after Clay was dead?"

The sheriff groaned. "Don't get me started."

"If the killer was also a ventriloquist, he would know how to throw his voice. Also the couple across the hallway swore it was Rowdy's voice they heard."

"The dummy wasn't singing after Wheaton died." The sheriff said it in a way that meant it was the last he wanted to hear anything different.

Jaden nodded. "Not singing."

Brandt gave him a warning look. "I don't want this foolhardy theory getting spread around."

"My lips are sealed."

"Really? So how did the Thompsons know it was a murder?"

"They're a smart couple," Jaden said. "Crime techs combing the room, the yellow tape on the door—I think they figured it out."

The sheriff looked contrite. "Sorry. You're right. I had hoped to keep the lid on this as long as possible."

"You forget where we live? In this part of Montana where nothing happens of much interest, even the birth of a calf is news." It wasn't quite that bad. But Fortune Creek was so small that little went unnoticed. Didn't help that everyone knew everyone else's business.

"The killer must have been looking for the dummy and that's why he was in the room so long," Brandt said. "Period."

Jaden didn't dare look at the sheriff, let alone mention the singing again. "Right. In theory, we find Rowdy, we find the killer."

"Maybe," Brandt said. "Also keep your eye out for an old paperback copy of *East of Eden*. It might have been discarded somewhere on the grounds. It was used to prop the door open on this floor's fire escape exit. Bag it for prints if you find it. Also, there's a couple of women on their way to Fortune Creek who are very interested in Rowdy's whereabouts. It won't take much to turn this case into a rodeo if we haven't found that dummy before they get here."

"I just heard that Kitty is on her way," the deputy said checking his phone.

"Good. Get her to help you search this hotel for that damned doll and if you discover that paperback just lying around—"

"Right, don't touch it. Bag it as possible evidence." Jaden smiled.

"I'm going to check Wheaton's pickup," Brandt said. "Strange his keys are also missing, but the pickup is still out there. The coroner said they weren't with the body either."

Had the killer taken them, and then changed his mind about taking the truck? Or had he wanted something from inside the vehicle? Or maybe to leave something in the pickup?

"Hopefully Rowdy's in the truck," Jaden suggested. "You need me to open it for you? I've got my slim jim in my rig."

"No, you stay here and help Kitty look for Rowdy," the sheriff said. "I can get into the pickup."

Chapter Three

Molly couldn't believe it took this long to rent a car—let alone how many hours she'd already been traveling since getting the news about her father. She'd taken the last flight out of New York City and after two stops, had spent a restless short night in an airport hotel in Kalispell. This morning she'd taken an Uber to the car rental agency since being informed of the distance she still had to travel. Now all she had to do was get the car and drive to Fortune Creek, wherever that was.

She was thinking that it might have been easier to buy a car, when the clerk at the rental desk finally found the car she'd ordered online from the hotel.

"How long do you want the car?" the clerk inquired.

"I don't know at this point. Make it a week. Can I extend it if I need it longer?"

"Yes, but you will be charged at a last-minute day rate."

Molly sighed, telling herself this shouldn't take more than a week. "Fine, a week." She noticed another woman waiting. Auburn-haired, about her own age, the woman was dressed much like she was, suit, heels and clearly just as impatient.

"I would suggest a larger SUV," the clerk said. "This is Montana—our weather is unpredictable, but this time of year it can snow."

"You can't be serious." Clearly the woman was. "It's spring."

"In some places," the clerk said and laughed. "Just not Montana."

"Fine."

"Where are you headed?"

"Fortune Creek."

The clerk's eyebrows rose. "If you're going that far north, you definitely want the larger SUV. That's almost to the Canadian boarder."

Great. She sighed and looked over again at the woman waiting. She saw the surprise on her face as well—also her sudden interest.

"I'm sorry," the woman said as she approached. "Did you say Fortune Creek?"

Molly held her tongue for a moment. The woman didn't look like a journalist, but you could never tell. "Yes."

"That's where I'm going."

"What are the chances you're both going to Fortune Creek," the clerk said with a cheerful chuckle.

Yes, Molly thought. "Journalist?"

The attractive brunette laughed. Molly caught the hint of a southern drawl in her voice. "No, I'm an insurance agent, Georgia Eden."

"Molly Lockhart, financial analyst. What takes you to Fortune Creek, if you don't mind me asking?"

"One of my clients passed away."

"Really?" Molly said. How many people could have died in Fortune Creek recently? She had no idea. Was it possible her client was Clay Wheaton? She couldn't imagine him buying an insurance policy on himself. With a start, she realized who he would buy a policy for though. Her heart began to hammer wildly. "Let me guess. Your client is Clay Wheaton."

Georgia looked startled. "How did you—"

"And the policy isn't on Mr. Wheaton, but on Rowdy the Rodeo Cowboy."

The woman was more than startled now. "I'm sorry, how—"

"I'm Clay Wheaton's daughter."

"Oh, I'm so sorry for your loss."

"Don't be," Molly said. "My father and I have been estranged for years."

"Do you want the extra insurance?" the car rental clerk interrupted. "We recommend it since your insurance—"

"Sure, whatever," Molly said and signed the form the woman put in front of her.

"That could explain then why we're both going to Fortune Creek. I didn't realize Clay had any family let alone a daughter," Georgia said.

"He had Rowdy," she said. "That's all he needed."

"Yes, he was quite attached," Georgia said and chuckled at her joke, but quickly sobered at her inappropriate choice of words.

Molly laughed but was unable to hide the bitterness in it. "Rowdy was like a son to him."

Georgia nodded sagely. "I never saw him without Rowdy. Is it true that Rowdy is missing?" Molly nodded and they both fell silent as Molly signed more forms and was finally given a key fob to the rental car. "I understand he was murdered."

"I have an alibi," Molly said flippantly. "I wasn't even in the state."

Georgia seemed startled at first, then realizing it was a joke, chuckled. "Clay was quite the character. Not father material I take it?"

"I guess not, unless you're a dummy."

The clerk explained where she could find her SUV and Molly started to roll her suitcase out to the rental lot as Georgia stepped up to the rental agency desk.

But Molly hadn't gone but a few feet when she turned back impulsively. "I've just rented the car for a week. I don't know how long I'll be staying, but since we're going to the same place for the same reason…"

Georgia seemed surprised. "I appreciate the offer and would jump at it, but it shouldn't take you very long to handle your father's affairs. I might be forced to stay longer than a week. I can't leave until Rowdy is found. So it makes it difficult since we aren't going for the same reason."

"I suspect we *are* going for the exact same reason."

"Yes, but…"

"I could have handled my father's…affairs by phone. I've come all this way because of Rowdy as well."

"Of course. I can understand why he has sentimental value for you—"

Molly's laugh was the first real one she'd had since getting the call about her father's murder. "*Sentimental?* That old puppet is nothing more to me than a piece of wood with some metal and cowboy clothing."

Georgia's mouth opened and closed like Rowdy's did. "That old puppet you're referring to is insured for a whole lot of money."

Molly blinked. "I know my father thought Rowdy was priceless, but worth a whole lot of money? You have to be kidding."

The woman shook her head. "It's why I'm here. Rowdy *has* to be found. Once he is, I have a museum interested in purchasing him for a long-term exhibit, so if it's money you're—"

"I don't care what that dummy is worth," Molly said waving away even the thought. "I plan to chop that piece of wood into kindling," she supplied. "So how about that ride to Fortune Creek?"

THE SHERIFF USED his own lockout tool, a thin strip of spring steel, to open the older-model pickup. Newer cars had more technology built in and were harder to get into. The crime scene techs had gone to breakfast. He didn't want to wait for them. If the dummy was in the pickup, it would save him a lot of headaches—two in particular who could be arriving in Fortune Creek at any time.

He popped the lock, pulled on gloves and opened the pickup door. It groaned and he caught a familiar smell. Huckleberries.

For a moment, he stood frowning as the scent dissipated and he wondered if he'd only imagined it. A quick search of the pickup brought him no closer to finding Rowdy. The dummy wasn't here. Nor was there anything of interest in the glove box, or under or behind the seat.

The only thing he found was a takeout container that had been jammed in the passenger-side-door cubby. He took a photo before pulling it out, wondering who had put it there. Someone Clay had given a ride to? He bagged it and the plastic spoon sticking out of it for prints, again catching a whiff of huckleberries and noticing a dark smear on the small white box.

The sheriff smiled. If a piece of huckleberry pie had been in the box, he had his first lead. Alice Weatherbee at the café made the best huckleberry pie in the county. But who had eaten it? He hoped the crime techs could get DNA off the plastic spoon. Whoever it was hadn't wanted to litter so had stuffed the container into the cubbyhole in the door? After bagging it, he put the evidence back.

Satisfied he wasn't going to find anything else of interest in the pickup, he locked the doors. Once the forensic team was finished, the truck would be stored down in Kalispell until the investigation was over. He'd let the crime techs take the evidence to the lab. The truck as well as the take-out box would be tested for prints and DNA. He felt as if he was making headway. If only he'd found the damned dummy.

FROM A SPOT in the woods on the side of the mountain over-looking town, gloved fingers tightened on the binoculars now trained on the young sheriff searching the ventrilo-quist's truck. Clay Wheaton was dead. The news had already rocked the town. Murder had a way of doing that. But the worry was the repercussions.

The young sheriff moved away from the ventriloquist's pickup, his cell phone pressed to his ear. Troubling was the evidence bag the lawman had been holding earlier. He had found something in the pickup?

A curse erupted in the pines, sending a bald eagle airborne and making a squirrel chatter angrily from a bough overhead.

The gloved hands slowly lowered the binoculars. A fool-ish mistake had been made, but with luck it wouldn't amount to anything. It was always the little things that got missed. The little things that put a person behind bars.

But not this time. The only one who should have to pay was Clay Wheaton.

And now he had.

THE SHERIFF WAS at his office that late afternoon when the rental car pulled up out front. He saw a slim blonde climb out from behind the wheel. She wore a navy suit, white blouse and heels and a look of all business on her pretty face. The whole outfit serving as armor, as she headed for the door.

From the other side of the car, a woman also in a suit climbed out, removed a suitcase from the back of the SUV and headed across the street to the hotel.

A gust of spring air wafted in as the blonde entered the

small sheriff's department building. It smelled of pine and water and fresh green grass. Even before she was close enough for him to see the intent in her blue eyes, he knew she must be the daughter of the deceased.

"I'm Molly Lockhart," she announced to Helen.

"I'm Sheriff Brandt Parker," he said behind her, making her turn to face him.

"Have you found my father's dummy yet?"

"Why don't you step into my office, Miss Lockhart."

"I assume that's a no," she said without moving. "Sheriff, I can't imagine that we have anything to talk about until Rowdy is found."

"That's not quite the case. We have murder to talk about. Please. My office."

She sighed and entered but didn't take a seat.

He followed, closing the door behind him before going behind his desk. As he sat down, he took her in. He doubted the woman had shed a tear for her father. "Sit down, Miss Lockhart. I'm in the middle of a murder investigation. I need to ask you a few questions if you can make the time."

MOLLY HEARD THE contempt in the sheriff's tone. She'd already seen it in his narrowed pale blue eyes as she'd looked around his tiny office from his Stetson hanging by the door to a photo of him riding a bronc on his desk. The cowboy didn't like her, and she resented being judged by this small-town sheriff. She didn't want to deal with any of this and found herself almost wishing that she had just taken care of it on the phone.

But then again, there was Rowdy. She'd always promised herself that one day that dummy would be at her mercy. She pulled out the plastic chair he offered, sitting rigidly, her purse in her lap. Furious that she'd been forced to come here and be judged, she also felt shame warm her face.

This sheriff thought she couldn't care less that her father had been murdered. He had no idea the years she'd hoped Clay Wheaton would someday want to be a father to her. Instead, she'd always been disappointed and hurt. Resentment and bitterness had formed a shell around her heart. It would take more than this cowboy's condescending judgment to crack it open.

The thought of how hardened she'd become because of her father brought tears of anger to her eyes. She hurriedly brushed them away. "You said you had questions?"

"I'm trying to solve your father's murder." His tone softened a little as he said, "Do you have any idea what he was doing in Fortune Creek?"

She shook her head. "My father and I haven't been in contact in years."

That seemed to stop him. "May I ask why?"

"You'd have to ask him. He left me and my mother when I was nine. All he took with him was Rowdy. Rowdy was his life, the son he never had. He had no interest in a daughter."

The sheriff leaned back in his chair, clearly taken aback. "I'm sorry."

"So am I. Sheriff, I'm only here to take care of arrangements for my father's cremation and to pick up Rowdy."

"Well, you're going to have to wait on both counts until the investigation is completed and the dummy is found," he said. "I can't promise you Rowdy will be found." He held up his hand to stop her from replying. "We believe that the killer took Rowdy with him. So the sooner we find his killer, the sooner you might be able to get the dummy—if your father left it to you. Do you know if he left a will?"

She shook her head, alarmed. She'd never considered he

might have left the dummy to someone else. "Without a will, wouldn't my father's possessions, including Rowdy, go to his next of kin?"

"I would assume so," he said, clearly irritated with her again since the dummy seemed to be the least of the man's worries. "Now do you want to help me find his killer or not?"

She straightened in the uncomfortable chair as a tense silence filled the small room. She couldn't help but wonder how many murders this sheriff had solved. He appeared to be about her age, maybe a little older. There was a confidence about him. He definitely spoke his mind. Under other circumstances, she would have admired that. Nor was he bad looking. Quite the opposite if you liked that rugged cowboy type. She did not.

He studied her, curiosity in his intense blue eyes, clearly planning to wait her out. She didn't like thinking about what he saw. His silent appraisal of her forced her to speak.

"Like I said, I have no idea what Clay was doing here." It wasn't much of a town. A few buildings on a dead-end road back in the mountains, miles from anywhere. She couldn't imagine why anyone would live here, let alone why her father would have come here. But she could see that the sheriff wasn't going to let it go at that. "Was he scheduled for a performance?"

"Not that we're aware of."

"Did you find Rowdy's case, the one he traveled in?" she asked.

"No. Can you describe it?" He took notes as she described a metal case the size of a child's suitcase with the brand and Rowdy the Rodeo Cowboy printed on the sides. He looked up to ask, "The dummy had his own brand? Can you describe it?"

She silently questioned why that would be important just

as she had with the case, but said, "The brand was burned into the side of the case under his name. I suppose I can describe it. I could probably draw it better."

He produced pen and paper, and shoved both across his desk to her. She noticed how clean his desktop was. Must not have a lot of crime. She also noticed his hands. Suntanned with numerous small scars. A working man's hands. She wondered how long he'd been sheriff.

She picked up the pen and began to draw. She was no artist, but finally satisfied that it was a close enough replica of the brand, she pushed the paper and pen back across his desk to him.

"A backward *C* with a small *r* inside it."

"The whole thing appears to be on a rocker, if that makes sense." She saw his expression change. "What?"

"There's a ranch not too far from here with that brand. You have any idea why your father would have chosen this particular brand?" She shook her head.

"This is at least a lead." He sounded extremely pleased. He even smiled, giving her a glimpse of the handsome rodeo cowboy that was much easier to take than an officious sheriff. Also, a lead meant that she wouldn't be here long. She couldn't help the relief she felt. Once she took care of Rowdy, she would be on her way back to New York City, back to her life.

She would finally put her father and his dummy behind her for good.

Chapter Four

Ash Hammond had been watching from the front window of the hotel. He saw the young blonde go into the sheriff's office while a young brunette got out of the passenger side of the SUV and walked across the street toward the hotel. As rare as murder was in Fortune Creek, two visitors who looked like these two women was even rarer.

No longer on a major two-lane paved highway, let alone the interstate, Fortune Creek saw few visitors aside from the tourist months of summer. If someone showed up in town with out of state license plates any other time of the year, it was a good bet that they were lost.

From what Ash could tell, these two women had come here intentionally so they had to be the two the sheriff had mentioned. They'd come about the murder. He tried to remember the last time he'd seen a woman in high heels crossing Main Street, let alone wearing a suit. Only the undertaker from Eureka, the closest town of any size, wore a suit.

Ash hurriedly left the window to take his place behind the registration counter as she pushed open the door. She stopped just inside it to blink in the cool semidarkness of the hotel's lobby. He saw her gaze take in the Western decor, much of it original, before she made a beeline for him.

He straightened, aware of his T-shirt and jeans, not to mention his worn boots. All the other guests, there'd just been the three recently, were gone, having either died or checked out.

"Afternoon," he said as he saw her glance at the cubbyholes behind him and the keys attached to wooden burls large enough that guests seldom pocketed them—let alone forgot to return them. "What can I do for you?"

"I need a room?" she said as if it should be obvious since she was dragging a carry-on with wheels.

"For how long?"

"Possibly a week. Can I pay daily?"

"Suit yourself," he said as he stepped to the computer.

She glanced toward the stairs. "This is where Clay Wheaton was staying, right?"

"Only hotel in town. I'll need some form of identification and a credit card." A Wheaton family member? This one didn't seem like a grieving relative though. That left…journalist. It had been a long time since he'd had a microphone shoved into his face. He hadn't missed it and wasn't looking forward to it happening again.

She dug in her purse, pulled out two cards and passed them to him. Georgia Eden, a resident of Chicago. He looked up at her, wondering why he'd detected a southern accent. The credit card was in the same name.

No hint as to what she did for a living or why she was interested in Clay Wheaton and his dummy. It had been years since anything had happened in Fortune Creek to warrant ink in a newspaper, let alone airtime on television, but this murder could go national because of a missing dummy— if not the once-famous ventriloquist. On top of that, this woman looked as if she could be a television anchor with her long, burnished hair and shapely figure, not to mention her ready-for-her-close-up face. He supposed she could be someone famous.

Still it surprised him that there would be even this much interest in Wheaton's death. From what he could gather online, the man and his dummy had enjoyed fame, but that had been years ago. Then again, Clay Wheaton *had* been murdered. They say nothing improves character like death.

"You doin' a story on him?"

"No," she said quickly. "Has the entire hotel been searched for Rowdy?"

It took him a moment. *"The dummy?"* he asked, his gaze drawn from the computer screen to her in surprise.

"Yes, the dummy."

"Sheriff's department is still searching every room, though I doubt they'll find it since all the rooms were locked the night of the murder." He heard the sound of boots coming down the stairs. "The deputy must be finished. I hear him now."

As Deputy Jaden Montgomery descended the stairs, she looked at him so expectantly that Jaden stopped in midstep. For a moment, it almost looked like love at first sight—both of them frozen, eyes locked.

Then Georgia Eden broke the spell—if there had been one. "Well?" she asked.

The deputy blinked and came the rest of the way down the stairs to the lobby. "Beg your pardon, miss?"

"Tell me you found Rowdy."

"The doll?"

"Yes, the doll," she said, clearly getting exasperated. Jaden held up his hands in surrender, his look saying *take it easy*. Jaden broke wild horses and had a patient, easygoing way with them that people said was nothing short of amazing.

But it apparently didn't work on Georgia Eden. "Do you have any idea how hard it is to get to Fortune Creek, Montana, from pretty much anywhere in this country and that after flying from Chicago to Denver and sitting there for almost five hours, not even to mention the endless drive to get to this…town?"

"Yes, I am aware of that," Jaden said. "It's why I stay right here. It alleviates that problem."

She stared at him as if at a loss for words.

He grinned and introduced himself with that same easygoing tone of his. "Deputy Jaden Montgomery. Welcome to our little town. Now that you're here, I hope you'll enjoy your stay. It's a peaceful place where you can get the rest you obviously need." With that he touched the brim of his Stetson and gave Ash a nod before walking out the front door of the hotel.

She bristled at the deputy's words, seeming still at a loss for words herself as she watched him walk out of the hotel. Ash had to hide a smile as he returned her credit card and driver's license and handed her the key to room 403. "You might want to take the elevator since your room is on the top floor." He motioned to the ancient elevator.

"Don't have something closer to the ground floor?"

"Sorry, we're renovating. We started with the fourth floor because it has the best views."

She stared at him. "Views of *what*?"

"Our scenery. You know, mountains, trees, our famous big sky."

The woman shook her head as she grabbed the burl attached to the key and the handle on her luggage, and marched to the elevator. He watched her go until he heard the front door open again.

"What are you smiling about?" Ash demanded as Jaden came back inside the hotel after Georgia Eden had disappeared into the elevator.

Jaden laughed. *"Who was that?"*

"Seems she's here looking for the ventriloquist's dummy."

He gave the deputy a pointed look. "Don't be fooled by her looks. You definitely don't want to mess with that one."

Jaden chuckled and rubbed the back of his neck as the elevator rose to the fourth floor with a clank. "I don't know. I do like a challenge."

Ash shook his head. "You really need to get out of Fortune more often."

BRANDT SAW THAT Molly was surprised that the brand might be helpful. Not impressed that he'd recognized it, but surprised it meant anything. She obviously didn't have much faith in him.

Nor did she know what brands meant in the state of Montana. They were registered; people held on to the rights for years even after they sold their ranches. He had several old branding irons from his grandfather's place and still held the registration on several of the designs.

After he explained this to her, she said dismissively, "I doubt the brand means anything."

"Was your father raised on a ranch in Montana?"

"No, he was raised back east, Boston, I think he said."

"Yet his costume and the dummy's were Western attire. As I understand it, his show was Old West stories and classic Western songs about life on the ranch."

"My father was a phony—everything about him was fake."

He heard the acrimony again and could understand it to a point. Yet, he'd thought he'd seen some sentiment when she'd first sat down. Even if the man had left her, hurt her, she must feel something for him. He thought of his own father, wishing he was still alive.

"Lockhart? Married name?"

"It was originally Wheaton. I took my mother's maiden name when I left home."

He guessed that at some time she'd been close to her father. Otherwise, she wouldn't be this bitter. "Is there anything else you can tell me?"

She shook her head. "I know nothing about him since I haven't seen him in years."

He had to ask. "Did you ever see him perform?"

She looked away. "The first time he showed us Rowdy and performed, he was terrible. My mother and I laughed. I'm sure we hurt his feelings. Why he wanted to be a ventriloquist, I have no idea."

Brandt realized she hadn't answered his question, but he let it go. "I wondered about that myself when I heard what he did for a living. Not necessarily your father, but why anyone went into that line of work. My deputy said he thought it was a way for a person to say things he didn't either know how to say himself or was afraid to say."

She scoffed at that. "Sounds like an excuse to me."

He nodded, kind of agreeing with her. "I assume you're staying at the hotel across the street?" Past her, he could see the woman who'd been in the vehicle with her now headed this way.

"Since it appears to be the only place in town to stay."

"Right. You know that's where he was killed on the top floor. In case that's a problem."

"No problem," she said getting to her feet.

"I saw that you brought someone with you," he said as the other woman reached the sidewalk outside the office.

"Georgia Eden. She's here for the same reason I am. But you'll find out soon enough. Please let me know as soon as—"

"—I find Rowdy," he said finishing her sentence and making her actually smile. She had a pretty smile, but this one never reached her pretty blue eyes.

"Yes. Also, I need to know when my father's body will be released."

He nodded. "One more question. I have to ask. Where were you night before last around nine?"

She gave him an incredulous look. "At home in my apartment in New York City. I worked late at the office where there are witnesses and when you called yesterday morning, I was at my desk at work. I'm sure you're aware how many flights you have to take to even reach a town with an airport in this state, let alone a place where you can rent a car. That a good enough alibi for you?" She didn't wait for an answer as she started for the door.

"Are you really not interested at all as to who murdered him?" he asked of her retreating backside.

She stopped at the door and turned slowly to look at him. "Only as far as Rowdy is concerned. I'm sure whoever killed my father had his reasons." With that Molly Wheaton Lockhart walked out and Georgia Eden walked in, the two women sharing nothing more than a nod, he noticed.

After his visit with the insurance agent, Brandt looked up to find Helen in his doorway. "You're not going to want to see this," she said. He hadn't had a moment to catch his breath since he'd gotten the call last night that someone at the hotel wasn't responding after an apparent fall.

Earlier, he'd barely gotten Molly Lockhart out of his office before the other woman, an insurance agent named Georgia Eden, came through the door.

He was still shaking his head after his conversation with Ms. Eden. "What now?" he asked as Helen stepped around his desk and called up a video on his computer. He instantly recognized Toby and Irene Thompson, the couple he'd met at the hotel this morning, doing a televised interview. "No," he said, knowing right away what he was about to see.

"It only gets worse," Helen said and left, closing his door after her.

He watched the interview, swearing under his breath. The guileless couple no doubt began telling people they met along their trip about their night in Fortune Creek. Not just about the murder, but what they called the eeriest thing they'd ever heard—the ventriloquist's dummy singing a good half hour after its operator had died. There was a grainy clip of Clay Wheaton with Rowdy, the dummy singing "Home on the Range." "Isn't the Fortune Creek Hotel already haunted?" the interviewer asked. "I thought I'd heard stories about strange goings-on."

The couple paled, saying they'd had no idea.

Oh, great, Ash was going to love this, Brandt thought as he switched off the interview. The last time a rumor about the hotel had gotten started, it brought all kinds of strange people to town wanting to see the ghosts—then getting angry when they didn't.

He rubbed a hand over his face, recalling his visit with Georgia Eden who had informed him that she'd written a million-dollar insurance policy on Rowdy.

"On a *puppet*?"

"A vent figure," she'd corrected. "Clearly you have no idea how much an original ventriloquist's dummy is worth. The most famous one, Charlie McCarthy, is in the Smithsonian. The *Smithsonian*. People are fascinated by them."

"Really? They kind of give me the creeps," he'd said. A mistake given her reaction. "I'm doing my best to find Rowdy and the man who killed Clay Wheaton," he'd assured her, hoping by his inflection that she realized the murder was more important to him. "It would help if you knew why Mr. Wheaton was in Fortune Creek."

She hadn't, but added, "Oh, but this might help. The man over at the hotel…"

"Ash Hammond?"

Georgia had shrugged. "As I was leaving, I heard him mention that Clay asked for room 401." She'd raised an eyebrow. "Apparently, Clay had stayed there before."

"That is interesting," Brandt had said. "Back to possible enemies… Was there someone who might have been jealous of him? Another ventriloquist possibly? Or someone he ridiculed in the audience at one of his shows? Someone with a grudge?" She hadn't known anyone.

"I really need Rowdy, Sheriff. I have a museum interested in him for an exhibit," she'd said.

"The Smithsonian?"

"No," she'd admitted. "But still it would be an honor for this museum to display Rowdy and they are willing to pay handsomely."

"I have to ask," he'd said. "If Rowdy isn't found, does that mean you'll have to pay the million dollars?"

"Not me personally, but yes, my insurance company."

He'd seen that it would probably mean her losing her job, which would explain why she was so upset over the dummy. "Who gets that money?"

She'd hesitated. "Clay's beneficiary." Clearly, she hadn't wanted to say, so he'd merely waited until she'd finally said, "His daughter."

That had gotten his attention. "Molly Lockhart?" She'd nodded, looking uncomfortable. "Does she know that?" He couldn't help thinking about how adamant Molly had been about him finding Rowdy.

"I… I don't know," she'd admitted. "Possibly. Possibly not."

"Then I would think that if she did know, she wouldn't want Rowdy being found so she could collect the money."

"She says she has her own reasons for wanting Rowdy found that have nothing to do with money."

"Isn't that what she would say even if she was hoping he wouldn't turn up?" Brandt had asked. "I couldn't help but notice that the two of you arrived in town together. Had you known each other prior to this?"

"No, we met at the car rental agency. We traveled together as a matter of convenience."

"Because you both want the same thing… Rowdy," he'd said, seeing that she wasn't so sure about that now. "Did Miss Lockhart say why she was so anxious to get her hands on the dummy?"

"She says she wants to destroy it."

He'd raised a brow. "But if it is worth money—"

"Apparently she has issues with the dummy—and her father." Ms. Eden had gotten to her feet. "Please. Find Rowdy and let me know as soon as you do. I'll be staying at the hotel." With that she had gone, leaving him wondering who had the most to gain—or lose—by Clay Wheaton's death and Rowdy the Rodeo Cowboy's disappearance.

Chapter Five

Early that evening, Molly answered the knock on her hotel room, not surprised to find Georgia standing in the hallway. She'd heard the quick click of her heels earlier and surmised that she was staying in the room next door.

"It's been a long day. I need a drink," the underwriter said, making her smile. Earlier Georgia had been wearing a suit. She'd changed into a sweater, jeans and ankle boots.

"I saw a Mint Bar sign at the end of the street," Molly said. "Come on in while I change." She grabbed clothes out of her suitcase and disappeared into the large bathroom, leaving the door slightly ajar so they could talk. "I heard you wandering around the hotel earlier. Find anything interesting?"

"You mean like Rowdy?" Georgia called back as Molly heard her move to the window. "I didn't find him. Can you believe this so-called view? It's just mountains and trees as far as the eye can see and nothing else but sky. People actually come all this way out here for this?" Molly heard her move away from the window. "I wanted to see the room where Clay was staying, but the door is locked although the crime scene tape has been removed."

Molly pushed open the bathroom door. She'd changed into jeans and a top. After moving to her suitcase she found socks and the pair of sneakers she'd thrown in when she'd packed in a hurry. She sat down on the bed to put them on.

"He was in 401 at the end of the hall near the fire escape stairs," Georgia said still looking out the window. "He asked for that particular room next to the fire exit stairs, so he's been here before. You don't have any idea why?"

"For a fast getaway?" Molly only half joked about the room by the exit, wondering if her father had been strapped for funds and hadn't planned to pay his hotel bill when he left.

"Why would he come here?" Georgia asked after chuckling at Molly's joke.

"For the view?" She shook her head as she finished putting on her sneakers. "Your guess is as good as mine." She stood. "It does seem strange if it's true that he's been here before. Did you tell the sheriff?"

"He seemed interested." She thought about the brand, which the sheriff said matched a nearby ranch. Maybe he'd already figured out that Clay Wheaton had been here before.

"You're a regular Sherlock Holmes," Molly said as she grabbed her coat and they left the room.

"I like gathering facts, which is helpful in my business," Georgia said as Molly closed and locked hotel room 404's door. "For instance, ventriloquists are rather unique. There are less than four hundred professionals in the world."

Molly glanced over at her, surprised by her.

"Ventriloquism is apparently easy to learn," Georgia continued. "You can pick it up in a few weeks. The trick is learning to use your tongue to speak but not moving your mouth or face."

The hallway was dim with shadows that played on the carpet. Molly found herself trying to imagine her father here alone. Alone, except for Rowdy. Why here?

"I like facts. For instance," Georgia was saying. "Did you know that there are sixteen Mint Bars in Montana? I wondered what the mint part was about. Apparently as legend has it, the mint moniker was associated with the mining boom in Montana. Mind if we take the stairs?" she asked changing topics abruptly. "That elevator gives me the willies."

Molly agreed. "Everything about this place creeps me out."

"Well, there was a murder just down the hall." She chuckled. "Sorry, I keep forgetting he was your father."

"You're not the only one." As they reached the stairs next to the elevator, she turned to look back at room 401. What had he been doing in this town, in this hotel, in that particular room? Like Georgia, she wanted inside the room, even though she knew Rowdy wasn't there.

She kept asking herself, who had her father been? Not that she thought she would find any clues here to answer that question or the one that haunted her most. Why had he left her and her mother all those years ago? Just as strange was why he'd left her number as one of the people to call should anything happen to him, she thought as they exited the hotel and she breathed in the cool mountain air.

After a short brisk walk, Georgia pushed open the door to the Mint Bar. The wooden front door was weathered and warped. It took the two of them to pull it open.

Once inside, Molly had to take a moment for her eyes to adjust to the dim darkness. The building, long and narrow like most of those in town, looked as if everything in it was original including the old metal ceiling tiles that had been painted red at one point.

To her surprise, Georgia seemed right at home as she made a beeline across the uneven wood floor for two empty stools at the end of the bar. Molly followed, noting the cracked vinyl chair covers, the scarred tabletops and a variety of different dark stains beneath her feet before she reached the bar.

Rustic was the only polite word she could come up with to describe the decor.

Climbing up on a worn, wobbly Naugahyde stool that had been repaired with so much duct tape she could no longer discern its original color, she started to set her purse on the marred bar top but changed her mind. A couple of older men wearing Western attire were at the other end of the bar laughing with the gravelly voiced elderly bartender.

"You tell 'em, Betty!" one of the men called after her as she wandered down to Molly and Georgia's end of the counter. Molly marveled how women of a certain age often dyed their hair red. Her own mother had and her grandmother. She feared she might too at some point, though had to wonder about the motivation.

"What can I get ya?" Betty asked, her voice more like a low growl. A pair of dark brown eyes peered out from a fallen lock of dyed red hair.

"I'll take a cosmopolitan," Molly said.

"Not likely," Betty shot back.

Molly glanced at the bottles of alcohol behind the bar. "How about a margarita?"

The bartender made a dismissive sound and looked over at Georgia.

"We'll take two bourbons on the rocks."

Betty smiled. "I like you," she said to Georgia and gave Molly the side-eye as she went to make their drinks.

"Seriously?" Molly whispered to her companion. "What is this place?"

Georgia shrugged and leaned her elbows on the questionably clean bar. "The end of the earth?"

"I'm sorry, but why do you seem so comfortable here?"

"Grew up in towns like this, bars like this." She shrugged. "Reminds me of home."

Molly studied her in surprise. "Home?"

"West Texas."

"You don't have much of an accent."

"I would if I got around my family—I'd pick it right back up."

Molly realized she knew nothing about this woman she'd offered a ride to so quickly as Betty brought their drinks. She took a sip. It wasn't that bad for well liquor.

Georgia saw her expression and laughed. "You should be glad I didn't order you a tanglefoot."

"I'm almost afraid to ask," Molly said.

"Don't."

"Got it," she answered laughing as she took another sip of her drink. She felt the alcohol go to work since she hardly ever imbibed. "How did you get into the insurance business?"

Georgia shrugged. "Straight out of a two-year college, I was offered a job. Just that simple. I kept moving up in the company until I ended up in Chicago. I thought I had it made." She took a gulp of her drink. "Now I could be starting all over."

Molly could hear the pain in the woman's voice. "What happens if Rowdy doesn't turn up?"

Georgia drew a finger across her throat then turned on her stool to face her. "You really don't know what happened to Rowdy?"

She shook her head, surprised by the question. "I haven't seen my father in years—let alone his dummy."

"You wouldn't destroy it, would you?"

"I would—I will," she said picking up her drink rather than looking at her companion. "Let's just say Rowdy has been a thorn in my side most of my life. Hard to admit that my father preferred a dummy over his own daughter, but," she said raising her glass, "he did."

"I'm not sure that's entirely true," Georgia observed as if choosing her words carefully. Molly finally looked over at her and frowned in question. "You really don't know?"

"Know what?" Molly said, thinking how little she knew about her father during his life, let alone his death.

"The insurance policy on Rowdy? Your father made you the beneficiary."

Earlier she'd thought he might have thought of her and her mother all those years ago and taken out a life insurance policy. "If he was thinking of me, he would have purchased an insurance policy on himself."

Georgia shook her head. "You were right the first time. He only insured Rowdy."

"Of course, he did and here I was hoping he might have thought of me and my mother."

"Is your mother still—"

"No, she died almost ten years ago."

"Did your father—"

"Know? I doubt it. It wasn't like he stayed in touch more than a few phone calls now and then as I was growing up."

"Well, he hadn't forgotten you," Georgia said, and apparently seeing how unimpressed Molly was, added, "What if I told you that if Rowdy isn't found, you get a million dollars?"

Molly stared at her. When Georgia had said that her father had insured the dummy, she'd never thought... She let out a laugh. "He valued Rowdy at a million dollars? Why am I not surprised?"

"It was the most my company would ensure the vent figure for," Georgia said. "But the point is, he made you his beneficiary so if anything happened to Rowdy... He was thinking of you."

"That makes no sense at all," Molly snapped. She was

starting to feel the alcohol. Betty poured on the heavy side. "If he cared about me, he would have insured himself."

"He wasn't worth a million dollars," Georgia said bluntly.

"But Rowdy is?" She took another drink.

"He couldn't have known that he was going to be murdered and that the murderer would take the dummy," Georgia argued. "Unless…"

Molly saw the glint in the woman's eyes. "Wait, you can't think that he planned this whole thing?" Another shrug. "That's delusional."

"Maybe he was desperate. Wanted to make it up to you with one grand gesture. Hired someone to kill him and take Rowdy so the insurance company would have to pay you."

Molly finished her drink. She couldn't believe this. Of course he would insure Rowdy. But a million dollars? The thought made her even angrier at him and especially Rowdy. "It's just a dummy," she mumbled under her breath.

They drank in silence for a few minutes. Molly started to order them another, but Georgia stopped her. "I'll have a shot of tequila."

Her new friend grinned making her laugh. "You got it, sister."

After they'd downed their shot chased with salt and a slice of lime, Molly coughed for a few moments, then laughed. "Maybe you're right," she said. "I did wonder why anyone would want to kill him—let alone take Rowdy. Can't you save your job if you can prove that he set this whole thing up?"

"Maybe," Georgia said. "I just hope you weren't in on it with him."

"Are you serious?" she demanded. Just when she thought they were becoming friends and that staying here until Rowdy was found wouldn't be so awful. "I don't need or want the money. I haven't been in contact with my father for years and I—" She stopped herself. "Why am I defending myself?"

Opening her purse, she pulled out a twenty and threw it on the bar. "I know you're desperate to keep your job, but I had nothing to do with any of this." With that she stormed out, her mind whirling, the alcohol warming her blood and making her feel lighter on her feet.

Everything had seemed so simple when she'd first heard about her father's death. Someone had murdered him and taken Rowdy. Law enforcement would find his killer and get the dummy back. She hadn't even thought about what she would do with her father's ashes once she had him cremated. Her only thought was destroying that damned dummy.

She'd seen how appalled the sheriff had been when she'd shown no interest in helping find Clay Wheaton's murderer. All she'd cared about was Rowdy—but not in the way anyone would understand how she could hate an inanimate object. They would have had to grow up in its shadow.

Now Georgia had her wondering if Clay had planned his own murder and Rowdy's disappearance so she would get a million dollars. Had he really thought she would want that? Who would do something like that? All to leave the daughter who he'd never had any interest in money? It made no sense.

By the time she reached the entrance to the hotel, she'd convinced herself that Clay Wheaton's death had been a random murder and the murderer had taken Rowdy thinking it might be worth money or just for the heck of it. By now Rowdy could be in a dumpster somewhere.

As she started to push open the hotel door, it was flung open as Sheriff Brandt Parker came out.

"I was just looking for you," he said. "Want to take a ride?"

He didn't seem to notice that she swayed a little and probably smelled like eighty-proof. Nor that a ride was the last thing she wanted after a day of traveling. But he was the law and he was actively looking for Rowdy—as well as her father's murderer.

"Give me a minute to freshen up and I'll be right with you," she said as she headed for the elevator, knowing she wasn't up for the stairs.

Chapter Six

The Crandell Ranch was next to the Canadian border some miles from Fortune Creek. Brandt didn't mind the drive on such a beautiful afternoon. Clouds drifted in an endless deepening blue in stark contrast to the deep lush green of the pines. The breeze was cool. In Montana there was often the promise of snow in the mountains. He remembered one Fourth of July when they'd had a snowball fight in downtown Fortune Creek.

He glanced over at the woman next to him. She'd made it clear that going to the Crandell Ranch to follow up on the brand was a waste of time.

"I really doubt Rowdy's brand has anything to do with a real ranch," she'd argued when he told her where they were headed. "Nothing about Clay Wheaton was real. He made it all up. He wasn't the man you seem to think he was."

He thought she might be right. But he couldn't quit thinking about the brand Molly said was on Rowdy the Rodeo Cowboy's case. Maybe Clay Wheaton had picked the brand out of thin air. Or maybe he had a good reason for choosing the Crandell Ranch brand. The same way he'd chosen the Fortune Creek Hotel in Fortune Creek, Montana. The fact that Clay had been killed here and might have stayed at the hotel in the past made Brandt think the ventriloquist had some connection to this area. That connection could be the Crandell Ranch.

As he drove, he pointed out mountains by name, told stories about hard winters, strange things that had happened like the moose getting stuck in the creek and how it had taken most of the residents of Fortune Creek to get her out. Molly made the appropriate responses, but he could tell her mind was elsewhere.

"Want to tell me about it?" he finally asked. She glanced over at him in surprise as if she'd forgotten he was there. He didn't take offense. If anything, he appreciated that she didn't seem in the least enamored by the romantic myth of the cowboy, maybe especially the cowboy sheriff. Her father had destroyed that Western fantasy for her.

He wondered if she thought of him as playing the role of the cowboy sheriff, like in the movies where even outlaws were given a silver star if bad guys were coming to town.

More than likely this New York City lady didn't think of him at all, he told himself. And if she did, it was to wonder if he was capable of solving this murder and getting Rowdy back, but not in that order.

"What's got you over there scowling like that?" he asked.

"My father was murdered."

He shook his head. "We both know that's not it." For a few moments he thought she was going to take offense.

"Georgia told me that I'm the beneficiary of a million-dollar insurance policy on Rowdy."

"You hadn't known?"

"How could I?" she demanded. "I haven't seen or talked to my father in years. I know Georgia's worried that she'll lose her job if her company has to pay out, but…"

"But?"

"She all but accused me of working with my father to rip off the insurance company by having him murdered and Rowdy stolen."

He'd considered that the moment he'd heard about the million-dollar policy. People plotted murder for a lot less money than that. "You're saying you didn't?"

"No," she snapped indignantly. "Why would I come here demanding you find Rowdy if I didn't want him to be found?"

"For show, to make yourself look innocent because you knew the dummy would never be found? Or to make sure that it isn't found." He saw her angry expression. "Just spit-balling here. You did ask."

She sat back, crossing her arms over her ample chest and sighing angrily.

Ahead, he concentrated on the turnoff into the ranch and slowed. He knew of the Crandell family. He might have met the old man years ago at a rodeo in Eureka. What he did know about them was that they stayed to themselves. He'd heard there'd been some kind of accident, a death involving one of the sons. Didn't seem like that was why they'd isolated themselves from the community at large, but he supposed it was possible. Out here, the ranches were so far apart, it was easy to keep to yourself if it was what you wanted.

Bringing Molly along had been impulsive and yet he'd hoped she might open up to him on the drive. There was also the chance that she might see something out here at the ranch that would jar a memory about her father. Right now, he'd take any help he could get solving this murder.

As he drove into the ranch yard though, he worried about the kind of reception he might get. Even though he was in his uniform, driving a patrol SUV with the sheriff's department logo on the side, it wouldn't be the first time he'd found himself facing angry armed men.

This time he realized wasn't going to be any different as he saw a man come out of the first house carrying a shotgun.

MOLLY HAD ALREADY decided that this was a mistake even before she spotted the angry-looking elderly man with the shotgun. The sheriff had made it sound as if they were just going for a ride, but he was much cagier than she'd realized. He had an ulterior motive in bringing her along. He wanted to question her about the million-dollar payout if Rowdy wasn't found.

Just because he was sheriff and lived in a small town in the middle of nowhere didn't mean he wasn't sharp and knew what he was doing. She hoped that was true as she considered the man with the shotgun.

"Stay in the car," the sheriff said as he parked and climbed out. He didn't have to tell her twice as she watched the man standing on the porch shift his shotgun.

"Afternoon," she heard the sheriff say congenially.

"You're trespassing," the man said in a deep scratchy voice. He looked to be close to ninety or older, a big man who'd once been bigger, but still appeared in decent shape for his age. "Unless you have a warrant—"

"Not that kind of visit," the sheriff said. "Just need to know if any of you have heard of a man named Clay Wheaton." No response.

Molly could see that this wasn't going to get them anywhere, just as she'd thought. She looked around the ranch seeing a couple of old barns, some smaller houses, a few outbuildings, farm machinery and a large tree next to a creek.

Her pulse jumped at the sight of the black tire tied to a rope hanging from one of the largest of the tree's limbs. The tree was huge, looked old. Even from where she sat in the patrol SUV, she could see the scarred trunk. It almost looked as if there were names carved into the trunk's base.

She opened her door, feeling like a sleepwalker, as she got out and walked toward the tree. She heard voices behind her, including the sheriff's trying to call her back, but she kept going. She had to see what was carved into that tree.

Even as she kept walking, the logical part of her brain was arguing that she wouldn't find her father's name carved there. That it was only a made-up story, one of many stories Rowdy told about growing up on a ranch. The sheriff and his theories about Rowdy's brand were just that. Fiction. She'd be lucky if the old man didn't shoot her in the back. It would be all the sheriff's fault since he was the one who'd brought her out here, she told herself.

A few feet from the swing, she stopped. There were names carved in the tree's trunk—just like she'd thought. Seth, Jo, Pat, Gage, Cliff, Wyatt, Ty—there were more but the one name she'd expected to see hadn't been there. No Clay. Someone grabbed her arm, dragged her back from the tree.

"Are you trying to get us both killed?" the sheriff whispered hoarsely. "We need to leave." She heard the urgency in his voice and yet she found herself trying to pull away. Clay had to be there. She'd heard the story about this tree and the names. She'd been so convinced that she would find it… "We need to leave. *Now.*"

With a jolt, she realized how foolish she'd been. Clay wasn't there because he'd made the story up for Rowdy to tell. It wasn't even an original story, a tire swing, a big old tree, a pocketknife and a lazy warm summer day, plenty of time to carve a name in a tree. Probably every kid who didn't live in an apartment in the city had done the same thing.

She let the sheriff pull her back from the tree. As she turned, she saw that there were more men now standing in front of the other houses, all armed, all looking angry. "Sorry," she called to them. Their responses were steely glares.

As she tried to swallow, her mouth gone dry, she couldn't

believe how foolish she'd been. The sheriff was right, she could get them killed and for what? Some story she'd once heard out of the mouth of a dummy?

The sheriff opened her car door and practically shoved her inside. She didn't hear what he said, but he seemed to get behind the wheel quick enough. As they were driving away, she saw him glancing back until they reached the county road and were off the Crandell Ranch.

"What the hell was that about back there?" he demanded.

She was embarrassed to tell him, especially after she'd told him that nothing about Clay Wheaton was real. Or that she hadn't seen her father's shows or cared about him or what he'd left her. Yet, she'd bought into it the moment she'd seen that tree and the tire swing next to the creek. It was exactly as he had described it. Rowdy had described it, she reminded herself with a sigh. "You were so convinced that Rowdy's brand meant something…"

"I was wrong, but that still doesn't explain what you were doing getting out of the car when I told you not to. Those men with guns were serious. You could have been shot. Going on someone's property without permission—or a warrant—is serious business in this state. Well?"

Molly could hear in his voice that he wasn't going to quit asking until she told him, as embarrassing as it was. "When I saw that tire swing and that big tree, I remembered this story Rowdy used to tell as part of his act. I don't even recall the punch line, just that as a boy he'd carved his name into a big ol' tree with a tire swing hanging from it out on the ranch." She looked over at the sheriff, surprised he hadn't said anything.

"Was his name there?"

She shook her head. "It was just a silly made-up story like

all of them that he told." She looked away. "I can't believe I bought into it. But if the brand really meant something…"

Molly expected him to call her on blaming him for the foolish thing she'd just done. Instead, he drove in silence for a few minutes before he looked over at her and asked, "When did you go see his show?"

She realized her mistake. She'd told him that her father had performed for her and her mother, that he'd been terrible, that he'd left them. She'd made it sound as if she'd never seen him again.

A lump formed in her throat. She hated being caught in a lie. She swallowed before she answered, feeling that almost getting them both killed he deserved honesty, for once. "In college. I went with some friends who wanted to go." She shrugged. "I didn't talk to him." But he had seen her. Their eyes had met. He'd sent a note that he wanted to see her. She'd balled it up, tossed it in the trash on the way out of the auditorium.

The sheriff was quiet again for several miles. "I'm sorry the trip was a wild goose chase. The men I spoke with swore they'd never heard of Clay Wheaton. How about something to eat in the big city of Eureka before the café closes?"

BRANDT'S EMOTIONS VEERED back and forth from furious with Molly to feeling sorry for her. When her stomach growled in answer to his question, he felt a kinship since he was starved. "When was the last time you ate?"

She had to think apparently. "Yesterday, on the plane?"

"Well, we need to remedy that and fast since Trappers Saloon closes at eight."

"Eight in the evening?" She said it as if she couldn't imagine eating before nine.

"It's still off season here. You're not in New York anymore," he said with a laugh.

"Tell me about it," she added, looking out the window. It was already dark as he drove into Eureka. "I always wondered why my father chose the cowboy outfit for him and Rowdy. All of it seemed so fake, the cowboy hero, so big, so strong, so capable. Yet since I arrived here, all I see are cowboy hats, boots and trucks."

He laughed. "It's real—it's just not as glamorous as some people try to make it out to be. For many in this state, it's a way of life, a dying one for some since ranching isn't always profitable."

"What keeps Fortune Creek alive?" she asked once they were seated inside the Trappers Saloon. They'd called it close. The place would be closing for the day soon. For that reason it was almost empty already.

He watched her studying the menu. "It's home for a lot of us. Some, like Ash, came back after a successful career and invested in the town. Me, it's home, way up here in the northwest corner of the state near the boundary line with Idaho and Canada. See something you like?"

She glanced up and grinned before diving back into the menu. "Montana sushi? Thin-sliced sirloin, served medium rare or rare only, on a bed of lettuce with sweet chili huckleberry sauce." She looked up at him again. "Huckleberries?"

"They're delicious, picked around here in the summer. You should try them. Might want to try the Wild Thing elk burger."

"Elk? I think I'll stick with chicken. It is really chicken, right?"

He grinned. "It's not sage hen, I promise."

"Sage hen?"

"Sorry, local joke." He ordered the Hang Over burger with

huckleberry slaw and she went with the Pacific salmon served with couscous & veggies. "Don't feel like living dangerously, huh?" She shook her head. "Tell me about yourself. What does a financial analyst do?"

"I'm sure you'd find it boring—most people do." He waited and she finally said, "I work for a stock brokerage. I examine financial information in order to help clients looking for businesses to invest in."

"No kidding."

She smiled and this one reached her eyes. "Told you it was boring."

"It must not be for you."

"It's not. It's something solid. Numbers don't lie."

He was no psychologist, but he couldn't help but wonder if the job hadn't attracted her because of what her father had done for a living.

Their food came. She picked at hers. He offered her a bite of his hamburger, then his huckleberry slaw.

"This is delicious."

He motioned to the waitress to bring them another burger and slaw and take away the salmon. They split both meals. After that she seemed to relax as the restaurant closed and they left in a companionable silence.

"You must think I'm heartless," she said as they headed back to Fortune Creek. "I'm sorry my father was murdered. I'm just so angry with him."

"I get it. Parents often disappoint us, some worse than others."

"Not many take off to be ventriloquists."

"No, that's true enough." He felt her gaze on him.

"I just don't understand why the killer took Rowdy," she said.

He shook his head. "Professional jealousy?"

"Not hardly. I don't think my father's been performing for quite a few years now. At one time, he had a show in Vegas and was doing well. Then he just disappeared."

So she *had* kept track of him more than she'd admitted, he thought. "Would you really chop up Rowdy?"

"I don't know." She turned to look out the window. "Pretty petty being jealous of a dummy, huh."

"My dad had a dog that he loved more than me and that dog used to bite him all the time for no reason." He felt her gaze again. "I'm serious." That bow-shaped mouth turned up a little at the corners, her gaze saying she wasn't sure what to believe about his story—let alone him.

She was quiet most of the ride back. He left her with her thoughts, enjoying the drive and the company. She kept surprising him. He was glad that his first impression of her had been wrong.

"Thank you for tonight," she said as the lights of Fortune Creek appeared high on the side of the mountain. "I loved that restaurant. Next time I want to try the elk burger."

He smiled. Next time? That made it sound as if she was planning to hang around for a while. "You'll have to try Alice Weatherbee's huckleberry pie at the Fortune Creek Cafe. It's the best. You haven't tried it yet, have you?"

She shook her head.

He'd been fishing, wondering about the take-out container he'd found in her father's pickup. He was still waiting for possible fingerprints and DNA. Still wondering who her father had given a ride to.

Molly hadn't flown to Montana earlier than she'd said, but she could have driven and stayed out of sight. Against his better judgment, he was hoping like hell that she had nothing to do with murder—let alone deception.

Chapter Seven

The next morning while having a mug of coffee in his office, the sheriff looked up to see a pickup with a camper on the back pull in. Arkansas plates? That was a new one in Fortune Creek, he thought.

A young woman stepped out. Her black hair hung in a long braid. She wore an ankle-length flowered dress and what looked like combat boots as if she'd been dropped from the 1960s. The camper, he saw, was covered in activist stickers with a smattering of political ones too.

"Oh boy," Brandt said, just imaging how some of the conservative older cowboys were going to react. Helen was already staring out the window, her mouth gaping open, as the young woman headed for the front door.

"I'll handle this one," he said, stepping out of his small office to greet the newcomer. "I'm Sheriff Brandt Parker. Can I help you?"

She grinned, cocking her head to the side. "Howdy, Sheriff. You're just the person I want to see. I'm here about Clay Wheaton."

That took him by surprise, but only for a second as he wondered how many more people would show up. He couldn't wait to hear why this woman was interested in the ventriloquist. Or, like the other two women, was she here about Rowdy the dummy? "Why don't you step into my office?"

"Mind if I bring in my dog first?" She turned to Helen. "You wouldn't have a small dish of water, would you?"

"No," Helen said, but the woman either didn't hear or ignored her as she went back out to her truck and opened the passenger-side door. He couldn't see because of the sun glinting off the windshield, but he was expecting something large. He was amused when she brought in a tiny white ball of fur.

"Her name's Ghost," she said as she handed the dog to Helen, who, startled, took it automatically even though she was no fan of dogs. "Just a little water would be great." With that the women headed for Brandt's office.

Offering her a chair, the sheriff walked around his desk to sit down. He could see Helen still standing in the middle of the outer office staring at the fur ball in her hands. "What can I do for you, Ms....?"

"Jessica Woods." She turned to look out the window at the hotel across the street. "That's where Clay was murdered?"

"Did you know him?"

She turned back around. "No, I heard about it when I was doing some investigating on another case next door in Idaho. I figured I'd better come up and check it out."

Investigating? Case? "Are you..." He was thinking undercover DEA.

"I'm a paranormal investigator." At his no doubt confused look, she added, "I have a PhD in parapsychology science with a masters in folklore. I'm here to investigate claims that Clay Wheaton's vent figure sang for a half hour after the puppeteer died. I would like to examine Rowdy the Rodeo Cowboy."

He nodded and leaned back in his chair as he searched for words. "I'm afraid you won't be able examine Mr. Wheaton's dummy. At this point, we suspect the killer may have taken it with him."

"Seriously? You don't have it?" She sounded devastated.

"No." He didn't mention that she wasn't the only one interested in Rowdy.

"That is so disappointing," she said. "But once you find the killer, you'll retrieve the dummy." She got to her feet as if the problem was solved. Her gaze went to the hotel across the street. "I guess Ghost and I will go check out the hotel then. I've heard this isn't the first paranormal event that has happened there. Let me know when you find Rowdy. I'll be staying in my camper down by the creek," she said as she left his office.

He watched her retrieve Ghost from Helen. To his amazement, Helen seemed taken with the dog and appeared reluctant to return it.

His cell phone rang. "Sheriff Parker," he said distractedly as he watched Helen say goodbye to Ghost as if the dog had become a long-lost friend.

"Thought you'd want to know."

He realized that he'd missed what the coroner had said. "Sorry, JP, what's that?"

"Got a hit on your victim's DNA. It came back a lot sooner than expected because he was in the military. That's not all. Are you sitting down?"

MOLLY HADN'T SLEPT WELL. Even the hot shower this morning hadn't helped. At one point she'd awakened from a dream, but as she sat up, she would have sworn that she had heard the last few refrains of Rowdy singing one of his cowboy songs.

Her heart had pounded in her ears as goosebumps raced across her skin. It had sounded so real. No wonder she'd had trouble getting back to sleep last night.

She was thinking about going back to bed when she got the call from the sheriff.

"Could you stop by my office?" He'd sounded so officious, so different from last night at the café in Eureka that whatever he wanted must be serious. She quickly dressed and headed for his office.

Last night after she'd returned from her trip with the sheriff, she'd gone for a walk. Only the bar had still been open. The convenience-grocery was closing. She'd stopped to visit with the older woman who ran the place. She'd glanced into the front windows of a narrow building after seeing a post office sign in the window. It had the smallest post office she'd ever seen along the right side at the front of the store.

"You the one from New York City?" the elderly woman had inquired pleasantly enough.

"I am," she'd admitted, amused by the way the woman had said it. "Have you ever been there?"

That got a crackle out of her. "Don't need gas, do you?" She'd told her that she didn't. "Good, cuz, I turn off the gas pumps at night." The pumps looked old, from another era. "You can come at six in the morning though, fill up and then come inside to tell me how many gallons you got and pay for your gas before you leave town."

"I'll keep that in mind, thanks. But I'm not leaving town for a while."

"Well, in that case." The woman had wiped her hand on her canvas pants and held it out. "Name's Cora. Cora Green."

"Molly Lockhart."

Cora had frowned. "Lockhart. I thought your name would be Wheaton." She had chin-length gray hair, green eyes and a fading beauty. Molly guessed that she'd given cowboys around here a run for their money when she was younger. Heck, she probably still did. "You're not married, divorced?"

"No, I just changed my name. It's a long story."

"All the sad ones are, aren't they? You have a nice night."

With that Cora went back inside the store-gas station and finished locking up behind her.

As the woman turned off the pumps and the lights, Molly had walked to the end of town, which wasn't far. It ended abruptly at a creek. She'd thought of the people who called Fortune Creek home, including the sheriff. She'd never met anyone who lived in a town a block long that dead-ended at a creek. There was only one way out of Fortune Creek—the way you came in.

This place was so different from New York City. Not just Fortune Creek, which wasn't much of a town at all, but the people. To say it was a simpler lifestyle was almost humorous.

As she'd reached the creek, she'd spotted a pickup and camper parked at the water's edge. She could hear the faint crackle of a campfire, smell the smoke and feel a chill as if suddenly aware of how the temperature had dropped.

She'd turned back, leaving the ambient light of the campfire to walk through the darkness of what felt like a ghost town. Suddenly, she was anxious to get back to the hotel as she recalled there was a killer out there somewhere.

Earlier she'd been glad that she hadn't run into Georgia after their argument—but on her walk to the hotel she'd been sorry she had no one to talk to about any of this. What friends she had would already be in bed back East. There was no man in her life, after parting ways months ago. She'd never felt more alone.

"Enjoy your walk?" the hotel owner had asked as she came in through the lobby.

"I did." She'd stopped, curious. "So have you lived here your whole life?"

Ash Hammond had nodded as if not the first time he'd been asked this. "I left for college, the NFL, but yes, I came back and bought the hotel and have been renovating it. And before you ask, no, I'm not expecting a lot of guests."

She had laughed as well since it was as if he'd read her mind. "Sorry, it is just in such an out-of-the-way place."

"We get tourists in the summer—some people get lost and end up here for the night," he'd admitted with a chuckle. "With the latest publicity, more will be coming, thanks to your father."

She'd frowned. "Him dying in your hotel?"

He'd shaken his head. "No, sorry, the dummy. The older couple who was in the nearby room swore they heard Rowdy singing after…you know."

"That's not possible. You do know the dummy doesn't talk without the ventriloquist, right? So with Clay dead, Rowdy wasn't singing."

Ash had shrugged. "Just telling you what they said they heard. Since they went to the press with the story, it will probably be like last time."

"What happened last time?"

"Rumors of the hotel being haunted brought ghost hunters out of the woodwork," he'd said and smiled. "I can see that you're a skeptic. Me too. I've had this place for over a year. Haven't seen a ghost yet."

"That's…comforting," she'd said. "Though it is interesting what the older couple in the next room said they'd heard. It could mean that the killer was still in the room manipulating the dummy."

He'd frowned. "Wouldn't the killer also have to be an impersonator? Seems unlikely."

"As unlikely as a dummy coming to life and singing because his master was dead?"

"You have a point," he'd said with another chuckle. He had a great smile and was handsome, if you liked that big brawny good-looking type. She preferred a leaner solid look. Like the sheriff. The thought had made her realize just how tired she was.

She'd said good night and gone up to bed, before falling dead asleep. But her slumber was haunted by weird dreams that left her feeling uneasy even in the light of day.

MOLLY SMELLED LIKE SUNSHINE, the sheriff thought as he led her into his office and closed the door. Her hair, long and blond, was tucked up into a rather messy ball at the nape of her slim neck. He thought that was the style nowadays. But he also thought she might have hurried after her morning shower because her hair appeared to still be damp. He feared he'd awakened her, which only made him wonder when she'd gotten to bed last night. From his upstairs apartment, he'd seen her wandering down the street toward the bar last night.

"Please have a seat," he said as he took his chair behind the desk. He couldn't help thinking about everything Coroner JP Brown had told him. There'd been so much off about this case right from the get-go.

"Peculiar case," the coroner had said earlier on the phone, once he knew he had the sheriff's attention. "Like the ink." JP had cleared his voice. "It was all over the fingers of the deceased's right hand."

"And this is important how?" Brandt had to ask.

"He was writing something with a leaky pen before he died."

The sheriff had chuckled. "He left a note on the hotel stationery with two names and phone numbers to be called in an emergency it said. There were ink drops on it and a smudge."

"*Before* he was murdered? As if he knew he was about to die?"

"Maybe. Maybe it was something the man did on a regular

basis, traveling alone and being of an age." He remembered something that hadn't struck him as terribly odd before. "Neither the leaky pen nor any of the hotel stationery that Ash supplies to the rooms was found."

"Can't imagine why the killer would have taken a leaky pen, let alone the stationery," JP said. "Maybe simply because it was free."

"I guess, but why would the killer leave the note Clay had written? Because the killer had wanted the next of kin notified? Or because it didn't matter?"

"Interesting," the coroner had said. "Didn't you tell me that the man's daughter is in town?"

JP's question had rattled him. If there was even a chance that the killer had wanted her to come to Fortune Creek, then Molly Lockhart could be in danger.

"Anyway, you're probably more interested in the DNA," the coroner had said and dropped the real bombshell.

As Molly took a chair across from him, Brandt met her gaze. This morning her eyes were like a tropical sea of blues and greens. "You were right about your father." Hadn't she told him that she thought Clay was a phony? She raised a brow. "Clay Wheaton wasn't his real name. When his DNA was run, it brought up his military service record. Did you know your father was in the military?" From her expression she hadn't. "He enlisted at seventeen with the name he was born with, Seth Crandell. According to the information he provided at that time, he was the son of Irma and Cecil Crandell with a rural address outside of Eureka, Montana."

"*Crandell? From the ranch where we went yesterday?*"

He nodded. "I believe that elderly man who came out with the shotgun is Cecil, his father. Did you see the name Seth carved in the tree?"

Her eyes widened. "*Seth.* I saw the name carved into the

tree trunk." He could see her putting the pieces together. "The story he told through Rowdy about the pocketknife and the tree hadn't been something he made up."

She hugged herself as if feeling a chill. "If that's the case then…then maybe the other stories were true too." She looked at him with a kind of wonder. She had a heart-shaped face with bow lips, her skin porcelain smooth. In the shaft of sunlight pouring into his office from the front windows he wondered how he hadn't noticed before how beautiful she was.

He blinked, realizing that she'd asked him a question. "Sorry?"

"Couldn't that explain what he was doing here if those people are his family?"

His thought exactly. "Your family too." He saw that she hadn't made that leap yet. "And there's more." She seemed to brace herself, looking expectantly at him, but also wary. "I'm sorry, but your father had cancer at a stage where if he hadn't been murdered, he would have had only weeks to live."

MOLLY TOOK THE news like a blow. Now she knew what her father had been doing here in Fortune Creek. "He'd come here to see his family before he died."

The realization came with the familiar bitter taste. Her father had come here to see his *other* family—not *her*. He'd come to see the Crandells, those odd people she'd seen yesterday.

It was as if the sheriff was thinking the same thing. "He might have had some loose ends to tie up here before he…"

She shook her head. "Before he came to tell me goodbye?" She was on her feet, angry with herself for coming here. All of this was too much to take in. She'd told herself she was doing this because she needed closure and destroying Rowdy would give it to her. The more she learned about her father, the more she didn't want to be here, the more she didn't care what had happened to him or his dummy.

"For whatever reason, he'd changed his name and became a ventriloquist," the sheriff said. "Maybe there is something about him he needed to hide behind Rowdy—and hide from you."

"His whole life was a lie even if his silly cowboy stories were true," she said. "So what if he was running from something? Hiding behind the dummy? Whatever it was, he'd come back here to…" She looked at him as if she expected him to fill in the blanks and remembered what Georgia had told her. "He'd been here before."

"Maybe," the sheriff said. "He asked for room 401 next to the fire escape, but given what we now know…"

"Someone could have told him to take that room," she said with a start.

"Maybe. There's a chance he'd been expecting company. We suspect the killer used the fire escape to enter and exit the hotel. There's no alarm on that door, but when closed, it's locked. That night someone had propped the door open with a book. Your father wrote the note with your name and phone number on it, along with his insurance agent's."

"He knew he was going to be killed. So basically, he was committing suicide by murder?"

The sheriff shook his head. "You realize this is all conjecture. We have no proof."

"He changed his name. Doesn't that sound like he had something to hide? Something to fear by staying Seth Crandell? If so, then he had to have known returning here would be dangerous. You don't think one of the Crandells killed him? His own family?"

"Not necessarily. But they might know who would want to harm him."

She groaned. "How could I not know this?" she demanded of herself more than the sheriff. "The clues were all there. That ridiculous brand on Rowdy's case. I never dreamed it was any more real than his cowboy costume or my father's."

A few moments ago, she'd wanted to walk away from all of this, regretting coming here. Now though, she knew she couldn't leave without finding out the truth. She said as much to the sheriff and saw his expression change.

"I'm not sure that's a good idea." He seemed to hesitate before he continued. "The killer took the pen your father used to leave your phone number and the extra hotel stationery. But the killer left behind the note with your name and number and Georgia Eden's." She waited, not sure what he was getting at. "The killer might have wanted you to come to Fortune Creek."

Molly frowned. "Why?"

"That's what I don't know. But you could be in danger."

She stared at him for a moment before shaking her head. "I'm not leaving until I know who killed my father—and why. I guess that means I'm going to have to go back out to the Crandell Ranch."

"Whoa!" He held up his hands, no doubt hearing the determination in her voice. "Way too dangerous. For all we know one of them killed your father."

"You're planning to go back out there, aren't you?"

"On official business this time."

She met his gaze. "Take me with you."

"Bad idea."

"Then I'll go alone."

"That is an even worse idea. Maybe you didn't pick up on the tension out there the other day. You could be shot as a trespasser. In Montana, that is definitely not unheard of."

"If you're trying to tell me that things are different here,

I've already figured that out." She gave him an impatient look. "If they have the answers, then I need to talk to them. Seth was their son. That makes me their granddaughter."

"If they killed one of their own, I doubt you being Seth's daughter will hold much sway with them," he said, trying to reason with her.

She dug in, seeing that it didn't really surprise him. "I'm going, one way or the other."

He swore under his breath. "Promise me you won't go alone…" He rushed on before she could speak. "And I'll let you ride along with me. But you have to do what I tell you. The Crandells could be dangerous."

"I have to know why my father changed his name, why he left here, why he came back and why he kept it all a secret to his death," she said. "Those people back at that ranch know."

"I suspect they might," he said, though sounding reluctant. "But that doesn't mean that they're going to tell me. Keep in mind, we're dealing with possible murderers."

"And kidnappers. Let's not forget Rowdy."

"Yes," he said with a groan. "Let's not forget Rowdy."

Chapter Eight

With time to kill before the sheriff could make the trip out to the Crandell Ranch again, he suggested Molly get some breakfast. "You wouldn't leave without me," she said, stopping in his office doorway to look back at him.

"No," he said, not appearing happy about it. "I wouldn't dream of it."

She nodded and left to walk down to the Fortune Creek Café. Along the way she passed several empty lots and the empty stone building that she'd noticed last night. The structure appeared to have been a bank. It was small with large windows across the front.

There was something about it that drew her closer. She stopped to peer in the windows. Inside, she was delighted to see an old tin ceiling, hardwood floors and oak cabinets that ran from floor to ceiling on one side. It appeared that after the bank closed, the building had been used as some kind of shop.

She could imagine it as a place that sold unique handcrafted one-of-kind items. People would drive all the way to Fortune Creek just to buy them. Maybe. If not, there was always an online business using photographs of a shop for promo. She decided she would mention it to a couple of the investors who might be interested. She'd work up a cost analysis when she returned, she thought with excitement. She'd ask the sheriff who owned the building and how much they might want for it.

Molly stopped herself. She needed to get breakfast so she'd be ready to leave when the sheriff was. But she couldn't get the building and the potential shop out of her mind since once she'd seen it, she could now imagine it as if it was already a done deal.

On down the street, she pushed open the café door to the smell of fried bacon and coffee. Her stomach rumbled as she started to step in and saw Georgia. She was sitting with a young woman with coal-black hair that had been plaited into one long braid. The two sat at a small table by the window.

She put her head down, pretending not to have seen them, and started for another table at the back.

"Molly," Georgia called to her. "Come join us. There's someone you need to meet."

She turned, pretending surprise to see the two of them sitting there, and headed for the table all smiles as if she and Georgia hadn't argued yesterday.

Georgia did the introductions as Molly took the free chair. "This is Jessica Woods. She's camped down by the creek."

Molly had seen the camp last night. But she couldn't imagine why Georgia thought she'd need to meet this woman with her hippie clothing and a little white furball of a dog in a basket beside her chair.

"And this is Ghost," Jessica said motioning to the dog. "She helps me with my research."

"Research?" Molly repeated.

"I'm a parapsychologist," Jessica said and smiled. "A ghost hunter and Ghost helps me."

"Guess why she's in Fortune Creek," Georgia said, then blurted out, "She's here about Rowdy the Rodeo Cowboy."

Molly stared at Georgia, then at the woman. Jessica was

younger than both she and Georgia but not by much. "What do you want with Rowdy?"

"The singing," Georgia said. "She wants to find out if Clay reached out to Rowdy from the other side or if Rowdy has always been the conduit for paranormal occurrences."

She stared at one woman, then the other, speechless. *She'd thought she'd heard Rowdy singing last night.* The memory came back so sharp and crisp that she would have sworn it had been real. But her father was dead so common sense told her that story was just part of this ongoing nightmare.

"I really doubt—" But Georgia cut her off, asking about the woman's dog's abilities. Fortunately, a plump brown-haired woman came out of the kitchen with a full pot of coffee. She filled a cup for Molly and took her order. "I'd like an egg white omelet with—"

"She'll take bacon and those delicious pancakes, you make, Alice."

As the woman refilled Georgia's coffee cup, she smiled. "You sure you don't want another pancake or two, Georgia? You could use some meat on those bones."

Georgia laughed and said, "The pancakes were delicious, but I'm full as a tick." The woman's laugh followed her all the way to the kitchen.

Jessica excused herself to leave for an appointment with Ash Hammond, the owner of the hotel. She scooped up the basket with the dog and left.

"What was all that about?" Molly demanded, slightly annoyed that wherever Georgia went she seemed to make friends. It wasn't a talent Molly had herself. "Ghost hunter? Pancakes and bacon?"

"You'll love the cakes," Georgia said dismissing her complaint. "It's also the special today so that's really all Alice is set up to make. That's why there aren't menus." She waved all that away and leaned conspiratorially across the table. "Do you believe this? Jessica is looking for Rowdy too. Who else is going to show up wanting the dummy?"

"That's the part you're having trouble believing?" Molly asked and then laughed, Georgia joining her. She marveled at this woman. She seemed at home no matter where it was. Even here in this strange little town.

"Maybe there's something to it," Georgia was saying. "Otherwise, how do you explain the dummy singing after your father was dead?"

She shook her head. That was just it; she couldn't explain any of this. Having just learned that Clay Wheaton was really Seth Crandell, the son of Cecil who'd almost shot her yesterday, she felt off-balance. That was enough to try to get her head around without attempting to understand why the elderly couple thought they'd heard Rowdy singing after her father had died. Clearly, they had been mistaken about the time.

"How'd your trip go with the sheriff yesterday?" Georgia asked as Alice brought out her breakfast and refilled their coffee cups, commenting on the beautiful day and complimenting the blouse Georgia was wearing.

Molly waited until Alice had gone back to the kitchen. Yesterday during their argument, she and Georgia had felt like adversaries. Which she now thought was silly. They both wanted the same thing. Kind of. Also, could she really blame Georgia for being suspicious of her given the million-dollar insurance policy?

But mostly she needed someone to confide in since who knew how long they would be here. She needed Georgia's down-home take on this mess.

"Turns out Clay Wheaton wasn't his real name."

The woman's eyes widened. "What do you mean?"

"Apparently, he'd changed it after he got out of the military before he'd met my mother. It looks like he might be related to a ranch family from around here."

"Well, that would explain what he was doing here," Georgia agreed. "Bad blood between him and the family, you think?"

"Looks that way since someone killed him and who else did he know around here?"

"Good question. I was looking on a map. The closest town of any size is Eureka."

"We went there last night. I highly recommend the Trappers Saloon, anything with huckleberries."

There was a twinkle in Georgia's eye. "You and the sheriff?"

"It wasn't like that." She felt a flush start at her throat and rise to her cheeks.

"Right. He's drop-dead gorgeous, or are you going to tell me you didn't notice?"

She'd noticed a lot about him. She'd felt his strength as he'd gripped her arm yesterday, seen his kindness and generosity when he'd shared his meal and ordered another and witnessed his fear for her when she'd defied him and gotten out of the patrol SUV at the Crandell Ranch.

She quickly changed the subject. "You're welcome to take the rental car if you want to go into Eureka. The sheriff and I are going back out to the ranch to see if anyone will admit to my father being a relative. Oh, and Clay was dying. He didn't have long at all to live."

Georgia was shaking her head. "I never would have guessed he had secrets. He seemed…sad."

Sad. Molly tried not to think about that, still angry with him for abandoning her without any explanation. "The sheriff mentioned that maybe someone my father knew had told him to ask for room 401 because it is right by the fire escape stairs. He could have even left the door propped open for his killer."

"As if he knew one of them would be coming for him."

"It's made me realize how little I know about my father," she said truthfully. "He left when I was nine. Not even my mother seemed to know much about his early years. I wish I could ask her, but she passed almost ten years ago now. There's no one to ask. Except the Crandells. And they might not be inclined to tell me anything."

"I'm sorry. All of this must come as a shock." Georgia seemed lost in thought for a moment. "It occurs to me that if you're right and Clay was from around here, a lot of people other than his family must have known him. You said he went into the military under his real name, right?"

"Enlisted at seventeen."

"So, his parents had to sign for him," Georgia said. "That's telling. But if he lived here seventeen years, then he must have gone to school, right? He must have had friends."

Molly nodded. "The answer does seem to be here. I'm staying around for a while to see what I can find out."

"I'm not leaving until I find Rowdy," Georgia said with a groan. "I might have to spend the rest of my life in Fortune Creek."

"Once the sheriff finds the killer…" Not even Molly held out much hope.

"I'm just worried that the killer could have already tried to sell Rowdy," Georgia was saying. "I've been watching for him online. I was thinking about offering a reward."

Molly hadn't thought that the killer had taken the dummy thinking it was worth money on the open market. For some reason, she'd thought it was more personal, like her own desire to get her hands on Rowdy. "Seems foolish to try to sell it if you were the murderer."

"Murder is pretty foolish when you think about it."

She couldn't argue that as she dug into her breakfast. Georgia was right. The pancakes were delish and so was the bacon. She couldn't help thinking that if the murderer was that clueless, then why not offer a reward and catch him?

"I think a reward is a good idea." They decided on a thousand dollars, Georgia saying she'd pay most of it since she had the most to lose but Molly insisted that they split it. "Okay, I'll get right on it."

Molly ate as if famished. She blamed all this fresh air up here in the wilds of Montana. When Alice came back to refill her coffee, Molly asked if Clay Wheaton had eaten his meals here.

"The man with the doll?" The woman belly laughed. "That was a first. Saw him talking to it like it was alive. I just figured he wasn't in his right mind. He seemed harmless enough."

Molly felt a wave of sadness for her father, realizing how lonely his life must have been. Had he come back here to die? To mend fences? Surely not to be murdered. But apparently, he'd known that it could happen—and it did. She thought of Rowdy and all those years he and her father were inseparable. Of course, the dummy didn't sing after her father was killed.

But if Rowdy could have, she realized he would have—just as the couple said, and that gave her a chill.

Chapter Nine

When Molly returned to the hotel, she spotted Georgia in what appeared to be serious conversation with Jessica, the younger woman she'd met that morning. She had a sudden strange uncharitable thought. What if the two were making some kind of deal? If one of them found Rowdy first—

"Molly." Georgia motioned her over to the corner where the two had been so intensely engaged. "Jessica wants in."

Still caught up in her thought of a behind-her-back deal, she said, "Wants in on what?"

"The reward," Jessica said. "I'll match whatever the two of you suggest."

"You will?" She couldn't help her surprise. Why had she gotten the feeling that Jessica might have to borrow money for gas to leave Fortune Creek? Because she hadn't had breakfast or even a cup of coffee at the café earlier? Or because she was staying in her camper down by the river? "Sure."

They decided to keep the reward at a thousand and not go any higher for the time being. Jessica took her dog and started to leave, stopping to talk to Ash for a moment. From what Molly could tell, the two were at odds. Ash was shaking his head and not looking the least bit happy as she left.

"You're sure about this?" she asked Georgia, who shrugged. "I thought we should at least ask her if she was interested.

She wants Rowdy as much as we do. I already told Cora Green at that little store about the reward." Georgia grinned. "As talkative as she is, I figure she'll let people around here know. I'm also putting it in the Eureka both print and online newspaper, *Tobacco Valley News*, and the local shopper."

"Sounds good," Molly said distractedly. She couldn't get Jessica off her mind. "What's with her and Ash?"

"She wants to investigate the hotel for paranormal activity while she's waiting for Rowdy to be found. Apparently, Ash isn't wild about the idea. She plans to get a room and do the investigating on her own. She seems very determined."

As the front door opened, Molly caught a glint in Georgia's eye as Deputy Jaden Montgomery strode in. He stopped in the middle of the lobby, pushing back his Stetson as he called out a hello to Ash.

"I'm going to do some investigating of my own with a little help from that handsome deputy," Georgia said with a grin. "Wish me luck." And with that, she was off, calling, "Deputy, a moment of your time."

As Molly started for the elevator, her cell phone rang. It was the sheriff.

BRANDT REALIZED THERE was no way he would have been able to keep a lid on the murder—even if the story about the singing ventriloquist's dummy hadn't gone viral. It wasn't every day that a ventriloquist was killed in Fortune Creek, Montana—let alone his dummy missing.

He was just getting ready to leave after his call to Molly when Helen came in with her "more-bad-news face." He groaned. "Now what?"

"A thousand-dollar reward is being offered for the dummy."

"Molly?" Helen nodded and waited. *"Georgia?"* Another nod and still she stood, hip cocked, in his office doorway. "If you tell me Jessica Woods—" She nodded and left, closing the door behind her so he could swear in peace.

"Jessica Woods?" he repeated to himself. She had a stake in finding Rowdy, but she didn't appear to be someone who had money to throw away.

He wished that they had asked him about offering a reward for Rowdy. Now the killer knew the dummy was worth something. Maybe worse, the killer might also realize that the dummy could be worth even more. He shook his head, reminded of who he was dealing with—three very determined young women.

As Molly came through the front door of the sheriff's department, he tamped down his anger and frustration. He could understand Georgia's desperation in finding Rowdy. He could even see Jessica wanting to get her hands on the dummy, but Molly? Was she really willing to pay good money to get Rowdy back so she could destroy it? Also, if found, she was out a million dollars.

That thought made him uneasy. Maybe she had her reasons for playing along pretending to look for Rowdy, offering a reward, saying she just wanted to put an end to the doll. Or maybe she and her father were in on this from the beginning, and she knew Rowdy was never going to turn up.

He shook his head, recalling the fact that Molly had a solid alibi. She'd been clear across the country when Clay had died and Rowdy had disappeared. But that didn't mean she hadn't had an accomplice here in Fortune Creek. But would that make the partner the killer?

Brandt swore, hating his suspicious nature, hating worse that he had no idea yet who'd killed the ventriloquist or who had Rowdy the Rodeo Cowboy.

Rising from his desk, he plucked his Stetson off the rack and walked out his door, mentally berating himself. Why did he want to suspect Molly? To keep her at arm's length? Quite possibly, since he'd had his heart broken not all that long ago by a big-city woman. His poor battered heart was still recovering and couldn't be trusted if he got too close to Molly Lockhart.

Attractive or not, Molly was off-limits because her life was in New York City. His life was in Fortune Creek. Not to mention, a very small-town sheriff would be the last man she'd be interested in. Except maybe for a fling with a cowboy. That he'd even consider a short-term romp with the woman had him shaking his head in exasperation. He needed to find Clay's killer and that damned dummy before he did something he would regret.

Molly was visiting with Helen as he came out of his office. Helen was usually a pretty good judge of character, and she seemed to like Molly. He reminded himself that she'd also liked that fluffy bit of fur Ghost too.

"Ready?" he asked at a break in the conversation. He saw both of their startled looks at the abruptness of his tone. He was determined to keep this all business. "Helen, you know where to reach me."

She nodded, her recently permed gray curls bobbing as she turned back to her own desk.

"Helen said you had a burr under your saddle," Molly said after a few miles of silence. "You'll have to translate that for me."

"Wish you'd talked to me about the reward before you offered it," he said without looking at her.

"I thought the idea was to find the murderer."

He looked over at her. "Is it?"

THEY RODE IN silence for a few more miles. Clearly, the sheriff was angry. Just about the reward? Or was there something else bothering him? She thought it might be the latter.

Molly let him stew in his own juices for a while longer before she said, "It was Georgia's idea. She would have offered the reward even if I hadn't offered to pitch in. She has the most to lose if Rowdy isn't found."

"What about you?" he asked, flicking a glance at her before quickly turning back to his driving down the narrow two-lane road. "You seem to have everything to gain by Rowdy *not* being found."

"Is that what's bothering you?" she asked with a laugh as she leaned back against the seat to stare out at the pine trees and mountains that blurred past outside the patrol SUV. Overhead white whisps of clouds skated across the big blue sky. "It's beautiful here." Maybe it was the surprise she too heard in her voice that made him slow down and look at her again.

"You just now noticed that?"

In the hours since his call about her father's death, she'd felt nothing but angry and inconvenienced, her emotions at war. Look how long it had taken for her to even notice how handsome the sheriff was. No surprise that she hadn't really appreciated the scenery. Or the lawman next to her.

Those blue eyes seemed to search her face as if he could find answers to his suspicions hidden there. Broad-shouldered, slim-hipped with long legs, everything about him sculpted in muscle, how could she not appreciate the view? Like his suntanned hands gripping the wheel. Hands of a working man. She wondered what he'd done before he'd climbed behind the desk as sheriff.

He was nothing like the men she'd dated in New York. Everything about him was strong and capable in this part of the country where such attributes could save your life. Not to mention determined, this man of the law. All of it made him more attractive than any man she'd ever known.

"What?" he asked still sounding irritated. She shook her head. He dragged his gaze away, slowing further to make the turn onto the country road into the Crandell Ranch.

She took a breath, let it out slowly, the cab of the patrol SUV seeming a little too cozy, a little too intimate. What was it about this cowboy that drew her, that made her want to know him and his secrets?

He hit a bump in the road and she wrestled her thoughts away from the sheriff as she prepared for her father's apparent family. Definitely not welcoming last time. She hated to think how much worse it could be this time.

As she glanced over at the sheriff again, she saw his shoulders tense as he turned down the even more narrow, bumpy road to the ranch. He too was concerned about the reception they would get. She told herself that the Crandells wouldn't shoot the sheriff. At least she hoped not as she saw the buildings ahead—and that huge tree with her father's name carved into it.

BRANDT BRACED HIMSELF as he pulled into the Crandell ranch yard again. He expected this time was going to be more confrontational. It was no secret that the Crandells didn't like visitors; they *really* didn't like the law.

But he was pretty sure the old man had lied about not knowing who Clay Wheaton was. Not that Brandt thought asking about Seth Crandell's murder was going to get him far either. At least he might be able to find out if they knew Seth had a daughter. Maybe they wouldn't care. He supposed it would depend on how they'd felt about their son Seth, he told himself.

"I want you to stay in the patrol car this time." He parked, shut off the engine and turned to her. "This could go a number of ways. If it goes completely south, lock the doors and get on the radio for help. Just push that button."

Her eyes widened in alarm. "Whatever you do, don't get out." As he opened his door, she grabbed his arm to stop him. He looked back at her, seeing her concern for him and smiling even as he told himself not to make too much of it. The drive here had been difficult enough. He'd never been so aware of a woman or his growing curiosity about her.

"It's okay," he said, sorry he'd scared her. "People seldom shoot a sheriff." She slowly released her hold on him and nodded, not looking the least convinced. He wasn't all that certain either.

He climbed out and closed the door before he headed toward the house. He hadn't gone far when the front door flew open.

The elderly rancher they'd seen the last time came out, the same shotgun in his hands, an even more irritated glowering warning on his face. "I thought I told you—"

"Cecil Crandell?" Brandt said. "I don't want trouble. I just need to talk to you about your son Seth."

"Never heard of him. Unless you have a warrant, you'd best get back in that rig and be on your way." He shifted the shotgun, definitely looking like he meant business.

"Put down the shotgun, Cecil. I'm investigating Seth's murder. I just need to ask you a few questions. We can do it here or at the sheriff's department."

"I don't know anything about it," the old man said lowering the shotgun only a hair. "Now get off my property."

With a silent curse, Brandt heard the door of the patrol SUV open behind him. He wanted to throttle Molly. He should have known she wouldn't follow directions.

"You aren't Seth's father?" she demanded. "Well, his DNA says otherwise," she said as she marched toward the house.

"If you don't care that he's dead, then you probably don't care that I'm his daughter and a Crandell. *Your granddaughter.*"

Cecil Crandell stared at Molly, eyes hard and narrowed. "I don't care who you are. You're not welcome here."

Brandt started to go after Molly but stopped when the door behind the man opened on a creaky hinge and an elderly woman stepped out drying her hands on her worn apron.

"Who did you say you are?" the woman demanded.

"Go back inside, Irma. I'm handling this," Cecil said.

She ignored him, stepping to the edge of the porch to motion to her granddaughter. Molly moved closer, even though Brandt wanted to pull her back. "You resemble him," she said, eyes squinted, her voice breaking. "What's your name?"

"Molly." She moved to the edge of the porch.

"Irma, don't make me—"

"Hush, Cecil, you old fool." Her gaze was fixed on Molly. "Come inside." She motioned to Molly, then shot a look at the sheriff. "You stay where you are." Turning to her husband, she said, "Cecil, you see to that tractor of yours. I want to talk to her alone."

For a moment, Brandt held his breath, afraid of what would happen next.

He didn't like the idea of Molly going into that house alone with the woman, but he also had heard clearly in the older woman's voice that he wasn't invited.

Cecil looked as if ready to put up an argument.

The sheriff, realizing how quickly this could go south, gave Cecil a way out. "I'll wait by my patrol car, as long as you promise me this young woman is safe."

Irma Crandell scoffed at even the idea of Molly not being safe in her home. Motioning to her granddaughter, she turned and headed back inside. Over her shoulder, she said, "And put that shotgun down, Cecil."

As Brandt returned to stand next to his patrol SUV, Cecil set down the shotgun, but he didn't go see to his tractor. Instead, he sat down on the porch in a weathered rocker, the weapon within reach.

Brandt didn't like anything about this, but under the circumstances, there wasn't much he could do. He had no evidence that these people had anything to do with Clay Wheaton's death so there would be no chance of getting a warrant. And he sure as hell didn't have any control over Molly Lockhart.

Chapter Ten

Out of the corner of her eye, Molly had watched Cecil as if he was a snake coiled up to strike. He'd leaned the shotgun against the house, but not before she'd seen his fingers shaking with fury.

She'd been almost relieved to get past him and inside the cold and dark old house. It didn't feel that much safer. Shadows seemed to hunker behind the large worn furniture. Irma Crandell led her back through the living room, down a long hallway and finally into the massive ranch kitchen. She followed the woman and the smell of boiled cabbage, her heart in her throat. She'd taken a chance, one the sheriff would be furious about, but she had to know more about her father.

If the information the sheriff had gotten on the DNA was correct, this jerky-tough, scrawny woman had given birth to him. Molly figured Irma Crandell had to be eighty but looked much older as if weathered by her hard life. As they traveled through the old house, Molly had tried to imagine her father growing up here with Cecil and Irma as his parents.

Irma motioned her toward a chair at the kitchen table and went back to her cooking at a huge old stove. "Tell me about Seth," the woman said, her back to Molly.

She had come here hoping to find out about her father—not to fill his mother in on the past half century. On shaky legs, she lowered herself into a chair. "I didn't know he was Seth Crandell." She waited for a reaction; getting none, she continued. "He'd changed his name to Clay Wheaton and became a ventriloquist."

The woman stiffened, then turned, clearly surprised. "One of them fellas that throw their voice to make a doll talk?"

Close enough, Molly thought, and nodded. "After he came out of the military and married my mother, he worked for a while as a mechanic before he became a ventriloquist. I was nine when he left my mother and me. I didn't know anything about his past."

Irma turned back to the stove. "How'd you find us then?"

She took another shaky breath, let it out. "My father came to Fortune Creek, to the hotel there and was murdered." No response. "When they ran his DNA, I discovered his real name and his connection to you. I thought he must have come back here to see you." Still no response. "I was hoping you could tell me about him since I know nothing about the first seventeen years of his life."

Irma lifted a lid on a pot, stirred and put down the spoon. She seemed to slump against the stove for a moment. Molly started to reach for her, afraid she might collapse, but the woman quickly caught herself and turned, wiping her hands on her apron again.

"He was a good boy, so sweet, so gentle," Irma said, her blue eyes filling. "Cecil…" She shook her head. "Seth didn't fit in here on the ranch. It was hard on Cecil even before…" She stopped, swallowed, looked away. "Before the trouble in town, before Seth had to leave."

"What kind of trouble in town?" Molly asked, her voice almost a whisper as the pots on the stove boiled and burbled, the only sound in the room.

"That girl." She waved a hand through the air as if to silence herself. "Where did my son live?"

"I don't know. I lost track of him. I was born in New York City. That's where I still live. I'm a financial analyst. I help businesses invest their money." She saw the woman's blank look along with absolutely no interest in her granddaughter's career. She tried not to let that hurt. What had she expected? Open arms? Any kind of recognition at all?

She refused to let this woman's lack of interest in her hurt her any more than her father's already had. After all, this woman and that man out on the porch had raised her father. Maybe the sheriff was right. Maybe her father could only communicate through a dummy after being raised here in this house.

"What girl?" she asked.

Irma shook her head. "Not diggin' up that old bone." She turned back to her stove. "New York City huh?" she mumbled under her breath before she said, "You should go. I wouldn't come back here if I was you."

Molly rose, studying her grandmother's years-hardened brittle frame for a few moments before she headed for the door. On the porch, she passed her grandfather, watching him from the corner of her eye as she tried not to show fear. She walked, head high, to the patrol SUV where the sheriff stood waiting for her. She wasn't going to let these people get to her.

"Next time I come out here, Cecil, it will be with a warrant," the sheriff said. Without another word, they both climbed in. The sheriff started the engine and drove down the road out of the Crandell Ranch. Molly felt a strange numbness, remembering something her mother used to say when she asked about her father.

Sometimes you don't want to know the truth.

BRANDT COULDN'T BEGIN to guess what had happened inside that house. He mentally kicked himself for letting Molly go in alone—even as he knew he couldn't have stopped her. Nor, he reminded himself, Cecil would never have allowed him in the house—not without a warrant. He suspected in the past this family had had other run-ins with the law and mentally made a note to check.

Glancing at Molly, he tamped down his anger knowing it rose from his worry about her because of the reckless, dangerous things she did. If anything, he felt a rush of sympathy. Whatever had happened in that house, it hadn't been healing. Her father murdered, her lack of a relationship with him and now finding out that she was the granddaughter of those people back there who he suspected didn't give a whit about her.

He couldn't imagine what she was going through. He tried to read her mood as he drove. She'd just met her grandparents. Not the reunion she'd hoped for, he would bet on that. She couldn't have expected much given Cecil's reaction. Hard to tell with Irma, but something told him that Molly wasn't going to be invited back anytime soon. He gave her time to process it, not pushing, not scolding her for doing exactly what he told her not to do.

"Okay, that was weird," Molly said as they reached the main road. She seemed to shake herself as if throwing off whatever had happened inside that house.

"Are you all right?" he asked, worried about what that old woman might have told her, even as he reminded himself that he had tried to protect her from her family.

She looked over at him. "Aren't you going to yell at me for getting out of the vehicle, Sheriff?"

"Would it do any good?"

"No."

"Then I guess not. Learn anything interesting a sheriff should know?"

"All she told me was that Seth never fit in on the ranch—Cecil was disappointed in him even before he got into trouble with some girl in town. I'm assuming she meant Eureka—isn't that the closest town?"

He nodded. "What kind of trouble?"

"'*Not diggin' up that old bone,*' Irma said and then told me I shouldn't come back to the ranch again. I suspect if she'd been disappointed in her son before, she was more so now. Apparently, she isn't a fan of New York City nor of ventriloquism."

Brandt chuckled, relieved that Molly seemed to be taking the rejection well enough. At least on the surface. She'd felt rejected by her father and now her grandparents. He wished there was more he could do. But there were things he couldn't protect her from. Maybe herself especially.

"If one of the family killed him," Molly said. "Irma didn't know about it. I got the impression she hadn't even known he was in the area. But if she finds out who killed her son… well, I think she might hurt them. I got the feeling she loved my father and that she blames Cecil for him leaving."

She turned to look at him, determination burning like tears in her eyes. "I want to dig up that old bone and find out why my father was sent away."

CECIL CAREFULLY PUT his shotgun just inside the door where he always kept it and walked into the kitchen. Irma didn't acknowledge him as she set the table.

"You want me to call everyone in for lunch?" he asked. After all these years, he knew this woman better than he knew himself. Just by the set of her narrow slightly stooped shoulders he knew she was furious with him.

She stepped to the flatware drawer, jerked it open and pulled out a large carving knife before she responded. "Did you see him?"

The question hung in the air. He studied her grip on the knife, the way her arthritic fingers clutched it until her knuckles turned white. A lie caught in his throat. "Seth?"

She turned then, knife in hand as she leveled her gaze on him, her warning as clear as the sharp point of the blade. The intensity of her look scared him. Seth had always been her favorite. She'd coddled that boy, and they'd fought about it endlessly until he'd left. Even after what had happened, she'd tried to stop him from signing the papers so the boy could go into the military, saying he was too young, too gentle. Cecil had hoped the army would toughen the boy up, make a man out of him.

What Irma hadn't understood was that Seth had to go and not just because Cecil couldn't bear the sight of his oldest son and she knew it. Her heart had hardened against him the moment he'd signed the papers that would send Seth into the armed service. Then he'd walked out, turning his back on the two of them as he'd silently hoped never to lay eyes on Seth again.

"He was murdered at the hotel in Fortune Creek," she said, her voice raspy and yet controlled. Too controlled.

He shook his head slowly, the lie coming easily at the mere memory of his son, a grown man, with that ridiculous doll. Making the puppet talk and sing, mocking him, mocking his way of life.

"Murdered?" He slumped into a chair and put an arm over his eyes. He could feel her watching him, almost feel the initial prick of the blade before he imagined the lethal, life-ending pain as the knife was plunged into him. He could see how badly she wanted to end this. He just hoped she would

go for his heart, puncture it and let him bleed out here in this house, here on this ranch that had been his life.

Time seemed suspended. He couldn't bear to look into her eyes for fear she would see the truth, and nothing could stop her from what he knew she had wanted to do for years.

"You'd best call the boys in," she said dropping the knife back in the drawer and slamming it.

Chapter Eleven

Cecil left the house feeling the weight of Irma's fury over him pushing Seth out settle familiarly on his shoulders. He blamed himself for letting her ruin that boy. He should have stepped in sooner when he saw her mollycoddling Seth. By the time he tried to take the boy in hand, it was too late.

He shuddered at the memory of the man Seth had become. He still couldn't believe him with that puppet on his arm—let alone the words that had come out of that creature's mouth. As if Cecil hadn't known it was his son saying those painful words, pretending the dummy was doing the talking.

Balling his hands into fists, he recalled his rage. He'd wanted to stomp that ridiculous doll into sawdust and lock his hands around his son's throat until he strangled the life from him. Why he had ever agreed to meet Seth after all these years was beyond him. He would regret it the rest of his life. If Irma ever found out...

And now Seth's daughter was in town asking a lot of questions, stirring the pot.

His son Gage came out of his house on the property before Cecil could call out to him. Gage's sons Cliff and Wyatt appeared next to him on the porch, making it clear that they had been watching the goings-on next door even before his son spoke.

"What was that about?" Gage asked. He sounded worried. Cecil wanted to tell him not to concern himself. "I thought you ran that sheriff off?"

Gage was the middle son of the three Cecil had been blessed with. He was thankful for Gage since Seth had been a huge disappointment and Ty... He didn't like to think about Ty who was buried up on a rise behind the house.

If it hadn't been for Gage and his two sons, Cliff and Wyatt, Cecil didn't know how they would have survived and kept the ranch going.

"Nothing to worry about. I'll take care of it," Cecil said and motioned them away from their house and away from their nosey wives inside. "Let's talk on the way over to lunch," he said. Every day, he had Irma make lunch for the boys so they could get back to work without a lot of female prattle at the table from their wives.

He wondered how much they'd witnessed of the sheriff and the young woman. Better to hear it from him than some fool at the feed store. Something like Seth's daughter showing up around here was bound to go countywide if not further. Still it made him angry. He didn't like anyone knowing his business, maybe especially his family.

"It's about that murder over in Fortune Creek."

"Why would the sheriff be asking you about that?" Gage sounded suspicious. Or worried, he wasn't sure which.

Cecil swore, stopping halfway between the houses to get this settled. He couldn't have them talking about any of it in front of Irma. "The man called himself Clay Wheaton." He saw that they'd already heard.

"He was one of them who could throw his voice," Wyatt said nodding. "Had this doll he called Rowdy who could sing. My friend Huck showed me on YouTube. Damnedest thing I ever saw. The man's mouth didn't even move."

"If you're through," Cecil snapped. "He weren't really Clay Wheaton. He made that up. His real name was…" He took a breath and let it out. "Seth. Seth Crandell."

Both of Gage's sons looked confused until their father said, "He was my older brother."

"I thought you said he died in the war," Cliff said.

Seth's name hadn't been spoken for more than half a century on this ranch. There were no photos of him in the house. The carving on the old tree trunk was the only sign that Seth had ever existed.

"What about that girl?" Wyatt asked. "The one who went in the house?"

Cecil growled under his breath. "Seth's daughter. She needs to go back from where she come from before she stirs up more trouble. Now I don't want to hear another word about any of this in front of Irma. She's upset enough. One word and—"

"Understood," Gage said as Cecil gave his grandsons a look that made them snap their mouths shut. "Too bad you can't shut up everyone in the county when this comes out."

Cecil grunted, wishing the same thing. He could feel Gage's questioning gaze on him as if he knew there was more and when it came out…

He knew only too well what it would mean if Irma learned even half of the truth.

In the meantime, he couldn't have Seth's progeny showing up here again. The question was what to do about Molly Lockhart. He considered what it would take to get rid of her like he had her father all those years ago. Whatever he decided, he knew he'd have to do it himself—and without Irma finding out.

BRANDT KEPT THINKING about what Molly had told him regarding Seth getting into trouble with some girl in town. While it might be what had sent him away from the ranch, the sheriff suspected it wasn't the reason Seth Crandell had come home.

But it very well could be what had gotten him killed. It was definitely a place to start by looking into Seth's past. Fortunately, Molly wanted answers as well.

"We could go on into Eureka and ask around about your father at the high school," he said as the patrol SUV idled at the crossroads. Normally, he wouldn't take a civilian on a murder investigation. But her wanting to know about her father would open doors to them that a badge wouldn't. Also, he felt the need to keep an eye on her. He had no idea what she might do next.

"Thought we could stop by the schools, see if anyone remembers Seth or some incident with a town girl about forty years ago," he continued when she didn't answer. "I know it's a long shot, but afterward I'll spring for an elk burger at Trappers."

She nodded as he started to turn left onto the highway toward the small tourist town rather than right toward Fortune Creek. His cell phone rang. It was JP from the coroner's office. "I need to take this." Pulling over to the side of the dirt road, he climbed out of the patrol SUV and walked up the road a way before he answered the call. He didn't want Molly hearing what he knew JP was calling about.

"I was just finishing up the autopsy," the coroner said. "You want to wait until I type up my report?"

"No, what've you got?"

"He appears to have been killed execution style. Shot in the back of the head. The bullet went into his brain. He would have died before he hit the floor."

"The other guests at the hotel said they heard a loud thud as he hit the floor. But they said nothing about a gunshot."

"He was killed with a .22 caliber handgun. Close range

aimed so the bullet entered the brain, powerful enough to pierce the skull and then ricochet around inside the cavity scrambling brain matter, but not powerful enough to exit and make a mess. A nice tidy quiet kill."

"A .22?" He couldn't help being surprised.

"Probably something like a Ruger Mark IV, the classic *Hitman* .22 suppressed gun," JP said.

"That's actually the name of the gun?"

"Yep. Short barrel. Anything you put through it would be quieter than the tapping of a pen." The coroner had a fascination with guns after only a few years on the job.

"You're saying the gun probably had a suppressor on it?"

"That would be my guess."

"So the killer would have had to apply for a permit. That should narrow down the suspects," Brandt said. "Also it takes months to get the permit and then the suppressor. He couldn't just buy one at his local convenience store. Clay Wheaton hadn't been in town that long. Unless the killer knew months in advance that the ventriloquist was coming to Montana…"

"There are ways to get around the law. I shouldn't have to tell you that," JP said. "The killer could have already had a weapon with a suppressor on it."

"Okay, let's say the killer got a suppressor for a gun like you mentioned. Clay Wheaton was a big man. The shot was fired at close range, right? So how did he pull that off?"

"It appears the victim was already on his knees. There was no sign of a struggle, but his nose was broken. It appears he fell face forward into the floor and didn't even have a chance to block his fall before he died."

"So there's a good chance that when he opened his hotel room door, he knew his killer."

"Maybe," JP said. "Open the door, someone is holding a gun on you. I suppose you'd do whatever the person said, even get down on your knees. Now what's this about the dummy singing after the ventriloquist died?"

"Pure fantasy."

MOLLY HAD WATCHED the sheriff on the phone in her side mirror. His reaction to whatever news he was getting made her certain it was about her father's murder. She watched him rub the back of his neck, kick at a small rock in the road and shake his head as if he was having trouble believing what he was being told.

She glanced away as he pocketed his phone and headed back to the patrol SUV, a scowl on his handsome face.

"Sorry that took so long," he said as he climbed behind the wheel.

"Something new on my father's murder?" she asked.

He glanced over at her. She saw him debating as to how much to tell her. "It was just the coroner filling me in. I believe we're looking for someone who knew your father and vice versa. Your father didn't put up a fight. Maybe because the killer had a gun on him. Or because he'd been expecting it."

She could tell he was leaving out a lot. "I'll be able to read the coroner's report at some point, right?"

"Once the case is closed," he said. "In the meantime, if it helps, he died instantly." She nodded and looked away as he started the engine. "If you want to go back to the hotel—"

"No," she said quickly. "Let's find out who killed him and took Rowdy."

"Yes, Rowdy. You haven't heard anything from Georgia about the reward offer?"

She shook her head, asking herself why she was going through this. Was it really to get her hands on Rowdy? Or find her father's killer? She suspected it was more complicated than that. She wanted to know her father. But she feared she might regret what she learned after meeting his family. *Her* family, she reminded herself as they left the pine-covered mountains to drop down into the valley.

Eureka in the daylight was like a metropolis compared to Fortune Creek, Molly realized. The other evening it was already dark as they'd entered town. She hadn't gotten a feel for its size. Nor had she realized how close it was to Canada. She saw a sign that said it was only nine miles to the border. She'd never been this far north in the US before. It gave her an odd feeling of being untethered from the world she had known.

With mountain peaks in the distance, she felt strangely more closed in here than in the sheriff's small hometown of Fortune Creek deep in the mountains and trees.

"Is this where you went to high school?" Molly asked as he turned off Highway 93, also known as Dewey Avenue apparently, and drove a block to the school.

"Yep. Good old Lincoln High," he said as he parked in the lot and turned to her. "Here's how I think we should play this. We're inquiring about your father, Seth Crandell. As far as we know, few people know Seth was Clay Wheaton since we just found out. People might be more anxious to talk about Seth under those circumstances."

She nodded. "Unless they're the killer."

"Yep," he said as they entered the high school. It smelled like every high school Molly had ever been in. As they walked down the hallways, she tried to see the sheriff here as a teenager. They passed a glass case with trophies. She slowed, noticing the names engraved on them.

"You were a jock," she said, surprised that she was surprised. It was no shock Ash at the hotel had been a football player. She studied the trophies. "Rodeo?"

"It is Montana," he said and pointed down another hallway. "Come on."

Still she lingered a little longer getting a sense of the teen-

ager he'd been—not all that much different from the man now
wearing the badge, she decided. Grinning, she let him lead
her deeper into the school. "I'm betting girls just flocked to
your rodeos."

"Don't start," he said looking embarrassed. "I was young."

"Young and obviously good at riding anything that bucked."

He shook his head at her as he stopped at a door marked
Administration.

"I see you didn't have any trouble remembering where to
find the principal's office. You ever get called down here?"

He grinned in answer as he pushed open the door. An
older woman looked up from behind the counter. Her eyes
widened as she cried, "Brandt? I thought you'd had enough
of this school years ago."

He laughed as she came around the counter to give him
a hug. "Good to see you, Elsie."

"So you weren't all that bad," she whispered as Elsie went
to see if the principal was free.

"It's all relative, but I don't miss this place. I have friends
who want to do it all over again. Not me." He glanced at her.
"What about you?"

"High school?" She cringed. "Once was plenty. When your
father is a ventriloquist, well, a lot of people think it's funny
and kids can be cruel."

"I'm sorry."

She waved it off. "I think I've heard every ventriloquist
joke there is and some even I was impressed with."

"Still, that had to be hard."

"Clearly, I have some issues when it comes to my father and Rowdy," she said with a laugh. "But I'm working
through them."

He gave her hand a quick squeeze before Elsie returned
and said they could go in. As they did, the sheriff put his hand

on the middle of her back. Even through her jacket, she felt the heat of his touch and missed it as the principal rose from his desk to extend a hand to Brandt.

Principal Hugh Griffith was a robust man with thinning hair and a florid round face. There was a large Stetson on one end of his desk and Molly would bet he was wearing boots. She'd seen rodeo awards in the case alongside Brandt's with that name.

"Brandt, it's almost like yesterday." His smile was genuine as he greeted them, shaking his friend's hand.

"Good to see you, Hugh," the sheriff agreed. "This is Molly Lockhart. She's staying up in Fortune Creek."

"Nice to meet you. Sit," Hugh said and plopped back into his chair. "And she wanted a tour of your old high school?" He lifted a brow in question.

"Not exactly. She just found out that her father's family is from around here. She was hoping to find out more about Seth Crandell."

"Seth?" He frowned. "Before my time. Any idea when he graduated?"

"He might not have. Joined the military at seventeen."

Hugh turned to his computer. "Give me some idea of when he should have graduated."

Brandt did the math. Seth died at sixty-two. "Forty-five years ago."

"Hmm. I show he was a student, but that's about all I can tell you," Hugh said. "Doesn't look like he participated in any school activities outside of class. You know who might remember him is Walter Franks over at the newspaper. Might even be something in the archives."

IRMA CRANDELL KEPT thinking about that snip of a woman who'd come looking for answers about her father. Molly, she'd called herself. Had some highfalutin job in New York City. Just the kind of young woman Cecil would find contemptuous—much like he had her father.

That was why she'd sent her away, telling her not to come back. She couldn't let Cecil get near that young woman. Look how he'd been with Seth. She wasn't going to let her husband destroy Seth's daughter as well.

Seth. For years she'd done her best to put her son from her thoughts. It hurt too bad. She'd gone through the years simply putting one foot in front of the other, making meals, doing what had to be done. If she had let him consume her thoughts, she couldn't have managed. It had been hard enough to crawl into bed each night next to Cecil, let alone let him touch her.

But now that she knew Seth had come back, that Cecil had met with him and lied to her about it… She found herself filled with a different kind of fiery rage that she couldn't extinguish. At the heart of it was the fear that Cecil had killed her son.

If he had, there was only one thing she could do, something she regretted not doing all those years ago. Now she just needed to dig up those old bones, a truth that had been buried in a deep, dark hole because she'd been afraid of it coming to light.

Irma was no longer afraid of facing the past. It was her present that terrified her to her aging heart. She thought of Seth's daughter. Her granddaughter. She couldn't let sentiment stop her as she planned what to do.

Nothing—and no one—could stop her once she made up her mind.

And her mind had been made up a long time ago.

BRANDT DIDN'T HOLD out much hope in discovering what had happened when Seth Crandell was seventeen. It was as if he was a ghost who'd left no footprint of his years in the area.

The newspaper office was housed in a narrow brick building on the edge of town that looked as if it had been built at least a hundred years ago. Walter Franks, a man about her father's age, explained that both employees were at lunch, but that he would be happy to help.

They sat down after he cleared a stack of newspapers off the chairs in his small office. "Of course, I remember Seth," he said. "Small class especially back then, you know." He rubbed his chin with his fingers as he looked to the ceiling. "Quiet, stayed to himself. He had one friend though who he spent time with I believe—at least at Bud Harper."

"Is Bud still around?" Brandt asked.

Walter shook his head. "Passed a couple of years ago. But Bud's sister still lives here, Lucy Gunther. She might remember something about Seth. Sorry I can't be more helpful. Whatever happened to Seth?"

"He passed away," Molly said. "I realized I knew very little about him."

Walter had to take care of a customer, but he led them back to a room where they could go through papers from that time on microfiche. They started with the year before Seth Crandell had left for the military.

"It would help if we knew what we were looking for," Molly said. "I haven't found his name anywhere. Apparently, he wasn't involved in any sports or events that might have gotten his name in the newspaper."

Brandt had noticed the same thing. "Some ranchers don't let their sons play school sports because they're needed back home for chores. Seth could have been one of them."

"Did you know Ruby Sherman?" Molly asked.

Her question surprised him. "She's kind of a cautionary tale around these parts," he said distractedly as he looked through old papers.

"There's a big long article about her car wreck. I wonder if my father knew her. They were about the same age."

Brandt was ready to give up when Molly said, "Here's something. 'Ty Crandell, son of Cecil and Irma Crandell, died of a gunshot wound.' That's all it says other than his death was being investigated. But it's dated…forty-five years ago. That would have been the year my father left for the service."

Brandt glanced over at the short article. "You're right. My father was sheriff back then," he said looking at the date of Ty's death. "There might be something in the case file. I'll check." He sighed. "Are you up to trying to locate Lucy Gunther while we're in town? Maybe we should have lunch first."

"I'm not very hungry."

His cell phone rang. He excused himself and took the call. "JP, you have something for me?" He listened. "Okay, on my way." He disconnected. "I need to get back."

"It's fine with me. I'm anxious to find out if there's been any response to the reward Georgia posted and I haven't been able to reach her by phone."

"Sure," he said, seeing the fatigue on her face. The more they found out, the more it appeared that Seth Crandell wasn't even a ghost. It was as if he'd never existed—at least not in any memorable way. "Let me know if you get a response on the reward."

MOLLY NODDED, wondering how she and Georgia would handle the exchange if someone did come forward—especially knowing the person could be a killer.

As the sheriff drove them out of Eureka and into the mountains toward Fortune Creek, she closed her eyes, suddenly feeling exhausted. Just that morning she'd met her grandmother and grandfather. It was hard not to be insulted by their lack of interest in her. Irma had acted as if she'd loved her son, that he might have been a favorite and yet she'd had no interest at all in his daughter.

The apple hadn't fallen far from the tree, she reminded herself. Her own father hadn't had any trouble cutting her from his life, preferring to spend all his time with Rowdy. She wondered if she would ever find out who Seth Crandell had been, this man behind the puppet—or if she wanted to.

The next thing she knew she was bolting awake lost in more of a nightmare than a dream, her seat belt keeping her from flying to her feet. She frantically looked around, unsure where she was. The sheriff, she saw, had pulled up in front of his office and shut off the engine. That must have been what had awakened her.

She'd fallen asleep?

"You all right?" he asked in concern.

She nodded even though she was still partially trapped in the nightmare, trapped in the Crandell kitchen with Cecil saying something about killing a bad gene. She shivered as the nightmare began to disperse like fog burning off in sunshine.

Her mouth dry, her pulse still thumping, she reached to open her door. She was anxious to get out, needing fresh air and both feet on the ground to assure her that she wasn't still in that nightmare about to die.

"Thank you for taking me along," she said as he climbed out on the other side. She looked across the hood of the SUV at him. He had that worried frown on his face. "I appreciate everything you're doing for me."

"I'm also looking for his killer," he reminded her. "But I'm glad I can help you as well."

She felt foolish. Of course, he hadn't done this all because of her. He was merely doing his job; their two agendas, if not exactly the same, were close enough that they could help each other. Flushing with embarrassment, she turned and hurried across the street to the hotel.

In the lobby, she saw that Ash wasn't behind the desk and was relieved. She wasn't in the mood for chitchat. Strands of that strange dream rolled in on the mist fogging her brain. She took the elevator, glad she didn't have to share it. She wondered if she and Georgia were the only guests in this place. The thought wasn't a comforting one.

At Georgia's door, there was no response to her knock. She tried again, then turned to her own room. After she unlocked her door, it swung open and she saw that someone had left her a note. It was on hotel stationery, a single sheet folded in half. It had apparently been slipped under her door.

Georgia, she thought as she picked it up. Had someone contacted them about Rowdy? Stepping in, she dropped her purse on the bed and unfolded the single sheet of hotel stationery.

Her hand began to shake as she blinked down at the childishly large handwriting randomly placed across the page. It took her a moment to figure out what it even said, especially with the numerous ink blotches that had spilled on the page.

Her heart leaped to her throat as the words suddenly made sense.

It was a ransom note.

Chapter Twelve

The sheriff had just returned to his office when he got the call. He ran across the street, having told Molly not to handle the note more than she already had, and to stay where she was.

He took the stairs to the fourth floor rather than ride up in the slow, antiquated elevator. He was breathless before he reached her room and knocked. She opened the door at once.

"Are you all right?" she asked as he leaned on the doorframe for a moment trying to catch his breath.

"I ran up the stairs, three at a time," he said between breaths. "Where's the note?"

She pointed to the bed where she'd apparently dropped it. Pulling out the gloves and evidence bag from his pocket, he approached the bed. The note lay open on the quilt covering. Just as she'd said, it was on hotel stationery.

What she hadn't mentioned, though, were the ink spots. He would have to compare them to the note Clay Wheaton had left before he was killed, but Brandt was sure they were going to match. The killer had taken the stationery and the leaky pen. Already planning to write a ransom note?

The note was difficult to read. The person writing it had tried, it appeared, to hide his or her handwriting so it wouldn't be recognized. Did that mean it was someone he knew, someone whose writing he would have known?

Whoever had written this hadn't known about the leaky pen, but they'd definitely been in Clay Wheaton's room—or someone they knew had been. If they had paid attention to the note Clay Wheaton had left on the bureau for his contacts, they might have noticed that the pen had leaked.

Was this from the murderer? It certainly could be. Didn't they realize how incriminating this was? Were they trying to get caught for his murder?

He couldn't shake the feeling that this note had been written by someone close to the killer—but not the killer himself. Someone who now had the hotel stationery and the pen. But did they also have Rowdy?

He shook his head. "I'm still trying to connect the dots— no pun intended," he said.

"He wants five thousand dollars," Molly told him as she joined him next to the bed.

Brandt could see that. Had whoever left this heard about the reward and figured the dummy was worth five times that amount? Or had the writer of the ransom note just picked a random number?

"I'll pay it." She sounded stronger than earlier, more determined. Her nap on the way home in the patrol SUV must have done her good.

"We can't know for sure that this person even has Rowdy," he said, then looked at Molly, studying her. "You want the dummy that badly?"

"I want the killer that badly," she corrected. "I can't imagine growing up in that house where my father was raised or why he would ever come back here. I want answers, but I also want justice."

He wanted to tell her that justice was illusive and often unsatisfying. It was seldom an easy thing to get. If Seth Crandell had done something that had made him flee here, join the military, change his name and never return—until recently—then justice might have already been meted out by the killer. Montana was famous for vigilante justice from back in the state's Wild West beginnings.

"The person wants us to bring the money tomorrow night to a spot in the woods." He shook his head. "Even if we were going to pay it, there isn't any way you could put together that much cash in such a short time."

"I can. At least I can try."

He turned to stare at her. "You do realize this could be a shakedown and that this person doesn't have Rowdy, never did."

"Or the person does because he was in my father's room that night after killing him, found Rowdy and took the case with the dummy inside."

Brandt was shaking his head again. "The first thing we need to know is who dropped off this note. Hopefully we can get a decent print off the paper." The person had been in the hotel, had known what room Molly was staying in and had left without being seen? He quickly called down to the desk. It rang four times before a winded Ash picked up.

Brandt recalled that Ash hadn't been at the desk when he'd rushed past. "Where have you been?"

"Brandt? I was down at the café getting something to eat. I still have to eat you know."

"Sorry. How long do you think you were gone?"

"Seriously?" A sigh. "Twenty, twenty-five minutes. But it wasn't like I couldn't see down the main drag if someone had pulled in and wanted a room."

"Is that the only time you've been away from your post?" the sheriff asked.

"Except for a quick bathroom break. What's this about?"

"Never mind." He disconnected and turned to Molly. "Ash

was away from the hotel. Anyone could have come in and shoved the note under your door. Anyone who knew what room you were in."

"You're that sure the note was for me?" she asked. "I wasn't the one who posted the reward."

He nodded, before he placed another call. Helen answered right away. "Any chance you might have seen someone going into the hotel especially in the past half hour?"

"I was on my lunch break, watching my stories on my phone," she said. "I wasn't sitting here looking out the window."

He disconnected. It struck him that anyone who knew the routines of this town would have known exactly when to enter the hotel without being seen. "Let's just hope we get a print off the note before we're contacted again."

"You mean when I'm contacted?"

He met her gaze. "Don't even think about not telling me if you get another note."

"Why would I get another one? This could all be over tomorrow night when we meet him in the woods," she said.

He glanced at her. Finding the note had scared her. Now that she was thinking clearly, he figured she was wishing she hadn't told him about the note. "*We* are not meeting him. When no one shows up, the person will get in contact again."

"If the note was left for me, the person knows who I am. I'm the only one who can go to the drop site since it says on the note, *no law.*"

If the person who left the ransom note, had purposely put it under her door, then they must know that she was Clay Wheaton's daughter. It was common knowledge in Fortune Creek and after the two of them had been asking questions around Eureka, word could have easily spread.

And then there were the Crandells. They now knew about

her. Maybe they'd known Seth had a daughter long before this if one of them had met with the ventriloquist—and killed him—and seen the note with her name and number on it.

"Please don't fight me on this," he said quietly. "I'm just trying to keep you alive." Under all her outrage and determination, Molly looked pale and vulnerable. Damn but he wanted to take her in his arms for all the wrong reasons. His gaze went to her mouth. The desire to kiss her was so strong that he had to make himself keep both feet firmly on the floor. He didn't dare take even one step toward her. She was already so near that he felt as if he could feel the electricity sparking between them. It would take so little to close the distance.

Her gaze locked with his, stealing his breath as he saw the flare of heat in her eyes and realized it wasn't all anger and determination. She felt the heat between them. Her gaze shifted from his eyes to his mouth. Her lips parted as if of their own will. He felt a pull stronger than all his determination and was too aware of the bed next to them. Too aware of this woman.

She'd pried open his closed heart in a way that felt more than dangerous. *You think you got your heart broken last time? This woman could very easily rip it out and stomp the life out of it—right before she drives out of town.*

She blinked and stepped back, either running from the need in his gaze or her own. Then again it could be just simple self-preservation. She wouldn't want to get involved with some small-town sheriff, knowing full well how it would end.

He swallowed, his mouth suddenly dry at the thought of how close he'd come to making a huge mistake with more than his heart. He picked up the bagged ransom note. Molly moved to allow him access to her hotel room door. He headed for it. "Call me when you get the next note."

She didn't answer. She didn't have to. He already knew that she wouldn't. Molly Lockhart thought she could handle this by herself. He swore as he left, practically bumping into Georgia as he closed the door.

MOLLY FELT AS if she'd just dodged a bullet. She was so wired by that tense exchange between her and the sheriff that she jumped at the knock on her door. She was afraid to open it, afraid it would be the lawman and that this time neither of them would call a halt to what had almost happened before. Her heart was still hammering, her blood running hot, desire simmering in places she'd seldom if ever felt before.

"Georgia," she said as she opened the door to the insurance woman. She felt a wave of relief—and disappointment that it wasn't the sheriff.

"I thought you might want to go to lunch. Are you all right?" The woman turned to look back down the hallway at the sheriff's retreating back. "Been doing a little entertaining in your room?" Georgia chuckled as if she was joking, but her look when she turned back was probing.

"Lunch," Molly said, needing fresh air and to escape the feelings the sheriff had evoked in her as well as to get out of her hotel room. Right now, she would go anywhere Georgia suggested.

"You don't seem all right," Georgia said as they walked down the hallway to the stairs. "You look like you've seen a ghost." Her eyes widened. "You haven't seen a ghost, have you?"

Molly shook her head. "I need air." She turned toward the fire escape stairs. She knew that the sheriff wouldn't want her talking to anyone about the ransom demand, so she couldn't blame that for her apparent frightened expression. "I met my grandparents this morning and survived it. Barely."

She pushed open the door and descended the fire escape. When they reached the bottom, , they headed down the alley to the café. "Seriously? You talked to your grandparents?" Georgia said, having to trot to catch up with her.

"It was more than strange and a whole lot disconcerting. My grandfather had his shotgun loaded the entire time and my grandmother…" She shook her head. "I think she loved my father. I don't think she knew he was murdered let alone that he'd been nearby in Fortune Creek."

"Do you think one of them killed him?" Georgia asked.

"I don't know. I'm not sure I want to know." Her thoughts kept shifting back to the sheriff, the heat of his look. She licked her lips unconsciously and tried to breathe. The last thing she needed to do was get involved with the cowboy sheriff. She couldn't trust her emotions right now—even if he wasn't the sheriff of Fortune Creek, Montana and she didn't live thousands of miles away in New York City.

Her libido teased her with the thought of a fling. Except that she didn't do flings and she had a feeling that neither did the sheriff.

Georgia was talking but she was barely listening as she pushed open the door to the café. "Hey, ladies. I just need to step out for a few minutes," Alice called. "I'm going to run some of my chicken soup over to May Greenly. She's feeling under the weather I heard. Take a seat. I'll be right back."

"Okay, something has you spooked and I don't think it's your weird relatives," Georgia said as they sat down at a table across from each other.

"Sorry," Molly said, shaking her head as if to throw off the chill she'd just gotten. "It's my father. Finding out that he's Seth Crandell, well, it could mean that a lot of his show with Rowdy was based on things that actually happened to him. It's kind of…spooky to be here and know that he grew up here. He might have known a lot of these people."

Georgia seemed to be waiting as if she knew there was more.

Molly looked toward the back door that Alice had gone out to take soup to her ill neighbor. "That name. May Greenly. It's…familiar. I think I heard Rowdy mention it in one of my father's shows." She frowned, repeating the name under her breath as she tried to remember what Rowdy had said about May.

"Okay, I can see where this would be weird for you. I mean meeting grandparents you never knew you had," Georgia said. "I hate to freak you out more, but we've received five responses to our reward notice. What do you think we should do now?"

Molly stared at her. *Five people claim they have Rowdy?* She sighed, feeling as if she was still in a nightmare. She'd dreamed again last night that she'd heard Rowdy singing. She thought of the ransom demand. Did the five people who responded to the reward know about the ransom demand? Or was someone hoping to double dip. So who was lying about having Rowdy? Maybe all of them—including the ransom demand writer.

"The sheriff was right. This was a mistake. How are we going to do this?"

"All we can do is agree to meet with each one, right?" Georgia was saying. "They all left phone numbers and first names."

Molly shook her head. "I definitely think we should tell the sheriff then. Don't look at me like that. This could be dangerous."

"All five said, 'no cops.'"

"Of course they did. Which is exactly why we need to tell the sheriff. One of them could be the killer."

"No sheriff," Georgia said adamantly. "What makes you think you can trust him anyway? Those dreamy blue eyes? Or the way his jeans fit that perfect bottom of his?"

It annoyed Molly that Georgia had noticed the sheriff's assets. "Very funny. Seriously, I think he knows what he's doing. I...trust him." That surprised her but she realized it was true. "If you want Rowdy back, then he should at least know about the people who contacted you for the reward. There's more going on than you know."

Georgia gave her an impatient look. "Between you and the sheriff?"

"On the murder case. Let's talk to him after lunch, please. You don't want to do anything that might jeopardize getting Rowdy back."

Georgia grudgingly agreed. "Once Rowdy is found, we can go back to our lives."

"Exactly." Even as she said it though, Molly knew that it had gone far beyond that. She wanted to know why someone had killed her father. She thought it might be the key that would unlock everything, including why he couldn't stay with her and her mother all those years ago.

BRANDT HAD JUST gotten off the phone when he saw the two women headed down the street toward his office. He groaned, definitely not in the mood after his call from the crime scene techs who'd processed Clay Wheaton's pickup.

"Got fingerprints and DNA," the tech told him. The sheriff had listened as he was told that both Gage Crandell's and his father Cecil's fingerprints were found in the pickup.

The only surprise was that the prints found on the take-out box found in the truck were Cecil's.

"All this proves is that Cecil and Gage had been in Clay Wheaton's pickup," the sheriff said, thinking out loud. "But it didn't sound like Cecil and his son had been at each other's throats if the older man had enjoyed a piece of Alice's huckleberry pie. Where were their fingerprints found in the pickup?"

"Cecil's on the passenger side door handles. Gage's on door handles and the steering wheel and the gear shift knob."

Brandt had sworn under his breath. "Gage drove the pickup? How did that happen?"

"Good question."

"I'd like to ask him," he'd said, not that he thought he'd get a straight answer even if he could get Gage in for questioning. He swore under his breath.

Since that awkward moment in the hotel room with Molly, he'd come back to work in a funk. He'd thrown himself into his work, tracking down information in his father's old files on Ty Crandell's death.

He'd just been debating finding Molly and telling her what he'd learned. He wasn't sure how Ty's suicide might tie into Seth's leaving Montana for the service, but he had a feeling it might. Ty had killed himself shortly after Seth left.

That's when he'd seen the two women crossing the street making a beeline for his office. Now he braced himself as they entered. He motioned for Helen to let them come on back.

"We've heard on the reward," Molly said the moment she cleared his office threshold.

"Someone says they have Rowdy?" He wasn't sure how to feel about that. They already had a ransom note. Could both be from the same person?

"Five people have responded," Georgia said.

Brandt groaned and motioned for them to sit down. This was exactly what he'd feared, a bunch of wild goose chases that would lead to nothing more than someone trying to make a fast buck. "What kind of information did they provide to reach them to make the trade?"

Molly and Georgia exchanged a look. He knew that look.

"The reward was Georgia's idea. She's handled it—she has the contacts. I don't. You're going to have to talk to her."

"It isn't something the two of you want to handle on your own," he said feeling his frustration rising. "This is dangerous. There is a murderer out there. He might want the money to skip town. You think he'd leave either of you alive to describe him?"

"I have phone numbers and what could be first names, but they warned us not to go to the sheriff," Georgia pointed out.

"Of course they did," he said. Clearly, Georgia had been against telling him. Which meant Molly must have talked her into it. He glanced at her, relieved one of them was taking this seriously.

He did, however, wonder if Molly had mentioned the ransom note to Georgia. He met her gaze, decided she had kept it a secret. He gave her the hint of a smile before he asked for the phone numbers.

"We're not reckless," Georgia said. "We were going to meet them separately in a public place."

He couldn't help thinking about the ransom demand. Did that person have Rowdy? Or were all of these people trying to cash in?

"The problem is, even if one of them really does have Rowdy, we don't have the cash yet," Molly said.

"Like any ransom demand, they need to prove that they have the dummy first," the sheriff said.

"Like a piece of Rowdy's clothing," Molly suggested.

Georgia turned to stare at her. "Would you recognize a piece of his clothing? I wouldn't."

"Bad idea, sorry."

"I might suggest having each of them text you a photograph of Rowdy in front of this week's *Tobacco Valley News* out of Eureka," the sheriff said.

Molly nodded. "I'll see about getting the money wired here in the meantime."

Brandt lifted a hand. "We need to start by running the phone numbers you were sent and see who's behind the reward demands, if you don't mind me making another suggestion."

Georgia groaned but handed over the list. He quickly checked out the phone numbers she'd been given. One was the main number at the high school office. The name with it was Monte. Another had used the number at a bar in Eureka, name Wild Bill. A third had used the number at the newspaper in Eureka where the reward notification had run, name Hank. Each of those had given a first name to ask for. The fourth had used a burner phone. Only one had used a phone number under his name. He recognized the name of a person he'd had to arrest for a number of infractions over the years.

Brandt swore under his breath and looked at the two women sitting across from him. "Here's what I'd suggest we do."

Irma Crandell waited until her husband, Gage and Cliff had gone to the barn to work on the tractor. She found her grandson Wyatt in the butchering room about to cut up the pig he had hanging.

He looked up, surprised to see her. In this family, women's work was inside the house. Everything else fell to the men and wasn't any of the women's business.

"I need to talk to you," Irma said, closing the door. She locked it and turned to see Wyatt's eyes as wide as a harvest moon. "You're going to tell me the truth, aren't you, boy." He nodded looking as if he wanted to make a run for it. "This is just between the two of us. You get my meaning?" Another nod as she took the knife he'd been sharpening away from him. "Tell me everything you know about Seth." She touched the blade of the knife, finding it plenty sharp. *"Everything."*

Then she listened as Wyatt stumbled over the words, his gaze going from her face to the knife in her hand.

When he finished filling her in on what he knew, she asked, "Who killed Seth?"

Wyatt looked like his bladder might fail him as he said, "I don't know. I swear, I don't." As scared as he looked, she thought he was telling the truth. All she could hope was that he feared her more than his grandfather. She studied him for a full minute before she put down the knife and reached over to cup his face. He was the most like Seth, something she knew her husband would try to kill in him.

The thought filled her with that familiar sense of desolation as she walked to the door and unlocked it. As she swung the door open, she came face-to-face with Cecil.

"Irma? What are you doing down here?" Cecil demanded, looking past her to Wyatt.

"Just telling the boy how I want my pork chops cut this time," she snapped and pushed past him. But as she walked away, she glanced back, catching Wyatt's eye and giving him a warning look.

Chapter Thirteen

"We need to weed out anyone who doesn't have the dummy," the sheriff was saying. Georgia tried each of the numbers, asked for the person whose name she had and then told the person who answered that she would need a photo of the puppet with this week's newspaper texted to her.

He noticed that Molly didn't seem to be listening. "There a problem?"

"Do you know May Greenly?"

He'd been right. She hadn't been listening. Because she wasn't concerned about the calls because she knew none of these people had Rowdy? Or was something else on her mind.

"May Greenly was my third-grade teacher. Why are you asking about her?"

Molly shook her head, motioning for him to move on.

Georgia finished and pocketed her phone. "So now we wait. I left the message for each of the people who contacted us."

Brandt sighed. "If you get a photo of Rowdy sent to your phone with this week's *Tobacco Valley News* paper, we'll set up a meeting with the person. But I will be the only person going."

"I don't like it," Georgia said. "They spot you and they could get rid of Rowdy."

"First off, I doubt we will hear from any of them. I'd be

shocked if one of these people had Rowdy and sent a photo. If you get any more hits on the reward, please treat them the same way. The point is to find Rowdy, right?" Both women nodded. "I'm serious about this being dangerous. Never forget, if you decided to follow up on your own, you could be meeting with the killer."

He didn't really believe that. He thought more than likely it would be the author of the ransom demand who they really had to worry about. But he didn't want Molly and Georgia taking the chance he was wrong.

Georgia got to her feet. She glanced at Molly who was still sitting, gave a shake of her head and walked out.

"Are you all right?" he asked after Georgia had left.

Molly stirred. "No, not really." She plastered on a smile. "I'm fine really." The lie didn't float and she knew it.

He let it go for now. "Thanks for not telling Georgia about the ransom demand you received. We'll handle it the same way once we hear from the alleged kidnapper again." She nodded but he wasn't all that sure she was listening. He reminded himself what she'd been through since arriving in Fortune Creek. She was dealing with a lot, some of it maybe just now hitting home.

As she started to leave, he detained her long enough to reiterate, "Let me know the moment you get another ransom note."

"I won't touch it. I'll call you at once," she said impatiently. "But you're not keeping me out of the loop either. You need me. Seems we need to trust each other."

He sighed as he met her gaze, rose and walked around his desk to her. She was in the driver's seat and they both knew it. From the look in her eyes, he'd pay hell slowing her down once she put her foot on the gas. He was along for what could be a very bumpy ride.

Swallowing, he held out his hand. "You have my word." She took his hand. Warmth spread up his arm as he was quickly reminded of earlier in her hotel room. He felt his pulse jump of its own accord. Desire feathered through him, bringing a rush of heat to places that had been forsaken for some time.

Helen cleared her throat. Brandt realized she'd been standing in the doorway behind Molly apparently for some time. "Two calls for you, Sheriff." There was a warning edge to her tone.

He let go of Molly's hand. "Talk soon," he said, his voice sounding rough with desire even to his ears—and no doubt to Helen's from the way she narrowed her eyes. "I'll take that first call now, Helen," he said pointedly. He knew she was only trying to look out for him. Didn't want him making a fool of himself like he had the last time with a city girl.

Brandt turned to his desk, thankful for the phone calls. Still, after he sat down, he took a moment to catch his breath before he picked up. "Sheriff Parker."

"We didn't get any viable fingerprints off the ransom demand," the tech at the lab informed him. "Wanted to let you know."

He thanked him and told Helen to put through the second call, hoping it would be more productive.

"Sheriff, it's Lucy Gunther returning your call."

He'd forgotten he'd called Bud Harper's sister. "Yes, I was calling about Seth Crandell. I understand he and your brother had been friends."

"Wow, I haven't heard that name in a long time. Seth? Now that I think about it, he and Bud did hang out some in middle school, maybe a little in high school? Didn't Seth drop out, join the service before graduation?"

"He left at seventeen. What can you tell me about Seth and possibly a girl he dated in town?"

"That was so long ago," Lucy said. "I wish Bud was still here. He might remember, but you know, I do have Bud's photo albums. He was always taking snapshots. Why don't I look through them and get back to you."

"Sounds great. Really appreciate this."

"I suppose you can't tell me why you'd be interested in Seth Crandell after all these years."

"Not at this point."

She chuckled. "You have me intrigued. I'll go dig out those albums. There have to be some shots of Seth, I would think."

Brandt hoped so as he thanked her again and hung up. It would seem that Seth had made little mark on the area in his seventeen years. But then again, that would depend on the kind of trouble he'd gotten into with some town girl like Irma Crandell had mentioned.

IRMA MULLED OVER everything her grandson had told her. None of it had come as a surprise. Cecil and Gage had gone to see Seth at the hotel one night late. How they'd known he was there was a mystery to Wyatt. But Irma figured Seth had contacted his father somehow to let him know he was in the area.

Why in the world would Seth be so foolish as to contact the man who'd hated him all those years, she had no idea. That Gage went along to see him gave her hope that her husband hadn't killed Seth—at least not that night.

"You have any idea what they talked about?" she had asked Wyatt who'd said he didn't. They'd come home even later that night, the two men then going their separate ways.

Which meant that all she knew for sure was that her husband was a liar. She had little doubt though that he could also be a killer.

When she'd heard about the reward being offered for the doll Seth used in his show, she'd been shocked at first, then curious. The dummy was missing. If her husband had killed Seth like she feared, then maybe he'd brought the dang thing home. Maybe he'd hidden it, though she couldn't imagine why he would do that.

Still, she had to search for it. The doll would prove what she knew in her heart. Cecil hated his son enough to kill him—and then lie to her face.

MAY GREENLY LIVED in a small cottage behind the café. The house reminded Molly of a gingerbread house found in the woods in a fairytale. There was a flowerpot up front full of marigolds, and cute lace curtains at the windows.

At the pretty turquoise door, Molly stopped, feeling as if she was opening up Pandora's box. But since hearing the woman's name, she hadn't been able to quit thinking that this might be a person from one of Rowdy's stories.

Did she really want to find out more of her father's secrets though? She'd never imagined that he had so many. He'd seemed like a man who had never lived much. Wasn't that why he'd become a ventriloquist—because something was missing? Or because he was hiding behind Rowdy? She felt as if she was close to finding out as she tapped at the door and waited.

It was a beautiful day, the sky so blue that it hurt to look at it. The pine trees gleamed dark green in the sunlight. The air was so clear and clean that she knew she'd never breathed anything like it before. She tapped again recalling what the owner of the café had said. May seldom left her house and she hadn't been feeling well. Molly was about to leave, thinking this wasn't a good time, when she heard movement inside.

A few moments later the door opened and a small gray-haired woman in a wheelchair appeared. No one had mentioned that May was in a wheelchair. Molly feared she should have called or come at another time and said as much.

"Don't be silly," the woman said. Her whole face lit, sparking the blue eyes and taking years from her round face. "Your timing is perfect." May continued to smile, not concerned in the least to have a stranger on her doorstep.

"I'm Molly Lockhart. I was hoping to speak to you about my father."

"Your father?"

"Seth Crandell," she said and saw from the woman's expression that she'd come to the right place. There was something so sweet and innocent in the woman's face. She guessed her to be in her late fifties or early sixties, close to Seth Crandell's age. "You knew my father."

The woman opened the door wider as she wheeled out of the way. "Please, come in. Would you like some tea? Or perhaps some coffee?" she asked as Molly followed her into the kitchen. The walls and shelves were filled with souvenirs from around the country and the world beyond. "No, thank you," Molly said distractedly as she gazed at the souvenirs. "You must have traveled a lot."

May laughed as she offered her a chair at the table. "Oh, no, dear, I've never left Fortune Creek. I lived vicariously through the wonderful things your father sent me."

Molly was about to take a chair at the kitchen table, but stopped in surprise. "My father sent you all of those?"

"You sound surprised," May said as she wheeled up to an empty space at her kitchen table. "He traveled with his show, but surely you know that."

Molly shook her head as she sat. "I don't know very much about my father. He left my mother and me when I was nine."

"I'm so sorry," May said. "That must have been very painful for you and your mother."

"How did you know my father?" She thought of the ventriloquist show she'd watched online. He'd said through Rowdy that May was his sweetheart.

"We grew up together. I was very fond of your father."

"He was very fond of you," Molly said. "At one of his shows, he said you were his sweetheart and that you'd broken his heart." May smiled, but said nothing. "Are you aware that he recently died?" She saw the answer on the woman's face. A sadness seemed to soften her features even more. Tears welled in her eyes.

"Yes, I heard. I was so sorry."

"I have to ask—did you see my father while he was here in Fortune Creek?"

May nodded, smiling. "He came to see me, and we visited just like old times." She looked so happy, as if lost in the memory.

"Did he tell you what he was doing in Fortune Creek?"

"He said he had some unfinished business here," she said. "He came to say goodbye."

"Then he told you he was sick?"

"Yes, I was so sorry to hear it. After everything he'd been through, I hated seeing him in such pain, both physical and mental."

"I'm sorry, you said everything he'd been through?"

May pursed her lips. Sunshine poured in the window and splashed across the kitchen table. She wiped at a speck of dust on the surface with the hem of her sleeve. "I love this room. It's my favorite because of all the light, but it always highlights any dust that I've missed." She chuckled to herself.

Molly could tell that the woman was stalling, not sure of how much she wanted to say. "Please, I would appreciate anything you can tell me about my father. I'm realizing more and more how little I knew about him or how many secrets he had."

"He loved you," May said. "He was so proud of you. He told me how successful you are and how beautiful." She smiled. "He wasn't exaggerating one bit either." The woman was still skirting around the question.

"What happened to make him leave when he was seventeen? I watched one of his shows and he talked about May Greenly being his first love. Of course he told the story through Rowdy."

"Of course, he did," May said laughing. "He and Rowdy traveled the world together. They were so close."

"Rowdy is a dummy, a puppet, not real."

"Are you sure about that?" she asked, a twinkle in her eye. "Rowdy was very real to your father."

"So you saw Rowdy, when my father came to visit."

May laughed. "Of course. He wouldn't have come without Rowdy. I loved them both and enjoyed Rowdy's stories and songs so much."

"You know Rowdy is missing?" Molly asked.

"I was so sorry to hear that. Rowdy had become his best friend. Rowdy was all that he had at the end."

"He had a family, a daughter he could have turned to, but he obviously chose not to," Molly said, hating the bitterness in her voice.

"I know, it does seem that way. But your father didn't want to burden you with the ghosts from his past, the demons that followed him through life."

"What demons were those?" Molly demanded.

May looked down at her hands in her lap. "You asked

why he left at seventeen. I wish I could tell you. It isn't that I don't want to or that I'm keeping secrets for him—I honestly don't know. For so many years I blamed myself for him leaving. We were in love, but we were too young. Even if our families would have agreed to let us marry, we couldn't. As much as I loved your father..." She shook her head. "It wasn't meant to be."

"Did you ever marry?"

"Oh, no, dear," May said. "I never met anyone like your father again. I know it sounds silly, but he was the love of my life. I didn't want anyone else."

"What was my father like when he was young?"

Her face lit up. "He was charming and so sweet and so loving and so generous. He saw beyond my handicap. He saw into my heart."

"Your handicap?"

"I had polio as a child. I've never been able to walk."

Molly stared at her, stunned. "I'm so sorry—I had no idea."

"Please don't feel sorry for me. I've had a wonderful life. Living here in Fortune Creek has been a joy. I have such close friends—it's such a wonderful community. I've always had love."

"There has to be a reason why he left the way he did, why he changed his name, why he was so...unsettled his whole life. Are you sure it wasn't because he was heartbroken that the two of you couldn't be together?"

"We both were heartbroken, but he promised that he would always stay here, that he would always be here if I ever needed him."

"He made that same promise to my mother. Seems he wasn't good at keeping promises." Molly thought about how easily he had walked away from her and her mother. Had he done the same thing to May? Or had something happened that he couldn't stay, that he had to go away and change his name and never be Seth Crandell ever again? "Didn't you ever ask him why he broke his promise to you?"

May shook her head. "I never needed to. I knew your father's heart. He wouldn't have left unless he was forced to. I always thought my family might have threatened him."

"Are any of your family still around?" she had to ask, but the woman shook her head.

"I'm so sorry you never got to know your father. He was a good man, though he had his demons. I never asked what they were. I'm just thankful that now he's at peace." She smiled. "I hope to join him one day. He'll be waiting for me."

Molly hoped so, but she personally wouldn't have counted on that.

CECIL CRANDELL WAS no detective, but it didn't take him long to find out that Molly Lockwood was staying on the same floor at the same hotel her father had in Fortune Creek.

Gage's daughter-in-law had come back from town with the news along with details about the reward. Cecil hadn't seen the ad in the newspaper, because he didn't take the paper, but Cliff's wife had picked it up on one of her many trips into town. Cecil didn't want to get started on how he felt about her constantly leaving the ranch.

"Someone's offering a reward for that doll?" he demanded.

"*A thousand dollars.* Shirley said everyone in the county is looking for that dummy." Gage looked at his father as if hoping Cecil had it.

"Craziest thing I've ever heard," was all Cecil had said and had gone back to work. But it kept nagging at him. A thousand dollars? That puppet doll couldn't be worth a plug nickel. It had to be a trap. The sheriff was hoping whoever killed Seth would try to collect the reward and then he would arrest him. All over some doll dressed like a cowboy.

Just the thought of that puppet and his son had him so worked up by that evening that he could barely eat. Right after dinner, he left without a word, got into his truck and drove off the ranch.

He'd seen Irma's face as he was leaving. She'd been watching him lately after years of not even looking in his direction. He had to put an end to this before things got out of hand.

Chapter Fourteen

Molly sat straight up in bed, her heart racing. Darkness. She hadn't been able to sleep earlier and was surprised that she'd fallen asleep. She felt as if she'd been startled awake.

Glancing toward the door now, she could see in the moonlight that there was no note. So what had awakened her? A dream? Or Rowdy singing again? She knew it could also be her visit with May Greenly that was haunting her sleep. All those things her father had sent May over the years, coming to Fortune Creek to see her. It had been true. Seth Crandell had loved the woman. Like a lot of things from her father's performances were true? She turned on the lamp beside her bed and reached for her phone. She'd wanted to get to know her father. Maybe she still could.

Many of Clay Wheaton's acts had been video recorded over the years. She found snippets, going from one to the next until she found a longer one. Sitting back against the headboard, she began to watch it hoping it was the one that mentioned May.

"What do you know about love?"

Rowdy swung his head around to look at Clay. "I'll have you know I've been in love. I had a sweetheart. Her name was May Greenly."

"I take it things didn't work out?"

Rowdy wagged his head. "We were too young, but I always

keep her in my heart." Then Rowdy began to sing an old cow-boy tune and she muted her phone.

She sat staring at the screen and the look on her father's face. Were all of his stories true? If so, the answer to what happened to him when he was seventeen might be in one of his performances. But she was too tired to try to find it tonight.

Molly turned off her phone and the lamp beside her bed. But as she lay back down, she doubted she was going to get any sleep. Lying there in the darkness, she heard a floorboard creak outside her room and froze, listening.

Another creak. Her eyes had adjusted to the darkness inside the room. A shaft of moonlight ran across the floor toward the door. In its ambient light, she saw her doorknob jiggle as if someone was trying to open it.

She'd never thought of herself as a screamer until the knob rattled louder and she heard the floor on the other side creak loudly as if the intruder was getting ready to bust down the door.

Chapter Fifteen

Molly blinked in the bright overhead light that chased away the shadows in her room. Ash had responded to her screams, then Georgia, then the sheriff, who'd left her and Georgia while he and Ash searched the hotel.

"Did you find him?" Molly asked when the sheriff returned.

He shook his head. "Someone went down the fire escape. It's possible they came up that way, but if so, they would have had to be let in. Unless they'd blocked the door open earlier. Ash is checking into it."

She shuddered at the thought that someone inside the hotel had helped the man get in. "Didn't I hear that the killer left a book in the door to keep it from locking on the night my father was killed?"

"So whoever tried to get into her room tonight could come back any time he wanted?" Georgia asked. "Even tonight?"

The sheriff shook his head. "He won't be coming back tonight. I'm leaving Deputy Montgomery on this floor until morning. You're safe."

"The deputy?" Georgia asked, trying to hide her smile as she rose to return to her room. "I should get back to bed."

"I'll also be staying around," Brandt added. "To make sure there are no more disturbances tonight."

Georgia looked a little crestfallen as she left, mugging a face at Molly as she went out.

After she was gone, the sheriff turned to her. "Tell me exactly what you heard."

She walked him through it feeling a little silly. "Maybe I overreacted. He just jiggled my doorknob, then a little harder and then I heard him shift on his feet as if he was going to try to knock the door down."

"You didn't overreact," he assured her. "What makes you think it was a man?"

"His boots, his step was heavy—he sounded fairly heavy."

"Whoever it was knows which room you're staying in."

"Just like the person who left the ransom note," she said suddenly, feeling wide awake again. "It could have been the same person. But how did he know my room number?"

"I'll be checking into that. In the meantime, maybe you should move to another room."

Molly shook her head. "No, we need the person with the ransom demand to come back so we can catch him."

"Yeah," the sheriff said. "We can do that without you being in this room, but we'll discuss it in the morning." He moved to her door. "You're safe. Try to get some sleep."

She looked at him as if he was delusional. "You think I can sleep after all of this?"

He smiled. "Try. I won't be far away. I'm staying in a room down the hall."

"As if that would help me sleep," she muttered under her breath. Just the thought of him nearby made her pull the blanket she was wrapped in around her. This time when she shivered it had nothing to do with the Montana cold night or her would-be intruder.

BRANDT WOKE FEELING DISORIENTED. He sat up and looked around. For a moment he didn't know where he was or what had awakened him. He'd slept fitfully after being called to the hotel last night. Even after he was sure the intruder was no longer in the hotel, he'd stayed in the lounge on the fourth floor before falling asleep and finally going to the room Ash had given him down the hall.

But once in the room, he'd kept seeing images of Molly wrapped in a blanket, her hair loose and wild, her face soft from sleep, her face flushed, her eyes shiny with fear. That alone had kept him awake for hours.

His cell phone rang, jarring him the rest of the way awake as he reached for it. "Sheriff Parker."

"I'm sorry, did I wake you?"

"Lucy," he said into the phone as he glanced at the time. Normally he would have been up and already finished with his first cup of coffee.

"Late night, but I'm up." He felt a shot of energy at just the thought that Bud Harper's sister had found something about Seth Crandell and his past that might help solve his murder.

"I've been going through old photos I told you about," she said. "I found several of Seth. He was definitely camera shy or Bud wasn't much of a photographer back then," she said. "I'm sending you the first photo."

He waited. His phone beeped. He opened the attachment. "What am I looking at?" he had to ask as he stared at a photo of a group of teens gathered in what appeared to be someone's backyard.

"Look at the two people deep in conversation on the top far left of the shot," she said. "The young male is Seth Crandell. You can't really see the young woman because she is out of the frame, but you can see part of her red dress. I'm sending another photo."

His phone beeped again. The young male had his back to the camera now, facing the young woman in the red dress.

From the woman's expression the two seemed to be having an argument.

"One more," Lucy said.

He opened the next attachment. The young man had turned, was stepping out of the photo, his arm outstretched. He had hold of someone's arm, the young woman's. Part of her red dress was still in the photo—along with her upper arm.

Brandt made the photo larger until he could see the grip the man had on the woman's arm. His fingers appeared to be digging into her flesh. An uncomfortable feeling settled in his stomach. It wasn't conclusive evidence, but it was disturbing enough to make it questionable.

"Who is the young woman?" he asked, hoping Lucy would know. She did.

"Ruby Sherman." The young woman who'd died in the car crash her senior year of high school.

His mouth went dry. "Seth and Ruby?"

"Personally, I can't imagine it, but in the photos it would definitely appear that they knew each other. Maybe more than that since they seem to be having a heated argument. His grip on her surprises me. Seth was always so shy, so nice and quiet as if he was trying hard to be invisible. I was surprised he was even at the party let alone possibly with a girl. But Ruby Sherman, the most popular girl at school? You know she died that night after her car left the road and landed in the trees. Apparently she was driving way too fast."

Brandt didn't know what to say. He kept thinking about what Irma Crandell had told Molly. *Not digging up that old bone.* "There could have been a side of Seth no one knew." Except maybe Ruby Sherman. "Was there drinking at this party where the photographs were taken?"

"It was behind our house so there wasn't supposed to

be, but you know how teenagers are. Someone could have sneaked in alcohol."

"You're sure this was the night she died?" he asked, his heart pounding.

"There's no date on the photos since this was before cell phones, but I remember the party and the cops showing up asking questions the next morning. Ruby's brothers swore that she would never have been driving that reckless unless someone was chasing her. To this day, they have believed someone was responsible for her so-called accident. My brother believed it too."

"You think it was Seth?"

She seemed at a loss for words for a moment. "He was always so sweet to me, the little sister who was underfoot all the time. I would have said the man couldn't have hurt a fly."

"Lucy, thank you so much for doing this. Could you please hang on to the photos? I might need them."

"There's something else." She sounded hesitant to bring it up. "Bud and Seth had a falling out before Seth left town. I never knew what it was about, but it wasn't long after Ruby died. Then Seth left and his brother Ty committed suicide. I've never put the three together before, but Ty Crandell was at the party that night. I found a photo Bud took of him. Ty was watching the party from the treehouse Bud and Seth built in our backyard. He must have been about fourteen at the time."

As Brandt disconnected, he had no idea what to do with this information. He quickly searched the *Tobacco Valley News* for the story of Ruby Sherman's accident. She'd died in late October. She'd been driving that night alone at a high rate of speed, missed a corner, the vehicle going airborne before crashing into the pines. She died at the scene. Alcohol wasn't involved, according to the coroner's report.

Ruby was the only daughter of Barnard and Nancy Sherman, owners of a company that mined gold and sapphires. The Shermans also owned a variety of local businesses, making them the leading employer in the valley. Her funeral was the largest in local history at that time.

Brandt had heard about her death growing up, a cautionary tale when it came to driving at night on these mountain roads. Also there were stories of people seeing her ghost on the spot where her car had left the road.

What her death could have to do with Clay Wheaton, he couldn't imagine. Yet he also couldn't shake the feeling that it was important to his investigation. But how it might lead him to the person who killed Clay Wheaton and took Rowdy was anyone's guess.

Chapter Sixteen

Molly could tell that the sheriff had a lot on his mind this morning. She'd been up, showered and dressed by the time he tapped on her door.

"Hungry?"

"Always."

"Thought we'd walk over to the café together."

"That sounds ominous," she said and laughed as she grabbed her jacket. He didn't even smile as she followed him down the hall.

"Mind if we take the stairs?" she asked.

He turned to look at her, frowning. "If this is about getting your steps in—"

"It's about not riding in that elevator," she said heading down the stairs. The moment she cleared the lobby and pushed out into the street, she turned to the sheriff. "So what's going on?"

"I just thought you might want breakfast," he said defensively.

She eyed him, not buying it. "I don't want to move out of my room."

"Fine." He started walking toward the café.

She had to run to catch up. "I'm not leaving town either."

"Whatever you say." He didn't even bother to look at her when he said it.

"I'm staying here until my father's killer is caught."

He stopped and spun around to face her, so abruptly she almost collided with him. "What? This isn't about Rowdy anymore? I thought that was the only reason you were here."

She glared at him, hands going to her hips. "You found out something you don't want to tell me." His mouth snapped shut as if he was shocked that she knew him so well. She was even more shocked that she'd been right. "You might as well go ahead and tell me and not ruin my breakfast with this mood you're in."

"Has anyone ever told you what an exasperating, infuriating, maddening woman you are?"

"Someone might have mentioned that before. Your point?"

He sighed, dragged off his Stetson and raked a hand through his thick sandy-blond hair before he settled those blue eyes on her again. "I hate how involved you've become in this murder investigation. It's put you in danger already and the more I learn, the more I wish you'd put your shapely behind on a plane back to New York City."

SHE SMILED, looking up at him with those big, luminous Montana-sky-blue eyes. "You think my backside is shapely?"

He groaned. "That's your takeaway?"

"No, I heard you say I was right. You found out something you don't want to tell me about." That smug look said she knew him too well. The worst part was that she did. How had this happened? He'd barely known this woman a matter of days and now he couldn't imagine a day without her around.

He stood in the street looking at her for a few moments before he shook his head and turned toward the café. "Breakfast first." He'd slowed down where she didn't have any trouble keeping up, studying her out of the corner of his eye and reminding himself that once the investigation was over, she'd be gone. She'd be putting that shapely backside on the next plane. That did nothing to improve his mood.

It was a beautiful spring day, the air crisp and clear scented with pine and falling dried aspen leaves. He led Molly out on the patio along the side of the café so they could have some privacy. "You going to be warm enough out here?" he asked. She nodded and took a seat. He watched her look toward the mountains before turning her gaze on him again.

He thought about apologizing for what he'd said about her, but had a feeling she'd heard worse. She was the kind of woman men would try to put a rope on, thinking they could tame that headstrong stubbornness out of her. But breaking Molly to his will was the last thing he wanted to do.

"I spoke with Lucy Gunther," he said after Alice had taken their orders and gone back inside. They were alone, no one within earshot.

"The sister of the man who was my father's friend," she said.

"She remembered Seth as a sweet, shy, nice friend of her brother's. That's about all she could tell me, but she said her brother took a lot of photos growing up and that she'd gone through them." Molly leaned forward, all her attention on him, the intent glow in her eyes stronger than the sunlight shining on them through the trees.

He cleared his throat. "She found some photos of Seth and a girl. They appeared to be arguing."

"That's it?" Molly said. "You think this is the girl he got in trouble with?"

"Maybe. The thing is, the girl, Ruby Sherman, was the one you found the story on, the one who was killed in an automobile accident the night the photos were taken of your father and Ruby."

"Am I missing something?"

"Her parents have both passed since then, but she has two older brothers, Tom and Alex. Whenever their sister's name comes up, both brothers claim she had to have been chased that night by another vehicle that forced her off the road. It was never proved. As far as I know there was no evidence to substantiate this claim. But she's kind of become a folk heroine. There's a shrine out on the highway where her car went off the road." He looked away. "There have been people who swear they've seen her ghost. Legend has it she can't rest until—"

"Her killer is brought to justice," Molly finished for him. "You think my father might have chased her that night?"

He shrugged. "Truthfully, I don't know what to think. When your grandmother told you that Seth had to leave because of some young woman, I figured maybe he'd gotten a girl in town pregnant, something like that. I never imagined it might have something to do with Ruby Sherman, let alone possibly her death."

Alice brought out their breakfasts and retreated back inside the café. Molly picked up her fork, but didn't begin to eat even though her stomach was growling. "Is it possible he was responsible for her losing control and crashing into the trees? If so, he killed that girl and he never came forward. But why?"

"Also, why would he have been forced to join the military unless…"

Molly nodded. "Unless his father found out what he'd done."

Chapter Seventeen

Molly thought that she wouldn't be able to eat a bite after the sheriff had told her his news. But hunger won out and while she barely tasted the food, she dug in as she tried to process what he'd told her. "So he could have chased her, not realizing how dangerous it was or how tragically it would end," she said between bites. "I guess I can see that happening and if he was this sensitive guy Lucy thought he was, he would have been traumatized. So why not come forward that night? Don't you feel like there is more to the story?"

The sheriff nodded as he ate.

"I wonder, if they were arguing at the party, what it was about," she said thinking out loud. "You don't chase someone you barely know, right? If he did chase her." Molly wasn't expecting an answer and didn't wait for one. "It just doesn't sound like the man everyone thought my father was."

"His brother Ty was also at that party that night," the sheriff said lifting a fork. "What that might have to do with anything I have no idea. But Ty committed suicide after Seth left the ranch."

"I wish we knew more about the family dynamic between Seth and his family especially his brother Ty," she said. "Maybe if they were close and Seth's leaving pushed him to take his life…" Molly looked up at the sheriff. "You're thinking Ruby fits into this puzzle, aren't you." He looked as if he was about to warn her not to be telling him what he was thinking.

"Don't bother denying it, Sheriff," she said with a shake of her head. "I'm thinking the same thing. How did Ty get to the party? I guess he could have come with friends."

"He wasn't with friends at the party."

"So if Seth left right after Ruby, how did Ty get home? He wasn't driving, not at… How old was he?"

"Fourteen."

She finished her breakfast and pushed her plate away. When she looked up, he had finished eating, had leaned back and was now studying her openly. *"What?"*

"Since you seem to know me so well, maybe you can call me something besides sheriff. My name's Brandt."

She smiled, but she wasn't sure that was a good idea. Thinking of him as sheriff seemed to put an invisible barrier between them. The memory of yesterday in her hotel room was still fresh. If either of them had even blinked they could have been lip-locked. Then there was last night in her hotel room. She didn't doubt that one kiss would have led to another and with the hotel bed right there in the room…

"Brandt," she said trying out his name on her lips and saw him staring at those lips. His look sent a fissure of heat to her center. "Yeah, maybe I'll stick to sheriff."

BRANDT SWORE TO himself as Alice came out to clear their dishes. He saw her curious look as she glanced at him, then Molly, then him again. Unfortunately, the entire town—who was he kidding—the entire county probably knew about his last disastrous love affair. Not that he and Molly were headed for a love affair.

But it was clear that some people in town were worried that he was headed down that precariously rutted road again.

He dragged his gaze from her to look out the window and felt a start as he saw Ash Hammond coming down the street with Tom Sherman. Brandt couldn't remember the last time he'd seen Tom in Fortune Creek.

The two men stopped at a dark-colored SUV, talking animatedly.

"Now what?" Molly asked as she glanced in the direction he had been looking.

"Ash and Tom. I forgot they're cousins," Brandt said more to himself than to Molly. "They used to be close in high school. Played football together in high school. Haven't seen Tom around Fortune Creek for a while though."

"Is it my imagination or is everyone in this county related?"

Brandt chuckled. "Seems like it. Have to be careful what you say about just about anyone in Montana, especially in these small towns. As large as the state is, you'd be surprised how many people are related. It makes Montana a lot smaller. Alice is second or third cousin with May Greenly. Cora if I'm not mistaken is a distant cousin of the Crandells and half the county since her maiden name was Olson. Roots run deep here."

"But not for you?"

He shrugged. "We moved here when my father took the sheriff job. All my relatives are spread across the country. I always envied my friends who had more cousins than you could shake a stick at."

"Shake a stick at?"

"Sorry, my grandmother. She had a lot of sayings and some of them kind of stuck."

Molly looked to the street in time to see Tom's car window power down, Ash still talking to him in the middle of the street for a few moments before Tom Sherman drove away. She frowned. "Tom and Ash are first cousins?"

"Tom's dad was a Sherman, his mother a Hammond, like Alice and May Greenly, first cousins, I think, might be second or third. Hard to keep track."

She gave him an impatient look. "All these cousins who can just come and go in Fortune Creek with no one thinking anything about it? If Tom and his family suspected Ruby's accident wasn't an accident like you said and he found out about Seth and Ruby…and Clay Wheaton…"

He chuckled. "I know where you're headed with this," Brandt said. "I'm already there. Tom had access to the hotel. Shall we go?" At her nod, he tossed down his napkin, rose from his chair and reached for his Stetson. He was already thinking about what he would say to Ash when they reached the hotel. He warned himself to be diplomatic. Tom Sherman was Ash's blood. Not that blood could save you when it came to murder.

Chapter Eighteen

The sheriff had a steely look in his eye as they walked up the street to the hotel. Molly could feel the determination coming off him. She hadn't realized how hard his job was here in this small town. He knew everyone, had spent a lot of his life in this town with these people. How hard it must be to have to arrest one of them, to put his feelings aside, to do his duty.

She wanted to touch one of those broad shoulders, to offer sympathy, but she knew it wasn't what he needed right now. So she kept her mouth shut and simply walked through the beautiful morning on this mountain. The air was so pure up here, the scents so filled with pine and aspen and earthy smells, she didn't recognize it as air. She'd grown up in the city smelling exhaust.

At the hotel entrance, the sheriff opened the door for her, ushering her in. She headed for the stairs as behind her, she heard the sheriff say, "Ash, need to ask you a few questions" in his authoritative lawman voice.

She was thinking about how their conversation might go, when she realized that she hadn't seen Georgia this morning. She climbed the stairs, taking her time. She kept thinking about earlier in the café with Brandt—the sheriff—she quickly corrected. Best keep that silver star between them.

Molly knocked at Georgia's door, but there was no answer. That seemed strange. There weren't that many places to go in Fortune Creek. Maybe she'd taken off with that deputy she seemed to have a crush on. If so, Molly envied her. It would be freeing to just let go and take what she wanted.

The thought startled her as she reached for the key to her room. The huge key fob weighed a ton and always fell to the bottom of her purse. Take what she wanted? Where had that thought come from followed on its heels by the image of Brandt lounging on her hotel room bed?

Groaning to herself, she opened her hotel room door. Her bed was made, no half-naked sheriff on it. Instead, there was a folded sheet of hotel stationery lying on the floor just inside the door in a shaft of sunlight.

Her pulse jumped at the sight before she closed the door and reached for her phone.

Chapter Nineteen

"What are you trying to say?" Ash demanded. "You can't possibly think that Tom had anything to do with this."

"Don't make this any harder than it is. Did you see him the day Clay Wheaton was murdered?"

"No." He shook his head but even as he did, he frowned. "I…" Ash swallowed. "Maybe I did." The new hotel proprietor looked miserable.

"He was in the hotel that day? What time?"

"Afternoon." Ash looked sick. "He would have no reason to kill anyone let alone some old ventriloquist who was staying here."

"He might have a reason," the sheriff said. "Did he go upstairs?"

Ash sighed and nodded. "He asked about the remodeling project and if it was all right if he ran up to check it out. I'd gotten busy with a guest and told him to go on up."

"Did you talk to him again when he came back down?"

"I…" He shook his head. "I was busy. He was in a hurry. He just waved on his way through the lobby."

"Did he seem upset?"

"I don't know." He swore. "Tom wouldn't—"

Brandt's phone rang. He saw it was Molly and excused himself to take it. He had begun to worry that they weren't going to hear from Rowdy's alleged kidnapper again so was glad to hear there was another ransom note. "I'll be right up. Don't—"

"I know," she said. "I'll be waiting out in the hall for you."

He disconnected and looked at Ash who appeared sick. "Please don't mention this to Tom."

"I just don't understand why you'd even think—"

"I can't explain right now. Just keep it between the two of us." Ash nodded and Brandt hurried upstairs, hoping Molly had done as he'd asked. He found her standing in the hallway, just as she said she would be.

"Did you read it?" he asked when she unlocked the door.

"No, you told me not to touch it." She stood back to let him enter first.

"Yeah, but you hardly ever do what I tell you to," he said over his shoulder as she followed him inside. "You don't follow orders all that well."

"I don't like taking orders." He could see how much all of this was weighing her down. He wished there was some way he could help her other than to find out the truth about her father—and find the murderer.

"I've noticed." The problem was that he wasn't sure finding Clay Wheaton's killer would help her though. It took all of his strength not to step to her, put his arms around her and try to ease her pain. But he couldn't cross that line, especially now when she'd just poured her heart out to him. She was confused, looking for a reassurance he couldn't give her.

He pulled out the gloves and unfolded one of the evidence bags he always carried. After pulling on the gloves, he finally reached down and picked up the folded sheet of hotel stationery.

"What does it say?" Molly asked as he unfolded it. She moved closer to read over his shoulder. Like last time, the note was written on Fortune Creek Hotel stationery. Only this time, the alleged kidnapper hadn't used the leaky pen. This time it was also more threatening toward Rowdy.

"It gives us a different place to drop off the money," he told her.

"I saw," she said as she stepped back. The sheriff smelled really good today. Standing that close to him earlier, she'd taken in the male scent of him, breathing a little too deeply. It wasn't good being this aware of the man. "The person is threatening to destroy Rowdy unless the money is left at the drop site. So what are we going to do?" she asked. "I don't have the money yet."

"We're not going to hand over five thousand dollars. What we're going to do is find out if the person has Rowdy. Then arrest him or her either for extortion or murder or both. You might remember I'm trying to catch a murderer?"

"I'm aware of that. But I thought we were going to try to get Rowdy back—and catch the killer when the person picked up the money."

The sheriff studied the note again. "This appears to be an inexperienced kidnapper. He should have given us a phone number so we could talk to him and make arrangements. Instead he expects us to drop off thousands of dollars in the woods? He's kidding himself."

"So we do nothing again?"

"I dropped off a note at the last drop site demanding proof that he had Rowdy. The person either didn't check the site or doesn't have Rowdy. Clearly, he's inexperienced at this, but he's not fool enough to just quit if he has the puppet. He probably isn't the killer." He finally looked at her. "Are you okay?"

"I'm okay," she said and sat down on the bed. "It's just all of this." She sighed. "I keep wondering. Who would my father open his door to knowing that they had come to kill him?"

"We don't know that was the case."

"Don't we? We know he came back here to say goodbye because he had unfinished business. It might have something to do with Ruby's death or his brother Ty's suicide or something else entirely. My father came here knowing he was already drying. He wasn't afraid of whoever he opened that door to the night he died or he wouldn't have come back here."

The sheriff raked a hand through his hair. "Wait, you think your father came here to say goodbye?"

She met his gaze. "I guess I didn't mention it. I doubted it would interest you."

He groaned as he got the chair from the corner, dragged it over and sat down in front of her. "You'd be surprised at what I'm interested in." His impatient look seemed to ask if he was going to have to pull the words out of her.

"He and May Greenly were in love when they were young," she said finally. "Did you know that? Apparently, he never got over her. She says she doesn't know why he left at seventeen, why he changed his name, why he did everything that he did. But he did go see her when he got to Fortune Creek. He went to tell her goodbye."

Brandt seemed to process all that for a moment. "So that's what he said he was doing in Fortune Creek."

"Not entirely. She said he had unfinished business to take care of."

"She didn't know what?"

Molly shook her head. "I'm learning things about my father that I never knew. I listened to one of his shows online where Rowdy said that May Greenly was his true love. I suspect now that all the stories he told through Rowdy were based on some truth. Everything I needed to know about him was there had I paid attention. I didn't think anything about his act was real."

"I wonder if what happened to force him to leave and change his name is also somewhere in those stories in his act," Brandt said thoughtfully.

"I thought of that too," she said, though she doubted the name of the killer was there. "I'm just afraid there is something much darker, much worse to find out. What if he followed Ruby, forced her off the road that night? What if he could have saved her but didn't?"

"We don't know she was the young woman your grandmother mentioned. But I feel as if it is getting more dangerous for you to be here. You know you don't have to stay in Fortune Creek. In fact, I really wish you would go back to New York."

She narrowed her eyes at him. "You've made that perfectly clear. I'm not going anywhere."

"What about your job?"

"It'll be there or it won't. At this point I'm not sure I care. I think I became a financial analyst because of my father. I wanted a career that was real. Numbers don't lie. I didn't want to be my father. I wanted something solid under my feet that I could count on. Now... I'm not sure it's what I want to do with the rest of my life."

"I wouldn't make any hasty decisions about your future if I was you. All of this has come as a shock. Give yourself some time and I'm sure you'll be winging your way back to New York City and your life there."

She met his gaze then, measuring his words. "Maybe." Rising, she then walked to the window and looked out. She turned from there to look at him. "Are you going to leave another note at the new drop site?"

"That would be sheriff's department business."

Molly was looking at him as if she could read his mind. "You're planning to set up some kind of trap for him, aren't you?" She didn't give him a chance to answer which was just as well since he didn't plan on telling her anyway. "I'm going with you."

"No, you aren't," he said as he rose from the chair and put it back where he found it.

"I have to," she said. "I'm the one who should leave the note. If you're spotted, you'll scare the person off."

"This is Fortune Creek. Even if not related, everyone knows everybody's business. The kidnapper knows that you told me about the note—trust me. There're no secrets here."

"I'm not so sure about that. My father had secrets and so far we haven't been able to dig them all up. I think there's more going on than you think. You didn't even know about May Greenly."

He sighed. "I know you went to visit her."

"Oh, yeah?" she challenged. "Did you know about her and my father? Did you know that he sent her little treasures from every place he performed? Did you know that they were in love, that their parents wouldn't let them marry?"

"I knew that she had a boyfriend years ago. Someone who broke her heart and that's why she's never married. If you're suggesting that she killed him…"

"Of course not. That's why she's always stayed here as if she thought he would come back. He did come back. To die. To pay for some past sin. To tell her that he loved her, and she told him that she loved him. It's a tragic love story and I'm part of it now, which is why I'm the one who's getting the ransom notes."

BRANDT GROANED INWARDLY. This woman was so independent, so determined, so dangerous. Those blue eyes of hers met his. He saw her fiery spirit, all that defiance burning bright. He actually liked that about her. Except for the part where she was going to make his job much harder—and he feared get herself killed.

"You can hide in the woods or whatever it is you do to set your trap," she said, rushing on before he could speak. "You just let me know where to pick you up."

Right now he wished he wasn't the sheriff. He wished he was just some cowboy standing in a pretty, young woman's bedroom wishing to hell he had her on that bed. "You're going to make me regret this, aren't you?" he asked.

She took a step toward him. "It depends on what you're thinking you're going to regret," she said.

He had to smile because damned if he wasn't positive that she really could read his mind. He saw her eyes shift to the bed and then up at him. Not an invitation—not exactly. But apparently, they were at least at the same rodeo.

Brandt had never wanted an investigation to be over as much as he did this one. This woman was like none he'd ever met. He told himself she'd be the death of him if he wasn't careful. He wished that wasn't so close to the truth. He had to keep his wits about him, reminding himself he was on the trail of a murderer. And he felt he was getting close.

Which meant he had to keep Molly at arm's length—at least until the investigation was over. That was if she ended up staying that long. She swore she was seeing it through to the very end. It would be like her to do just that and get herself killed.

He couldn't let that happen. How he was going to stop her was another thing. The worst part was that he knew what would happen once the investigation was over. After she had Rowdy and put her father to rest, she would go back to her life. She'd be gone before he could say lickety-split. Fortune Creek was no place for a woman like her. This woman couldn't be corralled like some wild horse. He told himself he was too smart to even try.

"Okay," he said, clearly surprising her. She'd been winding up for a battle and now he laid down his weapons and surrendered.

She was staring at him as if not quite believing it as he picked up the bagged note. "You aren't just trying to mollify me, right?"

He shook his head. "Like you said, you're the one getting the notes. You should be the one to take our response to the kidnapper out in the woods in the middle of the night." Molly eyed him with suspicion, making him laugh. "I'll be going with you—not where anyone will know I'm there except you. Still, it could be dangerous. But you only live once, right?"

"You're trying to scare me."

"You should be scared," he said more firmly. "This isn't a game. There's a killer out there. Remember last night the person outside your hotel room?" He saw her swallow. "Right. He could be the person you're so willing to meet in the woods alone in the dark."

"If you're trying to talk me out of it—"

"No, because you're right about him wanting you to deliver the money late tonight. I just want you to know that this might not be about Rowdy at all. It could be about you, the ventriloquist's daughter, and the killer wanting to finish what he started."

Chapter Twenty

Irma Crandell parked the old pickup in the trees at the edge of town where she had a view of the hotel. She saw in the soft earth that she wasn't the first person to park here recently. She thought of her husband. Or maybe Gage. Or maybe one of his sons.

She couldn't worry about that right now as she considered what she'd done—taking a ranch truck for a second time and leaving without telling Cecil or anyone else. It seemed a minor thing, especially considering what she was about to do. Last night she'd heard Cecil get up in the middle of the night and leave the ranch in his truck. That was when she'd known she couldn't wait any longer.

She hated herself for not taking things into her own hands years ago. Her precious son had been lost to her and now he was dead. She had no doubt that Cecil had killed him rather than let him return to the ranch and her. She would deal with Cecil later. It was Seth's daughter she'd come to see.

She'd sat in this same spot yesterday. This morning she'd seen the young woman leave with the sheriff to walk down the street to the café. Interesting how close the two walked together. Maybe too close. They'd both gone into the hotel. Finally, the sheriff emerged. No sign of the girl. What Irma was waiting for was the hotel owner. Yesterday he'd come out at one o'clock on the nose, walked over to the convenience store. He'd eaten his lunch on the bench out front and when his hour was up, he'd walked back to the hotel.

Today a friend had joined him, and Irma had worried that he might change his routine. But when he and the friend came out and headed for the convenience store, she knew it was her chance.

She popped open the pickup door and headed for the hotel. Just as she'd hoped, the lobby was empty. It didn't take her long to figure out what room Molly was in. Only two keys were missing from rooms on the fourth floor. She took the stairs even though it was slow going up the flights.

Once she came out on the top floor, she took a moment to catch her breath and make sure she still had the knife in her pocket. Cecil had handguns, but most of them he kept locked up and she didn't have a key. She wasn't about to come to town totin' his old shotgun.

She knocked at the first door she came to, tapping lightly with her free hand. The other hand gripped the handle of the knife.

Chapter Twenty-One

After leaving Molly, Brandt drove into Eureka. He found Tom Sherman behind a large desk in the office of one of his deceased father's businesses. He looked the part in chinos and a button-down shirt, his blazer tossed over a nearby chair.

"I can give you a few minutes," Tom said offering him an empty chair. "I have a meeting."

"I need to ask you about the night Ruby was killed."

Tom blinked, his face going stony. "Too bad the law didn't care all those years ago."

"You've been pretty vocal in the past about what you think happened. As I recall, you suspected Seth Crandell was responsible. I need to know what that suspicion was based on. I'm sure you remember that night."

Tom sat forward in his chair, forearms on his desk. "I wish I didn't remember. Ruby had just turned seventeen. Dad let her go to a party at the Harpers' house. Alex was fourteen and got to go to a sleepover. I was eight and mad that I had to stay home. I just remember waking up to cop cars in front of the house, my mother hysterical, my father furious and demanding answers."

"Did he get answers?"

"Over the next few days it became pretty clear. Alex and I had overheard Ruby complaining about this Crandell boy following her around, refusing to leave her alone. Dad said he would handle it, but he didn't get around to it. Then when we heard that Seth Crandell had been seen at the party with Ruby and they'd been arguing... Seth had left right after she did and seemed in a hurry." He sat forward, his gaze intent. "He chased her. It is the only thing that makes sense. She would have never driven that fast unless she was afraid and trying to get back to the ranch and safety."

"That is one theory," Brandt said.

Tom sat back, his face flushing with anger. "It wasn't just a theory. Your dad dragged his feet on arresting Seth and the next thing we knew he'd gone into the military to escape punishment."

"Had there been any solid evidence—"

"*Solid evidence?* Everyone knew what he'd done. He was responsible for killing my sister and destroying my family."

"Destroying your family?"

"My parents split up by the end of that year. Alex and I were forced to move to Colorado with our mother... Yeah, he destroyed our family. My mother never got over Ruby's death. I don't think my father did either. Put them both into early graves."

"Did you ever see Seth again?"

Tom looked away for a moment, his jaw working as he tried to tamp down his anger. "I tried to find him when I got older. No luck."

"What would you have done if you had found him?"

His gaze came back to Brandt. After a moment, he shrugged. "Beat him up."

"Kill him?"

Tom scoffed and got to his feet. "Thanks for this trip down memory lane, but I really need to get going or I'll miss my appointment."

The sheriff rose as well, waiting for Tom to ask why he was looking into Ruby's death after all these years. Or why he was asking questions about Seth Crandell. He didn't inquire as Brandt left.

MOLLY WAS ON the phone with her boss when she heard the soft tap at her door. She assumed it was Georgia who she hadn't seen all morning. She hoped the woman hadn't taken it on herself to meet with the people who claimed to have Rowdy.

"Take all the time you need," her boss was saying on the other end of the call. "Your father dying… You've had a shock." He had no idea. "Don't make any rash decisions." Same advice the sheriff had given her.

"I have to go." She disconnected and was headed for the door when she heard another tap, this one louder. "Hold your horses. I'm coming." She threw open the door.

The smile on her face turned to shock at the sight of Irma Crandell standing in the hallway.

"We need to talk," Irma said, pushing past her and into the room, where she stopped to glance around as if she'd never seen a hotel room before. "Close the door."

Too surprised to argue, she closed the door as her mind raced. What was Irma doing here? Her grandmother had told her not to come back to the ranch. Molly had assumed that meant she would never see any of the Crandells again, especially her grandmother.

"You need to leave town," Irma said glancing toward the closet and Molly's suitcase. "It's not safe for you here."

She wondered if this woman was so used to being ordered around that she thought she could do it to the granddaughter she had pretty much denied. "I'm not going anywhere until I find out who killed my father."

Irma's dark gaze pivoted to her. "He was my son. I'll see that the killer gets what's comin' to him."

"If you know who killed my father, you need to tell the sheriff."

The older woman scoffed. "You don't know nothing about it."

Molly crossed her arms, standing her ground even as her pulse thundered a warning in her ears. "I know about Ruby Sherman." She'd thrown it out there, unsure how it would fly.

From the stricken look on Irma's face, it had hit its mark. "You don't want to be saying nothing about that."

"Tell me what happened that night," she said, aware she was taking a hell of a chance pushing this woman. "Why did he chase her?"

Irma stood stone still, one hand in the pocket of her long jacket, the other clenched at her side.

"Please," Molly said. "Help me to understand." For a moment she thought the woman would come flying at her, Irma's gaze was so deadly intense.

When she spoke, it was in a whisper. "He was just a boy." She slowly dropped down on the edge at the end of the bed. For a moment she seemed distracted by how soft the mattress was. She placed her free hand on it, her other hand buried deep in the pocket of her old coat. She finally looked up at Molly.

"He didn't know no better, followin' a girl like her around, spyin' on her, thinkin' he could… That she would… She was playin' with him, makin' him a fool behind his back like he weren't nobody." Her voice broke.

"The night of the party," Molly clarified. "According to the sheriff, there were photographs of Ruby and Seth having an argument. Also a photo that showed that Ty was there too, watching from a treehouse on the property."

"Ty." Irma's eyes filled with tears. "It weren't nothing but a crush. He were fourteen. He didn't mean no harm. You know that girl lead him on. Then she was going 'round saying things about Ty, about the family. Seth wasn't about to let that stand."

Not Seth, but Ty? She thought of the photo the sheriff had told her about. Seth arguing with Ruby. About what she'd said about his brother? "So he did follow Ruby that night?"

Irma shook her head as if irritated that Molly hadn't been listening. "Ty's the one couldn't stay away from that girl. Seth was just tryin' to save 'em both. He spotted Ty hidin' in the back of 'er car. Seth went after Ruby scared at what Ty might do. Or what that girl might do, when she seen Ty hidin' in the backseat. But he didn't catch up till...till it were too late."

The pieces finally fell into place. Seth had been arguing with Ruby over how she'd been treating his younger brother. Ty must have overheard. When Ruby left the party, Ty was hiding in the backseat of her car. Seth saw him and went after them. "Ty wasn't hurt when Ruby crashed her car?" she asked.

"Nar a scratch cuz he was in the backseat. Seth hauled him out. Ruby was gone, nothin' he could do, couldn't stick around, weren't no purpose. Ty had her blood all over him, cryin' sayin' he loved her, wanted to die with her. Seth brang him home, cleaned him up. When the law came round askin' questions, Seth lied for his brother. Cecil could tell he were lyin'." She shook her head. "Seth wouldn't tell on Ty, just kept lyin'. Cecil wanted him gone. Been comin', weren't nothin' I could do 'bout it. Should-a stopped Cecil. Should-a ended it right there."

"Seth had to know that leaving the way he did made him look guilty," Molly said. Irma had fallen silent, no doubt lost in the past. "Ty...he took his life?"

"Couple weeks later. Left a note tellin' what he'd done. I burnt it." She looked up, something behind the dampness in her eyes that gave Molly a chill. "Ty were Cecil's favorite. Let 'im live thinkin' Ty done it cuz of Cecil sendin' Seth away."

Molly felt sick at the hatred that ran so deep in that family. Her blood, she reminded herself, thinking of how she'd never been able to forgive her father for leaving her and her mother. Wasn't that why she had to see this through? She couldn't make it up to her father. But she could see his killer was caught.

She realized her father had been lucky to leave here and the Crandells. But his upbringing had scarred him. Only seventeen, he probably left blaming himself for all of it.

"Who killed my father?" she asked her grandmother.

"Told you," Irma said as she rose stiffly and closed the distance between them. "Don't mind yourself with that. Best pack up and leave while you can."

"Aren't you worried I'll tell the sheriff what you told me?"

Irma was so close Molly could smell the sour scent of cooked food on her clothes. "You go blabbin' to the sheriff…" She seemed to finger something in her coat pocket where her one hand had remained since she'd walked into the room. "Too late to brang shame on us anymore. You do what you got to do."

With that, her grandmother walked slowly to the door, her gait filled with both physical and mental pain as she stepped out, closed it behind her and was gone.

Chapter Twenty-Two

Brandt noticed that Molly still seemed to be upset as she told him about Irma's visit. "Well, that solves one mystery."

She seemed to notice his lack of surprise. "That's all you have to say?"

"Sorry, I figured it might be something like that. One son sent away, another commits suicide shortly thereafter because he is actually the guilty one. I'd looked into the old case. Didn't find anything, but the timing had bothered me because of Seth's leaving. I'd just never put it together with Ruby Sherman's car accident. Now all three are dead. Doubt Irma would come forward with her story on the record. Not that it would change the past."

"But it could be why Cecil Crandell doesn't want it to come out."

Brandt agreed. "I spoke with Tom Sherman after I left you."

"Ruby's brother?"

"He was only eight the night she died, but what he told me fits with what Irma told you. Ruby had complained about a Crandell boy following her around. She'd just apparently not told them which one."

"So that's why they thought Seth was responsible," Molly said. "Which gives Tom and his brother a motive for murder."

"Alex isn't in the country."

"But Tom is," she said.

The sheriff nodded. "He definitely blames Seth, said after he grew up, he tried to find him. Said he might have beat him up if he had."

"What else would he admit to a sheriff?" She seemed to see his hesitancy. "You think he's capable of murder?"

"I think everyone is capable under certain circumstances." He didn't mention that he was tracking down anyone in the area who had a legal permit for a gun suppressor—or as they called them on television, a silencer. As for illegal suppressors, he didn't even venture to guess how many there might be.

"What?" Molly asked as if seeing him fighting what he needed to say.

Damn. It seemed she could read him like yesterday's newspaper. "I think Irma was right. You should go home."

She gave him a sideways look as those blue eyes fired with impatience.

"You're not safe here. I wrote a note asking for a photo of today's paper and Rowdy. I dropped it off at the second ransom demand spot. If the alleged kidnapper finds it before tonight…"

"He'll either come with a photo of Rowdy or not show up at all," Molly said. "If this person has Rowdy…" Her voice broke. "Then he's the killer."

"Not necessarily," he said, but she wasn't listening.

"Don't try to stop me. I talked to my boss today. He tried to talk me out of it, but I have to see this through even if it means quitting my job."

"Molly—"

"I can't leave." Her voice broke. "I owe it to my father who I'm only now getting to know. He tried to reach me through Rowdy. I wasn't listening. I'm listening now. I was going through his old performances when Irma stopped by. But now

I wonder if we don't already know who killed my father. We just need to catch him at the drop site tonight."

Brandt was momentarily at a loss for words. "This is all my fault. I shouldn't have involved you in this investigation." He saw her expression and quickly added, "You *did* help. A lot. But I can't let you risk your life. The murderer has already killed once. I suspect it will come easier the next time."

They both started at the sound of a knock at her door. They exchanged a look and Molly rose to answer it as Brandt stepped out of sight.

"WE NEED TO TALK," Georgia said the moment Molly opened the door and the insurance agent rushed in on a cool burst of spring air. Her face was flushed, her eyes bright.

"You found Rowdy?" the sheriff asked.

Georgia looked surprised to see him there and confused for a moment. "No."

Molly was in no mood to play games after her talk with the sheriff. He was trying to scare her. She didn't need him to tell her that she was out of her lane. Her life had been carefully planned and executed—until now.

But that didn't change how she felt. She wasn't going anywhere—except to the spot where the ransom note had told her to go tonight.

She turned her attention to Georgia, ignoring the lawman. "Then what are you so excited about?" she demanded.

"The deputy," Georgia whispered as if this hadn't gone as well as she'd thought it would. "He asked me out."

"So you haven't heard back from any of the people who'd contacted you about the reward?" Molly asked.

Georgia shook her head and glanced toward the sheriff as he made his way toward the door. Clearly, she hated that the sheriff had been right.

"I will leave you...ladies to your...celebration." His gaze moved to Molly. "Remember what I said." She mugged a face at him as he left.

"What was that about?" Georgia asked.

"Nothing," Molly said, waving it off. "So you and the deputy?"

Her new friend beamed; her excitement, while dimmed earlier, was now back. "I can't remember the last time I had a real date where I didn't have to swipe right or go Dutch. But I need something to wear."

"Don't look at me," Molly said. "I brought a minimum change of clothes thinking this trip wouldn't take long."

"Can we go into town shopping? Please. I want to buy something special."

"You'll look good in anything you wear," Molly tried to reassure her. But she could see that Georgia wanted a new outfit to wear on this date tonight. She glanced at the time. She still had plenty of it before the ransom note drop. "Fine, let me grab the keys to the rental." She stepped away, thinking a shopping trip was exactly what she needed after Irma's visit and then the sheriff's. Actually, she might buy a black outfit to wear tonight since she would probably be hiding in the woods. "Let's go," she said to Georgia. "What time is your date?"

"Six."

They had plenty of time. "Is there any place in Eureka to shop?"

"I looked online. There are several places."

Molly couldn't help smiling as they climbed into the rental car and headed for what they now thought of as the big city. "You and the deputy? Is it...serious?" she asked as she drove.

"It's just a date."

"And you're just excited because you haven't been on one for a while."

Georgia laughed. "Jaden is a hunk but after Rowdy is found, I'll be on a plane home."

"Are you telling me that this is just a wild fling?"

"Haven't you thought about having a fling with the sheriff?"

Molly smiled. "Whatever happens in Montana, stays in Montana?"

"Exactly." Georgia's phone rang. She checked it and didn't take the call, but she looked upset.

"Was that the insurance company calling about Rowdy?" Molly had to ask.

Her friend shook her head. "Just…an old boyfriend." She turned on the radio and began to sing along to the country station as they drove toward Eureka.

An hour later, Molly's feet hurt. She found a bench just outside the last store she and Georgia had visited. Finding the perfect dress had turned out to be quite an ordeal. Fortunately, she'd found one inside this store since it was the last one in town. The dress had been beautiful on her, Molly thought smiling to herself.

She realized that she hadn't felt like that about a date since… She laughed to herself. She couldn't remember if she'd ever felt giddy over a man. She thought of the sheriff. A few plucked heartstrings and several slightly indecent thoughts didn't count.

Georgia came out of the store beaming just as the clerk put out the closed sign. "We have to hurry," she said sounding breathless as she checked the time. The day had cooled.

"Don't worry, I'll get you back in plenty of time." Molly rose from the bench laughing as they started to cross the street.

A truck came flying around the corner pulling a horse trailer. Molly jumped back, dragging Georgia with her. She was about to shout at the driver when the driver threw on the brakes and jumped out. The passenger side of the truck flew open. At first she thought both were coming to apologize and see if she and Georgia were all right, when she got a good look at what appeared to be two people wearing rubber Halloween masks that covered their entire heads.

The larger of the two grabbed Georgia. Before Molly could react, the other one grabbed her, wrenching her purse away as they half dragged her to the open stock trailer door and shoved her inside. She fell to the trailer floor, Georgia joining her as the door was slammed shut. As Molly stumbled to her feet, the truck engine roared and the trailer began to move, knocking her to her knees.

"What is going on?" Georgia demanded.

Molly didn't know for sure, but she feared it had something to do with her father's murder and his missing dummy. She moved over next to Georgia as the truck and stock trailer sped out of town. "Do you have your phone?" She had to raise her voice over the rattle of the trailer and roar of the truck engine.

Georgia shook her head, looking as if she was in shock. "He took my purse." She was clutching the bag with her new dress inside to her chest as if it was a life raft and they were at sea and sinking. "Who... What..." She burst into tears. "This is not what I was hoping for when I came to Montana. I'm going to be late for my date and I can't even make a call."

Molly wanted to reassure her, but from what she could see of the landscape flying by through the gaps in the side of the metal trailer, they weren't headed for Fortune Creek. They were headed away from Eureka and into the wild country outside town.

Molly looked around the stock trailer. Even if she could unlock the door and open it, the truck was going too fast to jump out. Nor did she think she could talk Georgia into leaping out onto the highway as dark pines rushed past.

But she had to do something. While she had no idea who these kidnappers were or what they had planned, she wasn't naive enough to hope that she and Georgia weren't in trouble. Worse, she feared it had something to do with her and her father's death. Was it possible one of them had killed her father? What if they had Rowdy and there was no doubt at least one of them was capable of murder?

Not that it mattered at this point. There was nothing in the trailer to use for a weapon let alone a way to free themselves. She looked over at Georgia.

"Give me your necklace."

"What?" she said letting go of the package with her new dress to touch the beads around her neck. "What do you want—"

"The necklace, hurry."

Georgia pulled it over her head and handed it to her. The beads were large and brightly colored, catching the dying light of the early spring day. Molly put the necklace in her jacket pocket and pulled hard, breaking the beads apart, then she moved to the stock trailer door and began feeding the beads out the back.

"Seriously?" Georgia said joining her there.

"Well, we don't have any bread crumbs."

The insurance rep seemed to shake herself out of the trance she'd been in over their abduction. "Do you really think that's going to help?" she asked as she watched her necklace go, the beads bouncing on the quickly disappearing highway as the truck began to slow.

"Sorry about your date," Molly said seeing her friend's expression.

"Silly huh. We're probably about to die and I'm thinking

about how much I paid for a dress I'll probably never get to wear."

They were thrown together as the truck turned and the stock trailer swayed before it bounced along the bumpy dirt road.

"Any idea where we are?" Georgia asked.

"No." Molly was busy tossing beads out at intervals. She was almost out of beads and thinking it really had been a dumb idea. No one was looking for them. The sheriff had made it clear that she wouldn't be going with him tonight. How long before the deputy thought he'd been stood up and went home? Would he realize Georgia hadn't stood him up? Would he come looking for her? Doubtful since they hadn't told anyone where they were going.

She tried not to dwell on that as the truck slowed again and turned. She tossed the last couple of beads out and said a silent oath as the truck turned yet again before pulling to a rattling stop.

Chapter Twenty-Three

"I just saw the damnedest thing," the caller said. "Could have been a stunt. You know young people these days. But I swear, the two women looked scared and those two wearing the masks—"

The sheriff got the gist from the caller, then asked about the truck and stock trailer and which direction it had gone. A quick call to Ash at the hotel and he had a pretty good idea who the two women had been.

"They went into Eureka shopping," Ash told him. "Nope, haven't seen them since."

The clothing stores were closed by the time Brandt reached Eureka. He feared he would have to call the shop owners and clerks and that would take valuable time. As it was, he had no idea how long the women had been missing, but he could feel the clock ticking. He had to get them. He could feel the urgency making his fears rise with each second.

Fortunately, he got lucky. He found Molly's rental car parked in front of one of the closed shops just down the street.

"They were here," the owner told him when he called. "The one couldn't make up her mind. I sent her down the street to Marigold's place."

"Did you notice anyone hanging around or watching the two of them?"

"Sorry, I was busy with the picky one. Didn't have time to look around."

He thanked her and tried Marigold next. Her shop was only a half block away. The women would have walked to it.

Marigold hadn't been working today but gave him her salesclerk's number. Tina answered on the fourth ring. He could hear the television in the background and children's voices along with the clatter of dishes. He'd called right at supper time. He quickly asked about the two women, not surprised that Tina remembered them.

"It took a while, but I found the perfect dress for the one."

"Where was the other one?"

"She went outside to sit on the bench in front, said her feet were killing her." Tina chuckled. "I think her friend had dragged her to every store in town. As it was, I was late closing."

He asked about anyone hanging around, anyone paying a lot of attention to them and got the same answer. "Did you see them leave?"

"I walked them to the door and locked up." He heard her hesitate. "I saw them start to cross the street when a truck and stock trailer pulled up and almost hit them. I shut off the lights and left by the back way. I didn't see them again."

"You didn't happen to recognize the truck and stock trailer by any chance or see which way it was headed, did you?"

As THE TRUCK engine shut down, Molly heard the two kidnappers get out. She braced herself, watching the rear door of the stock trailer, terrified of what happened next. She couldn't see any lights in the semidarkness or tell where they had stopped. For all she knew, it could be in the middle of nowhere.

She realized she'd been waiting for some time. The two

hadn't come back for them. She looked over at Georgia who was hugging herself and the package with her dress inside.

Neither of them said a word, both apparently listening. Molly picked up the sound of male voices. One male's voice was louder than the other one.

"What the hell were you thinking?"

"He said he wanted her gone. They were together. What else could we do but bring them both?"

The louder one swore. She heard a door slam and looked over at Georgia. Just as she'd feared, this was about her. "I'm sorry."

"I'm sorry about earlier," Georgia said. "Crying over a date. The thing is…" Her voice broke. "I might as well admit it, since I'm about to die…" Before Molly could correct her, she rushed on. "I haven't been on a date in a very long time. I feel like all I do is work for that damn insurance company night and day and they don't appreciate me in the least."

"If you don't make your date tonight, you will tomorrow."

Georgia laughed. "Are you always such a Pollyanna?"

Molly leaned toward her friend and hugged her. "No one goes on real dates anymore so I'm happy for you. We're a generation so busy we have to meet men online."

"Except now I've been abducted and am never going to meet anyone," Georgia said. "It's been so long since I've met someone…nice, safe. I could be serious about a man like Jaden Montgomery."

Molly nodded, thinking of the sheriff. "I know how you feel. I'm really sorry," she said again thinking how grateful she was for her new friend. "You heard what they said. They only wanted to kidnap me."

Georgia waved it away. "I'm in this as deep as you are. I was the one who insisted you go shopping with me." They both fell silent for a few moments.

Molly felt a start as realization hit her. "Exactly. How did they know we were in town?"

"We went to every shop that sold dresses."

She shook her head.

"Someone was watching the hotel?" Georgia suggested.

Molly thought of Irma's earlier visit. She had to have come through the lobby when Ash wasn't at his post. But if anything, Irma had seemed to want to protect Molly. But if not Irma, then who had seen them both leave?

Everyone in Fortune Creek, she thought with a curse. But maybe someone else as well.

"How are we going to get out of this?" Georgia asked. "I should have my gun in my coat pocket." She began going through her coat pockets, pulling out tissues, coins, lip gloss.

"You have a gun?"

"I never go anywhere without it—except today to go shopping. Don't look so surprised. I checked it at the airport."

"A weapon of some kind might be nice," Molly agreed, though surprised that Georgia carried a gun usually. She checked her own pockets. Empty except for a piece of folded-up paper. Frowning, she realized that she didn't recognize it. In the dying light, she unfolded it and tried to make out what was written on it.

"What's that?" Georgia asked.

"A note." At second glance, she saw it had been written on a page from a Bible. She held it up to the light coming through the cracks in the stock trailer. Someone had circled "An eye for an eye." Written in tiny painful-looking script were the words, *Seth's killer heading for hell.*

A shock wave moved through her. "Irma must have slipped this into my coat pocket when she came to visit me earlier today. My coat was lying on the bed next to where she sat down."

She handed it to Georgia who read the note and said, "Old-time vengeance," and handed it back. Somewhere in the distance a door slammed. "We could use a little of that right now."

Molly could hear someone coming. She and Georgia hadn't had a chance earlier to put up much of a fight. It sounded like they were still outnumbered badly. "I think we should go along with them—until we know what's going on."

Georgia didn't answer as they heard the driver's side door of the truck open followed by the passenger side as two people climbed into the cab. Their abductors? The engine roared and moments later, they were moving again.

Molly felt her heart drop, terrified as to where they were taking them now and what they planned to do with them.

IRMA HEARD CECIL come into the house. She could tell by his heavy step that he was in one of his moods. She'd heard Gage's boys return from town. She knew the sound of each old vehicle they owned. From her kitchen even with pots boiling, she had listened for years to the day-to-day running of this ranch.

She knew she'd been waiting for the sound of her husband's old pickup, afraid of where he might have gone. But apparently he'd just been making himself scarce. Cecil thought he could hide the truth from her even after all these years. One look at him and she knew.

Out of the corner of her eye, Irma saw him pull out a chair at the table and drop into it. She didn't turn around. After spending years with this man, she had no illusions. She thought about what she would tell the mortician to write in his obituary. Cecil Crandell loved the land and his family. He would have done anything for them. Even kill to protect them.

She put down the spoon she'd been stirring their dinner with and, wiping her hands on her apron, turned to look at him. He sat, shoulders hunched, head down, looking like a kicked dog.

Irma took a breath and let it out, her heart pounding so hard it shook her entire body. She could feel the years in her bones, forcing her to remember all the times he'd come into her kitchen with bad news.

"What have you done, Cecil?"

THE SHERIFF DROVE FAST. There was no traffic this time of the evening, let alone this early in the year on this backroad so he didn't need lights and siren. He hadn't gone far when his headlights began to pick up something shiny in the road.

He saw one small flash of light, then another and another. What the heck? He kept going until he reached the turnoff that would take him into the Crandell Ranch via the back way. As he started to turn, he saw another of the shiny objects in the road ahead.

Pulling up, he opened his door and picked up one. It appeared to be a large bead, brightly colored and made of clear plastic. He'd seen it before, he thought as he slammed the door and hit the gas. Georgia was wearing a necklace just like this the last time he saw her. Ahead more of the beads caught in his headlights.

Brandt shook his head, thinking about the two women locked in a stock trailer, purposely leaving him a trail to follow?

As he came in the back way to the Crandell house, the bead trail stopped. In his headlights, what the sheriff didn't see was a truck and stock trailer, he realized, his heart dropping.

Ahead, he saw a large figure step into the road, a shotgun

in his hands. As Brandt roared toward the figure, he put on his lights and siren.

The man didn't move. Instead, the man raised the shotgun.

THE TRUCK PULLING the stock trailer stopped abruptly. Molly had felt every bump on the narrow road, then the wider gravel road. She'd been surprised when the truck had pulled onto pavement.

"Where are they taking us?" Georgia whispered, her tone sounding tight and as frightened as Molly felt.

She didn't answer, but she suspected it wouldn't be good. That was why the paved road had worried her. How far were they going?

The truck slowed, then came to a stop. Molly could see light through the crack of the stock trailer. This time, the driver didn't cut the truck engine and the two of them exited the vehicle.

She and Georgia shared a look as the back of the stock trailer was flung open. "Get out!" the larger of the two ordered. Both were wearing their masks but were no longer brandishing weapons. From the size of them, Molly was sure they were both males although their voices were muffled by the masks.

It took a moment for them to rise. Once on their feet though, they moved to the door. One of the kidnappers helped Molly down. The other grabbed Georgia and pulled her to the pavement.

Looking around, Molly realized that they were back where they'd started—in downtown Eureka. The shops had closed and there was little light on the streets.

"Get out of here!" the larger of the two said as they shoved their purses at them. "Get out of town. No one wants you here." With that the kidnapper shoved past Molly to return to the driver's side of the truck.

"Sorry," the other said, his voice sounding hoarse. He hesitated as if there was more he wanted to say before hurrying around to the passenger-side door. The engine revved and the truck and stock trailer roared away.

"What was that about?" Georgia said, sounding as breathless as Molly felt.

"They weren't supposed to take us," Molly said, still shaken. The street was empty, the darkness around it intense. "Let's go." She was digging into her purse for her keys. "You can still make your date."

THE SHERIFF HIT the brakes just yards from Gage Crandell standing in the road, the man pointing the shotgun directly as his windshield. He was reaching for his weapon, when Cecil Crandell stepped out of the shadows to grab the shotgun away from his son.

In the headlights, he watched the two arguing before Cecil headed toward the patrol SUV and Brandt. Cecil looked older in the harsh light. He reached the sheriff's side window, the shotgun dangling awkwardly from his left hand.

Brandt whirred down his window; his other hand was on his weapon. "What's going on?"

"I killed him," Cecil said, his gravelly voice heavy with emotion. "I killed my son, Seth."

The sheriff looked out his windshield. Gage still stood in the center of the road, head down. Behind him a smaller figure emerged from the shadows. Irma.

"Where are your grandsons?" Brandt asked.

"Coming back from town, alone." They met gazes in the ambient light.

"The women all right?" Cecil nodded. "I'm going to get

out now," he told the older man. "I need you to put down the shotgun."

Cecil seemed to hesitate before he threw the shotgun away behind him. It disappeared in the darkness as the elderly man stepped back to let the sheriff exit the vehicle.

Brandt felt the hair stand up on the back of his neck as he watched both Gage and his mother out of the corner of his eye. Neither moved as he put the cuffs on Cecil. After reading him his rights he checked to make sure he didn't have another weapon on him, then opened the back of the patrol SUV and helped Cecil inside.

As he closed the door, he saw that Irma had faded back into the dark. Gage hadn't moved. He tried Molly's number, hoping to hell the old man was telling the truth. It rang three times, his heart pounding as if it was an eternity before she picked up. "Are you okay now?"

"Yes. You know what happened?"

"Yes. Where are you?"

"Georgia and I are headed back to Fortune Creek."

"Good, I'll see you there later. We can talk then," he said as he climbed behind the wheel. He felt a wave of relief wash over him. She sounded shaken, but all right. His heart seemed to slow a little. He'd been so afraid something horrible had happened to her because of all this.

With Gage still standing in the road, Brandt had to back up to turn around. As he headed out the back way from the ranch, he saw more of the beads lying in the road. They shone in his headlights like diamonds. He shook his head, wondering whose idea it had been to try to leave a trail for him to follow.

Fortunately, he'd had a pretty good idea of who had taken the two women after the shop owner had described the truck and stock trailer—and the direction it had headed out of town.

He glanced in his rearview mirror. Cecil was leaning back in the seat, eyes closed. Beyond him through the back window, his son had dropped to his knees in the middle of the road. Irma was nowhere in sight.

Chapter Twenty-Four

It had taken a while to book Cecil and get him into a cell. He'd refused to make a statement other than to say that he'd killed Seth. Brandt had him sign the confession. Cecil had declined to call anyone, including a lawyer.

"What about your son's puppet, Rowdy?" he asked.

Cecil shook his head. That was all. Either he didn't take Rowdy or he had and had since disposed of the puppet.

Brandt had a lot of questions but few answers. Cecil had confessed. Now it was up to the prosecuting attorney to take it from there.

He was anxious to see Molly and get a statement from her, although he had known who had taken her and Georgia on a ride out to the ranch. The question was whether or not the women wanted to press charges.

As he opened the hotel door, his deputy and Georgia appeared to be on their way out. Georgia was all dressed up and so was Jaden. He raised a brow. "I had hoped to take your statement," he said to Georgia.

"Molly can fill you in," she said smiling. "I have a date."

He nodded grinning as he saw that she at least hadn't been too horribly affected by the kidnapping in the stock trailer. "Come by my office tomorrow." As the two left, he heard Jaden ask, "What was that about?"

Georgia's response had been. "It's a long harrowing story. I'll tell you sometime."

He climbed the stairs to Molly's room and knocked. When she opened the door, he caught the sweet scent of her fresh from the bath. Her hair was still damp. She looked so damned good. All he could think was that he was so glad she was all right.

Brandt couldn't help himself. He reached for her and to his surprise, she stepped into his arms. He held her for a long moment, his cheek pressed to her hair, breathing her in, not wanting to let her go.

As he drew back, he looked into her face and felt the impact of his next words. Once he voiced them, she would be leaving. "Cecil Crandell confessed to killing your father. It's over."

She nodded as if not surprised. Her eyes filled with tears. "We don't know why he killed him?"

Brandt shook his head. "Maybe it will come out if it goes to trial."

"Yes, I forgot that there could be a trial," she said as she stepped out of his arms and moved to the hotel window, her back to him. "It will be held here?"

"Probably down in Kalispell."

"What will happen to Cecil?" she asked.

"It could depend. Given his age…"

She turned then to look at him. "Are you saying he might not go to prison?"

"He's confessed to murder. He'd have to go before a judge who can pronounce a sentence. It might not go to trial. Either way, he will probably die behind bars."

She shook her head, her face contorting as she fought her emotions.

"I'm so sorry, Molly," he said as he moved to her. He took her shoulders in his hands. "I wish there was more I could do."

She looked up at him, then whispered, "I think I need some time alone."

He let go of her and took a step back. "Of course. I will need you to stop by my office before you leave town to make a statement about what happened earlier. You have the option of pressing charges."

"I won't be pressing charges," she said.

He nodded, then stepped to the door and stopped. Turning, he asked, "Whose idea was it to drop the beads?"

Her smile couldn't hide the pain he saw etched there, but still his heart did a little bounce. "Mine."

He smiled. "I knew it. Quick thinking."

AFTER THE SHERIFF LEFT, Molly burst into tears. It felt as if she'd been holding back everything, like a dam that now had broken, letting it all out. The pain threatened to overwhelm her. For years she'd said that she hated her father for what he'd done to her. She had wanted his love so badly and blamed him when she didn't get it.

She'd known he was dead, but it hadn't hit home until Cecil had confessed to killing him. Like the sheriff had said, it was over.

She thought about the one chance she'd had to talk to her father when he'd sent her a note that night after his show. Foolishly, she'd wadded it up and thrown it away. If only she could rewind to that night. If only she could have spent a little time with him. Maybe he would have tried to explain.

More than likely wouldn't have, but it still broke her heart that she hadn't even tried to talk to him while he was alive. As May had said, Seth Crandell had demons that followed him his whole life. They'd caught up with him here in Fortune Creek, here in this hotel. Not even changing his name and hiding behind Rowdy could save him. Had he just been counting down the days before he returned here to his fate?

She cried until she was exhausted. She thought about when he'd left her and her mother. She'd cried then too, always hoping he would come back. Finally she wiped her eyes. She'd cried her last tears for her father.

Sitting up, she then climbed out of the bed and went to the window again. She'd never seen so many stars. The pines looked black in the darkness. There was nothing keeping her here now. She wouldn't stay around to see what happened to Cecil. She couldn't think of him as her grandfather.

What would happen to Irma? She had her son Gage and his sons and their wives. But Molly wondered if they would provide her any comfort. Somehow she doubted it. Whether she hated Cecil for what he'd done or not, his being gone had to leave a huge hole in Irma's life. All those decades married…

Molly couldn't imagine it. Or at least she couldn't before coming here. She'd never wanted to plant roots. Lately she'd been feeling as if she'd already spent too much time in her job, in New York.

She thought about the sheriff and felt herself smile. She wished she was more like Georgia. But the last thing she wanted was a fling with the cowboy sheriff. Something warned her that she wouldn't be able to walk away unharmed if she did. Best leave the man to his life, no matter where the wind took her.

After getting undressed, she crawled into bed. She'd told herself that she wouldn't be able to sleep. But she must have drifted off because shortly before midnight, she was startled awake to pounding on her door.

The last part of Rowdy's song he'd been singing in her dream stopped abruptly. But not quickly enough that she didn't realize that this time, she hadn't dreamt it—let alone imagined it.

The thought made her turn on the light and look around the room as if she expected to see her father and Rowdy sitting in the chair by the window watching her.

Whoever was at the door was also not part of a dream, she realized as the pounding started up again.

She felt thrown off-balance by all of it as she grabbed her robe and called out, "Who is it?"

THE SHERIFF HAD done some paperwork before going up to his apartment over what locals referred to as the "cop shop." He wasn't hungry. He wasn't even that tired. After opening his bedroom window, he crawled out onto the roof and sat down.

From here he could see the entire town, not that that was anything to boast about—even in the moonlight. He looked across to the hotel. In the summer, he'd often come up here while the town dozed. He would crack open a beer and count his blessings or curse the latest fool thing he'd done.

Tonight he realized that he'd done it again. He'd fallen for a woman he couldn't have. Even as he thought it, he bemoaned the fact that he hadn't even tried to kiss her. The thought made him laugh softly on the nighttime spring breeze.

They'd both known what would have happened if he had kissed her. Molly was no fool. He, on the other hand…

A thought careened past. He grabbed hold of it, sitting up a little straighter. Tomorrow he would have to go out to the Crandell Ranch and talk to Irma, Gage and his sons and daughters-in-law. Was it possible one of them knew what Cecil had done with Rowdy the Rodeo Cowboy?

Maybe more important, was it possible that they knew more about the murder? He was reminded that Gage's fingerprints had been found in Clay Wheaton's pickup. But so were Cecil's and he'd confessed.

Earlier he'd gotten an anonymous tip that had led him to

the murder weapon. The gun was now with forensics in Kalispell. Had the tip come from one of Cecil's relatives? Hard to say. He was pretty sure that Gage's sons had kidnapped Molly and Georgia earlier. Just as he was pretty sure the women wouldn't want to press charges. Cecil had his reasons for confessing and not wanting a lawyer or a trial. Once he was sentenced by a judge, his family could begin the healing process, Brandt thought.

Things were typing up neatly. Maybe too neatly. Wasn't that what was bothering him?

From his perch, he saw Jaden bring back his date. The two kissed and parted; Jaden drove back to his house in the direction he'd come from. Georgia had disappeared inside the hotel, only stopping for a moment, to wave goodbye to the deputy before he drove off.

Would she leave without Rowdy being found? What choice did she have? As annoyed with Molly as he'd been originally about her single-mindedness about Rowdy, he wished he could find the dummy for her before she left.

Even as he tried to tell himself that the murder was solved and he could relax, he couldn't help the feeling that this had been too easy. Or maybe it was that something was niggling at him, but he couldn't put his finger on it. Tomorrow, he'd sort it out, he told himself as he climbed back into his bedroom window. He took one last glance over at the hotel where he hoped Molly was now asleep and then closed the window and pulled the shade.

"Who is it?" Molly asked again, this time in a less sleepy croak as she approached the door.

"Me. I have to talk to you."

She groaned at the sound of Georgia's voice. Was she

really up to listening to every detail of the date? What time was it anyway?

"I was sleeping," she said as she opened the door and Georgia rushed in.

"I just heard that Cecil Crandell confessed?" she cried as she looked around the room. "Do you have Rowdy? You didn't destroy him, did you? Please tell me you didn't."

Sleepily, Molly moved back to the bed and sat down trying to wake up. She kept thinking about hearing Rowdy singing. Not in a dream. Not in her imagination. But why would someone want her to think that she'd heard Rowdy singing? The same way they'd duped the elderly couple who'd been in a room nearby the night her father died?

"I don't know anything about Rowdy," she said seeing that Georgia was waiting for an answer.

"But if Clay's father confessed...?"

"You'll have to ask the sheriff in the morning," Molly said and mentally kicked herself even as she asked it, "How was your date?" But she needed to get her wits about her, and she couldn't with her new friend here.

Georgia plopped down on the bed beside her, throwing herself back to stare up at the ceiling. "It was amazing just as I'd known it would be."

Molly half listened in between falling asleep sitting up. "Sounds perfect."

"It was."

"Are you still leaving Fortune Creek?" Georgia was quiet for a little too long. Molly lay back and looked over at her. "You aren't seriously thinking of staying."

Her friend wiped away a tear as she shook her head. "Stay somewhere because of a man? Please! I've done that before. Good thing I got a job within the same insurance company because the guy dumped me a few months later. Of course

I'm leaving. As amazing as the date and Jaden are, I have to go home." Georgia sat up. "The sheriff really didn't say anything about Rowdy?"

"Sorry, I forgot to ask."

"Does that mean you don't want to destroy Rowdy?"

Molly thought about it for a moment as she too sat up. "I guess not."

"I'd ask what changed your mind, but I'm just glad. Sorry about your dad though."

She nodded. "Thanks."

"Looks like you've worked through some of your issues," Georgia said.

"I'm still a work in progress. I wanted to tell you. If Rowdy isn't found, I don't want the insurance money. If you don't have to pay out, you should be able to keep your job, right?"

"Are you serious?" Georgia was staring at her. "You'd turn down a million dollars?"

Molly nodded. "I can sign something or talk to your boss. Just let me know what you need."

"Wow, that is so nice of you. But I can handle it. I'm just surprised."

She shrugged. "I have everything I need."

Her friend's eyes widened. "The sheriff?"

"No." She looked away. "But it would have been nice."

Georgia laughed. "Nice? I hope it would have been a whole lot better than that. Listen, if you ever get to my part of the country, give me a call. We'll go have a drink together. My treat."

Molly leaned over to hug her. "I'll do that. But only if you will now let me get some sleep."

Her friend rose chuckling. "Goodnight. I'll lock the door behind me. Go to bed. It's late."

Molly climbed back under the covers. Images of the sheriff kept popping up. If it wasn't so late, she would have called him. He'd believe her about the singing, wouldn't he?

She had just nodded off when she heard a sound that made her eyelids fly open. She lay perfectly still for a few moments before she looked toward the door—and the sheet of hotel stationery folded neatly in half illuminated by moonlight shining through the window onto the floor.

Molly started to reach for her phone but stopped herself. After rising from the bed, she padded across the floor and used her big toe to unfold the note.

Her heart began to pound wildly as she read: *If you ever want to see Rowdy the Rodeo Cowboy again, you will meet me now. I'll give you twenty minutes. If you don't show alone, I'll destroy the dummy. Meet me by the big rock you can see from your hotel window.*

The note was nothing like the other ones and for a moment she didn't trust that it was real. She definitely knew the large rock. She'd stared out at it enough times.

But go now? In the middle of the night? Not to meet a killer, she told herself. Cecil had confessed. If she got Rowdy back, then Georgia could definitely keep her job.

Even as she thought it, Molly knew it was more than that. She wanted to get Rowdy back for her father. She liked the idea of Rowdy the Rodeo Cowboy being in a museum and thought her father would too. It was wrong for whoever had taken him to keep him—let alone destroy him.

She hurriedly dressed, telling herself she should call the sheriff. But then whoever had Rowdy might destroy him. She pulled her phone from her purse, telling herself that she could call him if she got into trouble. She didn't have much time, she thought as she headed out the fire escape exit.

Chapter Twenty-Five

Brandt bolted upright in bed. Something was wrong. It took him a moment to remember the thought that had awakened him so abruptly. After swinging his legs over the side of the bed, he rose and quickly pulled on his jeans.

He realized that he'd fallen asleep for longer than he'd thought. Moonlight shimmered over the tops of the pines as he rushed downstairs to his office muttering to himself, "Where did I put that?" It took a good twenty minutes before he found what he was looking for. He'd made a copy of the note Clay Wheaton had left on his hotel room bureau top.

The photocopy still showed the ink spots from the leaky pen the ventriloquist had used along with the names and numbers of the two calls he'd wanted made in case of an emergency.

Dropping into his office chair, he called the second number and listened to the recorded message telling him that the insurance company office was closed. He hadn't remembered the name of the company, but now that he had it, he called their New York office, which should have just opened since it was two hours earlier there.

Waiting for the call to be answered, he mentally kicked himself for not doing this sooner. He kept telling himself he was wrong as he listened to it ring. He wanted to be wrong. But something had been bothering him and had finally awoken him with a start as he realized what he might have overlooked.

"Hello," a woman said as she answered. She rattled off the name of the insurance company. "How can we help you?"

He quickly told her who he was and what he needed. "It's a matter of life and death." He gave her his identification information and explained what he needed.

"This is highly unusual. Let me see what I can do. Please hold."

The wait seemed interminable before she came back on the line. "I'm sorry, but I had to check your credentials. You're at the sheriff's office now? I will call you back."

"Please hurry." Even as he told himself that Molly would be in bed sound asleep at this hour, he couldn't help the urgency he felt and the worry that he might be too late. He'd thought about calling her, waking her up and then what? Telling her about the crazy theory he had and to keep her door locked and not let anyone in?

The office phone rang. He quickly answered it. "Sheriff Brandt Parker."

"I have that information you called about." He listened, his heart dropping. From the start of this investigation, it had been about Rowdy. It had always been about Rowdy. He'd been such a fool. He was busy looking for a murderer, thinking the dummy had nothing to do with it.

He hung up and quickly called Molly as he hurried upstairs to finish dressing. His pulse quickened as the call went straight to voicemail. She must have turned off her phone. Swearing, he headed for the hotel at a dead run.

THE WOODS WERE DARK, shadows lurking under the thick pine branches. Rays from the moon fingered through the boughs and bathed the top of the huge rock in moonlight. Through the branches, Molly kept getting glimpses of the rock, assuring her she was headed in the right direction.

She gripped her phone in her hand. She knew she shouldn't be out here alone. But then again, she wasn't alone. Someone was waiting for her.

As she walked, she tried to make sense of everything that had happened. Did it surprise her that Cecil had confessed to killing her father? From what she'd seen, she thought the rancher certainly was angry enough to do it.

In her memory, she called up the image of him standing on his porch, the shotgun in his hand. As she did, she recalled something that made her frown. His hands had shaken. She'd blamed it on his fury at her and the sheriff being on his property.

His hands had been shaking still when she'd crossed the porch right next to him and gone in the house to talk to Irma. She'd only noticed out of the corner of her eye. The shotgun leaning against the side of the house. Cecil trying to hide the trembling fingers of his hands. Trying to hide his weakness.

Molly felt a start and almost stumbled into a tree limb. His fingers were clawlike. Arthritis? Would he even have been able to fire the shotgun?

Her mind leaped to the ransom notes. There was no way he could have written them. Someone had tried hard to make it look as if he had though, or that they had been written by someone trying to conceal their real handwriting, but it hadn't been Cecil Crandell.

Molly stopped. The rock was only a few dozen yards ahead. The person waiting would have heard her approach. They would be ready for her.

But who was waiting for her?

THE SHERIFF GRABBED the spare key for Molly's room as well as Georgia's from behind the hotel desk. He would try to rouse Molly by pounding on her door, but if that didn't work, he was going rogue.

She must have turned off her phone since it had gone straight to voicemail, he told himself as he charged up the stairs to the fourth floor and down the hall to pound on her door. No answer. His heart was thundering as he inserted the key, knowing he was breaking the law. But if he hadn't gotten the second key from downstairs, he would have broken down the door, screw the consequences.

The door swung open. In the shaft of moonlight coming through the window, he saw at once that the bed was empty. He rushed in. "Molly?"

Within in seconds, he knew with certainty that she wasn't here. As he started to head for Georgia's room, he saw the sheet of hotel stationery lying on the table by the door. He swore as he read it, wondering how much of a head start she'd had.

At the window, he looked out at the huge rock visible beyond the pines. Why would she go alone? Because she was determined to see this through to the end. Because she didn't trust him? Or because this was something she wanted to do on her own?

He swore and quickly left the room and went to Georgia's. He knew before he opened the door that she was gone.

Out the window, a light flashed on near the large rock. Brandt took off at top speed. He had to get to Molly before it was too late.

ALL MOLLY'S INSTINCTS told her to turn around and run. But if she ever wanted to know the truth… Whoever was waiting for her turned on a flashlight. It went off quickly, but she knew now where the person was—on the dark side of the huge rock.

She took a step forward then another. The cold air was filled with the scent of pine and the creek nearby. A breeze moaned softly in the tops of the pine boughs as she walked toward the rock on the soft bed of dried needles.

She hadn't gone far when the trees opened to a small meadow next to the rock. Standing at the edge of the trees, she saw him waiting for her. She was startled for a moment because of his resemblance to Cecil, and to her own father. He was a large man, like his father and brother.

"Did you bring the money?" Gage asked.

She patted her purse. There was a couple hundred dollars inside it. She hoped he wouldn't demand to see the money first. She'd come here wanting answers. She'd love to save Rowdy for her father, but mostly, she wanted to know who killed him. The theory was that whoever killed the ventriloquist had Rowdy.

"Where's Rowdy?"

Gage Crandell stepped to one side revealing Rowdy's case resting against the base of the rock.

"Please open it."

Gage scoffed. "You're not very trusting, you big-city types." He opened the case and she got a glimpse of Rowdy's painted face before he snapped it closed again.

"If your father killed mine, then how is it that you have Rowdy?" she asked staying where she stood, a half dozen yards away.

"How do you think?"

"You're going to let your father take the fall for this?"

Gage laughed. "Believe me, he's safer in prison. When my mother finds out that he confessed to killing Seth, her favorite son, he's a dead man. She already blames him for not telling her that Seth was in the area, let alone for seeing her son without telling her. There is no happy ending here."

Molly didn't know what to say. This man standing before her was her blood. That alone was a chilling thought.

"You just don't get it," Gage said taking a step toward her. "My father and I went to the hotel that night to kill Seth. I'd left a book stuck in the fire escape door so we could get in. He hadn't wanted me to come with him. I jumped into his truck as he started to leave."

"You knew he was going to the hotel to kill your brother?"

He huffed. "He had his gun with the silencer on it. Yeah, I knew. It had been building up ever since we'd gone to the hotel the first time to see Seth. My old man had killed Seth in his heart, in his mind, in his very soul. I wanted him to do it. That's why I went along."

Molly felt sick to her stomach listening to this.

"But he couldn't do it. Even when he had Seth down on his knees waiting for the bullet to enter the back of his head, my father couldn't do it." He sounded both disappointed and disgusted. "I watched from down the hall as he dropped the gun and left. Maybe he was hoping Seth would take his own life."

She had trouble finding her voice as she realized that she had done what Brandt had feared—she'd met a killer in the woods all alone. "What did you do?" Her voice came out a whisper.

"I left the book in the door and followed my father down the fire escape. He was driving off, leaving me there as if he'd forgotten me. Nothing unusual about that. I was the forgotten son, the one who'd gotten trapped on the ranch after the only two sons my parents ever cared about were dead and gone."

Molly heard the bitterness in his voice. She swallowed knowing in her heart what happened next. "You went back to your brother's room."

Gage nodded, looking as if he was reliving that night. "Seth had made it so easy for my father. He wanted him to kill him, or maybe he was already dead, you know, maybe sending him away like he had, had already killed Seth and that's why he changed his name, that's why he had that silly doll that talked for him."

"You went back and killed him."

He looked at her and blinked. "No. When I reached his room, Seth was already dead. The gun was gone. I just took the pen and some paper."

She stared at him. Was he telling the truth? "What about Rowdy?"

"My father had the case when he left. Not sure what he planned to do with it, not sure he even knew. Destroy it probably. But when he reached the bottom of the fire escape stairs, he just threw the case into the bushes. I retrieved it, hiding it until I went back upstairs to finish what he'd started. Maybe I planned to kill Seth—I don't know. But I didn't have to. I took his pickup keys and left. I got my son Cliff to follow me back to Fortune Creek to leave the pickup behind the hotel."

"If any of this is true, then who killed your brother?"

"I don't know. But I need that five thousand to be able to leave, to buy my freedom. This is my chance to escape the prison my brothers left me in. I was forced to stay here, be the good, loyal, hardworking rancher's son who couldn't abandon his parents especially after they'd lost their other sons. Both Ty and Seth are now free. I'm tired of envying them for getting away from this life. I want to be free too."

"That works out well then," said a voice from the trees behind Molly an instant before she heard the gunshot and saw Gage grab his chest and slowly slump to the ground next to Rowdy's case.

BRANDT'S HEART DROPPED to his boots at the sound of the gunshot. He'd been moving quickly through the pines, the large rock in sight. He'd put it all together—but not fast enough. Maybe not fast enough to save Molly. His chest contracted at the thought, making it hard to breathe.

The rock was not far now. He could hear voices. But a sound closer made him stumble. Someone was directly behind him.

The blow seemed to come from out of nowhere. He caught only a flash of movement. He went down hard in the dried pine needles. Then in a blink there was nothing but blackness.

GEORGIA STEPPED FROM the darkness of the trees into the moonlight.

Molly stared, stunned to see the gun in her hand now pointed at her. "You really did bring a gun."

She smiled. "I told you, I never leave home without it."

"What's going on?" She felt confused by this Georgia holding the gun pointed in her direction.

"You could say that I'm saving you and getting Rowdy back." She tsked. "I thought you were going to tell me when you heard from the person who had the puppet? I trusted you."

Her mind raced, unable to understand what was happening. "You shot Gage."

"Yes, well…you forgot to mention that there'd been a ransom demand for Rowdy. If I hadn't heard about the notes being found under your door, I might have given up and left town without the dummy. But I knew someone had it and if anyone could find it, it would be you or that damned cowboy sheriff. Couldn't leave without knowing where Rowdy was."

Molly still couldn't get her head around what was happening. "Why would you shoot Gage? He was about to give me Rowdy. It would have been over. You would have had the dummy and saved your job."

"Yes, my job that I hate," Georgia said. "When your father came in wanting to ensure Rowdy, I saw a way out. I didn't know some fool was going to murder him and take the dummy. That hadn't been part of the plan. I figured the way Clay Wheaton looked when he came in to sign the paperwork that he didn't have much time left. You still don't get it, do you?"

She didn't. She was still too shocked to make sense of any of it.

"I changed the beneficiary. You were never going to get a million dollars. Your father signed a fake one with you as the beneficiary. I had him sign another page—this one—so when he died and Rowdy didn't turn up, I would collect the insurance."

"But only if you split it with me," came another voice behind Molly, another one she recognized.

BRANDT SURFACED WITH a blinding headache.

He pushed himself up. He could hear voices coming through the trees, his memory returning like a swift kick to his solar plexus. He rose, staggered for a moment, then began to move toward the sound, telling himself that as long as they were talking, Molly might still be alive.

MOLLY TURNED TO see Jessica Woods, the alleged paranormal investigator she'd met at the café. Jessica came out of the trees from the direction of the road out of town. Like Georgia, she was armed. Molly had a sudden flashback of that day in the hotel when she'd thought that the two of them were in league together. It had been such an uncharitable thought that she'd felt bad about it. Now she realized that her instincts had been right. Just too late to do anything about it. Georgia and Jessica had been in this together.

"You were both *pretending* you were looking for Rowdy," she said.

"Oh, we weren't pretending," Georgia said. "We definitely needed Rowdy not to be found before we could get our hands on it and destroy it so we could collect the insurance money. You, Molly, with all your righteous behavior, were the fly in the ointment. Would you really have given up a million dollars to help me?"

"I would have," she said. "You were my friend. I didn't want you to lose your job."

Georgia laughed. "Didn't I tell you, Jess? She's a saint, straight arrow, gullible as all get-out. Her and the cowboy sheriff."

"I see you have your phone," Jessica said. "I wouldn't bother trying to call him. The sheriff won't be coming to save you. I ran into him in the woods. I left him out cold."

Molly's body went limp. She staggered, terrified to think what Jessica had done to him. The phone had been her backup. Now there was no one coming to save either of them. "Was the deputy part of your plan too?" she asked, surprised that her voice sounded almost normal to her ears.

"Jaden?" Georgia laughed. "He was just for amusement and information. I figured he'd know if Rowdy was found and tell me. But he didn't even know about the ransom demands. You and the sheriff kept that bit of information to yourselves."

"We should get moving," Jessica said. "Grab the dummy and let's go. I can finish this up." Georgia moved toward the rock and the case with Rowdy inside. Gage hadn't moved.

"Leave the case—that way no one will ever know if the dummy was in there or not."

Finish up? Molly held her breath afraid she already knew what they had planned.

"Sad that your uncle killed you, Molly. But at least you got off a shot that ended his life as well. Jaden will find an unregistered gun lying by each of you with your prints on one and Gage's on the other. Shouldn't have come out here by yourself. Should have called me." Georgia was saying. "When I hear what happened, I'm going to be devastated. We'd become such good friends." Georgia reached down to open Rowdy's case.

Gage's hand shot out. Molly caught the glint of a gun an instant before she heard the shots. Two of them, fired quickly in succession. Georgia went down hard next to Rowdy lying inside his open case. Behind her, Molly heard Jessica swear and instinctively rush forward.

The moment she did, Molly lunged for her and the gun in her hand.

Two SHOTS ECHOED through the trees. Brandt didn't know how long he'd been out as he struggled to his feet. Too long. He ran toward the rock, terrified of what he would find. As he burst out of the pines, his own weapon drawn, his head pounding, fear gripped him as he took in the sight before him in the moonlight. Near the rock, there was no movement. He could see Gage slumped over, Georgia on the ground in front of Rowdy's case.

At first he didn't see Molly. Everyone seemed to be down. But then he saw movement. Molly and Jessica grappling on the ground. The shine of the gun in Jessica's hand in the moonlight as the two rolled, Jessica coming out on top.

He charged toward them, terrified of taking a shot for

fear he would hit Molly and yet at the same time, terrified not to take the shot. The bang of a gunshot was followed by a second one. Both seemed to fill the small meadow, echoing off the large boulder.

For a moment, nothing moved. Brandt blinked. Jessica was still looming over Molly, the gun in her hand. And then Molly wrestled the gun away and Jessica slowly collapsed to the ground beside her.

Brandt rushed to Molly, dropping to his knees next to her, his gun still in his hand as he stared at her in the moonlight. He'd been terrified by all the blood, convinced Jessica had shot her.

"Are you hit?" he cried and felt a drowning wave of relief when she shook her head.

"I got it all," Molly said as he took her in his arms.

It wasn't until hours later after reinforcements had arrived, Gage had been rushed to a hospital and that he and Molly were in his office, that Brandt understood her words. She'd recorded everything on her phone.

Chapter Twenty-Six

Brandt listened to the recording on Molly's phone a second time. It was all there, the truth and not just about Gage, but about Georgia and Jessica. After Molly had told him about hearing Rowdy singing at night, he'd done a search of her room and the one adjoining it on the opposite side as Georgia's.

He'd found the small recorder in the air vent and known only one person could have put it there. He almost had everything he needed to release Cecil from jail—and arrest the person he now believed had killed Clay Wheaton, a.k.a. Seth Crandell.

He just needed proof.

Molly was at the hotel, no doubt packing to leave. He told himself this shouldn't take long as he grabbed his Stetson and drove to Eureka. After everything he'd learned, he thought the prosecutor could make a pretty good case.

The sheriff just needed a few things clarified.

Tom Sherman looked up in surprise at finding Brandt standing in his doorway. "Sheriff," he said as he got to his feet, placing both hands on his desk. For support? Or so Brandt didn't see how nervous he was? "I heard you caught Seth's killer. Congrats."

"Guess you haven't heard the latest." He saw a tick around Tom's mouth. "Cecil Crandell didn't kill him."

"I thought I heard you found his gun?"

"Did through an anonymous tip after Cecil was arrested."

"I should think that would be sufficient to put him away for a long time."

Brandt nodded. "I have crime techs breaking down the weapon as we speak. That's the thing about killers. They just assume they can wipe prints off a gun, but they always miss a spot. All we need is one clear print."

He saw Tom swallow and shift nervously on his feet, waiting. "I suspect the killer was worried there wouldn't be enough evidence against Cecil, even though the man had confessed. Oftentimes people confess to cover for someone else."

"His son Gage," Tom said quickly. "I thought of that myself."

"Gage didn't kill Seth."

"What?"

"I'm going to need your fingerprints, Tom."

The man had the look of someone about to make a run for it. "Why?"

"I'm betting we are going to find Seth's prints in your SUV. You did meet with him before the night you killed him, didn't you? Did he tell you what happened the night your sister died? Or did he continue to cover for his brother Ty? I'm also betting that you've been watching the hotel, waiting for an opportunity to get what you believed was justice."

"You can't prove—"

"That's just it—I think I can. I forgot to mention," Brandt said. "Seth's small recorder was found. He'd recorded Rowdy's songs on it, probably liked to play them at night. I would imagine that's what the elderly couple a few doors down heard the night Seth died. The night you murdered him, you retrieved the recorder when you heard Ash coming up on the elevator. You sure you didn't leave your fingerprints on the recorder? How about the tape inside?"

"You can't prove anything," Tom said, sounding more confident than he looked.

"Jaden," Brandt said to his deputy who'd been waiting in the hall. "Would you please read Mr. Sherman his rights?"

As the deputy approached him, Tom's expression crumpled. He dropped into his chair. "Someone needed to get justice for Ruby. Your father sure as hell didn't."

"But you killed the wrong man, Tom. Seth wasn't responsible for your sister's death, Ty was. I suspect that's why he killed himself."

Tom's eyes widened. "I want a lawyer."

"I'm sure you have one you can call," Brandt said. "But I'm curious. Why did you leave the recorder in the hotel, set up where you could operate it remotely in the room next to Seth's daughter?" he asked after Jaden had read Tom his rights.

Tom shook his head. "If that ridiculous dummy hadn't been missing, she and the others would have left town and it would have been over. I could have put Ruby to rest, finally after all these years."

"You tried to scare away the wrong person," Brandt said. "All you did was make her more determined to find her father's killer and find Rowdy."

"Rowdy," Tom said with a bark of laughter. "That damned puppet. You're right. Seth and I did meet. He didn't even have the guts to tell me the truth about what happened to my sister. He had the puppet do it. I should have killed them both then."

Brandt watched Jaden lead the man out of his office toward the patrol SUV parked outside thinking what a tragedy it had all been. If Cecil hadn't dropped his gun that night in the ventriloquist's room, maybe Tom never would have picked it up and killed Seth.

The irony was that if Tom had waited, Seth would have died of natural causes and Tom wouldn't be arrested for homicide right now.

Chapter Twenty-Seven

"I don't want you to go."

Molly turned to look at Brandt. She smiled at the handsome cowboy sheriff in the noisy Kalispell airport. It had taken a while before she'd been able to smile after everything that had happened.

Tom Sherman's arrest had rocked the county. Tom's fingerprints had been found on the tape recorder cassette as well as a partial on the trigger of the gun.

The townfolk of Fortune Creek had been more shocked when it came to Georgia Eden. Like Molly, everyone had liked Georgia. She'd fooled them all, especially Molly.

That was what made it so hard, she thought now as she picked up the case with Rowdy safely inside. Her suitcase was already being loaded onto the plane. She'd thought she'd found a friend.

"I have a feeling that we'll see each other again," she said meeting Brandt's gaze.

"Not soon enough to suit me," he said stepping to her. His kiss was pure honey, his hand cupping her neck warm and reassuring. "You sure about this?" he asked as he drew back from the kiss.

"I want to personally deliver Rowdy to the museum," she said. At least that part of Georgia's story was true. The money would go to Gage, her uncle who had helped save her life. He was still in the hospital, but doctors said he should make a full recovery.

When he did, Molly wanted him to have the option of leaving the ranch that he'd felt trapped on all these years.

"You know that he probably won't leave," Brandt had said when she'd told him of her plan.

"Probably not since his sons are there, his mother and father. He might not realize how strong those roots are that have held him there," she said. "But I like the idea of Rowdy maybe saving Gage's life since he'd saved Rowdy."

"I never thought you'd really destroy it," Brandt said now, motioning to the case with the Crandell Ranch brand on it.

She smiled, wondering if that was true. "It took my father's murder for me to finally get to know him." She shook her head ruefully. "I wish he knew how sorry I am."

The sheriff scoffed. "You risked your life to save Rowdy and now your father's memory will live on at the museum. I think he knows." He drew her to him as tears welled in her eyes.

As her flight was called, he let go of her. She wiped her eyes. "If you're ever in Fortune Creek again, give me a holler."

ON THE WAY back to Fortune Creek, Brandt stopped by a bookstore and picked up a copy of *East of Eden*. Jaden had remembered it from high school, but Brandt wasn't sure he'd gotten around to actually reading it. Back in those days, rodeoing was all he'd cared about.

It hadn't taken him long to read it once back in Fortune Creek. He'd known how the story would end. Two brothers, one the father's favorite, a deadly rivalry between the two. He thought of Gage Crandell, who would have been fifteen the year Ruby Sheridan died and his brother Seth joined the military and his younger brother Ty killed himself.

Brandt had wondered if there was a reason *East of Eden* was the book stuck in the door the night the ventriloquist died. Or had Gage randomly chosen the book?

He'd taken the book by the hospital. "Have you read this?" he asked Gage who shook his head. "I think you might want to. Might make you feel like you weren't alone."

One son loved, one son hated, one son feeling unloved, he'd thought as he'd left the hospital.

Chapter Twenty-Eight

Helen spotted her first. The dispatcher had been getting Ghost a drink when she saw the car pull up out front.

Brandt heard her exclaim in the room outside his office and looked up. Helen, the woman who always said she didn't like dogs, was holding that ball of white fluff that had been rescued from Jessica Woods's pickup.

The sheriff had been planning to take it to the shelter, but Helen wasn't having any of that. She'd scooped up the furball and the two had been inseparable ever since. It had surprised him, but not as much as learning that Jessica really had been a ghost hunter by profession. How she and Georgia had crossed paths was still a mystery.

"Well, I'll be darned," Helen said. "Would you look at that."

He looked past her in time to see Molly standing by what appeared to be a new SUV. He smiled so hard that it hurt his face. She had come back?

For weeks, every time they'd talked, she'd said she was tying up loose ends. He hadn't pressed her, knowing it would be a mistake. As it was, he couldn't imagine what a woman like her would do in Fortune Creek. Would she even last a week if she did come back?

He'd warned himself not to get his hopes up and yet here

she was. He pushed himself up from his desk and walked toward the door. The look on her face was definitely one that said, *And you thought you'd never see me again*.

It was true. Not that he could blame her. They were from two completely different worlds. Murder had thrown them together. That and a dummy named Rowdy the Rodeo Cowboy. But it would take a lot more to keep them together, Brandt thought as he pushed open the sheriff's department door and stepped out into the sunshine. It would take a love strong enough to last forever.

Summer had come to Fortune Creek slowly; after all, this was Montana and only miles from the Canadian border. His father used to joke that the weather kept out the riffraff—until summer.

Today was one of those early summer days when the sky was a blinding blue, the sun a lolling ball of heat, making the pine-covered mountains shimmer with light. People fell in love with Montana in the summer.

"You came back," he said as he stopped on the sidewalk to take her in.

"Couldn't stay away."

He glanced at the SUV. It was packed to the top. "Almost looks like you're moving in."

She grinned. "Don't believe me? How about you come over here, cowboy? I think I have just what will convince you."

"That right?" he asked as he stepped toward her. He had no idea what had brought her back, let alone what might keep her here with him.

But when he reached her, she stepped to him and kissed him.

He felt his heart take off like the bald eagle he'd seen earlier flying across Montana's big sky. It had been free to go anywhere it wanted, but it stayed here in this isolated part of the state—just like him.

Brandt drew back from the kiss to look at her. "What in the hell are you going to do in Fortune Creek?"

"You mean after I marry you? See that building down the street? I want it. I'm going to open a business." He cocked a brow at her. "Don't worry—I'm a financial analyst. I know what I'm doing."

He laughed and pulled her into his arms. "If that was true, you wouldn't be interested in marrying a small-town cowboy sheriff."

"Try me," Molly said and kissed him again.

When their kids asked one day, Brandt planned to tell them that it was a kiss that had done it. Their mother had stolen his heart with one amazing kiss—and the rest would be history.

"Ask the woman to marry you, fool," Helen said from the doorway.

As he pulled back, he saw that half the town had come out into the sunshine. It was true that nothing much ever happened in Fortune Creek, that even the birth of a calf made news.

So he wasn't that surprised that he and Molly were making a stir.

He dropped to one knee right there in the main street and dug out the ring he'd been carrying for months, thinking himself a fool. He looked up blinded by this woman's beauty and strength. "Marry me," he said.

"I thought you would never ask," she joked and then she was in his arms. Some of the people who'd gathered cheered. Some just went back to their business. Helen huffed and took her new dog back inside the sheriff's department.

Brandt wondered how many people would be taking bets

on whether the marriage would last. He smiled to himself. He had a good feeling about this. He was putting his money on the two of them.

There was going to be a wedding in Fortune Creek! He couldn't wait to make this woman his wife.

* * * * *

Whispering Winds Widows
Debra Webb

MILLS & BOON

Debra Webb is the award-winning *USA TODAY* bestselling author of more than one hundred novels, including those in reader-favourite series Faces of Evil, the Colby Agency and Shades of Death. With more than four million books sold in numerous languages and countries, Debra has a love of storytelling that goes back to her childhood on a farm in Alabama. Visit Debra at debrawebb.com.

Visit the Author Profile page
at millsandboon.com.au.

CAST OF CHARACTERS

Reyna Hart—Reyna writes the stories of people who are suffering from illnesses that steal their memories. The stories allow them to hold on to their pasts.

Ben Kane—Thirty years ago, his father and his two best friends disappeared without a trace. Ben would do anything to solve that mystery, more for his beloved grandfather than for himself.

The Widows—Lucinda Kane, Deidre Fuller and Harlowe Evans have secrets they can never tell. Did they murder their husbands? How far will they go to keep their secrets?

Father Vincent Cullen—He knows the truth but his vows prevent him from telling another living soul...but there are other things he can do. How far will he go to see that the secrets are revealed?

Deputy Gordon Walls—He was supposed to marry Lucinda, until she cheated on him and married someone else. Was it revenge for that betrayal that caused three men to vanish thirty years ago?

Wade Landon—He was the most succesful high school football coach in state history, but he has secrets too...secrets he can never tell anyone.

Sheriff Tara Norwood—Her father was the sheriff thirty years ago when three men disappeared. She feels obligated to finish that case for him.

Chapter One

The Light Memory Care Center
Lantern Pointe
Chattanooga, Tennessee
Sunday, April 21, 10:00 a.m.

"Are you certain you want to do this, Reyna?"

Reyna Hart smiled—as much to reassure her friend as to brace herself. She was going to do this. "I absolutely do want to do this."

Eudora Davenport's eyes shone with excitement. "I knew you'd never be able to resist." She placed a frail hand against her chest. "You don't know how much this means to me."

Reyna had a fairly good idea. She had been visiting Eudora, a sweet woman she'd enjoyed getting to know, for nearly a year now. Each Sunday from 10:00 until 11:00 a.m., sometimes until noon. Generally, they sat in the two chairs positioned to take in the view out the one large window in her room. Their tea on the table between them. They had become friends. Good friends.

"There aren't many who will talk to you," Eudora reminded her. "Others will say plenty just to hear themselves talk." She drew in a deep breath. "Some will attempt to mislead you. Folks don't always tolerate change very well. Particularly if that change prompts the unknown."

"I'm aware." Reyna considered herself a good judge of character. When she'd been pursuing her original career dream, she'd spent most of her research time interviewing people—and Eudora was right. The best interviewers learned to recognize the difference between a thoughtful and forthright person and a conversational narcissist. Reyna had spent most of her life, even as a child, watching people. Her mother always said that particular skill was one of the things that made Reyna so perfect for the art of storytelling. She was a natural at slipping into the thoughts and dreams of characters.

Reyna had certainly expected she would spend her life writing fiction. She'd been writing short stories since she'd been old enough to string sentences together. The first contract had come quickly and somewhat easier than she'd anticipated. Her debut novel had made a brief and distant showing on the bestseller lists. Not so shabby. But that book had been the one and only.

Just call her a one-semi-hit wonder.

The marketable ideas had stopped coming, and her publisher had moved on.

For a while Reyna had drifted—career wise. She'd held on to her New York City apartment that was about the size of a shoebox for another year, and then she'd opted to take a break from the dream and spend some time in reality.

Not so much fun at first. Coming back to Chattanooga to start over hadn't been easy. She'd tried out a few different career hats—none worth remembering. And though the process had been painful, the timing had turned out to be important: her beloved grandmother had been diagnosed with Alzheimer's. From that moment there had been no looking back for Reyna. She'd become her grandmother's primary caretaker even after she'd had to move to this very facility. Throughout the remainder of her life, her grandmother's greatest fear had not been of dying but of forgetting who she was and what her life had been before, so she'd asked Reyna to write her story. Then, anytime she wished, she could read her story and remember.

Reyna would have done anything for her grandmother, so she'd thrown herself into the task. The story, mostly a narrative written in first person, had given her grandmother much pleasure the final months of her life. When she'd passed, others at the facility had pleaded with Reyna to write theirs. So, she'd decided to give the possibility a go.

Now, two years later, work was steady and surprisingly lucrative. Reyna had been featured in the *Chattanooga Times Free Press*, and several other newspapers had carried her work in their lifestyle sections. She'd even received an award from the city for innovation in supporting quality of life for the elderly.

"You've decided how to start?" Eudora asked, drawing Reyna out of the past.

"I have." She gave her friend a nod. "I'm starting with Ward Kane Senior."

Eudora's thin gray brows rose. "He may not talk to you. At the ten-year anniversary of the disappearance as well as the twenty, he refused to give an interview. He's a stubborn man."

Reyna had heard this from her before. "He's also the only remaining father."

Eudora's gaze turned distant. "Sometimes I forget how much time has really gone by." She sighed. "Thirty years. It's hard to believe."

Eudora Davenport remained a beautiful woman even at eighty-two. Her hair was that perfect shade of silver that required no dyes or anything at all to give it luster or to add thickness. She wore it in a French twist with pearl pins. At this stage she spent much of her time reclined in her bed or in her favorite chair, but her loungewear was always tasteful and representative of her elegance and class. Eudora insisted aging was a gift, one that should be respected and embraced with dignity.

"I will call him," she said then, her tone determined. "Perhaps I can persuade him."

"It couldn't hurt," Reyna agreed. "I've read everything about the case that has been released for public consumption. Anything he hasn't shared could prove helpful. The FBI agent who assisted the sheriff's office in the investigation has passed away, but the deputy detective, Nelson Owens, who worked the case, has agreed to meet with me tomorrow."

Eudora picked up her cup of tea from the table between them and sipped. When she'd set it aside once more, she searched Reyna's face for a long moment before speaking. Reyna hadn't quite decided why this case was so important to Eudora. She was not related to one or more of the three men—the Three, as they were called—who had disappeared, nor the wives and children—if any— they had left behind.

The only thing she had told Reyna when she'd commissioned her to write the story that was technically not even hers was that she wanted to know the truth before she lost herself completely or died—whichever came first.

Eudora stared straight ahead for a long moment, her gaze reaching somewhere beyond the window. There were times like this when she stopped speaking and drifted off. Sometimes for minutes, others for hours. Her grandmother had done the same. Reyna had learned to be patient or to come back another time.

"She never comes to see me anymore," Eudora said, her voice as distant as her gaze.

"Who?" Reyna asked, though she wasn't sure the eighty-two-year-old was speaking to her or if she was still aware Reyna was in the room. It happened more and more lately.

Her pulse reacted to a prick of emotion. She truly had begun to consider this woman family. There was little left of Reyna's. She still had her mother, who had remarried recently and was quite focused on her new husband. Not that Reyna resented this one little bit. Her mother had been madly in love with Reyna's father, and his death had devastated them both. It had taken a decade and a half for her mother to even consider having dinner with a romantic interest. Now she was happily married to the second love of her life, and Reyna was incredibly grateful for her second chance.

Reyna, however, was still waiting for her first chance. But she had time. Thirty-five wasn't so old.

Wasn't so young either, an evil little voice chided.

"Eudora, who do you mean?" Reyna prodded.

Eudora blinked, turned away from the window to meet Reyna's gaze. "I'm sorry—what were you saying?"

"You said she never comes to see you anymore."

A frown lined the older woman's otherwise perfectly smooth brow. The woman had beautiful skin with so few lines one would think she'd had multiple cosmetic surgeries, but when asked, Eudora always laughed and insisted it was simply good genes. "Just an old friend. No one important, dear."

"Well." Reyna stood, walked over to her chair, reached for her hand and gave it a little squeeze. "I should be on my way. I can check in at the bed-and-breakfast after lunch. I'll spend some time getting the lay of the land, so to speak."

Eudora held on to her hand when Reyna would have pulled it away. "No matter what happens, I so thoroughly appreciate that you have agreed to do this for me. Please know that if you don't find the answer quickly enough or at all, don't despair. Knowing what happened is important to me, but it is not your fault if I go first."

Reyna smiled and gave her hand another squeeze. "I'm sure you'll be fine, and if I can uncover the truth, I will revel in writing the story."

Eudora released Reyna's hand and clasped hers together in her lap. "Oh, I have no doubt you'll find the truth. From the moment I met you, I was certain you would know exactly how to do what no one else could."

No pressure.

"I'll talk to you soon," Reyna promised before leaving.

This lady had a great deal of faith in her. She surely hoped she wouldn't have to let her down. A thirty-year-old missing persons case that no one else had been able to solve was a tall order.

In time, evidence grew faint, disappeared, as did memories. But there was a flip side. The passage of vast amounts of time often loosened tongues and added to the weight of guilt. Reyna exited the facility and drew in a deep breath of cool spring air. So much had started to bloom already—it gave her hope that anything could happen.

Even solving a very, very cold case.

Whispering Winds
1:00 p.m.

LEGEND HAD IT that the air in Whispering Winds was never still. The small community was an old one, nestled against the state line, nearly in Georgia. The tourist guides called it one of Lookout Mountain's lesser-known gems. Like most of the small niche communities on the mountain, the tiny town proved a powerful draw for tourists with its incredible views and ghost stories that were nearly legend in themselves. Not the least of which was the story of how three young men—Ward Kane Junior, known as JR, Duke Fuller and Judson Evans, ranging in age from twenty-eight to twenty-nine, all three with wives, one with a child—had just vanished into thin air, never to be seen again.

Reyna turned into the small parking area of the lovely historic home that had been turned into the Jewel, a bed-and-breakfast located right as you entered Whispering Winds. The house was the first of many grand old residences that had been well maintained and remained occupied. A bit farther down Main Street the town shops and offices lined both sides. Tourism kept the little shops thriving. Many of the residents worked in Chattanooga, but there were a good number of retail and service jobs available locally.

The sheer number of thriving little communities on the mountain had surprised Reyna. There was Dread Hollow and Sunset Cove, and both had their own tourist draws. Funny, when Reyna had returned to Tennessee she'd expected to end up in Nashville after spending some time with her grandmother, but fate had seen things differently.

Now she owned her grandmother's cottage in the city's historic district. Growing up, Reyna had found the little cottage filled with hidden treasures and treats. Since Reyna was the only grandchild, her grandmother had loved creating little treasure hunts and mysteries to solve whenever she'd visited. As a child, Reyna had been convinced her grandmother had secret fairy friends. She was also certain she had inherited her creativity from her dear grandmother.

The city wasn't so far, and Reyna could have opted to drive back and forth for the next few days while she did this deep dive into research, but in her experience, there was no substitute for living among the folks from whom she wanted answers.

Reyna parked her vintage Land Rover—also inherited from her grandmother—in a spot reserved for guests and climbed out. Owning a vehicle in New York City had been far too much trouble. The better route had been just to rent one when needed. But here, in the South, a vehicle was a must. Reyna had always loved the Land Rover, and her grandmother had insisted she take possession of it as soon as she moved back home. Even for a vehicle nearing forty years old, it had very low mileage and was in pristine condition, aesthetically and mechanically.

She grabbed her bag from the back seat and headed up the walk. Spring flowers were blooming, and the trees had sprouted new leaves. The world was coming alive, her grandmother would say, after its long winter's sleep.

The porch was exactly what one expected of a grand Victorian home. It spread across the front and wrapped around one side. More than a century old, the home stood three floors high and covered better than thirteen thousand square feet. Lots of stone taken right from the area made up the foundation and the walkways. But it was the fountains and gardens that took her breath away before she even reached the entrance. Truly beautiful. So well-thought-out.

Stepping inside, Reyna found exactly what she'd anticipated. Soaring ceilings and grand chandeliers. Furniture made during a time when craftsmanship had carried a higher standard. Shiny wood floors and well-loved woven rugs.

The registration desk was staffed by the owner. Reyna recognized Birdie Jewel from the website's About page. A lovely woman of somewhere in her late seventies, with the gray hair to prove it. Her hair hung in a long, loose braid. She looked up and smiled, and her eyes were bright in a face that showed a light hand toward cosmetics. As natural as Birdie Jewel's gray hair and minimal makeup suggested she might be, her style in clothing was the show. Flamboyant fabrics in brilliant colors. Lots of exotic jewelry that tinkled as she moved around the counter to meet Reyna.

"Welcome. You must be Reyna Hart."

Her voice was as musical as her jewelry. Pleasantly so.

"Hello." Reyna dropped her bag at her feet and shook the woman's outstretched hand. "This is genuinely lovely." She gazed around the lobby.

Birdie's smile widened. "Oh, I adore hearing guests say so. Come sign the guest book." She hurried behind the counter once more and turned the large guest book around to face Reyna. "We do things here a little on the old-fashioned side. None of your personal information will be in the book, but we do love for you to sign your name. Even if only your given name."

"Love that." Reyna accepted the pen and signed her name on the next available line. She passed the pen back to the owner.

"Now I'll need your credit card."

"Of course."

Once the paperwork was done, Birdie grabbed a key from one of the numbered boxes behind the desk. "Follow me," she said.

Reyna picked up her bag and trailed after Birdie, who

led the way up the grand staircase, her bohemian skirt flowing around her. It wasn't until they neared the top that Reyna noticed the older woman was barefoot. Her toenails were painted a bright orange. Reyna smiled. She preferred bare feet herself when working at home.

The owner paused in front of room seven. "This one is for you. It has the balcony that overlooks Main Street."

"Lovely." Some might prefer one of the views provided from the elegant home's cliff-side location, but she was interested in what was happening among the people, so a view of Main Street was perfect.

"Make yourself at home," Birdie said as she placed the key on the table near the door. "If you need anything at all, just let me know. I'm always here. Breakfast is served each morning from seven until nine. Snacks are always available, but we serve no other organized meals."

"Perfect," Reyna assured her.

When the lady had gone, after closing the door behind her, Reyna quickly hung up the clothes she had brought along. She put away her suitcase and left her toiletry bag in the bathroom. The claw-foot tub was center stage in the room. Very romantic.

Reyna walked out onto the balcony and simply stood there for a long while. She watched the slow pace of the cars moving along Main Street and the even slower stride of the pedestrians. The small town had a very sedate air about it. Peaceful, content. And yet thirty years ago the Three had disappeared without a trace.

The wives left behind remained, to this day, widowed. For thirty years all three had stuck with their stories of having no idea what had become of their husbands. Never a single deviation, not even a little one. Those closest to the families had given mixed messages, according to the many, many articles Reyna had read. Most were certain the couples had all been happily married. Churchgoing, deeply in love, happy people with no financial issues or other known troubles.

The men had been lifelong best friends. Different jobs, different family backgrounds. As adults they'd remained friends, and the women they'd married, Lucinda, Deidre and Harlowe, had been best friends their entire lives as well. They'd attended school together, parties, vacations, and they'd all married the same summer—only days between their weddings.

So strange that the men would abruptly disappear together and the women would know nothing of the reason. Not one had ever remarried. Not one had ever spoken against the other.

Reyna walked back into her room, closed the French doors to the balcony and decided she would drive around a bit and get the lay of the land.

Tonight she would call Eudora and tell her all that she'd seen. The woman couldn't wait to hear everything.

Eudora was such a good storyteller in her own right that developing her narrative would be incredibly easy. Reyna had videoed their sessions using her phone's camera, as she did with all clients, and then she would use those to help bring their voices to life.

The sun was shining and the temperature was perfect for a leisurely stroll, but Reyna wanted to drive to a number of locations first thing, so she opted to head out to the Land Rover. She'd grab some lunch somewhere before returning to the Jewel.

Excitement had her belly tingling as she descended the staircase. To tell the truth, she hadn't felt this much enthusiasm for an endeavor since her own book. She enjoyed all her work, but this was the first time she had felt so drawn toward a project. She wanted to find the answers that no one else had. When she'd written her novel, a mystery loosely based on an actual event, she had loved the research aspect. The digging into the dirty details in search of previously unearthed facts.

Perhaps that was what had put the fire in her blood this time. Her goal was to find the answer to a thirty-year-old mystery. Had the young husbands taken off for parts unknown in search of wealth or new love? Had they met with untimely deaths from someone to whom they had been in some sort of debt?

Or were the Widows actually murderers who had decided for whatever reasons that their husbands had to die?

The Widows of Whispering Winds. The perfect book or movie title. For the first five or so years after the disappearance of the Three—no remains had ever been found—there had been lots written on the Widows and the long-lost husbands. But the story had eventually fizzled as they all did. Once in a great while a retired cop or private investigator or investigative reporter would come to town and dig around. But no one had ever found an answer.

Reyna refused to allow that reality to dampen her spirit. In all such unsolved cases, there were no answers until someone found one. It was only a matter of time and interest. And maybe luck.

She had the time and the interest. Just maybe she would get lucky.

The idea that this could be more than the memoir for Eudora dared to flirt with her thoughts. This could be Reyna's next book.

Eudora herself had suggested as much.

"Don't get ahead of yourself, girl."

Reyna started her Land Rover and prepared to back out of the parking lot. A knot tightened in her stomach. She wasn't getting her hopes up about anything more than what was. She would write the memoir and dig as deep into this mystery as necessary to find answers for her client.

Nothing more…for now.

If more developed…well, that would be incredible. For now, all her focus needed to be on finding answers.

The knot loosened, and Reyna eased the Land Rover out onto Main Street. She surveyed the lovely shops and the happy-looking pedestrians. It was all picture-perfect. Like a Norman Rockwell painting. The quintessential little village filled with the best of what life had to offer.

But there was something unpleasant or perhaps evil hidden here.

All Reyna had to do was find it.

Chapter Two

Kane Residence
Lula Lake Lane
3:30 p.m.

"Ben, I think that faucet in the bathroom under the stairs is dripping a little too."

Bennett "Ben" Kane drew his upper body from under the kitchen sink and looked over at his grandfather. "I'm just about finished under here, so I'll have a look at that one next."

He swiped his hand over the interior floor of the sink base cabinet to ensure no water had dripped from the P-trap he'd replaced. Dry as a bone. Good to go. He grabbed his tools, elbowed the cabinet doors shut and got to his feet.

"That's a wrap on this one. Good thing too. The old one was just about rusted through."

Ward Kane Senior, arms crossed over his chest, gave an approving nod from where he was propped against the counter overseeing the work. "A man can't complain when anything lasts fifty years."

Ben placed the wrenches in his toolbox. "No, sir, he sure can't."

His grandfather's father had built this house. Fifty

years ago his grandfather had renovated this kitchen after inheriting the place. Ben's own daddy had been born in this house. There was a lot of Kane history here. It was home.

For the past year, Ben had been living here…*again*.

"I'll make a pot of coffee." Ward Senior moved toward the sink, his gait unsteady still.

The hip-replacement surgery had gone well but, as the old man would say, nothing had worked the same since. His hand shook when he reached for the carafe. A frown tugged at Ben's brow. The shaking hands was different. He'd keep a closer watch for any worsening. His grandfather would be the first to say that at eighty-five things started to wear out, but Ben felt it was his obligation to keep a running list of anything the doctor might need to hear about. Otherwise, the good doctor would likely never know.

"I'll be right with you," Ben promised. He grabbed his toolbox from the counter and headed for the bathroom beneath the stairs, which was more a powder room with just a toilet and sink.

He tapped the newel-post as he passed it, as was his habit. He'd spent a lot of time on those bottom three steps as a kid. He could sit there and watch through the glass in the front door for his daddy to come pick him up. Not that Ben hadn't enjoyed spending time with his grandparents— he had. But his father had worked long hours in the city. Sometimes late into the evenings. So on the occasional Saturdays or Sundays when his parents had left him with his grandparents, he'd always been anxious to get home. He'd loved his daddy and hadn't had nearly enough time with him.

Ben pushed the memories aside. No point going there

today. Today was for his grandfather—his pops, as he had fondly referred to him since he'd been old enough to talk. There were things around the house that needed a little tweaking, and until now, his grandfather had refused to allow Ben to take care of them. He'd insisted that as soon as he was recovered from his surgery he'd intended to do it himself. Here they were nearly a year later, and finally he'd relented and agreed to have the work done.

Ben placed his toolbox on the toilet lid and studied the fifty-odd-year-old sink faucet. Sure enough, about every five seconds a drop of water slipped free. His grandfather's eighty-five-year-old body might've been giving out here and there, but the man's hearing was perfect. Lying in bed at night, he probably heard every drop hit that porcelain sink basin. Ben chuckled.

Ward Kane Senior had spent his whole life from age twelve until just last year as the local handyman in Whispering Winds. He'd been taking care of folks' around-the-house issues for all that time. His son, Ward Junior, had started helping him when he'd been twelve as well. But then when he'd married, his wife—Ben's mom—had insisted that she wasn't living that life. She'd wanted a husband with a "real job that paid real money." So his father had gone to work for a plumbing company down in Chattanooga, and Ben wasn't sure his grandfather had forgiven his mother yet.

Ben was fairly confident the two would never do more than merely tolerate each other and would only do that because of him.

Some family rifts just couldn't be repaired. Maybe if his father had still been with them things would have turned out differently.

"Enough of that," he grumbled as he focused on changing the washer in the faucet.

The truth was Ben hadn't done the right thing either. His mother had insisted that he go to college, so he had. He'd spent the past twelve-plus years as an architect in Chattanooga, helping out his grandfather here and there. But last year, with his grandfather's health declining and his longtime helper having moved away, Ben had had to move in for a while.

The wrench slipped, and he popped his knuckles on the sink rim. He swore under his breath.

Well, he could have driven in from the city and then back home at night, but his two-year relationship with the woman he'd expected to marry had ended, and he'd decided that going home no longer held much appeal. Not that he could blame his ex-fiancée so much. The trouble had been more his fault than hers. He'd been so focused on work that he'd allowed their relationship to disintegrate. It would be far easier to blame her for finding someone new, but then, it might not have happened if he had been paying attention.

He wasn't sure they had ever decided what they'd wanted for the future. They'd never talked about starting a family or any aspect of long term. Once they'd been engaged, things had just sort of stalled there. In hindsight they'd probably rushed into the engagement thing too quickly anyway. Better to move on before things got any more complicated.

No hard feelings was always the best way if it was doable.

At some point he would likely put his house in the city on the market. He was perfectly happy here for now. His mother, on the other hand, was not happy at all. She wanted him back in the city and getting on with his life. Not going backward, as she called it.

"Coffee's done!" his grandfather shouted.

Ben smiled. Coffee with his grandfather on a Sunday afternoon was always a good thing.

Ben finished up, grabbed his toolbox and headed back to the kitchen. "Next week I need to get up on this roof," he said as he left his tools on the bench by the back door. "Those April showers have given me a pretty good idea where the leaks are."

There were only two and those only showed up during a serious downpour, but they needed to be taken care of before they worsened.

"No need." Ward filled his cup and settled at the table. "I called Johnson's Roofing. I'm just gonna have the whole thing replaced with one of those nice metal ones. They have a special right now. Ten percent discount."

Ben blew out a long, low whistle as he filled his own cup. "Standing seam metal roof—that'll be a pretty penny, Pops."

"I've got plenty of pretty pennies," he said with a pointed look in Ben's direction. "Planning to get the place painted too."

Now Ben was worried. "You planning on selling? Or are you just trying to make me feel unneeded?"

"The place hasn't been painted in thirty years," Ward declared. He gingerly sipped his steaming brew.

"I thought you liked the chippy-white-paint style." Ben grinned at the hard look cast his way. "You know, I'm a pretty good painter."

"You've got enough on your hands with taking care of folks in the community and still doing projects for that firm of yours."

"Technically," Ben said, "it's not my firm."

"It's got your name on the sign."

"I'm a partner, Pops." He opted not to mention that he'd discussed stepping back for the foreseeable future. He would still do projects and be a part of the firm, but he wasn't spending whatever time his grandfather had left focused on expanding the business and working sixteen-hour days.

Turning thirty-seven with a major breakup under his belt had been a hard wake-up call about where his life was and where it was heading.

He wanted a family. A home. A life. His gaze settled on his grandfather. Their lives had fallen apart when Ben's father had disappeared thirty years ago, and things hadn't been right since. Ben had gone on with his life, sure. But not the life he heard his grandfather speak about. The real family where you did things together. You built a home life and a work life that were woven together with love and time spent together.

He wanted that.

And he wanted his grandfather to be around to see that it could still be done.

"Seems to me," Ward said, leaning back in his chair and cradling his coffee mug, "they'd be expecting more from a partner than video conferences and long-distance project management."

So, he'd picked up on what Ben was up to. "I'm not going back to full-time work at the firm, Pops. I'm stepping back in order to build up the family business and to get my personal life in order."

Ward's gaze narrowed. "You found someone around here I don't know about yet? Because this decision sure as heck better not be about taking care of an old man and the fleeting legacy his daddy built."

Ben sipped his coffee for a while before going for the snap. This discussion would need to go down strategically. Like a hard-fought state football championship. Otherwise the opposing team would be closing in for the win.

"No, sir. I haven't found anyone. I haven't been looking. Not really, anyway."

Ward harrumphed. "In my opinion, there's trouble if you aren't looking at all."

"And I'm not giving up anything just because I'm needed around here." He opted to stick with the career decision rather than go down the relationship road. When his grandfather would have said more, Ben interrupted, "This is not solely about you, old man. Mom is fifty-eight. She needs me a little more these days too."

Another of those unimpressed harrumphs sounded.

Yeah, well, he got why his grandfather felt that way, but Lucinda Kane was Ben's mother, and he loved her no matter that she could be judgmental and stubborn and nosy. A lot like the man eyeing him right now.

"I just want to do what's right," Ben admitted. "I'm seeing the decay of family more and more—call me old-fashioned, but I want what you and Mimi had. If I'm lucky enough to find it."

Ward stared into his mug for a time. "Women like your mimi are hard to find." His gaze settled on Ben's. "But they're out there." He exhaled a big breath. "That's an admirable goal. Just don't cut yourself short on the follow-through. You're a good man, Bennett. Just like your daddy was. Any woman would be lucky to have you as a husband. Remember that too."

The smile that tugged at Ben's lips wouldn't be ignored. His grandfather only called him Bennett when he was really serious. His mother had refused to allow her child to be Ward Kane the Third. Instead she'd chosen her maiden name for his given name. The story was that his grandfather hadn't spoken to her for a month after Ben had been born. But Mimi had brought him around. Like he'd said, his mother and his grandfather were the two hardest-headed people he knew.

"I'll keep that in mind," Ben promised. "But in all seriousness, this is what I want. I'll have the work that goes along with that hard-earned degree Mom wanted me to have, but I'll also have this, and I love *this*."

Ward nodded. "You won't get any more argument from me."

Ben was glad to hear it. "So, you'll let me paint the house?" It wasn't that big. Two stories. Three bedrooms, two baths. He could handle it.

"As long as it doesn't get in the way of your search for that special someone."

A strangled laugh burst out of him. "Oh, man. I have a feeling I shouldn't have been so brutally honest."

"Honesty is always the best policy." His grandfather nodded. "In fact, that oldest Burton girl just got divorced. I see her at church with her mama. She's—"

"Pops," he warned, "don't even go there."

"Just trying to give you a hand," Ward suggested.

The buzz of the ancient doorbell saved Ben from having to respond. He slid off his stool. "Finish your coffee— I'll get the door."

"Suit yourself." Ward lifted his mug in a sort of salute.

Ben glanced out the window as he stepped into the front hall. He didn't recognize the vintage Land Rover that sat in the drive next to his truck. The idea that his grandfather hadn't argued about answering the door suddenly pinged him. He already knew who it was. There was one thing most of the older folks around here had in common, he'd noticed: they liked knowing who was at their door or calling their phone. And they liked knowing it first.

If the visitor was the Burton girl, as he'd called her, with a Sunday-afternoon casserole, Ben was not going to be happy. He braced himself and opened the door.

Fiery red hair. It was the first thing that captured his attention.

"Good afternoon," the woman standing before him said.

Green eyes. Ben blinked. Not the Burton woman. "Afternoon, ma'am." Confusion furrowed his brow. He glanced at the Land Rover and then at the lady. Not from around here, for sure. Everyone knew everyone else in a small community like this one. "You lost?"

She smiled. He blinked again. The lady was pretty, for sure, but when she smiled...wow. Okay, so maybe the conversation with his grandfather had left him off balance. This was not his normal reaction to meeting strangers— even gorgeous ones wearing snug jeans and a green sweater that brought out the green in her eyes.

"I hope not." She looked around the porch and then at the front yard before meeting his gaze once more. "I'm here to see Mr. Ward Kane. He's expecting me."

Ben's frown deepened. "Okay." He stepped back and opened the door wider. "Come on in. We were just having coffee in the kitchen."

She stepped inside, and he closed the door behind her. She surveyed the front hall, studied the staircase and the line of photos that marched up the wall to the second floor. He hadn't looked at the place from a stranger's viewpoint in forever. Natural wood floors. The matching wood treads of the staircase were worn from time and use. Plaster walls that pushed up to ten feet where an ancient ceiling fan turned slowly—its only speed. It was a well-loved and timeworn home.

He gestured for her to go ahead of him. "Right through there."

These old center-hall farmhouses were mostly all the same. The staircase and a wide welcoming area split the downstairs in half. On the left was the parlor, or living room. On the right was a dining room. Straight ahead, beyond the stairs with its neatly tucked bathroom, was the kitchen that took up the better part of the area across the back of the house. Next to that was the one downstairs bedroom, which had its own bath that had been added half a century ago.

Upstairs was far smaller with only two bedrooms and a shared bath. But the hall on the second level was broad enough for a small office area or den. That hall also led out onto an upper porch that overlooked the backyard.

The design was nothing like the more space-conscious and elegant designs of today, but it was practical and functional. More importantly, no other place had ever felt like home to him. If he was completely honest with himself, he wanted to raise his future family here in this house.

He banished the thought. He really did need to get his brain on track and off his current single status. It wasn't like time was running out for him to find someone. In his entire life, he could not remember ever being this totally preoccupied with not being in a relationship.

When they entered the kitchen, Ward had cleared away the coffee mugs, and a pitcher of lemonade and three glasses sat on the big table they used for casual eating as well as for a workspace, much like modern islands. Stools lined two sides.

"Miss Hart," Ward said with a broad smile. "I hope you had no trouble finding me."

The two met in the center of the room and shook hands.

"Your directions were spot-on." She surveyed the room. "You have a lovely home, Mr. Kane."

"No, no," he argued. "You call me Ward."

"You should call me Reyna."

While his grandfather gushed, Ben did a double take when his gaze landed on the plate of cookies sitting just beyond the pitcher and glasses. What in the world was this about? His grandfather did not bake. A quick glance around the counter and Ben spotted the white box from Sweet Feed, the local bakery. Since the shop wasn't open on Sundays, he'd had to pick up the cookies on Saturday—which meant he'd had this appointment scheduled for at least a day.

Something like denial twisted with irritation started a climb up Ben's spine. If this was some sort of matchmaking—

"This is my grandson, Ben."

He snapped from the thought and looked from his grandfather to the woman.

"It's a pleasure to meet you as well, Ben." She thrust her hand in his direction. "I genuinely appreciate your time."

His hand wrapped around hers. Small, soft… Warmth flashed through his senses. "I'm afraid I'm at a loss here."

Reyna Hart looked from Ben to Ward, but before she could question his confusion, his grandfather said, "Sit, please. I made fresh lemonade, and those cookies are the best in the county." The grin on his lips softened the edge of frustration closing in on Ben. "Storytelling," his grandfather went on, "calls for lemonade and cookies."

Storytelling?

Reyna settled on a stool, and Ward poured the lemonade. Watching in a sort of dismay that had him feeling as if he wasn't actually here and was seeing this from someplace else, Ben took a stool and waited for the other shoe to drop.

As soon as he'd placed glasses of lemonade in front of their visitor and Ben, Ward picked up a cookie and took a bite, then hummed his approval. "No one makes a chocolate chip cookie like Carol McVee."

"That sounds like a challenge to me," their guest proposed as she snagged a cookie of her own and took a bite. "Hmm. You may be right, Ward. This is excellent."

Ben could only stare.

As if she'd picked up on his confusion, Reyna turned in his direction. "Your grandfather has kindly agreed to help me with my research on the Whispering Winds Widows."

Her words landed like a blow to his gut. He flinched. "Research?"

She nodded. "Yes. I'm a writer, and I would very much like to solve the mystery that surrounds the disappearance of the Three."

Now he got it. He laughed, but the sound was far from pleasant. "So you hope to do what no one else has been able to do in thirty years?" He laughed again, couldn't help himself. "What dozens—and I mean dozens—of other people, cops, PIs, investigative reporters, have tried to do. To no avail?"

Ben paid no attention to the glower his grandfather was sending his way.

Her head dipped in a slow nod. "Yes, I hope to do exactly that. Is talking today going to be a problem?" She

looked from Ben to Ward. "If so, I can come back at another time."

"It is not an issue," Ward said firmly, with an equally
hard look in Ben's direction. "No one wants the truth
about what happened to my son more than me and Ben.
Isn't that right?"

For most of his adult life, Ben had pretended his father
had died—since there had never been any other explanation and he hadn't come back and no body had been
found. What else was a kid to do? His mother had refused
to speak of what had happened. She'd had no choice in
the beginning while the official investigation had been
in full swing. But after that she'd never spoken of what
had happened or of her missing husband. Ever. It was like
she wanted to erase the memories so she no longer had
to feel the pain.

If Lucinda Kane were in this room right now, she would
simply walk out. She wouldn't ask questions, wouldn't
shout her frustrations or anger—she'd just go. By the time
Ben had left for college, he had pretty much taken that
same path. God knew he'd asked enough questions and
done enough digging himself, once he'd been old enough.
But no amount of wondering or digging or feeling sorry
for himself had ever changed one thing.

His father and two other men—his friends—had vanished, never to be heard from again.

That had been thirty years ago.

His mother had a point. Always looking back and wondering was too hard. It was far easier just to look forward
and not think about it.

Before his brain could catch up with his mouth, Ben
was nodding and saying in answer to his grandfather's
question, "No one."

This woman—this stranger, a writer who wanted to delve into his most painful past—smiled brightly. Her green eyes flashed vibrantly. Her cheeks flushed the tiniest bit. "That's great. I can't tell you how much I'm looking forward to working with the two of you. This is such an important endeavor."

The two of them? He glanced at his grandfather. What had he promised this woman?

"Do you work for a newspaper or other media outlet?" The question had only just bobbed to the surface through all the disbelief and confusion fogging Ben's brain. His gut was in knots, his chest tight enough to bust open like an overinflated tire.

"No. I'm an independent writer. This is a story that I want to write, but before I can do that, I need to find the facts."

This just got worse. This woman intended to write the story of the Widows and the Three. His mother would go ballistic, even if only inside, where no one else could see or hear. Right or wrong as to how she looked at the past, Lucinda Kane was Ben's mother and he had an obligation to look out for her.

"If you're expecting me to help with this in any way, you should know I won't go down any path that puts my mother in a bad light."

Reyna nodded her understanding, her eyes searching his. "I would never expect you to disparage or hurt your mother in any way. Whatever you think of the people who've tried to solve this mystery, I'm not here to find what I want at all costs. I'm not that sort of person. I'm here to find the truth…if I can. Your and your grandfather's help will go a long way in guiding my search in the right directions. I look forward to your input and your oversight."

As much as part of him wanted to argue, to question her seemingly carefully laid-out sincerity, he couldn't bring himself to do it. There was something about her. Not just the way she maintained direct eye contact or the way she stuck to her guns about wanting to do this right... but the genuine passion he heard in her voice. All of it coalesced into something he couldn't ignore. Couldn't deny wanting to see through. Not to mention that he didn't want to embarrass his grandfather by refusing to help.

"All right." He gave a nod. "We can start first thing in the morning." He glanced at his grandfather. "Works better for my schedule, actually."

A frown lined her pretty face and punctuated the scattering of freckles across the bridge of her nose. "Why not start now?"

"Because I need to find out exactly who you are, and when we start, in the morning," he repeated, "we'll start with who my father was and go from there."

"All right, then." Challenge rose in her eyes. "Name the place and time, and I'll see you in the morning." She looked to his grandfather. "If that's all right with you, Ward. We can reschedule our interview." Her gaze returned to Ben. "I wouldn't want anyone to be uncomfortable."

"Works just fine for me," the older man assured her. The tightness in his voice warned he was not happy about his grandson's reaction.

Ben gave her a nod then. "We'll meet at eight sharp at the old Henry place on Shadow Brook Lane."

She scooted off her stool and thrust out her hand for another shake—maybe to seal the deal. "I'll be there."

Ben gripped her hand tightly. "See you then."

He released her hand, and she stepped back. "I can see myself out."

When the front door had closed behind her, his grandfather swung a glare in his direction. "Are you really planning on making her talk to you while you're renovating that old house? For God's sake, boy, it's a mess over there."

Ben shrugged. "You can serve her lemonade and cookies when she interviews you, if that makes you happy, Pops. But if she wants to know about the Kane family from me, then she'll follow me around and see with her own eyes what we're about."

"If you don't want to be a part of this," Ward argued, "just say so, but don't try these antics in hopes of running her off—because I do want to be a part of it."

That was the part that hit Ben the wrong way. "Why? What makes you believe for a second that she can find anything no one else has? Do you even know her?"

He nodded. "You're damn straight I know her. Eudora Davenport sent her. If Eudora trusts her, then I trust her."

"Ms. Davenport is very ill, Pops. We can't be sure she knows what this woman is all about."

"You can help me with this," his grandfather growled, "or you can stay out of the way. I want the truth."

He started clearing the table.

Ben didn't move. Couldn't move.

The sudden urge to have things repaired when Ben had been on him for months to let him do the maintenance that needed to be taken care of hit like a punch to the gut. The decision to paint the house. Holy crap.

"Are you sick, Pops?"

His grandfather glared at him. "What I am is old.

Eighty-five. I won't live forever, boy. I want the truth before I go."

The decision came swiftly and profoundly. No way in the world would he stand in the way of something his grandfather clearly wanted this badly. "I've never tried to figure it out," Ben admitted. "Not really. Not with real effort. Let's face it—whenever I have tried talking to Mom, she cuts me off. You and Mimi were too deep into the search for the truth to have time to figure out how I could fit in."

Hurt passed over the older man's face. "That was never our intent, Ben. We were devastated. We couldn't see beyond finding him…at least for a long while."

"That wasn't a criticism, Pops. It was just the way it felt. I knew even then that the two of you were doing the best you could. The way I survived all of it was to, in time, let it go. Leave it to the reporters and cops who from time to time developed an interest. To go on with my life."

But had he? Was he really any different from his mother or his grandparents? Had he really, deep down, let go?

Maybe not. Maybe that was why he hadn't been able to hang on to the relationship with his ex-fiancée. How could you move forward with the now if part of you was still mired in the past?

Ben took the three strides that separated him from his grandfather and hugged him. When he drew back, he gave the old man a nod. "We will find the truth. No matter what it takes, and if this Reyna Hart can help us, then I'm all in."

The emotion that shone in his grandfather's eyes was all the confirmation Ben needed to know he'd made the right decision.

The strangest sensation—a bit of anticipation mixed with something a little like fear—welled inside him.

Thirty years was a long time to wait for the truth. He just hoped that truth wasn't more painful than not knowing.

Chapter Three

The old Henry place, as Mr. Kane had called it, was just that—old and run-down. But like the other old places Reyna had seen in the area, it had a loveliness about it. When restored it would be the sort of farmhouse seen on television renovation programs.

Reyna put the Land Rover in Park and shut off the engine. She'd spoken to Eudora at length last night. She'd asked all sorts of questions about the town and the people Reyna had met so far. Not so many, really. Just Birdie Jewel at the B and B and Mr. Ward and his grandson.

She imagined he—the grandson—was in there looking out a window now. He obviously wasn't happy she was here. Not that she could blame him, really. She'd scoured the internet for stories about the Widows and the missing husbands. So much of what had been published about the families cast a negative light on them. Though no evidence of foul play on the part of any of the three families had been found, doubt, suspicion and accusations had been all over the place.

How was it that all three Widows had remained single and living right where they'd been when their husbands had disappeared? Even Reyna couldn't deny the oddity of that reality thirty years later. The possibility that one or more of the Widows knew some little something that could break the case was possible, maybe even probable. Yet for three decades their stories had remained the same without deviation.

Reyna wondered, if one were to become terminally ill, would that change?

Not that she wished any such thing, of course, but it would be interesting to see what happened at that point.

For now, Reyna thought as she reached for the car-door handle, she would try this the old-fashioned way—with hard work and a heavy dash of relentlessness.

She really hadn't come prepared for this sort of endeavor like this morning's meeting in a renovation project, but between her and Birdie, she'd pulled together something to wear. Her hiking shoes and the jeans she'd brought along were fine, but she hadn't bothered with any casual-work sorts of shirts. Birdie had lent her a couple of sweatshirts that were perfect for this cool day. The fact that the sweatshirts sported logos of flowers and birds suited Reyna just fine. She had a feeling that beneath all her exotic jewelry and flowing clothing, Ms. Birdie Jewel was an old hippie at heart.

By the time Reyna reached the steps, Ben was waiting for her on the porch.

"Morning," he said with one of those male nods that you had to be looking for to spot.

"Good morning to you." She climbed the final step and set her hands on her hips. "Why don't you show me around the place and tell me what your reno involves?"

He shrugged. The movement involved only one shoulder and was nearly as negligent as the nod. "Or we could just get straight to the point as to the relevance of this house to your research. This house was the last place the Three were known to be together. No one saw them here that day, of course. But the wives all stated that there was a meeting here."

He gestured to the door, and she went inside.

Reyna was surprised at his bluntness and to find lights on inside. Though there would have been some light anyway since it was morning, the interior would have been shadowed without interior illumination.

"I had temporary power restored on Friday," he explained, noting her attention to the vintage fixtures hanging from the ceilings and the sconces on the wall near the fireplace.

Reyna wandered to the staircase. It was a bit more ornate than she'd expected for a farmhouse. The flower carvings on the newel-post were particularly interesting. She traced the surface, her fingers noting the slight irregularities in the pattern that suggested it had been hand carved. The front edge of the treads reflected the same carefully hand-carved design.

"My father and grandfather's work."

Reyna turned to Ben. "Your father worked in the city," she said, not arguing with him but surprised by the information.

"The summer before he disappeared," Ben began, "my father left his job in the city and started working with my grandfather again. My mother was most unhappy. She had bigger plans than Whispering Winds and hoped to move down to the city in time."

So there had been trouble with at least one of the cou-

ples. The three men had disappeared on October first—
the upcoming October would be thirty-one years ago. It
had been a Saturday, and the men had met here at this
house for a card game. They'd played cards twice a month.
Had for years. To anyone's knowledge, nothing had been
different or amiss that time except for the meeting place.
Considering that it was well away from the men's homes,
privacy might have been the motivating factor.

Reyna turned around in a slow circle, taking in the
front hall and the parlors on either side. She let the idea
that this was the place where they'd met up for the very
last time on that fateful day soak in.

"Who owned this house at the time?" Reyna asked,
moving to the parlor on the left side of the hall. The mir-
rored overmantel of the fireplace was dusty but in perfect
condition. Even the tile around the firebox looked great.

"Duke Fuller. He and his wife, Deidre, wanted to re-
store the home and turn the farm back into a thriving
property. Deidre didn't care for the plain details, so she
hired my grandfather to add a few distinctive ones. Like
the carving on the staircase." He gestured to the fireplace.
"And the overmantel."

Judging by the condition and the layers of dust, Reyna
assumed the house had remained empty all these years.
"The restoration was never finished?"

"No. Deidre left it just as it was, and it sat here all this
time. She decided to put the place on the market and asked
me to get it back in shape."

"You have a team or a couple of employees?" Otherwise
this was going to be a long wait for the lady.

Ben laughed. "Just me and my pops, though there isn't
a lot he can do these days. I have a few sources—friends—
who help out from time to time if the need arises."

"I guess it's a good thing she's not in a rush, then." Reyna moved back into the front hall and crossed to the other parlor.

"Guess so," he agreed.

Reyna didn't wait for an invitation; she moved on to the kitchen that spanned the back of the house. The layout of the first floor was very similar to the one at the Kane home, with the exception of no bedroom downstairs. The only other room on the first floor was a smaller parlor that, considering all the bookshelves lining the walls, had been a library.

"There was no blood or other evidence of violence found in the house or anywhere outside," she said.

"Nothing," he agreed.

"What was the overall condition of the house at the time?" Reyna searched her memory for the details. "No one had lived in it for a number of years, correct?"

"That's right." He crossed to a broad window and stared out over the landscape. "The Henry family had all died out, and the place had been empty for about fifteen years. It was in pretty good shape. Just needed an update and whatever options the new owners wanted to add."

"Was there any connection between Ms. Fuller and the previous owners?" Deidre Fuller's maiden name was Henry.

"The last owner was her uncle," Ben said. "He had no children, and when he passed, the property went to Deidre. She was a teenager at the time, so her parents held it in trust for her. Judging by some of the photographs I've found in my mother's old scrapbooks, they used this place as a hangout a lot in their younger days."

"Before they married?"

"Right. Like a private teenage hangout."

And then their husbands had disappeared here. In Reyna's opinion, that had to mean something.

"I know what you're thinking," Ben said. He leaned against one of the bookcases, arms crossed over his chest. "I'm sure you read how about ten years ago ground-penetrating radar was brought in. They found no remains anywhere on the property. Not in the garden, not in the basement. Nowhere. The properties where the Three lived were checked as well."

She had read the articles. A private investigator with his own television program had talked his producers into paying for the venture. Deidre Fuller had agreed to the only interview she'd done in twenty years. Reyna guessed because it would be part of the episode to air on television. Who didn't love that fifteen minutes of fame? Although, in Deidre's case, it had been more like three minutes. The main focus had been on the search for remains.

"There's nothing here," Ben said, "that's going to tell the story of what happened that day." This might not be true, but whatever was here, he wanted to be the one to find it.

Truth was he and Ms. Fuller had made a deal. He'd bought the place from her. No one was to know. He didn't want his mother or his grandfather to know, and she didn't want the public stir that would've surely followed the sale. So they'd executed a private transaction. He'd used the firm's little-known development company to buy the property so no one would easily attach his name to it.

At this point he wasn't really sure why he'd done it. Maybe it was reaching that age where life felt as if it were slipping by or maybe it was the breakup, but he'd suddenly needed desperately to do something. To figure out the past. To force it all to make sense somehow. Though he was fairly confident it never would.

But for some reason he had to try.

He hadn't quite determined the reason, but he intended to do all in his power to get it done.

The idea that it perhaps had something to do with his grandfather's advanced age wasn't lost on him. The realization shook him, though this was not the first time he'd considered losing the man who had been his rock, his mentor—his world for most of his life. Ben did not want his grandfather to die never knowing what happened to his son. It just wasn't right.

Clearly the man wanted to know or he wouldn't have agreed to work with this…Reyna Hart.

His gaze settled on her as she wandered around the room looking at empty shelves as if the dust settled there might give her some insight.

He shook his head. How the hell would he get this done?

Reyna turned to face him. He flinched. The curiosity that captured her expression warned she hadn't missed his lingering attention. To cover, he said, "What's going through your mind right now?" He shrugged. "I mean, you're not from around here. You don't know any of the folks involved. You're not a cop or a reporter. What does all this—" he turned his arms up "—say to you?"

She walked around the room, did a little more looking at the dust and cobwebs because God knew there was nothing else.

"It says there are secrets," she announced, stopping maybe three feet away. Close enough for him to see those little freckles that made him want to trace their faint path.

He chuckled, mostly to cover the ridiculous thought about those freckles that had popped into his head. "I hate to tell you this, Miss Hart, but that's hardly original and definitely not news."

She gave him an acknowledging nod. "However, the point you're missing, Mr. Kane, is that there are secrets and then there are *secrets*."

His gaze narrowed as he searched her face, looking for some hint of where she was going with this. "I'm listening."

"We all have secrets. Little things we do or say or that happen which we want to keep to ourselves. A little something we did or a habit that isn't flattering. A mistake we made. That sort of thing."

He got it now. "But you're saying the secret or secrets about the Three is a different kind. The sort that has to stay secret no matter what. The kind that turns worlds upside down." The twist in his gut told him she was right about that.

She nodded. "Exactly. Someone knows something. Someone right here in this little town. Someone you probably know. Maybe one or all of the Widows. And this thing they know could potentially reveal everything or just the first step in the right direction."

"But how do you find that...thing?"

"You ask the right people the right questions, and you keep looking. It's here. It has to be. It's basic physics. All things that exist must be somewhere. The bodies—if the Three are dead—are somewhere. The weapon—if they were murdered—is somewhere. The murderer is somewhere."

"All right." Made sense so far. "I'll tell you now I've searched this house top to bottom. I've walked this property step by step. I've found nothing."

"Not finding it doesn't mean it's not there," she countered. "What it means is that you need additional direction. The only way to get the right additional direction is to go to the source."

"The Widows."

"Yes. They were married to the missing men. They knew them and each other better than anyone—intimately—since they were lifelong friends. One or all of them knows something that can help us. All we need is a point in the right direction. We need at least one to give us that direction."

The need to protect his mother nudged him. "You're saying one or all three of the Widows have been lying all this time."

"Not necessarily. It's possible that she or they don't understand the importance of what is known. Or it could be fear. Until you know why the three husbands went missing, you won't know the motive for keeping the knowledge secret. And there will be a motive. Does that motive pose some sort of threat to the Widows? Who's to say? But that is the typical reason secrets are kept."

The idea wasn't a new one. It had been discussed in previous investigations, but nothing had ever come of it. One investigator had even gone so far as to say that until it was known why the Three had disappeared there would never be any other answers.

Evidently, he'd made a valid point. Thirty years felt a whole hell of a lot like *never* at this point.

"You want me to get you meetings with the Widows," Ben suggested.

"Your grandfather has already offered to do this, but if you'd rather be the one to make it happen, I can work with that."

His mother would say no. He knew this up front. Ms. Fuller might be eager to get her point of view in first.

She'd been easy to talk to when Ben had purchased the property. Then again, money had been involved. She might not feel the same when it wasn't. He couldn't say how Ms. Evans would react, but he was willing to try to make it happen.

"I'll get the meetings," he agreed. "While I work that out, how about I take you on a tour of the property and then our town. You'll have a better understanding of the place and the people then."

"I would really appreciate that. Believe it or not, getting the feel of a place and the people can often sharpen your instincts."

"I can see that." Made sense.

Funny, he hadn't expected to like this woman. The very last thing he'd wanted was someone else involved in what he felt he had to do.

Now it seemed exactly like the right move.

Then again, it wouldn't be the first time he'd made a mistake.

Chapter Four

Reyna liked this town already. Small, quiet. Everyone seemed to know everyone else. Then again, she had been hearing about it from Eudora for months. Reyna felt at home here because of all that she'd learned and studied about the place. She'd spent so much time thinking about it, it was as if she'd lived here herself.

The reality of it, though, was even nicer than her expectations. The real place felt…peaceful.

This conclusion felt a bit strange since a possible triple homicide had taken place thirty years ago that remained unsolved. How was it that three grown men had vanished in a town so small and no one had a clue what had happened?

There was no logic in the notion.

Reyna studied the man seated across the table from her. Ben Kane's father had been one of those three. How had he gone on through life all this time and not fought harder to know the reason? Then again, perhaps he had. Eudora had said little about Ben. She'd mostly spoken about his grandfather, Ward. Reyna suspected the two had had a connection at one time—perhaps a brief affair after his wife had passed away. A retired schoolteacher, Eudora had never been married. She had no children.

Ben looked up from the menu he'd been perusing. "If you've got a question, the best thing to do is ask it. Staring a hole through me isn't going to get you any answers."

"Why now?" she asked. "In the past I'm sure you've followed along with the investigations. Maybe even been involved on some level, but why decide to go the extra mile, so to speak, now?"

And that was the impression he'd given when he'd shown her around the Henry property. He wanted very much to find the truth. She had felt the tension in him when he'd spoken of his grandfather's pain all these years, of how the disappearance had certainly sent his grandmother to an early grave.

Whatever his mother wanted, he hadn't mentioned. Reyna suspected, based on Eudora's conclusions about the Widows, that none of them wanted the past shaken or stirred ever again.

The trouble in that was this man—and Reyna. They both wanted answers. This wasn't personal for her. She didn't really know these people or this community, but it felt important. It felt like something she needed to do.

Ben placed the menu on the table. Reyna hadn't even really looked at hers. She wasn't hungry for anything except answers.

He held her gaze for long enough to have her wondering if he intended to answer. Finally he said, "My grandfather is eighty-five. His health is really good, in my opinion, for a man of his age. That said, I can't deny the idea that I could lose him anytime. I know he wants answers. He tried harder than most to get those answers before admitting defeat. If I can somehow find those answers, it would be the most important thing I could possibly do for him. I want to do that for him."

Reyna smiled and gave him a nod. "I can't imagine a more noble reason."

A gray-haired gentleman wearing an apron with the diner logo swaggered up to their booth. "Afternoon, folks." He nodded to Ben. "You ready to order?"

Ben eyed him skeptically. "Since when did you start taking orders, Harold?"

Ah, Reyna got it now. This was the owner, Harold McGill. Eudora had said he was a very generous man—always feeding and taking up donations for those in need.

"Well now, Ben," Harold said as he eyed the two of them, "that would be your fault for waltzing in here with this pretty stranger. You're gonna have the whole town talking."

"It doesn't take much," Ben said under his breath.

She smiled and reached out to the older man. "Reyna Hart. It's a pleasure to meet you, Mr. McGill. I've heard wonderful things about you from Eudora Davenport."

"Mercy me." McGill grinned. "I hope she's doing well. I haven't seen Eudora in ages."

"She's doing well enough," Reyna said. Eudora wasn't keen on anyone knowing the extent of her illness. "In fact, one of the projects I'm working on is Eudora's life history."

McGill's eyebrows reared up. "Now, that's a story I'd love to read. They say still waters run deep, and Eudora Davenport's ran deeper than most, in my opinion."

"I'm including the mystery of the Widows and their missing husbands as well."

His expression turned to one of surprise as he glanced at Ben. "Is that so?" He pursed his lips and nodded. "It'd be a good thing, I suppose, to finally know what happened all those years ago."

"You knew my dad pretty well," Ben said. "Anything come to mind about that time frame? Any sort of trouble or issues?"

To Reyna's surprise, the older man walked over to a table, grabbed an empty chair and dragged it to the end of their booth. He settled his short, stout frame into it and propped his elbows on the table. "Your daddy," he said to Ben, "was a good man. Better than most, I'd wager. Just like his own daddy."

"You going to take their order or wag your tongue?"

Reyna shifted her attention to the woman who now stood behind McGill. She had the same gray hair as the owner, but it was twisted high on her head in a bun. The name tag pinned to her uniform said Vinnia. His wife. Reyna recognized the name.

"Ben'll take the cheeseburger plate," McGill said. "With a glass of water."

Ben nodded. Obviously the man knew his preferred lunch.

"The lady..." McGill turned to Reyna.

"Will take the same," she filled in for him. "Reyna Hart," she added for Ms. McGill's benefit.

"I'd ask what brings you to our town," Vinnia said as she scratched the orders onto her notepad, "but I couldn't help overhearing the subject of the conversation."

Reyna doubted that was the case since the diner was busy and hummed with conversation in addition to the soft music from a local radio station playing from the speakers. Most of the customers were crowded around the

counter and spread around the diner far enough away from
the booth Ben had chosen to give them some amount of
privacy. If Vinnia had overheard anything it was because
she'd made the extra effort.

"We'd love to hear your thoughts as well," Reyna offered.

"I don't imagine Ben would care for my thoughts,"
the older woman said with a glance in his direction. "He
knows how I feel about his mama."

Ben mustered up a smile—a charming one in spite of
the woman's attitude. Reyna was impressed.

"I also know the feeling is mutual on my mother's side."

Vinnia shot Reyna a look. "You see, that's why we'll
never have the whole story on what happened. Those Widows are keeping it to themselves. Whatever you hope to
find, Ms. Hart, I'd start with Lucinda Kane. She's the one
who started it all."

Before Reyna could respond, the lady twisted around
and hurried away.

Ben said nothing. McGill's face had gone red.

"You'll have to overlook my wife," he said. "She has a
sore spot where your mama is concerned, Ben. That's not
news to you."

"No, sir," he agreed. "It is not."

McGill pushed back his chair and stood. "You two
enjoy your lunch, and if I can help in any way, just let
me know."

He returned the borrowed chair and disappeared behind the counter.

Reyna gave Ben a minute to comment. When he didn't,
she asked, "You want to tell me about it?"

"My mother was engaged to Vinnia's younger brother
before she married my father."

Now, there was a detail Reyna hadn't heard. "So there was bad blood between your father and Vinnia's brother?"

"Gordon Walls. He's a Hamilton County sheriff's deputy. There was bad blood, yes. But that was eight years before the disappearance. There hadn't been any trouble during my parents' marriage."

The other man's occupation cued up a whole other line of questioning. "Was Gordon Walls a deputy back then— during the time of the breakup with your mother?"

"He was in the Army. They were supposed to get married when he came back from training, but she married my father before that happened. Walls did his time in the military, then joined the sheriff's department."

"How long was he in the military?" Reyna's instincts were buzzing. She couldn't believe she'd missed this aspect of the story—if it had come up during the numerous investigations. She was certain it hadn't been part of anything she'd read.

"Six years."

Reyna added the information to her mental files and moved on. "Where is Gordon Walls now?"

"He married. Had a family. He and his wife live in Chattanooga."

"What are the chances I can get that interview with your mother today?" Reyna was itching to do some looking into this new aspect of the story and then to approach Lucinda Kane about it.

"I'll talk to her after we're finished here." He glanced at the woman behind the counter, who quickly looked away. Vinnia had been watching them since she'd taken their order. "But I'll need to speak with her alone first."

"I understand. I have other names to follow up on."

He held her gaze for a long moment before saying more.

"I wonder if finding the truth will actually give anyone peace."

Reyna wished she could assure him it would. But it might not. It might create more pain and more questions. But if he wanted to know, now was the time. The window of opportunity was closing. The players, and even the by-standers, from thirty years ago were getting older. Many were already gone.

Before long, there would be no one left who might actually know the answers or may have witnessed something relevant. Better to ask now than wish he had later.

Owens Residence
Rushing Stream Hollow
1:30 p.m.

RETIRED SHERIFF'S DEPUTY Nelson Owens had been sitting in a rocking chair on his front porch when Reyna had arrived. He had invited her to have a seat in the matching rocking chair. His home was a rustic cabin, well off the road and surrounded by thick woods. He kept a shotgun propped against the railing on the other side of his rocking chair.

She supposed there were all manner of wildlife in those woods. Having a shotgun nearby was likely a good idea. At his age, seventy-one, he probably had no desire to try outrunning a bear or any other predator. Better to scare them off.

He'd offered her a beer, but she'd declined. He'd had several already. Emptied and crushed cans lay in the corner, a few feet from where he sat. Whether this was his daily ritual or just the way he'd braced for her visit, she didn't know. As much as she would like to video all her interviews, she had found that the request generally put people off. So, she didn't take the risk. Better to take notes during or immediately after.

"We never found anything," he said in answer to her question. "It was really strange, if you ask me. Tarrence Norwood, he was the sheriff at the time—a good one, at that—he really tried to find answers. It just never happened."

"Everything I've read says there was no evidence found. No motives for anyone having wanted one or all three of the men gone," she said, recalling the words of the then sheriff. The few television interviews she had seen had shown a deeply, deeply disappointed man for having not been able to solve the case.

Owens shook his head. "It was the strangest thing. You know, usually you find something, hear a rumor or what have you. But we got nothing. Zero. It was like they just vanished. An alien abduction."

There had been plenty of speculation on that one over the years.

"You didn't find anything or hear anything from anyone you interviewed that prompted you to form any sort of scenario? Sometimes we don't have evidence, but we have ideas," she suggested.

He popped the top on another can, took a long swallow. "It's been thirty years," he said. "A lot of people have moved away. Others have died. And no one has ever figured out what the heck happened." Another swallow of beer. "But I'm gonna tell you something I've never told anyone before."

Reyna held her breath, hoped this was a true lead.

"I think the Widows know exactly what happened." He shrugged. "Heck, they might even have killed them. Seems strange to me that they still stick together after all this time and they never remarried or moved or anything else." He frowned at Reyna. "Don't you find that weird?"

"We all have our own way of grieving. Maybe theirs was to do exactly as they've done."

Another shrug. "Maybe. Just seems strange to me. Truth be told, most people around town think they're a little on the odd side."

"Why do *you* think they know what happened?"

"The next day after they disappeared," he explained, "the first call came from Lucinda Kane. She said she was worried because her husband never came home. We went out to see her, and she was so calm. It was like she was saying all the right words. That she was worried and that he'd never done this before…but she didn't seem worried or upset. She was just, you know, normal."

Reyna wondered if Ben was aware of his mother's behavior during the interview. "Perhaps she was in shock."

"Why? At that point we didn't know they weren't coming back. You'd think she would have been worried about an accident or something. She never went out looking for him. Nothing. Most people would have been driving around or calling people, you know."

"Are you sure she didn't?" Reyna certainly wanted his thoughts on the matter, but it was difficult to tell whether this was an opinion based on what had been happening or his perception of what should have been happening.

"We asked if she'd called the local hospitals or friends or looked for him at all, and she just said no. Not one additional detail. Just no."

The reaction was a little odd, she supposed. "When did the next call come in?"

"While we were interviewing Lucinda, Harlowe Evans called, all freaked out. Now, she had been out driving around. She'd called all the hospitals, driven out to the Henry place and called the other wives. That was the reaction you'd expect."

Reasonable point. "What about Ms. Fuller? When did her call come in?"

"Now, that's the really strange one." He opened another can of beer. "She didn't call. We went to her place and asked if her husband had been home. She said no, and then we asked her if that was out of the ordinary for him to leave and not come back. She just shook her head, said she didn't know what was going on."

"Did you or Sheriff Norwood have any reason to believe one or more of the wives were lying?"

He considered the question through two more deep slugs of beer. Then he said, "I always thought there was something Dede Fuller wasn't telling. Deidre," he clarified. "Most everyone calls her Dede. Anyway, she just didn't act right through any of it. She seemed zoned out or something. Maybe shock like you said, but I don't know. The truth is it was all just weird. All of it."

"Looking back," Reyna said, "is there anything you would do differently?"

Another extended consideration. "If I could go back, I'd watch those women day and night. I'd push them harder until one of them cracked."

Interesting answer, Reyna decided. "You're that certain that at least one of them was and still is hiding something."

He looked directly at her then. "I would bet my life on it. If you want to know what happened, that's where you'll find the answer."

He had little else to say after that. Reyna left one of her cards with him and urged him to call if he thought of anything else that might be helpful to her research.

As she drove away, she considered that he was likely right about the Widows, and she had every intention of finding whatever any of them was hiding.

Kane Residence
Thistle Lane
1:50 p.m.

BEN SAT ON the front steps of his childhood home for a while. His mother was inside and no doubt had noticed his arrival. She hadn't come to the door and wouldn't until he rang the bell.

She wasn't happy about his decision to stay in Whispering Winds. She'd been happier when he'd been in the city, focused on building his career. She wanted him to get married and have grandchildren for her to enjoy.

She wanted him to never look back.

Not such an easy task, all things considered.

With a heavy breath, he got up, crossed the porch and knocked on the door. Putting it off any longer wouldn't make it any easier.

She opened the door after his first knock. Oh, yeah, she'd been standing there watching and waiting. Didn't seem right that they had to have this standoff about his being back in Whispering Winds or the past.

She should want to know the whole truth. Maybe if he'd pushed harder when he'd been younger. He shook off the idea. Wouldn't have mattered even then. She had not wanted to discuss it. She had wanted to move on and pretend it was not relevant to the future.

A wide smile spread across Lucinda Kane's face. Even as she headed toward sixty, she was still a beautiful woman who liked taking care of herself, who liked looking nice.

Not a single strand of gray was allowed to survive in her dark mane. Her eyes and hair were the only features he'd gotten from her. Folks said he looked exactly like his daddy except for his mama's blue eyes and black hair.

"What're you up to, Ben?" She opened the door wide and gestured for him to come on in. "You're usually busy with work this time of the afternoon."

He stepped inside, waited for her to close the door. "We need to have a conversation about…things."

Her smile faded instantly. "Have you had lunch? I made a fresh pitcher of iced tea, if you're thirsty."

"No, ma'am," he said. "I'd just like to talk."

She inclined her head and gave him that look that said she so, so did not want to go there. "You know I don't like talking about the past. It's too hard. I don't know why no one seems to understand how difficult those years were for me. Shouldn't I be allowed my peace?"

"I know you don't," Ben agreed. "But I need you to do it anyway. And I need you to understand that I'm not backing off this time. I'm sticking with this until I have the answers."

She drew in a big breath. "Well, in that case, I need a drink."

Lucinda Kane had never been much of a drinker. Not even socially. But whenever the subject of her missing— presumed dead—husband came up, she wanted a drink. He supposed he couldn't blame her.

He followed her to the parlor, where she poured a shot of Jack Daniel's into a glass, drank it down and then settled into her favorite chair—the pink one with the rose-colored throw lying across one arm. Growing up, his friends had often ribbed him about all the pink in the house. But his mother loved pink and she loved roses. What was a boy to do?

When he would have kicked off the conversation, she held up a hand. "Don't tell me where to start. Believe me, I know. At the beginning."

He said nothing, just waited. He'd learned from experience that it was best to allow her to do this her own way or she wouldn't do it at all.

She folded her hands in her lap, closed her eyes as if sifting through memories only she could see. "It was a Saturday, October first. There was a new Halloween thing opening that weekend. A corn maze. Something scary that all your friends wanted to do. Your daddy said I should take you because he had to work over at the Henry place and then, of course, he had that silly card game."

Ben's father and his friends, Duke Fuller and Judson Evans, had played cards together since their college days. Twice a month. The games had moved to the old Henry place after the Fullers had bought it. As long as it had been under renovation and unoccupied, the men had had privacy. All three Widows had given the same statement about the reason their husbands had been at the house at the time of their disappearance. But the card table hadn't been set up. No cigars or glasses were around, as there usually would have been. None of the Three had smoked except when they'd played cards; then they'd puffed on cigars and drank whiskey.

"Dad never had any trouble with the others? I mean, surely at some point during their lives they'd had a falling-out."

"Nothing I know about," she said. "No one else could recall any issues either. But then, I suppose there were little things that no one ever heard about."

She wasn't going to like this one. "Gordon Walls couldn't have come back for revenge?"

Surprise flashed across her face. "What?"

"Gordon Walls. The two of you were engaged when he left for the Army. Then you met Dad, and when Gordon came back you were married to him. That couldn't have gone well."

Her glance at the old-fashioned bar cabinet that had stood next to the parlor's French doors for as long as he could remember warned she wished for a second drink.

"No." She fixed her attention on him. "It did not." She took a breath. "I'm going to tell you this once, and then I will never speak of it again."

This was a new tactic. "Okay."

"Gordon was gone for a long time. I was lonely." She shook her head. "I was young. For goodness' sake, I was barely twenty years old. I didn't mean to get involved with your father, but it happened. He and your grandfather came to my parents' house to repair something or the other. I don't even recall what." A smile tugged at her lips even when she obviously did not want to smile. "He was so handsome. I ran into him again at the county fair, and we walked around together. Rode a few rides. Shared some very innocent kisses."

Her eyes closed as if the rest were too difficult to look at. When she opened them once more, there was a shine of emotion that told Ben he'd been right. This was hard for her, and he regretted that it was necessary.

"We started sneaking around, and—" she looked straight into Ben's eyes "—as you are well aware, I found out I was pregnant with you, and so we got married."

"Did you want to get married?"

Her mouth rounded in shock. "Well, of course we wanted to get married. We just hadn't expected to start with being parents first. But," she said firmly, "I was thrilled when you were born, and I have never once regretted it."

"You're certain my father and Walls never fought about this? No harbored resentment or any bitterness?"

"I'm certain there were exchanges between them," she confessed, "but your father never discussed those with me. He and Gordon handled things very discreetly. I'm confident Gordon didn't want to be humiliated any more than he already had been. It was better to work things out quietly. He was away with his commitment to the military for several years after that anyway. When he came back, it was ancient history."

This was the same story his grandfather had relayed. "The one thing that bothers me," Ben explained, "is that he trained to be a member of law enforcement. Meaning he would know how to make people disappear without leaving evidence. Did any of the folks looking into the case really consider him as a potential suspect?"

"Of course. It was utterly humiliating to me, having to go over and over the details of our former relationship. Gordon had his own life by the time your father went missing. Why on earth would he have bothered with ours? Thankfully, Sheriff Norwood kept that irrelevant history out of the official reports or I would have had to go through the same humiliation every time some detective or reporter wanted to poke around."

"I don't know—the need for revenge is a powerful emotion," Ben said bluntly. "Some folks hold on to a grudge longer than others. Maybe it was an accident? Something Walls didn't intend to start, but once it started he couldn't stop it."

"Even if that were the case, why would he have bothered with the others? Certainly Duke and Judson had nothing in that fight."

"Wrong place, wrong time," Ben suggested. "There are a lot of unknowns when it comes to murder, Mom. Whoever did this had a reason. We just don't know what that reason was."

She looked away. "I don't want to talk about this anymore."

Therein lay the problem. "I have a friend. Reyna Hart. She's working with me to find the answers we all need."

Lucinda shook her head. "I don't need any answers. What difference would they make at this point? My God, it's been thirty years."

"I need answers," Ben said gently. "Pops needs answers."

Anger tightened her lips. "I knew you were doing this for him. You've always been more concerned with his happiness than mine."

And so went the ongoing saga of his mother's jealousy of his relationship with his grandfather.

"You should go back to the city, son. Go on with your life. Stop looking back."

"The way you went on with your life?"

It was a low blow, but he couldn't pretend anymore. His mother had lived in this house—the same one she and his father had bought when they'd married—for the past thirty years. To his knowledge, she had never even dated another man.

"Not fair," she argued. "I had a marriage. A man I loved. A child. My life was and still is complete."

He wasn't going to argue the point and upset her further. "I need you to agree to be interviewed by my friend."

He and Reyna didn't really know each other, but if calling her a friend would get his mother to agree, so be it.

And he did like Reyna.

Lucinda frowned, then rubbed her forehead. "I have a headache coming on. Check with me tomorrow. Perhaps I can speak with your friend then."

At least it wasn't a no. "Can I do anything for you, Mom? Make you some tea?"

She drew in a deep breath and managed a smile. "I'll just lie down, and then I'll be fine. Call me in the morning."

"One more question," he said before relenting.

She rubbed at her forehead. "Very well. Ask your question."

"If you knew anything—anything at all—you would tell me, wouldn't you?"

Her expression turned to one of pain. "Of course I would tell you. What a foolish question." His mother rose from her pink chair and left the room.

But it wasn't a foolish question. It was a completely legitimate one.

Ben stood. He figured Reyna was wasting her time interviewing the Widows. They were all going to tell the same story.

He sincerely hoped the reason was because it was true.

Chapter Five

Father Vincent Cullen had agreed to meet with Reyna at his home at the church he had served for most of his life. Reyna shut off the engine of her Land Rover and surveyed the area. The church was an old one, for sure. Nestled in the woods on the edges of Whispering Winds, the setting offered a sense of calm and serenity. Reyna grabbed her shoulder bag and climbed out of the vehicle, and she shivered a little with the crisp breeze.

Maybe it was more being at a church than the actual temperature this afternoon. Reyna hadn't been inside a church since her grandmother's funeral. It wasn't so much that she was a nonbeliever, more nonpracticing. For now, anyway.

Though Father Cullen was retired, he lived in the small church rectory. The priest currently assigned to the church lived just next door in the church parsonage. According to Eudora, even at ninety years old, Father Cullen helped out from time to time. The parishioners adored him, which was why the church had both a rectory and a parsonage.

No one had wanted to ask Father Cullen to move out, so the parsonage had been acquired.

Father Cullen waited on the steps of the church. "Good afternoon, Ms. Hart."

Reyna extended her hand as she approached the older man. "Thank you so much for taking the time to see me."

"Any friend of Eudora's is a friend of mine." He smiled, and Reyna got a glimpse of the handsome man he had been when Eudora and her friend Birdie had been so enthralled with him.

Reyna wondered if the man realized how many women in the community had been smitten with him.

"If you'll follow me," he said, "we'll have coffee or tea— whichever you like."

"Sounds perfect."

A cobblestone walkway wandered through the landscape, then split, with a narrower portion leading through a grove of high thick hedges and meeting up with a small addition to the church. The rectory, she presumed. Eudora had said it had been added in the 1940s for Cullen's predecessor.

The rectory was a small studio apartment with worn, cozy furnishings and book-lined shelving covering most walls. There was even a small fireplace. A chair, obviously favored by the current resident, sat near the stone fireplace.

"Sit wherever you'd like," he offered as he made his way to the kitchenette. He checked the kettle for water, then turned on the burner. "I'm a tea lover myself. What suits you, Reyna?"

"Tea would be very nice."

As he gathered the cups and saucers, he said, "So you want to talk about the Three, I presume."

Right to the heart of the matter. "I do. Eudora would

very much like for me to figure out what happened thirty years ago. She feels certain you can help."

Vincent Cullen's hair, though gray, remained thick and full. He was tall yet far thinner than in the photos Eudora had shown her. His voice remained strong and clear. Reyna hoped his memory was also. Even so, it was possible he might choose not to share whatever he knew, particularly if that information had been shared in confidence. This man, Reyna understood, could very well know the secrets no one else did.

"Cream and sugar?" The kettle's whistle underscored his question.

"Both, please."

He delivered her tea before preparing his own. When he'd settled into his chair, he rested his gaze on hers. "I wish I could help Eudora find the peace she desires."

Here it came.

"Unfortunately," he went on, "I have no idea what happened thirty years ago."

His answer surprised Reyna. She'd expected the usual response of being bound by the seal of confession.

"No one in the community has ever spoken to you regarding what he or she did or knew?"

"I'm afraid that's the case." He sipped his tea.

Reyna did the same. The peppermint flavor teased her taste buds.

"I'm sorry," he offered. "I should have mentioned that I only keep peppermint tea."

"It's very good," she assured him. "Do you have any personal feelings or conclusions related to what happened that you can share?"

He sipped his tea for a time before placing it on the table next to his chair. "JR—Ward's son—Duke Fuller and

Judson Evans were all very good men. I'd known them since they were born. Judson was the only one whose family didn't attend services here. I knew him through his relationship with JR and Duke. He came often with one or the other. They were popular in high school. Athletes. No trouble that I was ever made aware of."

There was a *but* coming. Reyna heard it in his tone.

"There was," he began, "a restlessness about the Three. They weren't troublemakers or bullies—nothing of that sort. It was as if they were exploding with the need to do something even they couldn't define. An energy, I suppose you'd call it."

"Do you suppose this restlessness could have prompted one of them to delve into territory he might not otherwise have ventured into?" This was the first time she'd heard or read anything that suggested any of the Three might have been poised to mix things up or launch some new something.

Father Cullen lifted his bushy gray eyebrows. "I can't say, of course. Really, anything I offer will be mere speculation. I can only tell you what I sensed, and I sensed a building need to act somehow."

"Were they still coming to mass here at the church fairly regularly?"

"JR was, of course. And Duke occasionally. Christmas and Easter, mostly. But I saw them around town. Spoke in passing quite regularly. I saw more of JR toward the end because he'd returned to work with his father."

"You sensed this restlessness in JR?"

He nodded. "I suppose I could go a bit further where JR was concerned. His family has always belonged to this parish, and it was easy to see that something was not quite right. Whether it was JR's relationship with Duke and Judson or his relationship with his wife, there were ripples in the water, so to speak."

This sounded like more than restlessness.

"Others have said—" Reyna placed her tea on a nearby table "—there was trouble between JR and Deputy Gordon Walls. Did you notice any lingering animosity between the two men?"

A frown furrowed the man's face. "There were rumors, of course. But Ward, JR's father, is a well-respected member of this community. Folks weren't going to say a lot—at least, not out loud."

"Did JR's friends, Duke and Judson, stand on his side of the situation?" Eudora had insisted the Three had stood together through thick and thin. But hers was only one person's perspective on the matter.

"As far as I was aware, yes. Those three always stood together."

"Father Cullen, what is your opinion of what happened to those three young men?" She turned her hands up. "Let's face it, the chances that they simply ran away or disappeared into thin air are basically nonexistent. Something happened to them. I really, really would appreciate your conclusions."

He held her gaze for a moment. "Just between the two of us? No passing my conclusion along to anyone else?"

"If that's what you require," she agreed.

"It's what I would prefer."

Reyna gave a nod. "Then I won't share your conclusions with anyone."

"I think those three got into some sort of trouble and had no idea how to get out. They had no history of trouble. How would they know what to do? If any one of the

Three survived that day, he's in hiding somewhere and will never return."

Reyna couldn't say she saw the situation any other way. "Do you feel that whatever happened was somehow connected to Deputy Walls?"

He smiled, settled deeper into his chair. "Unless you uncover an alternative, it certainly seems the most likely."

From there, the conversation moved on to the weather and local events. Reyna interjected more questions from time to time in hopes Father Cullen would reveal more with his guard down, but she learned nothing she didn't already know. As the conversation wound down, he invited Reyna to mass and urged her to pass his thoughts and prayers on to Eudora.

As she prepared to leave, Reyna gave him one of her business cards. Since he was feeling overly tired, she insisted he not walk her back to where she'd parked. She'd enjoyed meeting him no matter that she'd learned very little from a source who surely knew far more.

She sat in her Land Rover for a time and considered how those three young men had attended services here in this lovely old church. They'd maintained good reputations and been popular among the community.

Yet they had disappeared suddenly and seemingly without warning.

Reyna exited the church parking lot and headed back into Whispering Winds proper. She hoped to hear from Ben soon with news that she could meet with his mother and the other Widows.

Ben's mother had been the least cooperative in interviews over the years. Harlowe Evans appeared to always be up for them. Deidre Fuller had done much the same as Evans, though with less and less frequency over the years. Did that suggest Lucinda Kane had something to hide? Reyna hoped not. She liked Ward and Ben. If Reyna was going to find the truth—and she intended to give it her best shot—she didn't really want it to turn the world even more upside down for the Kane family. But her first loyalty was to Eudora.

Her cell phone rang, and Reyna reached toward the passenger seat for her bag, blindly feeling for the phone in the side pocket. This stretch of highway was far too curvy to take her eyes off the road and risk going over a cliff. The Land Rover suddenly lurched to the right. Reyna whipped the steering wheel to the left in an attempt to correct its path, but she was too late—the wheel slipped off the edge of the pavement. Her heart launched into her throat as she attempted to pull the vehicle back onto the pavement and away from the cliff, which only made matters worse. She pressed harder on the brake, and the Land Rover slid sideways, heading for the tree line.

A scream became stuck in her throat. Reyna fought for control, finally wrestling the vehicle to a complete stop just shy of a massive tree.

She shoved the gearshift into Park and sat for a moment, unable to move or to think. Her whole body shook with the receding adrenaline.

What the devil had happened?

Finally, gathering her wits, she released her seat belt, opened the door and climbed out. Her knees buckled, and she had to catch herself on the door.

Steadying herself, she surveyed the driver's side of the vehicle. No damage. The front end faced the highway away from the trees, so she moved around the back. Nothing on the rear. Thankfully. Squeezing between the Land Rover and the trees on the passenger side wasn't so easy. To her great relief there was no visible damage to that side of the vehicle either.

Except for the flat front tire.

So that was why she'd lost control.

"Damn it." She moved closer and peered down at the tire. Totally flat. She rose up and looked along the highway in both directions.

She needed a tow truck.

Making her way back around to the driver's side, she decided she would call Ben. He would know where she could get the tire repaired and a reliable towing service.

As she plucked her bag from the front passenger-side floorboard, she hoped there was no damage under the vehicle. She did vaguely recall bumping over the ground with some rather sharp jolts and jerks.

"Don't borrow trouble, Reyna," she grumbled as she fished out her cell phone.

This was not how she'd seen her first full day on this venture going.

Ben answered on the first ring. He promised to be there in ten minutes.

Reyna leaned against her crippled vehicle and studied her surroundings.

It really was a beautiful, peaceful place.

How could anyone—much less three full-grown men—just disappear in such a nice place?

Kane Residence
Lula Lake Lane
6:00 p.m.

THE SCENT OF vegetable soup stirred Reyna's appetite, had her stomach vying for attention.

"Mr. Kane," she said, "you really don't have to go to all this trouble."

Ward Kane shot her a look from his position at the stove. "Ward," he reminded her. "I make dinner every evening, so this is no trouble at all, Reyna. I've got to keep that boy fed."

"The boy" to which he referred was Ben, and he would be home soon. He'd insisted Reyna drive his truck back here while he waited for the repairs to her vehicle. He'd be along shortly, he'd insisted. That had been an hour ago. The flat tire hadn't been such a big deal, but there had been damage to some steering component that needed to be repaired. The mechanic had assured Reyna he could do it, but it would take a little time. Ben had wanted to hang around and supervise the work.

"I appreciate being invited to dinner," Reyna said.

"Did you have a productive day?"

She supposed that was his way of asking if she'd learned anything. "Ben showed me around the Henry place. We had lunch at the diner, where I met Mr. and Mrs. McGill."

"She's a sight," he pointed out. "Still believes my son duped her younger brother."

"She mentioned something about that." Reyna opted to see what Ward had to say before offering what Vinnia McGill had insinuated.

"Vinnia always has plenty to say about folks. Most of it's slanted to suit the point she hopes to make."

Reyna had definitely gotten that impression.

"JR had no idea Lucinda had agreed to marry Gordon when they started seeing each other. She lied to him. Lied to them both."

"I suppose there was quite the backlash when Walls came back and found out what she'd done."

"Not so much," Ward said as he scooped soup into a bowl. "If he'd made too much of it, he would only have looked like the loser. As I recall, he played it off like he was grateful to be rid of her."

Vinnia certainly hadn't appeared to think so.

"Wounds unattended have a tendency to fester," Reyna offered. "Especially as time goes by with nothing left to do but look at it."

Gordon Walls had remained in the Whispering Winds community. He'd had to watch the woman who was supposed to marry him grow round with another man's child… marry that other man and build a home together.

Ward placed a steaming bowl of soup on the table in front of her. Then loaded one for himself. "I can't argue with your reasoning," he said as he took a seat at the table with her. "But I can tell you that me and Jacob Evans pretty much ruled out Gordon's involvement in whatever happened to our boys."

"Jacob Evans?" Then she remembered that was Judson Evans's father's name.

"Judson's daddy. A few days after they disappeared, he and I picked up Gordon and had a little talk with him."

Reyna could just imagine how that had gone down. "Dare I ask how that played out?"

He eyed her for a long moment. "I'm certain you've seen enough movies to know when a man believes someone has hurt someone he cares about, things can get ugly."

Reyna nodded. "You might want to refrain from filling in the details."

He chuckled. "The end result was that Jacob and I were both convinced that Gordon had nothing to do with what happened to our boys."

Reyna picked up her spoon and took a bite of the soup. "Mmm. This really is delicious."

"It was my mother's favorite soup. Whenever times got tight, we lived on this soup."

The perfect opening for moving into another territory she'd wanted to explore. "Did any of the Three or their families have any particular financial issues during the time of the disappearance?"

"Everyone has trouble now and then. Some more than others." He shrugged. "But there was nothing out of the ordinary, to my knowledge. If the other families had any troubles—financial or otherwise—they kept them quiet."

Reyna ate for a while. Couldn't resist. She felt guilty for not waiting for Ben, but he'd insisted she shouldn't.

Eventually, she resumed her questioning. "Was there anything going on with JR or the others that had you concerned? Any sort of restlessness or dissatisfaction?"

"Lucinda was all torn up about JR quitting his job in the city. Duke Fuller had been talking about selling everything and moving to Nashville—even though he'd promised to fix up the Henry place for his wife. Judson Evans was pitching some new venture to his daddy. That boy never had to worry about a job. His daddy would always take care of him. I suppose those things fall into one or both of those categories."

Reyna agreed. She supposed that was what Father Cullen had been referring to. "The official investigation looked into the possibility of a kidnapping gone wrong."

He nodded, pushed away his empty bowl. "Never was a ransom demand. Truth is one investigation or the other looked into most every possibility of what could have happened. But it didn't bring them any closer to figuring it out."

"Based on the things you mentioned were happening, did you ever feel as if the guys were on the verge of something?"

"They were young. One or the other was always on the verge of something, but what's new? It's the sort of thing that drives treasure hunters and scientists alike."

Reyna hesitated a moment. She wanted to go for shocking, but she felt guilty doing so with Ward. Still, he wanted the truth. She wanted it. Why not just do it? "If you had to choose one of the Three," she said, "who was capable of killing the other two, which one would it be?"

The shock and anger she'd expected to see didn't come. Instead, he gazed steadily at her. "If I had to choose," he repeated, "I would say Duke for sure. He was older and more hotheaded. But—" he stared directly at Reyna "—I would bet my life that whatever happened was not prompted or carried out by one of those boys."

Reyna didn't remind him that they had been men—grown men—at the time of the disappearance. She understood that he was speaking as a father who would forever see his son as his boy.

If none of the three men had precipitated the event somehow, had it been one of their wives? Or one of the parents?

"There's plenty more," he said, gesturing to her empty bowl.

"I'm good, thank you. It was wonderful." Reyna studied the man who took their empty bowls to the sink. Who had wanted to hurt the Three or wanted to get rid of them badly enough to actually make it happen?

Ben arrived, and his grandfather insisted he join Reyna at the table while he ladled up his dinner.

Ben passed her keys to her. "Everything's taken care of."

"Thanks. I'm really glad there wasn't more damage."

He nodded, flashed a smile for his grandfather as he settled a bowl of soup on the table in front of him and produced a glass of iced tea.

Ben was clearly starving. Reyna occupied herself with tracing a bead of sweat down her own tea glass while he ate.

She thought of the parents of the Three who were still living. JR's mother had passed away. Duke Fuller's father had died, but his mother was still alive. Both Judson Evans's parents had passed. As awful as it was to think of a parent harming an offspring, it happened. But the age group of the men when they'd disappeared put the possibility lower on the probability scale.

"Thanks, Pops—that was great." Ben pushed aside his bowl and settled his attention on Rey. "Have you ever had any trouble with that tire?"

The question surprised her. "No. I mean, the Land Rover is old, so there are mechanical issues from time to time, but the tires are fairly new."

"No slow air leaks? No previous repairs?"

She shook her head. "Was the tire defective?"

"The best we could determine, the tire was cut, punctured in a way that prevented the air from seeping out until the vehicle was moving, and then it came out quickly. You're lucky it wasn't a rear tire, or you might have lost complete control of the vehicle. With a front tire, you still have some control with the steering wheel. Not so with a rear blowout."

Reyna drew back as if needing distance from the words he'd uttered. "You're saying you believe someone did this on purpose." It wasn't a question. Of course—that was what he'd said. But…why? How?

"Yes. I'm saying someone did this and it was on purpose—no question."

The idea was ludicrous. "It had to have happened while I was at the church. I went to Nelson Owens's house first, but we were on the porch the whole time with my vehicle in clear view. Then I drove to the church, and I was there maybe forty-five minutes. An hour, tops." This was crazy…and yet her nerves were suddenly jangling.

"Did anyone know you were going to the church?"

Reyna thought about the question. "Eudora, of course. I don't think I mentioned where I was going next to Owens." Not that she could see either one having anything to do with her tire being damaged.

This was too much.

"Maybe," Ben said, "going off on your own while you're conducting these interviews isn't such a good idea."

"This is the way I've always conducted interviews and done my research." How else was she supposed to do it? This was…disturbing. She felt violated.

"I'd feel a lot better if you would let me tag along."

Was he serious? "Don't you have work to do?"

"Nothing that won't wait."

Again, this made no sense.

"Why would you even want to do this? This tagging-along thing?" It wasn't that she was opposed to company, but—as unkind as it sounded—she needed to be clear on his motive.

He held her gaze for a moment before answering. "My father and his two best friends went missing thirty years ago. Since that time, no less than two dozen people—some official, some not—have looked into their disappearance, and no one has ever found a damned thing."

She nodded. "What does that have to do with your playing the part of my shadow?"

"In all that time, I've never heard about any of the folks doing the investigating receiving any sort of threats or being vandalized."

His words suddenly made way too much sense.

"This tells me," he went on before she could say anything, "someone is worried you might actually be the one to find what no one else has."

Chapter Six

Kane Residence
Thistle Lane
Tuesday, April 23, 10:00 a.m.

Ben stood at the kitchen window, staring out over the orchard. As a kid, he'd loved running through those trees and climbing them. Despite his father disappearing when he'd been seven, he'd had a good childhood. He'd had his grandfather and his mother had been there for him. She'd been different then. Always smiling and laughing. Always baking cookies and thinking up games to play. She'd seen that he'd had all the things a kid needed. He'd never once gone without food or clothing or the usual things kids thought were necessary.

But after the disappearance something had been missing—besides his dad. Never with his grandfather, but with his mother. There had been a distance. He hadn't recognized it in the earlier days of his youth, but as he'd grown into a teenager, it had become more and more clear. At the time he'd assumed it was the usual teenage angst that had created a gulf. But in more recent years, rather than see that gap close, it had somehow become wider.

For a long while he'd ignored it as nothing more than his

mother's way, but he saw it differently now. He'd gone through the possibilities. Maybe she was depressed. Sad. Lonely. But then he'd slowly realized it was something else. She was hiding something. The biggest visible change had started five years ago when a Chattanooga reporter had decided to do a twenty-fifth anniversary special about the Three. The dynamics between him and his mother had changed dramatically. Her connection with the other Widows—all the relationships he was aware of—had shifted.

He'd told himself that people changed when they got older. She'd been fifty-three at the time. Maybe she'd experienced a later-life crisis. Anytime he'd brought up the subject, she had bristled. Eventually she'd lowered the boom, letting him know that his questions were not appreciated and would no longer be tolerated.

"She's here."

Ben turned at the sound of his mother's voice. Instead of responding to her less-than-enthusiastic announcement, he said, "I was just remembering how I loved to climb in all those apple trees. Dad used to boost me up when I was really little."

She didn't smile. "I remember when you fell out and broke your arm."

That was Lucinda Kane. Always recalling the downside of the past.

By the time Reyna had climbed the steps and was just about to knock on the front door, he was there and opened it. Her fist hesitated in the air, then dropped to her side.

"Good morning," she said.

"Morning." Time would tell if it was a good one. "Come on in."

Reyna stepped inside and looked around, her gaze lingering on the family photos on the walls.

Ben closed the door and watched for a while as she walked toward one photograph in particular. It was the largest of the framed images. The last one taken before his father had vanished. Ben had just turned seven. The photo had been shot at his grandfather's home, down by the barn beneath Ben's favorite tree.

He didn't rush her, just let her look her fill. His mother would be waiting in the parlor, braced and ready for battle. The whole idea made no sense. Why couldn't she be glad that someone was trying to find the truth? Someone, he'd decided, who was in it for more than some misplaced hope of notoriety.

Someone who, apparently, just by showing up had disturbed the thirty-year-old cloak of silence that surrounded the disappearance.

"How was your night?" he asked when her interest shifted from the photographs to him.

She smiled. He liked her smile. He gave himself a mental shake. What he really needed was to get out more.

"Thankfully uneventful. Birdie showed me dozens of photo albums. Vintage photos of the town and the folks who live here." Reyna gave a nod. "I'm reasonably confident I know most of your secrets now."

If Birdie Jewel was doing the talking, Ben would bet Reyna knew plenty for sure.

"Let's head into the parlor. My mom's waiting there."

Lucinda Kane stood in front of the pink chair that had been her favorite for as long as Ben could remember. Each time the fabric grew worn, she had it recovered. She always insisted there was something to be said for good furniture.

"Mom, this is Reyna Hart," he announced when she at last looked up and acknowledged their presence. Deep down he hoped her reasons for always being so stubborn about this subject were genuine and not because she was hiding some secret he really didn't want to learn.

Reyna approached his mother, extended her hand. "It's a pleasure to meet you, Ms. Kane. I appreciate your time."

His mother reached out and grasped Reyna's hand ever so briefly before drawing away. "I'm certain my son told you that I'm only doing this to appease him."

"He did," Reyna said. "This is a difficult subject for you, so I can understand your hesitation."

Lucinda gestured to the sofa. "Please, sit. Ben, would you get our guest coffee or water?"

"Not necessary," Reyna hastened to say. "I filled up on coffee at breakfast. Birdie makes the best coffee."

"I'm sure you're finding her B and B welcoming." Lucinda settled into her chair.

"I am," Reyna confirmed. "She's an interesting lady— well versed in the history of Whispering Winds. She's had me enthralled since I arrived."

His mother cocked her head and eyed Reyna for a moment. "You can't always believe everything you hear, Ms. Hart, not even from Birdie Jewel."

Reyna smiled. "We all have our own way of remembering," she agreed. "We tell our memories from our own perspective, so what might feel like an error or oversight is more often simply the way a person remembers."

Ben looked from his mother to Reyna. "Interesting way of seeing things."

Frankly, he'd never thought of it that way, but it made sense. Maybe this was the problem with his and his mother's way of seeing the past. Definitely something to consider.

"My son says you have questions for me," Lucinda said, clearly ready to move on.

"I think we should just rip the Band-Aid off and start with the hard questions first," Reyna suggested.

Ben braced for his mother's rebuttal.

"Very well," she said instead.

Surprised but grateful, he relaxed marginally.

"Why did you change your mind about wanting to marry Gordon Walls?"

Even Ben was a little put off by the question. His attention swung to his mother, expecting to see anger and shock. Instead he saw a face clean of emotion and intently focused on the woman asking the questions.

"I was young. Gordon had all these big plans for getting out of Whispering Winds, and I wanted that very much. His Army uniform was impressive. It seemed like the perfect plan for getting away. I imagined traveling the world with him in the military." She sighed. "I was just a foolish girl with silly dreams."

Never once had he heard this version of his mother's decision. Strangely, it made a great deal of sense.

"But then you met JR," Reyna went on. "You knew him before, I'm guessing."

"We both grew up right here in Whispering Winds, so of course I knew him. But he'd just come back from college, and…he'd changed. Matured. He was very different from Gordon. Far more handsome, but also kinder, more deeply passionate about everything. As they say, he swept me off my feet."

"How did Gordon react to this?" Reyna asked the next logical question.

Ben held his breath. This was the aspect of her history that his mother most often refused to speak about.

"I think he was relieved."

Ben did a double take. Had she really just said that to basically a stranger?

"He put up a bit of a fuss to save face, but I personally believe he already had other plans and my decision gave him the out he needed."

"Why have you never said that before?" The question was out before Ben could tamp it back.

Lucinda smiled in his direction. "Because it was embarrassing. I didn't want to admit that Gordon had likely outgrown his brief infatuation with me." She sent him a pointed look. "Why don't you find those family photo albums from back then and show them to Reyna? She might find them interesting."

"I'd love to see them," Reyna agreed.

Ben pushed to his feet, his brain wobbling with disbelief. Who was this impostor, and where was his mother?

Evans Residence
Blackberry Trail
12:25 p.m.

DEIDRE FULLER HAD refused to meet with Reyna. She wasn't so surprised. Frankly, she'd been shocked that Ben's mom and now Ms. Evans had agreed to an interview. Ben, on the other hand, seemed completely surprised by Fuller's decision.

He parked his truck next to Rey's Land Rover. When he opened his door to get out, she did the same. The Evans home was typical of the area and not unlike the homes of the other two widows: farmhouse, two stories, well maintained. There were many houses of this style in the area, but what continued to amaze Reyna was the idea that these women had lived in the same ones for all these years. None had ever remarried, and none had sold the homes purchased by their husbands. Reyna would have thought that at least one of the Widows would have moved on by now, particularly since two had no children with the spouses who had disappeared.

Why stay in that same place with the same memories and no forward momentum during all this time?

On top of all that, the houses were very short distances apart. They were all on different roads on the fringes of Whispering Winds, but they were only a mile or so from each other.

"I enjoyed meeting your mother," Reyna said as she and Ben climbed the steps to the front porch. "The photo albums provided such a great sense of time and place for my research."

"Mother startled even me with her cooperativeness," he confessed. "I expected each answer to be like pulling teeth."

Reyna laughed. "Sometimes those closest to us surprise us the most." She wondered if he understood how lucky he was to still have his mother and his grandfather. She had no one left but her mother. As much as she loved her mom, she dearly missed her grandmother.

At the door of the Evans home, Ben hesitated. "I think we should have dinner together again so you can share your insights from the day."

She nodded. "I think we can work that out."

This research trip continued to throw her curveballs. She hadn't expected to have her tire vandalized, and she certainly hadn't anticipated being welcomed so whole-heartedly by one of the families she needed to investigate. Mostly, the unexpected attentiveness of this man astonished her.

As he knocked on the door, she reminded herself that this might very well be nothing more than his determination to know her every step. To be involved with how she conducted her research.

For now, she opted to believe his intentions were sincere and that there were no ulterior motives.

The door opened, and Harlowe Evans stood in the entryway. Younger than the other widows by only a couple of months, Evans kept her hair the same blond shade it had been in her youth. Her makeup was flawless, as was her spring attire—khaki trousers and a floral shirt with just the right hint of blue to highlight her eyes.

"Ben." She drew back. "Come in." Her attention fixed on Reyna as the two stepped inside. "Ms. Hart, such a pleasure to meet you. I read your book!" Her eyes twinkled, *"The Woman at the End of the Lane.* It was wonderful!"

"Thank you." Reyna couldn't help feeling a burst of pride when anyone mentioned having read her book. She doubted she would ever get past the blush that right this second heated her cheeks and the little stream of excitement that zipped through her. She suspected that feeling would never get old if she published a hundred novels.

"I have a little something prepared for lunch," Evans said, "if you're interested."

Ben patted his stomach. "Sounds good to me, Ms. Evans. I can always eat."

The older woman made a happy face. "Well, come on, then."

They followed her to the kitchen. This farmhouse had been gutted at some point, Reyna decided. Most of the first floor was a huge open space. Very different from the others. She wondered if the open floor plan happened before or after the disappearance. Not that it really mattered, but it would be interesting to know if Evans was the only one of the Widows who had moved forward in any manner.

On the massive island that stood between the kitchen and main living area Reyna spotted neatly halved sandwiches and other finger foods as well as a sweating pitcher of lemonade, judging by the sheer number of lemons floating in the otherwise clear liquid.

"We have my fave cucumber sandwiches and those ham-and-cheese ones I know you like, Ben." She looked to Reyna. "We can munch while you ask questions. I'll pour the drinks—you two grab a plate and fill it up."

While Reyna picked through the yummy-looking offerings, she asked, "You, Lucinda and Deidre have been best friends your whole lives, is that right?"

"It is," Evans said as she slid onto a stool and surveyed her plate. She went for a cucumber sandwich. "We knew each other in church, of course, and then we started kindergarten together. We were always inseparable."

Reyna had decided to approach this interview from a different perspective. "I'm sure the three of you struggled with the usual teenage issues."

Who hadn't?

Evans chewed for a moment, then swallowed. "Not so much. There were a few times we stopped speaking to each other but never for more than a day. We've always been extremely close."

"Getting married didn't change this?" Reyna nibbled a cucumber sandwich and hummed her satisfaction. "So good."

"Why, thank you." Evans gave a nod. "Now, to answer your question, I think we got a lot closer after we married."

She smiled at Ben. "When your mama had you it was like we all had you. So exciting and so scary at the same time."

Ben grinned. "My mom says you two spoiled me."

"We did," Evans agreed.

"Do you mind sharing why you never had children?" Reyna asked, steeling herself for a backlash. It was not the most polite of questions.

"I don't know if you've spoken with Deidre already, but she'll tell you that she never wanted children. As much as she enjoyed being a part of Ben's life, she didn't have any desire to go there personally."

Reyna chose not to mention that Fuller had passed on the interview.

"I, on the other hand, would have loved to have babies." She smiled sadly. "Unfortunately, my Judson had issues in that area." She leaned toward Reyna and whispered, "Low sperm count." Then she straightened. "I never wanted to make him feel pressured, and back then it was not so easy to do the things you can do now. Then he was gone, and I just let it go."

Felt like the perfect segue to another important question. "I find it curious that none of you have remarried or even moved from Whispering Winds. Have you discussed this between the three of you?"

Evans took a moment, drank some lemonade, picked at the food left on her plate. Then she met Reyna's gaze. "We were never going to talk about this, but—" she looked from Reyna to Ben and back "—I guess it's time we did."

Her comment had other questions jumping in Reyna's head, but she kept quiet for fear of causing Evans to change her mind about whatever she intended to say.

"After…what happened, we made a vow that we would not even look at anyone else or consider moving on with our lives until we had answers…" She exhaled a sad sound. "We really did expect them to come back. I mean, how do three men just vanish? It felt like a dream—a nightmare. We kept expecting to wake up and find everything the way it was before."

Except that had never happened.

"As the years passed, did you revisit this decision?" Reyna held her breath, hoping she would continue to answer the questions no one else had so far.

"We did once or twice. But no one wanted to say the words—that they were never coming back. It was easier to believe they'd come walking through those doors just anytime."

She stared at her front door as she said this.

Her words and her voice were so sincere. Reyna found it difficult to believe she wasn't being honest. But it felt like such a stretch. Who waited thirty years for a man to return?

"When was the last time the three of you discussed what happened?" Reyna asked.

Evans frowned. She blinked, once, twice. "Well, it's been a while. We're all busy, and life just kind of slips by."

Now she was evading. The change was easy to see and hear.

"With the three of you still being so close," Reyna said, redirecting, "I imagine you talk of those hard days fairly often."

The deer-caught-in-the-headlights expression was impossible to ignore. "Not as much as you'd think."

Another evasion.

"But you are still very close," Reyna suggested.

Slow, vague nod. "Like sisters." She picked up a cheese straw and poked it into her mouth.

"That's so unusual," Reyna pointed out, hoping to shift the tension. "I've lost touch with everyone I knew in school."

Evans only nodded.

Reyna had a feeling the interview was over.

Ben pulled his cell phone from his pocket and checked the screen. "Excuse me—I need to take this."

He stepped away from the table.

She decided to try one more avenue. "I love the open floor plan you've created in your house. It's really lovely."

Evans looked around as if she wasn't sure what Reyna meant. "It works."

Ben reappeared. "We have to go," he said to Reyna.

The worry on his face had her moving off the stool. "Everything okay?"

Rather than answer her, he said, "Thanks so much, Ms. Evans. We may call you again, if that's okay."

Reyna pulled a card from her bag and passed it to the woman. "Call me if you think of anything that might help."

"Absolutely," Evans insisted, her tone and expression back to open and sincere. "Y'all come back anytime."

They were outside and moving toward their parked vehicles before he explained: "Pops called. There's been a fire at the B and B."

Reyna's heart hit the ground. "Is Birdie okay?" As far as Reyna knew, there were no other guests… This was just terrible.

"Don't know. We need to get over there now."

Chapter Seven

The small Whispering Winds fire department had deployed both their fire engine and their fire truck. Thankfully no one had needed rescuing. Birdie had smelled the smoke, discovered the flames and made the call as she'd hurried out of the building.

With the fire department just down the road, the trucks had arrived in mere moments. The flames had been extinguished, and the building had been cleared.

Birdie sat on a bench in the front gardens, staring tearfully at her beloved bed-and-breakfast.

"I'm so glad you're okay." Reyna sat down beside her. She didn't even want to consider how things could have gone. Fires in old buildings were particularly ravenous. The older structures hadn't been built with the more modern deterrents. Not to mention the sheer age of the wood made it highly flammable.

Birdie worked up a smile. "My insurance agent insisted I install those smoke detectors years ago." She shook her head, swiped at a tear that had slipped past her hold on her emotions. "I'm so very glad I did."

Reyna looped her arm around the woman's shoulders and gave her a hug. "Me too."

Birdie turned to her then. "How's your research going? I've been hearing all sorts of rumbles from the natives." She smiled. "Everyone knows there's a stranger in town digging around in the most painful part of our past."

Reyna supposed she couldn't deny the description. "Progress is slow. I was able to interview two of the Widows—Lucinda Kane and Harlowe Evans. Deidre Fuller refuses to see me."

Birdie sighed. "Deidre was always a bit full of herself. The truth is she always wanted to give the perception of utter grace and wealth. You know the sort. Dory and I used to shake our heads at how some folks thought they had to prove they were above the rest of us."

"Dory?" Reyna suspected she meant Eudora, but she had never heard about any nickname from the lady.

She looked away. "Eudora. That was my nickname for her. We've known each other our whole lives."

Reyna felt guilty for being here two days already without another call to Eudora to update her. She'd have to call her tonight. She would be very interested in learning that Reyna had spoken at length with two of the three Widows. If she was feeling particularly lucid, she might even have some insights into how to prod Deidre Fuller into talking. It never hurt to ask.

"I'll tell her you said hello," Reyna promised. "I plan to call her tonight and catch up."

Birdie's smile widened, reached her blue eyes. "That would be very nice. Thank you."

Reyna studied the beautiful old mansion that had been lovingly transformed into a bed-and-breakfast. Birdie had done much of the work herself, and the gardens she had created were nothing short of spectacular. "Have they given you any sense of the damage inside?"

"I only know that the trouble was on the second floor."

Reyna's room was on the second floor. Her laptop was in the room. And her clothes. Nothing that couldn't be replaced, of course.

Ben had gone in search of the sheriff. Now there were three Hamilton County sheriff's department vehicles in the street. Reyna knew from her research that a small substation was here on Main Street, and the sheriff, Tara Norwood—the daughter of retired sheriff Tarrence Norwood—was a local from nearby Dread Hollow. Reyna imagined she kept her finger on the pulse of local goings-on.

"Oh my," Birdie said as she grasped Reyna's hand. "I hope your things weren't damaged."

If the laptop was ruined, it wouldn't be so bad. Reyna always saved everything to the cloud. Her notes and videos from Eudora—her work—everything was backed up. She usually typed up a sort of daily report each evening. This technique worked well for her.

"We're not going to worry about that," Reyna assured the older woman. "There's nothing in there that can't be easily replaced."

Birdie released her hand and pressed her own to her chest. "Thank goodness. Back when I was your age, to have the physical pages destroyed would have been the end of my work. Things weren't so easy back then."

Reyna was aware. The days of manually typed manuscripts and notes, with only a copy machine to back up the work, were a little unnerving. The writer's life was certainly simpler today—at least, in terms of saving and transferring one's work.

Ben walking in their direction had Reyna pushing the

thoughts away. She hoped for Birdie's sake that the damage was minimal.

"Is it bad?" Birdie asked, her hands wringing in her lap.

"It could have been much worse." Ben glanced back at the firefighters going in and out of the front entrance of the building. "The fire was contained to only one room." He turned to Reyna. "Yours."

She was pleased to know the damage had been contained to a small area, but that it was her room suddenly seemed odd. "I don't smoke, and I had no candles lit." She frowned. "In fact, I don't think there were even any candles in the room." She looked to Birdie for confirmation.

She shrugged. "None that I'm aware of. I've had guests bring candles and incense, but I've never had one start a fire."

Reyna flinched. "With me away all day, I can't imagine how it started."

"The fire marshal is conducting an investigation," Ben explained. "Sheriff Norwood said you wouldn't be able to rent any more rooms until the investigation is complete and cleanup has been done, Birdie."

She waved the idea off. "Of course. I'm sure the whole place smells like smoke."

He made a face. "Unfortunately."

Reyna drew in a big breath. "I'll need to find a clothing shop." Everything she'd brought with her was now beyond her reach…if it had survived the damage to her room.

Ben hitched a thumb back toward the entrance. "The sheriff said there was one smaller bag in the bathroom and it was okay. She'll bring it out for you."

Her meager cosmetics and underthings. Relief flashed through Reyna. "I would really appreciate that." She glanced down at her jeans and shirt. "I can just wash and wear this over and over." No biggie.

"Certainly you cannot. We can't have you conducting your interviews in the same clothes over and over," Birdie argued. "I have things you can wear. As soon as I'm allowed to go inside, I'll put together a little care package for you."

"Thank you," Reyna said. "That would be helpful."

A woman in a sheriff's uniform approached. "The fire marshal is almost finished," she said, her statement directed at Birdie. "We can go inside and go over everything with you once he's done."

"Thank you so much, Tara," Birdie said. "I just can't believe this happened."

Reyna felt terrible. The idea that the fire had something to do with why she was here made her feel ill.

"Sheriff Norwood," Ben said, "this is Reyna Hart. Her room is the one where the fire started."

Tara gave Reyna a nod. "I'm sure sorry we have to meet under such circumstances, Ms. Hart."

"Reyna," she offered as she pushed to her feet. "I'm just confused about how it started. There didn't appear to be any electrical issues in the room." She'd used her laptop and phone chargers in two of the outlets. The lamps had all worked fine. Oh, and she'd used the hair dryer in the bathroom.

"That's the odd part," Norwood explained. "There was a lit candle in the room, and it apparently fell over."

Reyna drew back as if she'd been slapped. "A candle? But there weren't any candles in the room, and I certainly didn't bring any with me." She shrugged. "I don't have matches or a lighter. Even if there had been a candle, I wouldn't have been able to light it."

Norwood held up her hands, palms out. "My statement wasn't an accusation. Based on the time you left your room—Birdie said before nine this morning—the candle would have burned out long before now. The fire marshal's report will give us a more accurate timeline. But I'm guessing it was lit around noon."

"I had lunch at the diner," Birdie said. Her mouth rounded for a moment. "I always leave the front entrance unlocked in case a guest returns while I'm away. You know I never go far."

"I wish you had video cameras," Norwood said. "Most of the shops along Main have added them in recent years."

She waved off the idea. "I'm too old to worry with that sort of thing. I'll leave it to the next owner to bother."

Norwood smiled patiently. "Let's go conduct a walk-through, Ms. Birdie."

She stood, then turned back to Reyna. "I'll bring you some clothes in just a few minutes."

"Thank you."

Reyna watched the two head back to the entrance and disappear inside. Then she turned to face Ben. "Sheriff Norwood didn't say it, but she has to see that whoever started the fire had targeted me in particular." She shrugged. "I mean, what else is there to think?"

Ben glanced toward the activity at the bed-and-breakfast. "She believes that's the case," he confirmed. "She asked me a lot of questions about who you'd been talking to and that kind of thing." He moved his head side to side, the gesture slow, worried. "I told her about your tire. I'm getting a bad feeling about all this."

"So am I." As unsettling as this was, Reyna would not be scared off. "Is there another motel around here?"

"You're going home with me," he said, his gaze settling on hers. "Sheriff Norwood thought it was a good idea as well."

Well, if the sheriff thought it was a good idea, how could she say no?

Kane Residence
Lula Lake Lane
8:30 p.m.

"I DIDN'T MENTION the fire when I spoke to Eudora," Reyna said.

Ben placed the final plate he'd dried in the cabinet. "It would only have upset her." He didn't know the elderly woman well, but he remembered her from when she'd been a schoolteacher. She'd still been teaching at Whispering Winds Elementary when he'd been a kid.

Reyna propped a hip against the counter and smiled. "I could hear the smile in her voice when I talked about Birdie. She misses being here."

He walked to the coffee maker and checked the water level. "You up for a cup of coffee?"

"Coffee would be nice."

"How about you, Pops?" He turned to his grandfather, who still sat at the table. He'd been listening avidly to their conversation about the fire at the bed-and-breakfast and the other events of the day.

"No, thanks." He pushed to his feet. "I think I'll turn in a little early, finish that book I started last week."

"Good night, Ward," Reyna called after him.

"Night, Pops."

Ward waved as he shuffled on out of the kitchen. He seemed more tired lately than usual. Ben hoped this business wasn't taking an extra toll on him. As much as his grandfather wanted to find the truth, was it really worth it at this point?

"You're worried this is too much for him," Reyna offered.

Ben went back to the business of making coffee. "Yeah. It's a lot to deal with."

"For you as well," she pointed out.

He pressed the start button on the machine and listened for the sounds that indicated it was beginning the brew process. Then he turned to his guest. "Not as much as for him." He reached into the cabinet for a couple of coffee mugs. "We're kind of programmed for losing parents." He set the mugs on the counter. Shrugged. "Maybe not at seven years old, but the concept is a part of growing up. But losing a child..." He shook his head. "No one is ever prepared for that."

"Valid point," she agreed. "I hadn't stopped to consider that even though your father was twenty-eight, he was still Ward's child—his only child."

The scent of coffee filled the room in the silence that followed. Ben waded through the years, searching for memories of his father. "I don't remember a lot about him. Pops tried to keep his memories alive for me. But Mom..." He shrugged again. "She turned it all off a few months after the disappearance. It was like she understood what had happened, had accepted it and wanted to move on. I resented her for a long time because of that."

Reyna searched his face, looking for the emotions behind his words. He didn't really want her to see them.

He hadn't actually meant to share quite so much, but there was something about the way Sheriff Norwood had watched him, scrutinized his every word today when they'd been surveying Reyna's room. The sheriff thought something was going on related to the Three as well. She hadn't gone out on a limb and said as much, but Ben sensed she'd been seeing it and trying to make sense of it.

Thirty years was a long time for someone to protect a secret.

In all this time with the dozens of investigators and re-porters who had poked around in the case, there had never been this sort of trouble or backlash. Why now? Why with Reyna Hart?

What was it about her or how she was going about her research that made someone nervous?

Once the coffee had brewed and mugs had been filled, they moved to the parlor. The quiet down the hall nudged Ben again. He should check on his grandfather. But then he'd only complain. Ward Kane did not like to be treated as if he were helpless or needy.

"Do you mind if I browse through the family photo albums again?"

He exiled the troubling thoughts about his grandfather. "I do not." He settled his mug on the table by the sofa and helped Reyna round up the many photo albums his grand-father had ensured remained safe through the years. Then they sat side by side on the sofa.

"My grandmother was the one who always made sure there were family photos of all the important events— holidays, birthdays and stuff like that. After she was gone, Pops took over and did a pretty good job."

"What about your mother? Her albums seemed thor-ough as well."

"Mostly. Sometimes Pops would make extra copies of photos he'd taken for her. Her documentation was more thorough before the disappearance."

Reyna turned a page in the older of the albums that included Ben as an infant.

"She seemed happy." She tapped a photo of Ben and his parents. He couldn't have been more than a few months old.

"Pops says they were happy." When Ben had gotten older he'd asked his mother about his father and whether they'd been happy, and she had usually changed the subject. Eventually he'd stopped asking. It was easier to believe what he wanted and to take his grandfather's word for how things were.

"Was this at your grandmother's funeral?"

Ben studied the photo and nodded. "Yeah." He tapped the Victorian-style house in the background. "You probably saw this place when you were driving through town. Addison Funeral Home. It's been here forever. They were one of the first funeral homes in the area to have their own crematorium." He laughed. "But no one wanted to use it. It was a long time before folks around here even considered going that route with a deceased loved one. But the Addisons liked being ahead of the times. They're one of the few funeral homes that hasn't sold out to a chain. Pops says you can do that when the family is independently wealthy."

Reyna smiled. "I like hearing stories from the past. It helps put life back then in perspective," she said, her attention back on the photos. "Your family seemed happy before the disappearance. You never sensed any issues?"

"Never." He shrugged. "But I was a kid. Kids don't always notice."

Reyna set the album aside. "But other people do, and everyone I've interviewed says the same," she began. "Eudora said the Three were happy, had beautiful wives and good lives. She always says it doesn't make sense that they just vanished. Birdie said almost the same thing. Your grandfather. There has been no one except Vinnia McGill who believes that things weren't storybook."

He saw where she was going now. "You planning to attempt an interview with Gordon Walls?"

"I think I need to," she said. "His role in your mother's life was a major one. Pretending that didn't happen or didn't alter attitudes and perceptions is just too much of a reach."

Yeah, he got that.

"Her relationship with Walls has always been downplayed or left out of the story," he offered, "whenever anyone talks about the Three and what happened."

She nodded. "I just find that odd, but maybe it's because I'm an outsider. They all knew one another. It's possible the idea is as nonsensical to those who know Walls as the opposite is to me."

"I guess so. I've never been around him that much. I've seen his name in the news when he's made major arrests, but that's about it." Ben thought about what he wanted to say next. "I feel like my grandfather would have been the first to go after him if he'd believed he might be involved somehow."

"He mentioned that he and Jacob Evans had a talk with Walls and felt comfortable that he wasn't involved. Still, I would be interested in hearing Walls's side of the story."

"He never told me that," Ben confessed. "Makes sense though. Pops wouldn't have played it off. He would have gone straight in and found out for himself."

"He didn't give me the details," Reyna explained. "Only that he was confident in the answer he got."

He imagined his grandfather thirty years ago kicking

the guy's butt and demanding answers. Not the sort of thing you told your grandson, he supposed.

She continued poring through photos, and the conversation lapsed.

Ben finished off his coffee and relaxed into the sofa. He hadn't gotten one thing done on the Henry place today. In fact, he hadn't gotten any work done at all, and still he was tired. But not too tired to continue talking to Reyna. Maybe he'd been out of the dating game so long he'd forgotten how good it was to have someone his own age—a woman, at that—to just talk with.

"Do you mind if I ask a personal question?" He decided turnabout was fair play. At least, he hoped so.

She put the latest album she'd been perusing aside and picked up her mug. "After the way I've been digging around in your life, how could I ever say no?"

"Why only one book?" He smiled. "I mean, it's only been five years, and maybe you have one in the pipeline as we speak. But I checked your website and your publisher's website. I didn't see anything coming up."

"There's a very good reason for that." She laughed softly, placed her empty mug on the coffee table next to his. "There is no second book. Not so far, anyway."

She sat back, curled her bare feet beneath her. He liked that she felt comfortable enough to do that despite the obviously uncomfortable question he'd asked.

"Sales were actually pretty good, but my publisher wasn't interested in another book—at least, not the ideas for the ones I offered." She was quiet for a moment before going on. "That sort of thing happens more often than you'd think, so I figured the best thing to do was just go on with my life and not consider my brief career as a published author a total failure."

Now he really did feel like a chump for asking.

"These memory books you write," he said, hoping to make up for bringing the subject into the conversation. "It sounds like the families really appreciate your work. It's an amazing thing you do for your clients."

"I enjoy the work, and I do feel it's an important service to my clients as well as their families." She turned her hands up. "I have to say being here and researching this long-ago mystery is making me yearn to dive into fiction again. Maybe something based on a true event."

"Like this one," he countered.

"I'm not so sure that would be appropriate. This is Eudora's memory. Whatever happens with this one, it's for her." Her gaze connected with his. "And maybe for the families involved."

A horn blowing sounded outside.

What the hell? Ben stood and walked toward the front window. The continuous sound was more like someone had laid down on a horn and not let up. There were no other vehicles outside. His truck, his grandfather's and Rey's Land Rover. But his was the one with the horn blowing—the flashing headlights confirmed as much.

"Is something wrong?" Reyna stood beside him now.

"The alarm on my truck went off." He sent her a pointed look. "Stay put, and I'll have a look."

He went to the front hall and grabbed his truck fob off the table they used for a catchall when it came to keys and hats. When he reached for the door, Reyna was next to him again.

"Never tell a woman to stay put," she warned.

"At least stay behind me."

She didn't argue with that one. He surveyed the porch before stepping across the threshold. As he crossed the porch, he scanned left to right and back. No movement as far as he could see. Since the porch lights only extended to where the vehicles were parked, it was quite dark beyond that point.

He clicked the fob—the horn died and the lights stopped flashing. Still no sign of movement. No other sound.

The breeze kicked up, and something on his windshield flopped. It was tucked down into the slot where the wipers sat in the resting position. Still watching for trouble, Ben reached into the shallow valley and pulled what was a single sheet of paper from beneath one of the wipers.

Three words were written in bold red letters on the plain white piece of paper.

MAKE HER GO.

Chapter Eight

Ben parked and shut off the engine. He'd suggested they ride together as a means of ensuring that Reyna stayed safe. Made sense, she supposed, since they were doing the rest of her research together.

Then came the call from the sheriff wanting a meeting with them both.

On the way over to the substation, they had talked about why Sheriff Norwood would want to see them this morning. Obviously it was about the fire or Reyna's research into the Three. But there was a third option and Reyna had hesitated to bring it up, but they were out of time now.

The sheriff was inside waiting for them.

"Do you think Gordon Walls found out I've been asking questions about him?" Reyna had assumed he wouldn't be happy about her delving into the past—his in particular. The same could likely be said of anyone involved, she supposed. Eudora had said there would be those who wouldn't be happy.

Last night's message coupled with the fire and Reyna's damaged tire were fairly solid proof that someone wasn't keen on her being here.

There were plenty of good reasons for that attitude. Reyna understood. Some folks just wanted peace. Others wanted to just keep moving ahead and not look back.

But all things considered, she had to wonder if this was about peace or about protection of secrets.

No matter that she hadn't been here very long—anyone could see there were several folks who might have reason to want to protect their secrets.

Ben glanced toward the substation. "I'm certain he knows. News travels fast in small towns, Reyna. No matter how nice and how pretty you are, folks are curious, and they're going to talk."

Reyna smiled, bit her lip. "I think I should say thank-you."

"Just stating the facts." He reached for his door. "People like keeping their secrets and twisting things around to get their way, but I've never been that kind of guy. I prefer going straight for the truth."

Her smile widened. "Good. I prefer the truth."

It was cooler this morning. She was thankful for Birdie's sweatshirt. The flowers on the front were springy. Reyna had tucked her hair into a ponytail. If she was going to be casual, she might as well go all the way. Her partner in crime wore jeans as well. A button-down shirt in blue that matched his eyes and a vest—the kind workingmen wore—completed the look, which was sharp. He looked nice. Very nice.

She dismissed the thoughts and focused forward.

Inside the substation there was a small lobby. *Small* might've been an overstatement. There was a bulletin board and one chair standing beneath it. The only other door besides the one they'd entered opened, and Sheriff Tara Norwood looked from Ben to Reyna.

"Thanks for coming in. Come on back here. Deputy Travers lent me his office."

They followed her down a short corridor, past a couple of other doors and into an office not much larger than the lobby. There was a desk with a chair behind it and two in front. Norwood took the one behind the desk. Ben waited to sit until Reyna had taken a seat.

"I'm going to get straight to the point," Norwood said. "I'm a little worried about what's happening around here. Generally, I'd leave this little community to the two capable deputies assigned to keep it safe, but this goes way back to my daddy's time as sheriff, so I have a bit of a personal stake."

Reyna was aware that Tara's father, Tarrence, had been sheriff when the Three had disappeared.

"I can assure you, Sheriff," she felt compelled to say, "that I did not come here with the intent to stir up trouble."

"I did a little research on you, Reyna, and I'm confident you did not. Frankly, I'm not sure why these anomalies are happening. We've had all manner of investigators poking around over the years. Never once have we had this sort of reaction from what I can only presume is a local."

Ben reached into his back pocket and pulled out the plastic baggie he'd tucked last night's warning note into. "This was tucked under my windshield last night."

Norwood studied the note. She looked over at Reyna. "You've been here three days and you've received three warnings. I feel like it's time to take this situation more seriously than you may believe is necessary."

"I'm fully aware there's a problem," Reyna countered.

"It's my hope that you won't see my presence as an issue for the community." She mentally crossed her fingers. "I feel like I'm onto something here, and I don't want to let it go."

"It's a free country, Reyna," Norwood assured her. "I'm not suggesting that you can't be here doing exactly what you're doing. To my knowledge, you've broken no laws. You have as much right to be here as anyone. All that said, you are in my county and that makes me ultimately responsible for your safety."

"I'm not letting her out of my sight." Ben spoke up. "She's my grandfather's guest, and I feel responsible for her immediate safety."

"I'm glad to hear it," Norwood said. "You two stick together, and I'll be satisfied for now. Anything new happens, I want to hear about it first. Like I said, this was my daddy's case thirty years ago, and whatever's going on now, I want to ensure that it's handled properly."

"Yes, ma'am," Ben said. "You'll be the first to know if anything else happens or if we find anything that will help with the answers we all want."

"I'm sure this is a little difficult for you, Ben."

"More for my grandfather than me," he countered. "At his age, he's just hoping to finally have some answers before…"

Norwood nodded. "I understand." She rose from her chair. "I should get on to my own office."

Ben stood; Reyna did the same.

"Thank you, Sheriff Norwood." Reyna extended her hand across the desk. "I'll really try to keep a low profile."

Norwood laughed. "In this town I don't think that's possible, Reyna."

Outside, Reyna reminded herself to take in the sunshine and the spring air as she climbed into Ben's truck. So often she forgot to fully appreciate the things in every-day life around her. Nearly every one of her memory clients had said in one way or another that their biggest regret was not taking more time to notice the little things.

Norwood's SUV bumped out onto the street and headed in the direction of Chattanooga. Reyna liked Norwood. Her reputation as a sheriff was excellent, and she seemed to really care about the community. But like everyone else related in any way to this case, she wanted answers and was keeping her finger on the pulse of what Reyna was doing.

Maybe she was right and there was no keeping a low profile when most everyone around you had a reason to watch you. Would she be the one to finally crack the case?

No pressure.

Reyna cleared her head and attempted to focus. She wasn't entirely sure where she and Ben were headed this morning, but he had mentioned going back to the Henry property. She wouldn't mind having a more extended look around there as well.

Just because Deidre Fuller had turned her down on the interview request yesterday didn't mean she wouldn't change her mind today. Reyna intended to try. It never hurt to ask. The worst she could do was say no again.

"Since you've decided to be my shadow and chauffeur," she said to the man who'd just started the engine, "do you mind if we make an unexpected visit to the Fuller residence and see if she'll talk to me?"

He reached for the gearshift. "Why not?"

A rap on Reyna's window made her jump.

Her heart lunged into her throat.

The man standing outside her door wore a deputy's uniform, but the baseball cap and the sunglasses prevented her from recognizing him immediately.

Then she did.

Gordon Walls.

Reyna glanced at Ben.

"Stay put," he warned.

This time she didn't argue with him. He got out and walked around to her side of the vehicle, where Walls waited.

"I need to speak to both of you," Walls said.

Ben glanced at her, and Reyna powered the window down. "I'm listening," she said.

"For the record, I'm more than glad to talk to you if you have questions," Walls said, his tone not exactly angry, more determined. "I'd much prefer that to hearing about you asking other folks questions about me."

"I planned to pay you a visit," she said. "But even so, it never hurts to have other people's perspective on the events that occurred thirty years ago."

Reyna wasn't about to be put off by this man or his uniform.

Walls exhaled a big breath, braced his hands on his hips. "I was not happy about what Lucinda did. That's a fact." He set his shielded gaze on Ben. "But my beef wasn't with your daddy. It was with Lucinda. She's the one who betrayed me. But I got over that before I was even back home. What was the point? She'd found someone new, and I was SOL—if you know what I mean. I moved on. Did it hurt?" He shrugged. "Bruised my ego a bit, but I got over it."

"Maybe," Ben offered, "you can give us your thoughts on what happened to my father and the others."

"You surely read my statement from the original investigation."

"I did," he confirmed.

Reyna had as well. Newly minted Deputy Walls had insisted that he had not seen or spoken with any one of the Three in months when they'd disappeared. Hadn't seen or spoken to Lucinda either.

"Then you know I had nothing to do with what happened."

"But you knew them," Reyna argued. "Knew their habits. Their hangouts."

"The Henry property was the place they were last known to be together before the disappearance," Ben pointed out.

Walls pursed his lips for a second. "They hung out at your granddaddy's barn a lot. That's where I confronted JR. We exchanged a few harsh words. Then I left." He shrugged. "I at least had to make an effort, give people something to say, otherwise they would just make it up."

"Any other places we should check out?" Ben asked. "Over the years, I've been every place anyone has told me about."

Walls weighed the question for a bit. "I remember some talk of those guys having a hangout on the Fuller property out by the lake. During the initial investigation, the property was searched, but nothing was ever found."

"There used to be a cabin out there," Ben said, "but the Fullers said it burned down when Duke was a kid. It no longer existed when they disappeared."

"That's all I can tell you," Walls said. He turned to Reyna. "I hope you'll direct any future questions straight to me."

He walked back to his SUV and climbed in. They watched until he'd exited the parking lot.

Ben suggested, "I say we take a ride out to the Fuller property."

"Should we call her and get permission?" Reyna hoped the answer would be no.

"This is land over by the lake, deep in the woods. I doubt she's been out there in years. She likely won't mind if we have a look."

Reyna fastened her seat belt. "Let's do it."

Trout Lake
11:45 a.m.

BEN HAD FISHED at this lake many times as a kid. First with his father and then with his grandfather. He hadn't been here in years. Truth was he hadn't been fishing in years. He'd spent too much time trying to be the man his ex-fiancée had wanted him to be. As soon as this was over, he was taking his grandfather fishing. Here, the way they'd done when he'd been a kid.

The old gravel driveway was mostly grown over with grass and weeds. He pointed to a leaning stone chimney. "That was the cabin someone in the Fuller family built a few generations back. It burned down right before the disappearance. It had been a long, dry summer. Lightning struck the roof, and it caught fire like dry kindling."

"It's beautiful out here."

Reyna was right. It was one of the most peaceful places on the mountain. Behind the original cabin was dense woods, but when you walked about a mile you hit a clearing that flowed right to the lake. The water was as blue as a cloudless sky, and there was nothing but the sound of nature all around.

"Just wait." He grinned at her. "You ain't seen nothing yet."

She gestured to the No Trespassing signs. "Maybe we should call Ms. Fuller."

"We're following up on a lead," he reminded her. He should call, but he wasn't taking the risk, not after Ms. Fuller had refused to meet with Reyna. What the woman didn't know wouldn't hurt her. They were only having a quick look. Mostly, he was just really tired of the evasive tactics and silence. He wanted answers.

The walk took a few minutes. The underbrush had grown out of hand, but it was worth the trouble. It was clear no one had been out here in years. Definitely no all-terrain or utility vehicles.

When they reached the clearing, Reyna gasped. "Wow."

"Yeah." He watched her take in the scene, her eyes wide with wonder, a smile on her lips. Watching her made his respiration pick up. Or maybe it was the trudge through the thick brush.

The lake was large, and the water was clean and clear. But it was the way it reached toward the cliff side, giving it an infinite edge, that really took your breath.

"What's that?"

He blinked, turned his attention to the woman at his side. She pointed toward the woods to the left of the lake. His gaze followed that path. He squinted. What was she seeing?

She started moving forward again. "In the tree line. I can just make out a structure or cabin."

"But the cabin burned down."

"There," she said, pointing again without slowing her pace in the same direction.

That was when he saw it. A roofline angling downward. How had he never seen this before? Maybe because he'd usually come here in the summer, and this early in the spring there were still a lot of trees with bare limbs, which allowed him to see beyond the tree line.

He was running now, and Reyna was keeping pace with him.

They reached the small cabin. Rustic. Old. How the hell was this here without him noticing? Ben gave the handle a twist and to his surprise the door opened.

"I should have a look first," he suggested.

She gestured to the door. "Hurry. I want to see."

The interior looked dark since the tiny structure sat back in the trees far enough to keep it shaded. The windows were cloudy from years of neglect blocking most of the light that would have penetrated the darkness. He reached for his cell, tapped the flashlight app.

He stepped inside and skimmed the light over the interior. Framed photographs on the walls.

Ben spotted a photo of his dad. He moved closer. There were more. A lot more. He stood in the middle of the cramped space and turned slowly, allowing the light to play over the walls. Dozens of framed photographs—all of them moments captured in time. Moments in the life of the three men who had disappeared. Not the kind taken from a distance the way a stalker would, but the sort snapped by someone with them...someone they knew.

"Look at this." Reyna had turned on her own flashlight app as well. "Their jerseys from high school."

Ben moved to the wall where the three jerseys hung. Numbers 21, Ward; 18, Fuller; and 14, Evans. "This is some sort of shrine."

"Maybe the Widows put all this together," she suggested. "Makes sense with the way it's all laid out."

Why wouldn't his mother tell him about this? He would have loved to share this with her. If she had been embarrassed, she shouldn't have been. He would have understood.

Before exiting the one-room cabin, they scoured the wall a foot at a time. Same with the ceiling and the floor. Both took dozens of pics, documenting the extensive efforts someone had gone to in order to create this memorial. Whoever had built the place had never painted it. Just left the natural wood, well aged and covered in memorabilia dedicated to the three men who had vanished without a trace.

Outside it took a moment for his eyes to adjust to the sunlight. His gut was in knots, and he wanted to call Lucinda and demand to know why she'd never told him. This was his father. Ben had a right to know about this... to see it. Damn it.

"Should we call Sheriff Norwood?"

"We should. Yeah." He doubted this was relevant to how or why they'd disappeared, but he was in no position to make that judgment. He was emotionally compromised, and he was no cop.

Ben studied the structure of the small cabin. It was well-built, not thrown together by novices. The roof was sturdy, and he'd seen no sign of leaks inside. Definitely built to last.

Had his grandfather helped his mother with this?

The quality of the work suggested his grandfather's level of craftsmanship.

He started toward the back of the structure. Reyna had already gone that way.

"Ben!"

The shock or fear in her voice had him rushing around

the rear corner to find her. She stood only a few feet from the back of the cabin in a small clearing that was overgrown with grass and weeds, but it was the three wooden crosses that had him stalling in his tracks.

Moving on autopilot, Ben stamped through the knee-high grass until he reached the crosses. Three in a neat row. No markings or names. Just three rustic crosses.

Ben went down on his knees and pressed his hands to the ground. He felt the surface, touched the wood where it had been driven in the ground.

Could his father and the others be here?

Could they have been here all along?

Reyna knelt beside him, put a hand on his arm. "It's time to call Sheriff Norwood."

3:00 p.m.

SHERIFF NORWOOD AND three of her deputies as well as the lead member of the county's crime scene investigation team had arrived and were going through the cabin and the area around it.

Reyna and Ben had been sequestered a safe distance from the structure. Norwood was not happy that they'd gone inside. But not going inside would have been impossible, even for Reyna. She glanced at Ben. He was tense. Ready to snap. She could understand why. If his father was buried here…had been for all these years…

He didn't want to tell his grandfather anything until they were certain. A good move, in Reyna's opinion. As hard as this was on Ben, it was even harder on the elder Kane.

The point that kept kicking around inside Rey's brain was the idea that Walls had basically sent them here. He had suggested they look at the Fuller property by the lake, and voilà, here was this shrine to the missing husbands. And grave markers. There was just no ignoring the idea that he might have known about this place. Whatever Norwood thought of the deputy, this was not something that could be easily overlooked. Walls had to have known or at the very least had some inkling.

"He knew." Ben turned to her with the words as if she had somehow telegraphed them to him. "This is no coincidence."

"We told Norwood the reason we came here," Reyna agreed. "She won't be able to ignore he had to know this was here."

Ben shook his head. "Why would he keep this from us all this time? What kind of man would do that?"

"One with something to hide," she warned.

Norwood exited the cabin and started in their direction.

"Let's see what she has to say now," he muttered.

"We're going to do some excavating back there. See what we find." She glanced back at the cabin. "There's no need for the two of you to hang around. This is going to take some time. If we find anything, I'll let you know."

"What about Deputy Walls?" Ben demanded, his voice taut with agitation.

"I've called him three times since you told me how you found this, but he's not answering. I've issued a BOLO for him, his private vehicle and his county SUV. We'll find him, and then we'll get some answers. Meanwhile, it would be best if you don't discuss this with anyone for now. We need to talk to your grandfather and to your mother," she said to Ben. "We need to find out what they knew before they hear about your finding it and our being here."

"They would have told me," Ben argued. "There is no way either of them knew about this."

Norwood nodded. "Maybe. But those photographs came from people close to those men. Either they were stolen from their homes or..." She exhaled a big breath. "You get where I'm going."

"I got it," Ben agreed.

"Call us," Reyna urged, "as soon as you find anything. It's been thirty years. They don't need to wait a minute longer than necessary."

Chapter Nine

Ben felt like he was in a sort of shock. He stared at the cup of coffee his grandfather had made for him. Somehow he'd lost interest, couldn't think about anything else. Finding that shrine to the Three…had emotions erupting inside him that he didn't fully understand. The anger and frustration he got. Thirty years was a long time to wait for the truth. But it was the other, the uncertainty, that he couldn't comprehend. The truth was what he'd waited his whole life to find, right?

Then why the hell did he suddenly feel like everything was about to change—and not for the better?

He'd tried calling his mother, and she wasn't answering. They'd dropped by her house and gotten no response there either. Her car was in the garage, but that didn't mean she was home. She could have gone to the city with a friend, one of the other widows. Frankly, they were the only friends he'd ever seen her do things with. Not so much in the past few years. If he looked long and hard at the situation, he would have to say that beyond Ms. Fuller and Ms. Evans, his mother had no actual friends. She went to church and did her shopping around town and was always friendly to everyone but never went to dinner or other outings with anyone or invited anyone to the house.

Growing up, he hadn't really noticed because the Widows had always been together. He'd had his grandfather and he'd had his friends from school. But looking back, he recognized that his mother had had a lonely existence beyond her association with the Widows. She never dated anyone. Never went on trips, cruises—nothing.

He tried calling her again. The call went directly to voice mail.

"She still not answering?" his grandfather asked. He pushed his own untouched cup of coffee aside.

Ben ended the call and tossed his cell onto the table. "Maybe she's with Sheriff Norwood. But the sheriff said she'd let me know when she spoke to her."

"She came here straightaway," his grandfather reminded him. "I'm sure she went in search of Lucinda immediately after speaking to me or maybe before."

"I suppose it's possible Norwood has spoken with her and Mom doesn't want to talk about it." His mother was like that—she didn't enjoy revisiting what had happened. Frankly, Ben was still stunned that she had opened up to Reyna as much as she had. For a little while she'd talked freely, and then she'd closed up once more. He just didn't get any of this.

He looked at his grandfather then. "How did we not know about the cabin?" Ben shook his head. "Ms. Fuller had to know. Gordon Walls sure seemed to know. He's fallen off the radar now too. Sheriff Norwood couldn't reach him."

"I wish I knew, son." Ward gave an affirming nod. "I

certainly had no idea. But we need to find out how that cabin came about. I'd say we need answers more than ever before."

Reyna walked into the room holding one of the old photo albums. She'd given Ben and his grandfather some privacy to discuss the find and how things had gone with Norwood. She hadn't exactly said that was what she was doing, but she'd wanted to look at photo albums again while they'd talked in the kitchen. Ben appreciated the space she'd given them. Not that he'd believed for one minute that his grandfather knew about that place by the lake. No way.

"I'm assuming," she said as she settled into one of the available chairs and placed the album on the table, "that all the teammates and the coach were questioned. Probably more than once."

"They were," Ward said. "Even though JR, Duke and Judson hadn't really stayed in contact with the others, every person they had known in high school, college and in their work lives was questioned. The football team in particular," he went on, "since those young men had all grown up here together. Most had moved to the city or surrounding area, but…" He made an aha face. "The reunion. Just a few months before the disappearance, JR attended his ten-year high school reunion. They all three did. I think the sheriff and the deputies investigating the disappearance hoped someone from the reunion would remember something one of them said."

"Did anything happen at the reunion that prompted the police to think this?" Reyna closed the photo album, her full attention on Ward now.

He frowned, struggling to remember probably. Ben had been a kid. He had forgotten all about the reunion until his grandfather had mentioned it. But now he vaguely recalled that there had been some disagreement between his dad and his mother about him not wanting to wear his team jersey.

"My parents argued about Dad's team jersey," Ben said, his mind still focused on thirty years ago. His mother had been furious, but Ben couldn't remember why. He could see her face…could see her clutching the jersey. The one—or one just like it—that hung in the cabin they had found. The memory had to mean something. His gut clenched. None of this could be coincidence. "I don't know if the argument was before or after the reunion."

"There was some argument at the reunion," Ward explained. His forehead furrowed as if he was working hard to recall some fact. "I remember now. One of the other guys who had played with JR and the others was bragging about how Coach Landon had insisted that his boy had that special something. The kid was going places. Anyway, Landon and Duke exchanged some heated words. If I'm remembering right, I think Coach Landon even left early that night."

Didn't make a lot of sense to Ben. "Duke didn't have any kids. I can't see him being jealous of what some guy said about his kid's performance on the team. There had to be something more than that, Pops."

Ward turned his hands up. "I'm just telling you how the story went as it made its way around town—at least, what I remember of it. Your daddy and your mama refused to talk about it, so I can't say anything with any measurable accuracy. The whole thing blew over." His gaze grew distant. "And then they were gone."

"We should talk to the coach," Reyna suggested.

"I'm not so sure that would be worth our time and

trouble," Ben explained. "Landon is wheelchair bound and a bit of a shut-in. Who knows how his memory is?"

"It's not like we're accomplishing anything sitting around here waiting," Reyna contended.

"She's right," his grandfather said. "The two of you should see what Landon can recall. I'll be here if you need backup." He chuckled. "Plus, I'll go around and check on your mama. Make sure she's okay—assuming I can find her."

Ben looked to Reyna. "Let's do it."

Landon Residence
Harding Drive
6:15 p.m.

THE LONGTIME FOOTBALL coach of Whispering Winds had retired just over twenty-nine years ago, after his home had burned to the ground. An electrical issue had started the fire, according to the articles Reyna had found on the internet. The man had been forced to jump from a second-story window to escape the fire. The injuries he'd sustained had been the reason he was wheelchair bound.

Reyna had called Landon and laid it on a little thick about needing to interview him for her next book. She'd played to his ego—considering everything she'd read from his heyday in coaching, the man appeared to have had a rather large one. No surprise there. It took a lot of ego for a man to take a bunch of kids, shape them into a team and then ensure they won more often than not.

Whatever his formula, it had been a successful one.

According to one article written a couple of years ago about the high school football team, they hadn't experienced a true winning streak since Landon had been forced to retire. His record of victories remained unbroken.

Reyna wasn't really interested in his coaching prowess. She wanted to understand the Three better from the perspective of a man who had known them well and who wasn't connected by blood or marriage. More importantly, she wanted to know why he and Duke Fuller had exchanged heated words at the ten-year reunion.

Ben parked in front of a small cottage along a short street lined with similar little cottages. Other than color, they all looked basically alike. Small. Neat and colorful enough to have been on a beach in Florida.

"I'm assuming we shouldn't mention the cabin," Ben said as they walked toward the man's door.

"Agreed." Reyna paused before reaching the entrance. She'd spotted the doorbell camera, which meant once near the door, the man inside could most likely see and hear them. "I'll take the lead, if that's okay with you. You've seen the man around. You certainly know him better than I do. I'd like you to watch him closely. When we're done, tell me if you think he was being completely honest with his answers or if anything I ask affects his emotions."

Ben nodded. "I can do that."

She walked the remaining steps to the door and knocked. The knob turned and the door opened. Coach Wade Landon rolled backward in his wheelchair.

"Saw the two of you on my doorbell camera. Come on in."

"Thank you for making the time to see us," Reyna said. She gestured to Ben as he closed the door. "I'm sure you know Ben Kane. He has kindly agreed to show me around town and introduce me to the folks."

"I sure do. His daddy was the best running back we ever had."

Ben smiled, though it wasn't one of his full-blown charmers. Reyna had come to appreciate his genuine smiles probably more than she should have.

He was a nice man. Handsome. Kind. How was it she'd never been lucky enough to meet a guy like him in her real life? Reyna banished the idea. This was real life. Just not hers. Well, it sort of was. This was her work.

"The living room is straight through here," Landon said as he turned his wheelchair around in the relatively wide entrance hall and headed toward the back of the cottage.

Reyna exchanged a look with Ben before following. She had a feeling this investigation was beginning to get to him in a way he hadn't expected. She wished it wasn't necessary to put him through these steps. But her first obligation was to Eudora.

The idea sat like a stone in her stomach.

Was it really?

Or was her first obligation to finding the truth for all concerned?

That conclusion seemed to suggest she had some special superpower that she didn't. All she could hope for was to dig around enough and turn over all the necessary rocks and maybe find something no one else had.

Like that cabin.

The realization still stunned her. Someone had built what could only be called a shrine to the Three. On Fuller property, no less.

Who? Why? When? How had the Fullers not known?

Then again, maybe they did.

Either way, Reyna wanted to find those answers. She'd wanted to track down Ms. Fuller and try again for an interview, but the discovery of the cabin had waylaid that possibility. The sheriff wanted to talk to her and to Ms. Evans first—the same as they had Ward and Lucinda. Now any additional interviews of the Widows were postponed until after the official notification and questioning was done.

"Sit anywhere you like," Landon said as he parked next to a table that was clearly where he spent a good deal of his time. A cell phone lay on the table. Next to that was a pair of glasses and, most important of all, the television remote.

"Coach," Reyna said as she settled on the sofa, "tell us about the Three around the time of the ten-year high school reunion."

He looked surprised at her question. "We mostly lost touch after high school," he said, choosing his words carefully. "I knew them better back in those days." He propped a smile into place, but it wasn't the same broad, open one he'd been wearing when he'd answered the door.

"They were good students," Reyna suggested. "Good team players. You had high hopes for Duke Fuller."

He nodded, lips in a tight line. "I did. Duke could have gone pro. Instead, he blew off his college opportunity and, well...you know."

"There was trouble at the reunion," Reyna ventured. "An argument broke out."

If possible, the man's face paled more so than it already was. He clearly didn't leave the house much.

"I had left by then." He shrugged. "Reunions are for the students. Some of us showed up for the first hour or so. It's expected."

Ben spoke up. "I was told that Duke Fuller was upset by something one of his old classmates said about his son and you."

A slow, stiff nod from Landon. "Oh, yes. I remember something about that." He shrugged. "Bradley Carson. His son, Jesse, had a very promising ability. Just a natural. I know a good player when I see one. I was lucky to be able to get the boy started when he was just a tyke in peewee football. I sort of recruited him. You may not be aware, but I helped out with the local peewee team. It was a pleasure to volunteer my time with those kids. Anyway, Duke and Carson had words that night. I don't know if what was said somehow made Duke jealous or what. The behavior was completely unexpected and actually very much out of character for him. That's all I know."

"Why would Duke," Reyna ventured, "have an issue with your praise of someone else's child? It just seems strange since he had no children. Why do you suppose he overreacted?"

Landon shrugged again. "Who knows? I think he'd been drinking, and maybe it bothered him that I had said the same things about him in his playing days, but he threw the opportunity away. The truth is I can't really say. I wasn't there at that point."

"What made you think he'd been drinking?" Ben asked.

More shrugging from Landon. "His words were slurred early on—before I left. He was kind of rude to me and my wife, if I'm being totally honest. Duke could be mean like that. As for why he would be jealous of Carson's kid, maybe it was about you." His gaze settled on Ben. "Your daddy didn't want you to play. Maybe Duke thought you should have and that you'd have been better than Jesse. I guess we'll never know."

"That's so strange," Reyna said. "Everyone I've interviewed said it was you who had that heated exchange with Duke."

The coach shook his head. "I mean, we talked, but I wouldn't call it heated. Like I said, my wife and I left."

"Only a few days after the reunion, your wife had her accident," Reyna said, moving on.

His face turned sad. "She did. Got up in the middle of the night to go downstairs for a glass of water and fell. It was the worst night of my life."

"Then the Three disappeared, and no one's life was the same," Ben said.

Landon nodded but kept his attention on his hands, which were clasped in his lap.

When neither man spoke for a bit, Reyna said, "The fire was nearly a year later."

Landon's gaze lifted to hers. "After my wife died, at least I still had my work, but then I lost that too."

"The report," she went on, "showed that you woke up to the house in flames and your only option to save yourself was to jump out a second-story window."

"I couldn't get down the stairs." He shuddered. "The smoke was so thick I could barely breathe. It was *go out the window or die.*"

"The fire marshal's report showed there were no accelerants of any sort in the house. The fire started and just kept going. No alarms notified the fire department, and your house was a fair distance from any others on the street."

"With me asleep—my neighbors too—no one noticed until it was too late."

"Your body was bruised, and there were a good many wounds," she noted, recalling all that she'd read when digging around in his past.

"My memories of that night are scattered, fuzzy, but the docs said I probably bounced off the side of the house and the porch roof. I was meaning to jump to the porch roof and then to the ground, but that didn't work out." He gestured to his chair. "All this damage occurred in that sudden stop when I hit the ground."

"It was a miracle you survived," she agreed.

He nodded.

"Had you been drinking that night?" she asked. "Maybe taken sleeping pills?" One article she'd read suggested he may have taken sleep medication, but the reporter had only been speculating.

"I don't drink," he said quickly. "Never have. I had sleeping pills. They weren't mine—they were my wife's. I may have taken one. I really don't remember. My wife always took them. I had trouble sleeping after she was gone."

"Is there anything at all," Reyna said, "you recall about the Three that might help us in our search for answers about their disappearance?"

He moved his head slowly from side to side. "I wish there was. They were good kids who grew up to be good men. It's a darn shame the police or the FBI have never figured out what happened to them."

Reyna couldn't agree more. It was a shame. The worst part was that someone somewhere—more than likely right here in Whispering Winds—knew exactly what had happened.

Maybe even this man who had known them so well. Who could say? The one thing Reyna suspected was without doubt correct was that he was not being completely honest.

As she and Ben walked back to his truck, she asked, "What were your impressions in there?"

Ben opened her door and then looked her straight in the eyes. "He was lying."

Exactly what Reyna had thought.

The Jewel Bed & Breakfast
Main Street
7:00 p.m.

THE CLEANUP CREW had done a spectacular job on the downstairs areas. Thankfully the smoke damage was minimal there. The bigger problem was in the room that had been Reyna's. There was fire, smoke and water destruction. The second-floor rooms would need a thorough and specific cleaning to remedy the smoke odor. But for the most part, the actual mess was confined to the one room.

"I'm so glad this isn't as bad as we feared," Reyna said to the woman who had become a fast friend.

"You and me both." Birdie nodded. "I'm extra grateful that it didn't happen at night while we were all sleeping."

The way it had for Coach Landon. He was lucky to be alive. Reyna thought of the wheelchair and wondered if there were times when he didn't feel so lucky.

Ben had gotten a call and was pacing the lobby. Birdie had ushered Reyna to the small parlor in her private quarters. The rooms were lovely and oh so vintage, with lots of color and sparkle, just like the woman.

"It's a little late for tea," she said. "Would you like a drink of something stronger?"

Reyna hesitated only a second. Then she nodded. "You know, I think I would love something stronger."

While Birdie prepared their drinks, Reyna wandered around her parlor and admired all the lovely framed photographs. So many were of her and Eudora. Clearly, they had been dear friends for a very long time.

On the mantel was a photo taken at the beach what appeared to be maybe fifty years ago. The intimate moment snagged and held Rey's attention. The two were holding hands. But that wasn't the thing… The thing was the way they looked at each other over their cocktail glasses.

Reyna's breath caught ever so slightly, and her heart started to pound.

"Here we go."

She set the photograph back in its place on the mantel and accepted the shot glass of something that looked and smelled quite strong.

"Bottoms up," Birdie said with a wink.

They turned up their glasses at the same time. The sweet burn rushed down Reyna's throat, and she barely stifled a cough.

"Oh, that had some heat to it." She laughed. "But it was certainly good."

Birdie winked. "It gets better."

Reyna gestured to the photograph. "You and Eudora love each other."

Birdie's gaze rested on the photograph. "We always have. Some days she doesn't remember, but I will cherish our every memory for the rest of my life."

"In love," Reyna clarified. "The two of you are a couple."

Birdie smiled. "In some places." She gestured to the photo. "The way we were in that shot in Cancún. But not here. Never here."

Reyna scoffed. "Please, there is no reason for you two to hide the way you feel. The world has changed."

She nodded. "It has, but sometimes in small towns it's easier to go with the way things have always been. Fifty-five years ago she was a schoolteacher and I was a wanderer trying to find my place. The way we found each other and lived our lives never mattered as long as we were together. We were happy and loved each other until I could no longer properly take care of Eudora at home.

Then she insisted I take her to the center, and I visit her every chance I get. We speak by phone every night that she's lucid enough to do so." The older woman took a deep breath. "She accuses me of not coming to see her anymore, but it's only because she doesn't remember I was there." She smiled sadly as she touched the faces in the treasured photo. "She will live in my heart just like this forever."

"I hope the two of you will allow me to find a way to incorporate your beautiful secret into her story."

"That is entirely up to Dory."

"I wish your friends in the community could have known and celebrated with you." Reyna sensed no resentment in Birdie.

"The only person who ever knew was Father Cullen." She laughed. "He knows everyone's secrets. Dory and I always called him the secret keeper." She shrugged. "I had moments when I was certain Ward Kane knew, but if he did he never said a word."

Reyna hugged her as firmly as she dared. The woman was eighty, after all. "Thank you for sharing your secret with me."

Later, Birdie walked Reyna and Ben to the porch and waved as they drove away.

"She's such a lovely woman," Reyna said, enthralled with the love story of Birdie and Eudora. "I want to be so calm and accepting. To live the life I have and not wait for some other thing to happen or come along."

Ben laughed. "I think you're doing just fine on the path you're traveling."

She laughed too. "I'll take that as a huge compliment, Mr. Kane."

"That was Sheriff Norwood who called. They found nothing buried in the back of the cabin. They're still trying to collect and prepare all the fingerprints for running through the system. A lot of local folks provided their prints thirty years ago, so she'll compare all those. She still hasn't been able to track down Mom. I tried calling her and it just goes to voice mail."

"That's so frustrating." Reyna had really hoped there would be something at the cabin. She wasn't really surprised his mother was avoiding the news. She felt sure Ben wasn't surprised either. As for the lack of discovery at the cabin, Reyna wasn't calling it done yet. There had to be answers they could find. She refused to accept any other conclusion. And that cabin was connected somehow. "They could still find something useful. We should keep the faith until there are no other options. Forensics can do magic these days."

Ben parked in the driveway at his home. The lights downstairs were on, except for the one on the east end that was in Mr. Kane's bedroom.

They sat in the dark silence for a bit. Reyna was waiting for Ben to make a move toward getting out of the truck. Maybe he was waiting for the same. Whatever the case, the two of them just sitting there quietly felt right for now.

Finally, she decided to mention, "Birdie said Father Cullen knew everyone's secrets. She and Eudora called him the secret keeper."

Ben chuckled softly. "Makes sense."

She turned to him. "This has been a really tough day for you. I'm sorry. I feel a little like it's my fault."

He shifted in his seat to face her. "No. It's not your fault. It just is. Is the fact that you're here poking around making things happen? It seems so. Are those things uncomfortable? A little. But they need to happen. We need the truth."

She put her hand on his arm, resisted a shiver at the tingle that fired where their skin touched. "We're going to find the answers. I won't stop until I do or you run me off."

He took her hand in his and traced her fingers with his own. "I don't think I could bring myself to run you off under any circumstances."

She laughed, the sound nervous. "Maybe you just need more time in the same house with me. I'm used to doing things my own way. I can be—"

Before she could finish, his mouth had closed over hers, and then he pulled back as if asking permission. She nodded, and he resumed. The kiss was soft and deep and over far too quickly.

"I probably should have warned you that I'd been dying to do that since the first time I laid eyes on you."

Her nerves were jangling and her body was shaking, but she wasn't ready to run... She was ready for more.

"Maybe you can do it again, just to be sure you scratched that itch."

He kissed her again, and this time it went on and on.

Chapter Ten

Ben opened his eyes and stared at the woman in bed next to him.

He had not seen that one coming. He'd thought about it, for sure, but he hadn't figured out whether she was drawn to him the way he was to her.

He wanted to touch her so badly…run his hands through that mass of red hair. It was spread across the white pillowcase like flames. Those freckles he'd noticed the first time he'd seen her seemed to become more vivid when she was alive with desire the way she had been last night. He'd tried kissing each one but his lips had just kept finding their way to her mouth, and then they'd gotten lost in the fever again.

Apparently, a guy never got too mature to be blown away by a woman's body…by her touch…her scent…and the way she looked at him. Like he was all she had ever wanted.

Whoa. He had to slow it down here. This was no romance movie—this was real life, and they were in the middle of a major mess that had roots deep in his life.

He doubted either of them would feel the same when the tension of finding answers was past.

His gaze flowed over the shape of her beneath that sheet, and his mouth went dry. Right now he couldn't see ever feeling anything less than a frantic need to touch her.

Her eyes fluttered open, and that brilliant green took his breath.

God, she was beautiful.

"Morning," he murmured.

"Morning." She smiled. "I think I may have lost my objectivity last night."

He grinned. "Just a little bit, maybe."

He'd lost his mind, and he'd loved every single minute of it.

"Will you be comfortable with me staying here after this?" she asked, her eyes searching his face for reaction.

He traced her cheek with his fingers, swept a lock of hair back. "I won't be comfortable with you anywhere else."

"Good." She smiled again. "I don't know about you, but I'm absolutely starving."

"As it happens," he said, bracing his elbow on his pillow and his head in his hand, "I am a very good cook. My pops taught me how to fend for myself."

"That means—" she sat up "—that I get the shower first."

She jumped out of bed and rushed toward the bathroom, laughing and pulling the sheet around her as she went, leaving him buck naked on the bed. He liked her laugh too. She might have gotten first dibs on his shower, but there was another one downstairs. Even a few steps behind, he would still finish first and have bacon cooking in a pan when she appeared in the kitchen.

HALF AN HOUR later Ben had the bacon frying and the biscuits in the oven. Making biscuits from scratch was one
culinary feat he had not mastered. In an effort to avoid
early morning disasters, his grandfather had shared his
biscuit-making secret—the frozen ones could be just as
good with the right amount of butter slathered on.

Ben frowned. Speaking of which, where was the guy?
He was usually up before Ben. He tossed the oven mitt
aside and would have headed to his grandfather's bedroom, but he spotted a sticky note on the back-door glass,
just barely visible beyond the curtain. When Ben had been
in high school, his grandfather had stuck notes on the door
glass to ensure he'd seen them before leaving for the day.
If Ben overslept, he might not go to the coffee maker or
the fridge, but he had to walk out the door.

Checking on a few things. See you tonight.

Ben frowned. Usually his grandfather talked to him
about his plans for the day. Maybe the news about the cabin
had upset him more than Ben had realized. He should have
gone to his room and checked on him last night.

But he'd been too busy with...

"Damn." He tossed the note onto the counter and went
back to the stove to turn the bacon.

"Smells great." Reyna walked into the kitchen in borrowed jeans that fit her as if she'd had them made just for
her and one of Birdie's flashy, low-cut shirts hugging her
breasts—body.

"Coffee's ready." He forced his attention back on the
frying pan. "The rest will be in about two minutes."

"Sheriff Norwood called me." She paused at the coffee maker and grabbed the mug Ben had set out for her.

"She needs my fingerprints to rule me out of the dozens her team has lifted."

"We can go by the substation first thing," he said. Norwood would likely want Reyna's prints sooner rather than later.

"Great." She savored her coffee for a moment. "I thought we might stop by the cemetery, if you're comfortable with that."

The idea gave him pause, but he pushed through it. "We can do that."

His father and his friends had been buried in the Whispering Winds cemetery, the one that was as old as the town. Of course, there had been no bodies in their coffins, only a few pieces of memorabilia. The families hadn't even declared them dead until a few years ago. No one had wanted to take that step.

It wasn't until Duke Fuller's grandfather had passed away that the family attorney had said they'd needed to do this right—the grandfather's property could not pass down to Ms. Fuller until Duke had been declared dead. The same with Judson Evans, except his mother had still been alive and she hadn't really wanted to do it. But when Lucinda had joined the *let's get it over with* side, Ms. Evans had gone along.

Putting aside the painful thoughts, he and Reyna ate, talked, laughed. It was comfortable. Surprisingly so. Ben had expected the morning after to be awkward, but Reyna didn't let that happen. Just something else he liked about her.

He wondered if she would think about him after she was gone. She had a life, a job. She would be getting back to all that. This was just a layover for research.

But it sure felt like more to him. Then again, he was pretty rusty at this romance thing.

Whispering Winds Cemetery
9:00 a.m.

REYNA SAT ON the bench that had been installed by the high school alumni in memory of the three classmates who had vanished.

The three headstones were the same. Black marble with silver etching revealing the names, dates of birth and death—disappearance, actually—as well as epitaphs for the memory of those entombed there, because memory was all they'd had to bury. The idea that none of the three families had been in a hurry to take this legal step seemed to indicate they wanted nothing that might feel like they were gaining from the deaths. No death benefits of any sort, including insurance. They wanted to go on pretending that the three men might come back one day.

Could Reyna say with absolute certainty that the Three were dead? Of course she couldn't. But it had been thirty years without a trace. The odds were against them being alive.

That said, it did happen. Most of those cases involved people who didn't want to be found. Nothing Reyna had uncovered suggested that was the case with the Three.

Ben sat down beside her. "I keep seeing those handmade crosses, and I can't help wondering who put them there. More importantly, why?" He gestured to the markers in front of them. "This was done nearly a decade ago. I mean, I guess it's possible what was done at that cabin goes back further than ten years. Forensics is working on putting some dates together, according to Norwood."

In the past three days, Reyna had learned a great deal about the people left behind, but she hadn't learned as much about the Three—the men who had actually disappeared.

"Tell me about your father." She turned to Ben and studied his handsome profile. He looked so very much like the photos of his father. If the man was anything like this one, he had been a great guy.

"He was always smiling. He…" Ben smiled, and Reyna's heart stumbled. "He had this laugh, kind of a low rumble that was contagious. Everyone—and I mean everyone— liked him. I honestly have never met anyone who didn't like him. If they knew him, they liked him."

"Do you ever remember him and your mother fighting?"

Ben shook his head. "Never. I mean, I'm sure they did, but they kept it private. My mom has never bad-mouthed him. I'd think by now if he'd ever given her any trouble I would have heard about it." He frowned. "But there was something around the time of the reunion that caused a disagreement. That meeting with the coach jarred the hint of a memory, but I haven't been able to grasp it yet."

"I think it's a reasonable assumption that your parents were happy. What about his relationship with his friends Duke and Judson? Any talk of trouble between them?" There was nothing in the many, many interviews and statements floating out there in cyberspace. But put three guys together playing sports and dating, it made sense that they wouldn't always see eye to eye.

"Pops told me once that the three of them used to work out any issues in the woods."

"In the woods?"

He nodded. "They would take off in different directions and run as long and hard as they could. When they couldn't run any further, they had to stop and find their way back to each other. It gave them time to think about what was real, distance to give them perspective, and the hard run drained the adrenaline. By the time they found each other, whatever the trouble had been, it didn't matter anymore."

What an ingenious idea. "Your grandfather is brilliant."

"He is. He thinks things through. Doesn't take sides."

"Have you spoken to him this morning?"

Ben shook his head. "He'd already left when I got downstairs. I'm a little worried. He doesn't usually avoid me."

Reyna was really sorry to hear this. "I'm certain it's not really about avoiding you. He may just need to work this for himself." She considered what she'd learned from the coach and the trouble that had cropped up at the ten-year reunion. "Has he ever mentioned anything about Coach Landon? Likes, dislikes? Doubts?"

"Pops has never talked about him in particular. In my experience, if he has nothing to say about someone, then he doesn't like them very much."

Made sense to Reyna. "I wish we had more information about what happened at the class reunion." That was the biggest hole in the puzzle she was putting together.

"I was thinking about what Coach suggested was the reason for the argument that night," Ben said. "You know, the Jesse Carson thing. Jesse was, like, three years older than me, but I vaguely remember him because he was the only boy born to anyone on the team besides me. All the others who grew up, got married and had children had girls." He put up his hands. "Don't ask why that particular fact occurred to me, but it did."

"We need to find out what that disagreement was about," Reyna pointed out. "It suddenly seems significant."

"Well, we could try talking to Ms. Fuller again," Ben offered. "We kind of skipped over that second attempt with all that's happened."

"I think that's a great idea." She stood. Surely the sheriff had spoken to Fuller by now. "Let's go for a cold call and see what kind of reaction we get."

Fuller Residence
Hawk's Way
10:30 a.m.

BEN DECIDED DEIDRE FULLER was hiding from them. Her garage was closed and without windows, leaving no way to know if her car was there. But she wasn't answering the door or her cell phone.

"Well," Reyna announced, "we tried."

Ben surveyed the house and yard. "We'll try again later."

He was not giving up until he talked to her about the things they had learned.

They had just reached his truck when another vehicle arrived. Truck. White. Tinted windows. Newer than Ben's. When the driver's-side door opened and a man emerged, Ben recognized him. Jesse Carson. Talk about a bizarre coincidence. Jesse and his family had moved to Nashville eons ago. Maybe six months or so after the Three had disappeared. It wasn't until this moment—after learning about the disagreement at the reunion—that their move seemed in any way relevant.

But that could very well be wishful thinking.

"Kane," the other man said as he strode toward Ben. "I haven't seen you since— God, I don't even know when." He thrust out his hand, glanced at Reyna as he did so.

Ben gave his hand a shake. "It's been a while, for sure."

He motioned toward the house. "I hope Ms. Fuller is in a good mood. I need to talk to her about her financial portfolio, and unfortunately none of it's good."

"You still working for that big-time wealth-building company?" Now that portfolios were mentioned, Ben vaguely remembered hearing about Carson winning some sort of award in the world of finance.

"I do, but it's a struggle in this economy."

"We knocked on her door, but there's no answer," Ben explained. "She's either out or avoiding us."

Jesse glanced at Reyna for the second time.

Ben gave himself a mental kick. "Sorry. This is Reyna Hart." He gestured to Jesse. "Jesse Carson." He gave her a look that said *you know the one*. "His father was on the team with the Three."

"Nice to meet you." Reyna shook his hand. "You played football around here too?"

"When I was just a little kid. We moved to Nashville when I was ten." He frowned then. "Now, why would someone as nice as Ms. Fuller be avoiding the two of you?"

"My bad." Ben explained, "Reyna and I are looking into the disappearance of the Three. We're actually making a little headway."

"No kidding," Jesse said. "Wow. It's crazy that thirty years later we still don't know what happened. My dad still talks about them."

"For sure," Ben agreed.

"Does your father ever talk about what happened?" Reyna asked.

Jesse turned to her. "I mean, he's talked about it from time to time, but not so much, really. Nothing in particular that I remember. Wait." He held up a hand. "There was this one thing I remember vividly. I guess I was, like, ten—it was just before we moved, in fact. Coach Landon had handpicked me from the peewee team to start on the middle school team a year early. I was super excited. It was a big deal to get picked for the team early by one of the most popular coaches in the state."

Ben frowned. "I don't remember you playing on the middle school team."

"I didn't. My dad pitched a heck of a fit. My mother would never tell me the details. I was pretty upset. But my parents just kept saying they didn't want me to play for Landon. So I didn't. In fact, we moved right around that same time—right after your dad and the others disappeared." He frowned. "Or maybe right before. Man, thirty years. I feel old now."

"I'm sure they had a good reason for not wanting you to play," Reyna offered, hoping to prompt more from him.

"Guess so." Jesse looked from her to Ben. "Well, it was good to see you, but I have to run. If you see Ms. Fuller, tell her I stopped by." He shook his head. "She's the only client I have in this neck of the woods, but Dad insisted I take her on as a client. I guess he thought she might need a trustworthy adviser. He said he owed her a big favor."

"Will do," Ben said. "It was good to see you too."

When Jesse had driven away and Ben and Reyna had climbed into his truck, she said, "Duke, your father and Judson played football their entire school careers, for Coach Landon. Why the explosion when he learned a teammate's son—the only son born to the group—was going to follow in their footsteps?"

"No idea." Ben shrugged. "It makes no sense at all."

"Exactly," Reyna confirmed. "We should ask Landon. Maybe if we tell him we spoke to Jesse Carson he'll be more forthcoming."

"Can't hurt to try."

As Ben headed in the direction of the coach's home, Reyna pulled her cell phone from her pocket to answer an incoming call. She listened for half a minute and then promised the caller she would be right there.

When she'd disconnected, she turned to Ben. "I have to get to Eudora. Can you take me back to get my SUV?"

"No need." He sent her a sidelong look. "I'll take you."

The only thing that worried him more than the idea that at some point Reyna would leave was the notion of letting her out of his sight until he had no other choice.

The Light Memory Care Center
Lantern Pointe
Chattanooga
Noon

WHEN THEY REACHED Eudora's room, Rey's heart surged into her throat. She looked so frail…so pale.

As they'd headed out of Whispering Winds, Reyna had somehow had the presence of mind to ask Ben to go by the Jewel and pick up Birdie. The three of them had ridden in silence the entire half hour it had taken to reach the facility.

Reyna waited for Birdie to approach Eudora first. The worry on her face hurt to watch. She took Eudora's hand in her own, and the frail woman's eyes fluttered open.

"My sweet Dory, tell me you're staying with me, please."

Eudora's nearly translucent fingers curled around Birdie's. "I'll always be with you, Bird. I'm just tired now, and I need to rest."

The words gored Reyna. Eudora had never talked so negatively about hanging in there.

"I brought friends to see you," Birdie said. She motioned for Reyna and Ben to join her. "Reyna is with me. She's working on the story, just like you wanted."

"Reyna." The elderly woman's eyes lit just a little. "I'm so glad you came. I need to tell you something, dear. It's very important."

"I'm listening, Eudora," Reyna assured her.

"I should have told you they would try to stop you. Birdie told me the things they've done."

"Who are *they*, Eudora?" Reyna asked. "I can't protect myself if I don't know who they are."

Eudora's expression fell. She looked beyond Reyna, and her frown deepened. "JR?"

Reyna's heart stumbled. She thought Ben was his father. "Eudora, it's—"

Eudora waved her off with one feeble hand. "Come closer, JR," she ordered, her voice stronger than before.

Ben moved closer. "Ms. Eudora, you're sounding stronger."

"JR, you need to tell that wife of yours that I'm onto her. I know what she did, and I fear she's in danger because of it."

He exchanged a look with Reyna. "Yes, ma'am, I'll tell her."

Eudora turned back to Reyna. She blinked slowly. "Are you listening, dear?"

"I am, but you never told me who I should be afraid of."

"Good gracious, have you not been hearing me? The Widows. You have to be careful because they will try to stop you."

Chapter Eleven

The Jewel Bed & Breakfast
Whispering Winds
3:30 p.m.

"I should walk you in," Ben suggested.

Birdie waved him off. "I'll be fine." She swiped at her eyes. "Thank you so much," she said to Reyna, "to both of you, for taking me with you."

Reyna reached for her hand, gave it a squeeze. "I wouldn't have left you out for the world."

"We'll just hang around and make sure you get inside okay," Ben said, determined to see that the lady made it into her bed-and-breakfast safely.

Birdie waved as she traveled the cobblestone path. She climbed the steps and crossed the porch. She unlocked the door—Sheriff Norwood had convinced her it was best—and stepped inside.

When the door had closed behind her, Reyna turned to Ben. "We need to find your grandfather and see if he can make sense of what Eudora said about your mother and the Widows and anything at all he remembers about the Carson family's abrupt move."

Ben's face told the story of the emotions whirling inside

him. They had tried repeatedly to reach his grandfather as well as his mother, and neither was answering their calls.

"Part of me wants to go to my mother's house and demand answers. The other part is still worried about Pops's early morning disappearing act. Something is going on with that man. He never does this kind of thing."

"Let's see if he's back home now." Reyna reached for the truck door, but Ben got it first. He opened the door for her.

"Thanks." She smiled when he lingered before closing the door. "Is there something you need to say?"

He stared at the sidewalk a moment. "I don't understand what's going on around here right now, but if it all means the truth is finally coming to the surface—I'm glad." His gaze connected with hers then. "And I'm glad you're part of it."

She laughed softly. "Don't go getting all sappy on me, Mr. Kane. We're not finished yet."

He smiled, then hustled around the hood to climb behind the steering wheel.

Reyna kept her biggest concern to herself. Whatever truth or part of the story that was coming next might not be anything Ben wanted to know. If that turned out to be the case, he likely would wish he'd never laid eyes on her.

The latter was the part that worried Reyna the most.

Kane Residence
Lula Lake Lane
4:00 p.m.

THE HOUSE LOOKED exactly as they'd left it. Ward Kane's truck was still gone. No new note from him on the counter or the door. No indication he'd been back.

Reyna watched Ben struggle with what to do next. The worry on his face had her wishing there was more she could do beyond offering moral support.

"Why don't you call your mom again, leave a message asking if she's seen or spoken to Ward. Maybe she'll call you back if she realizes you're worried about your grandfather. I'll call Birdie and ask her to check around with mutual friends. This is a small town. Someone must have seen or heard from one or both of them today."

Unless they don't want to be heard from.

Reyna kept that part to herself. Something else Ben didn't need to hear.

She stepped into the front hall to make her call and to give Ben some privacy for calling his mother.

Birdie's cell went to voice mail, so Reyna called the bed-and-breakfast number. When it went to voice mail as well, she left a message.

"Hey, Birdie, Ward Kane is still not home, and he hasn't called. Ben is worried about him. We haven't been able to reach Lucinda either. Can you check with friends and see if anyone has spoken to or seen them today? Thanks."

Reyna wandered to the parlor and walked around the room, admiring the many family photos. The family looked so happy in those photos. There were so many of JR growing up and plenty more of him and his young family. Ward's wife had been a beautiful woman. There were lots of photos of her and Ward when they'd been younger.

Where were the photos of JR and his football team? The jersey he'd worn had been hanging in that cabin, so it had been kept all those years. And what about photos of him with his two best friends?

Reyna made her way back to the front hall and surveyed the photos there. No team photos. No photos of JR and his friends.

She climbed the stairs, scanning the tread-to-ceiling framed photos hanging there as well. Again, there were none of what she was looking for. Upstairs, she went to the guest room where she was supposed to sleep. She smiled. She kind of liked Ben's bed better. No photos of the team or friends there either. The final room upstairs was Ben's. The door was open, so she went inside. It wasn't like she hadn't been in there before—though she hadn't been looking at photos, for sure. She checked all the ones hanging on the wall, then the ones placed about the room on the bureau and the dresser. There was a gorgeous photo of Ben with his parents when he'd been maybe five or six.

"Reyna!"

She jumped as if he'd caught her snooping. "Coming!"

He waited at the bottom of the stairs.

"Did you find him?" She hurried down, hopeful that Ward was home and okay.

Ben shook his head. "His phone goes straight to voice mail now, and so does Mom's. I tried her house phone too, and she's not picking up."

"Should we drive over?"

"The sheriff is going to drive by. If she's avoiding the two of us, it won't do me any good to go over there. Maybe if our poking around in the past is the issue, she'll respond to the sheriff."

Reyna frowned at the idea. "I really hope my being here and doing the research I'm doing hasn't upset your family." She rolled her eyes and gave herself a mental kick. "Well, that was a ridiculous statement. How could it not?"

"Reyna." He took her by the hand and pulled her down

to sit on the third step with him. "Pops wanted this. He wanted you to help him find what no one else had—actual answers. I, unknown to him, was starting my own dig into the past. So nothing you've done has caused anything that wasn't already going to happen."

She felt a bit of relief at his words. The thought that she might have disturbed so many lives wasn't an easy one to swallow. But he made sense. Still, there was that nagging question of who had reacted in such an extreme manner, with her damaged tire, the fire and that note. The answer might prove more painful than the not knowing.

The fact that Eudora had warned her about the Widows was eye-opening. Would they have hidden the truth all these years? Sadly, it seemed all too possible.

"Thanks. That makes me feel a lot better about my part in this." Another frown tugged at her brow. "What did the sheriff say about Ward still not being home?"

"He's a grown man with no known health issues, so we have to wait twenty-four hours. If he doesn't show by then, she can officially get involved. Driving by my mom's house is a simpler issue. It falls under a welfare check. Not that Mom would appreciate the gesture."

Reyna laughed. "I'm sure she would not. But it's the thought that counts."

He braced his elbows on his knees, hands between his legs, and turned to her, putting them almost nose to nose. Reyna smiled. She really, really liked his eyes. His face. The rest of him.

"What're you thinking?" He shrugged half-heartedly. "About all this, I mean."

Focus back on the research, Reyna.

"I think that a lot of people know a little something. Maybe each one believes their particular fragment doesn't matter in the grand scheme of things. But if we can get them talking openly, we might make some headway. In any puzzle, every little piece matters."

"What about the fire and your tire and that warning?" He shook his head. "I swear I've never known folks around here to be so bullheaded."

"The unknown is scary. Change is scary to some." Reyna considered the people she had met. "Sometimes it's easier to stick with the known, with the routine. Then you don't have to wonder what will happen if anything or everything changes."

He held her gaze for a long time before he finally responded. "You're right. For a year now, I've been pretending what happened between me and my ex-fiancée didn't matter. Was no big deal. But it did matter, and it was a big deal. But I'm okay with that. I'm beyond it—have been, actually. The trouble was I was holding myself back."

They had talked last night about prior relationships. Reyna had confessed to never having had a serious one. And though Ben had been engaged, he had realized over the past year that what he'd felt had not been the deep kind of love he'd hoped for. He'd been reluctant to try again.

"I was afraid, as you say," he admitted now, "of what moving on might look like." He laughed softly. "But now I know exactly what I want looks like, and I can't wait to see more."

Her heart nearly stopped as the meaning of his heart-felt words sank in. "I'm right there with you. Ready to see what could happen next."

Reyna watched him closing that tiny distance between them, felt his lips press against hers. Smiling, she closed her eyes and melted into the kiss.

His fingers forked into her hair. Reyna rested her forehead against his face. The feel of his afternoon stubble and the ridges and planes of his handsome face had tingles firing through her.

A knock on the door had them jumping apart.

Ben shot up to answer it. Reyna took a breath and a little more time getting up. She braced a hand on the newel-post since her head was still spinning.

"Sheriff Norwood."

Beyond Ben's shoulder, Reyna spotted the sheriff at the door. Her heart took a dive, and she hurried to join him.

"Is everything okay?" he asked.

"Maybe," Norwood said with a glance around the yard and driveway. "You mind if I come in for a minute?"

"Course not." Ben opened the door wider. "Come on in."

Reyna hoped this was not going to be worse news.

"I stopped by Lucinda's house, and there was no answer."

"I appreciate you stopping by," Ben assured her. "She may have gone to the city for a day of shopping. She doesn't always keep me up to speed on her agenda, but with what's been happening, I can't help but worry. She's not answering my calls."

Norwood nodded. "I get it, and I've got a bad feeling you have cause to worry."

There was a new development. Her voice told the tale. "What's happened?" Reyna asked.

"The fire marshal has determined that the fire at the Jewel was not an accident. The way the candle burned told him that it had been lying horizontal from the moment it was lit. So whoever lit that candle wanted it to turn into a fire."

Reyna shook her head. "Wouldn't it have been easier to just take my laptop and other stuff?"

"I'm with you," Norwood agreed. "Which tells me this wasn't really about your stuff. It was about sending you a message."

"So the note left on my truck windshield wasn't some sort of prank," Ben suggested. "It was another message, like the fire but not as aggressive. Don't criminals usually escalate?"

"It doesn't make sense, for sure," Norwood said, "but there was a point—and that point was to scare you off." The last she directed at Reyna. "The fire was set during a time when no one was around to be hurt and in the middle of the day so it was more likely someone would see the trouble and call for help. It's as if the person or persons sending these messages weren't actually trying to hurt anyone. Even the damage to your tire was not created for optimal potential damage."

"Which suggests our perpetrator," Reyna offered, "is either not a seasoned criminal or not someone who really wants to make me disappear altogether."

"That's my thinking," Norwood agreed. "Whoever it is just wants you to stop digging around in the past. That said," she added, "desperation could change what we're seeing. We have to view this as a dangerous situation."

"Have you talked to Birdie?" Reyna hoped this didn't mean she wasn't safe at the bed-and-breakfast. A thread of fear worked its way through her at the reality of what they were talking about. As strong as she wanted to believe she was, she was not a fool.

"I have, and she took it in stride," Norwood said. "Since she doesn't have any guests right now, she has agreed to keep the doors locked as a precaution."

"I can't help feeling like this is all the more reason to be worried about where my grandfather is," Ben admitted.

"I've looked up his vehicle registration info—I'll have my deputies keeping an eye out for it. You check in with me in the morning, and if he's not back or hasn't called, we'll get the ball rolling on an alert."

Ben thanked her again as she left. He closed the door and turned back to Reyna. "You mind taking a ride with me? I'd like to do a little follow-up for myself before it gets dark."

"Let me get my bag."

6:00 p.m.

FOR A WHILE, they didn't speak, just rode. Reyna was okay with that. She needed to think. To sort through the details that wouldn't quite gel.

"The way I see it," she said when he'd cruised down the next street, "we have two prime suspects—Walls and Landon. Both appeared to have some sort of issue with one of the Three."

She opted not to mention the Widows. They both knew they were suspects as well, but Reyna wasn't ready to go there until absolutely necessary. It was better to allow the possibility to evolve naturally. That way, Ben could come to the conclusion himself.

Ben made a turn back onto Main Street. "No one has ever mentioned trouble with Coach Landon beyond the disagreement at the reunion," he reminded her. "Likewise, most folks believe Walls is a good man who wouldn't have bothered with revenge." He lifted one shoulder in a half-hearted shrug. "But who really knows what a person is capable of if backed into a corner—even one of their own making."

"Being on the team was significant in the lives of the

Three," she pointed out. "To school kids, particularly in the high school years, being a part of a team is a big deal. The fact that those jerseys were hanging in that cabin with the rest of the stuff in what was obviously a shrine to their memories confirms as much."

Ben slowed as they passed the Jewel. Reyna wished she could find the truth—before it was too late for Eudora. Birdie would be relieved if for no other reason than it would allow the woman she loved so much to slip into the depths of her horrible disease with some semblance of peace.

"If only," Reyna said, her gaze floating over the lovely homes along Main Street, "the secret keeper would give us a clue."

"I think there's a vow that precludes that possibility." Ben pulled into the Shop and Save Market parking lot, turned around and headed back along Main Street in the other direction.

Reyna laughed. "Or there's a blackmailable reason the secret keeper is afraid to come forward."

"That too," he agreed.

They drove past the homes of the Widows, checked the Henry place and found no sign of anyone, including Ward. How did one man disappear so completely in such a small town?

The shock at her own question resonated profoundly through Reyna.

How had three men disappeared so completely from this little town?

Someone had to know something. The trouble was in finding that someone and prompting him or her to talk about the something.

"Before we call it a night," she said, breaking the silence that had fallen between them, "let's stop by to see Coach

Landon again. I want to ask him straight up what happened between him and Duke Fuller over Jesse Carson."

"He may not be willing to answer," Ben pointed out.

"But unless he's very good at the poker-face thing, we will get a reaction, particularly when we mention talking to Jesse just today. I'd like to see that reaction."

Ben glanced at her. "Now that you mention it, I'd kind of like to see that myself."

He turned left at the next intersection, drove around the block and headed back into town. Reyna did some research on her cell while he drove. She searched for more information on Landon and on Duke Fuller. She had already seen everything that populated the results, so she moved on to the Carson family. The typical social media hits about Jesse. Then she searched the name *Father Vincent Cullen*, the priest who had officiated at the memorial service for the Three when they'd finally been declared dead.

There were a good many hits, but none were the priest who lived in Whispering Winds—who had lived here for more than sixty years. She checked the church's website. Found no mention of him.

How strange was that? Other than the church website, she hadn't actually expected to find him on any sort of social media. He hadn't seemed the type. But she had expected newspaper mentions and that sort of thing. Just because he didn't do social media didn't mean he didn't get mentioned by other people.

But there was nothing.

Not a single mention.

Strange.

"You want me to go to the door? Or do you want to go together?"

Reyna jumped. She'd been so deep in thought she hadn't realized they had arrived at Landon's home.

"We're in this together."

Ben flashed her the kind of smile that reminded her that finishing this project was not going to be an easy wrap.

They climbed out of the truck and made their way up the sidewalk. She considered mentioning the oddity of finding nothing about the priest on the internet but then decided it was better to ask the priest personally and see his reaction. No need to suggest the local priest was on her list of potential suspects until she had something more than a lack of hits on the net.

Ben knocked on Landon's door, and they waited. There was no sound inside. No lights, and it was getting dark now. There should have been lights on inside.

Another knock. Then the seemingly endless minutes that crept by without a response. Reyna surveyed the block. A little on the shabby side, but nothing out of the ordinary. No dogs barking. No neighbors peeking beyond curtains.

Ben knocked a third time, and when no answer came, he gestured to his truck. "I suppose we can go. He is evidently out."

"Guess so. Let's take a ride past the church. See if Father Cullen is home."

"Maybe he's the keeper of secrets," Ben said.

Made sense to Reyna. He supposedly knew everything.

But Father Cullen wasn't home either. How was it that every single person they wanted to see was suddenly missing?

Reyna had a sneaking suspicion that all those secrets were building toward a crescendo.

The ride back to the Kane home was quiet—too quiet. Ben was worried, and his worry was only mounting. Reyna had to admit that all these folks ducking them and the little threats were worrisome. But none of it troubled her the way his missing grandfather did.

Once in the house, Ben did a walk-through—no matter that his grandfather's truck was not in the driveway.

Reyna figured they could both use some coffee. Maybe talking out the day's events would help one or both.

The scent of fresh-brewed coffee had just started to fill the kitchen when Ben came into the room.

"We need to look this up." He showed her a prescription medicine bottle for Ward Kane. Obviously he'd been prowling the man's room.

Reyna took the bottle from him and went to the table where she'd left her cell. She typed in the name of the drug. The words on the screen split through her with a vengeance. Her gaze connected with his. "It's primarily used in the treatment of Parkinson's disease."

The shock on his face made her chest tighten.

Reyna checked the details on the label—prescribed just weeks ago.

"I've known a number of people with this," she said, understanding what he was thinking. "It's not fatal. Not the way most people think. It can contribute to a short-ened life span, but there are medications like this one that can help control the symptoms."

The words sounded hollow even to her. Good grief, his grandfather was eighty-five. Clearly this was not a good thing for his life expectancy.

"Have you noticed any symptoms?" she asked. "Trem-ors? Trouble walking? Any psychosis?" She hadn't noticed any of those things in Ward, but frankly she hadn't seen that much of him. This was the very last thing Ben needed on top of the deep dig into his father's disappearance. If Reyna hadn't felt bad already for barging into his life, she did now.

"I should tell the sheriff about this."

The defeat in his voice, in his eyes, tugged at her heart. "You should," she agreed.

Was this why Ward had wanted to help Reyna find answers? Because he feared his days were numbered more so than before?

But all she'd managed to do so far was find more questions.

Chapter Twelve

Ben walked around the house, scanned the property for as far as he could see. His grandfather was still MIA.

Where in the world was he?

And why hadn't he told Ben that he was sick?

Ben set his hands on his hips and exhaled a big breath. Ward Kane had always been steady, easygoing. Never a hothead or one to go off on a tangent. This was so, so wrong. It was possible the illness—if he and Reyna were right about the Parkinson's—had caused him not to behave in his usual manner. Ben had lain in bed last night and gone over every minute with his grandfather over the past few weeks. He hadn't noticed any unusual symptoms. Yeah, he had a bit of a tremor, but the man was eighty-five—was that so unusual? He got around great, in Ben's opinion, for a man of his age. If there were other things going on, he'd kept them well hidden.

Then there was his sudden interest in poking around in the disappearance of his only son. For all his adult life, Ben had assumed that his mother and grandfather had come to terms with what had happened and chosen not to look back.

Had this diagnosis prompted a sudden urgency to find the truth?

Ben couldn't deny that deep down he'd considered wanting the same closure. Who wouldn't?

But wanting it and going after it were two very different things. Other people were involved, and not everyone wanted to stir the hornet's nest.

The question, in his mind, was *Why?* Who would be opposed to finding the truth? There was no reason, unless there was some sort of guilt. Ben hated the idea that someone in this town—maybe someone he encountered regularly or considered a friend—might have been involved in his father going missing.

Murder.

His father hadn't just gone missing; he'd likely been murdered.

Ben stared at the ground a moment. All these years he and his mother—his grandfather too—had tiptoed around the idea. They'd skirted the possibility without acknowledging or accepting it. Never allowed themselves to dwell on the idea that JR Ward had been murdered—that all three of the missing men had been murdered.

Alien abduction, escape to some tropical island, all the other options were easier to consider.

It was time to face the fact that none of those things were true. His father was dead. His friends were dead. And someone had murdered them.

That someone was still out there—assuming he hadn't died in the past thirty years—living his life.

Unless it was a *she.*

Ben thought of his mother and how Eudora had said she knew what she was up to. She'd thought she was talking to JR. Had Eudora meant that Gordon Walls was a threat because Lucinda had cheated on him with JR? She'd also said Reyna should be worried about the Widows. The Widows had been considered suspects in the beginning. They were the wives, after all. Whenever a spouse disappeared, the other half of the couple was the primary suspect. But what reason would his mother have had to kill his father? Ben had no memory of arguments or unhappiness. Their family photos showed no hint of dissension.

Surely his grandfather would have been aware of any issues between JR and Lucinda.

Ben walked back toward the house. His heart felt heavy and his mind was going in a dozen directions at once.

"It's always best to have coffee before thinking so deeply."

Ben turned to see Reyna on the porch, where she held two mugs.

He smiled, liked the way she looked in the mornings. The nightshirt Birdie had lent her was a little loose but fell against her thighs in just the right spot... It made his mouth dry. Her hair was a fiery mass of waves and maybe a few tangles. As much as he enjoyed their lovemaking, just having her next to him last night had felt comfortable...right. He hadn't felt that kind of ease with anyone in a long time. Not even his ex-fiancée. There had always been a tension or uncertainty between them. As if they'd almost fit but not quite.

"Thanks. I meant to get back in there and pour a cup, but I never made it."

He joined her on the porch, where she'd taken a seat on the top step. "He's still not home."

Ben stared into his mug of dark brew. "No." He turned to her. "I'm seriously worried about him, Reyna. This is way, way out of character. He never just takes off like this."

"Could be the disease."

He nodded. "Could be."

"I say," Reyna offered, "that we grab a piece of toast and head for your mom's house. Maybe stop by the Henry place. See if he's shown up at either place. We can check in with Sheriff Norwood, see if her search has found any-one who's seen him."

"That's a good plan." Tracking down his grandfather wasn't exactly part of Reyna's work here, but he appre-ciated her offer to help. He'd never been bothered about doing things alone, but somehow this was different. He was pretty sure that if she wasn't around he would be lonely.

He had no idea how he would remedy that issue when she was gone.

"Have you ever—" he stood, offered her his hand "—had toast with peanut butter for breakfast?"

She took his hand, and he pulled her to her feet. "I can't say that I have."

"A little protein goes a long way when you have stuff to do."

Henry Property
Shadow Brook Lane
9:00 a.m.

REYNA CLIMBED OUT of the truck and met Ben at the hood. The house looked as abandoned as it had the last time they'd stopped by. The disappointment on his face warned that his worry was escalating.

"We can walk through," he said, "though I don't expect that anything's changed."

"We're here." Reyna tried to sound chipper. "Might as well."

A methodical walk-through of the old house revealed nothing but dust and the tools Ben had left on-site. The doors had still been locked. From there, they exited through the back door and went from one outbuilding to the other. Nothing disturbed. If Ward had been here, he hadn't taken anything or left anything behind.

On the way back to the truck, Reyna asked, "We headed to your mom's house next?"

He nodded. "I tried calling her first thing this morning, and the call went straight to voice mail again."

Reyna didn't bother mentioning that his mother could have lost her phone or forgotten to charge it. None of those things were likely true, but they sounded logical. Whatever was going on, the rest of Ben's family had fallen off the radar.

Kane Residence
Thistle Lane
9:45 a.m.

REYNA UNDERSTOOD BEFORE they emerged from Ben's truck that nothing had changed here either. Her instincts were humming, and not in a good way.

This time after he knocked a couple of times, Ben tried the door. It opened.

He exchanged a look with Reyna, and the worry she'd been watching escalate all morning morphed into something closer to fear.

"Mom?" he called out as they entered the front hall.

No scent of morning coffee…no smells of prepared

foods. Nothing that suggested someone had been up and around doing anything at all.

Reyna's nerves were jumping. This was not good. Ben moved forward, heading for the kitchen. She ventured into the parlor, where they'd met with Lucinda just a few days before.

The photo albums they'd looked at were no longer stacked in neat rows on the coffee table but were scattered about. Some on the table, some on the sofa. A couple open. Reyna sat down and picked up the first of the two open albums. This one was in the couple's younger days. There were numerous photos of JR during high school. Several of him with Duke Fuller and Judson Evans. They were all smiling widely, their lives just beginning to evolve into what had come next.

Reyna set the album aside and picked up the other one that had been left open. The photos were mostly from just before the Three's disappearance. Taking her time, she moved through the images slowly, examining each one with a close eye. What had these men been thinking in the weeks and months before they'd just vanished?

Had there been marital problems? No one seemed to believe so.

Financial problems? None had been found.

There was the fact that Lucinda had dumped Gordon Walls for JR Kane, but that had been more than seven years earlier.

Then there was the disagreement over Jesse Carson between Duke Fuller and Coach Landon. Why would Fuller care if his former teammate's kid played on the team, was the coach's new chosen one?

Reyna paused on a photo of the Three. JR and Judson were goofing around, but Duke was sort of off to himself.

His expression appeared brooding. Reyna turned back and looked for instances of a similar scene—one with Duke Fuller looking sullen and separate from the others.

There were plenty of others. Rey's pulse sped up. In those final weeks before they'd disappeared, Duke looked as if he'd had the weight of the world on his shoulders and even his friends couldn't help him. Reyna set the album aside and reached for the one from their high school days. She studied the photos carefully. In all the team photos Duke looked distracted. Not really unhappy, just not as exuberant as his friends.

"Her car is in the garage," Ben said from the doorway.

She'd been so engrossed in the photos and what this thing plaguing Fuller might've meant that she hadn't heard Ben come into the room.

Reyna stood. "Did you check upstairs?"

Their gazes locked and held for a long moment.

He shook his head. "I'll do that now."

If his mother had fallen ill…

"Not going there," Reyna muttered. She reached for the album, and it slid onto the floor. "Dang it." She crouched down to pick it up, but something beneath the sofa snagged her attention. She leaned down to get a better look. The sofa was one of the higher-legged ones, so it wasn't difficult to see beneath it.

A cell phone lay face down on the floor.

Oh, no.

Reyna reached for it, turned it over and touched the screen to awaken it.

Dozens of missed calls from Ben.

This was his mother's cell phone.

"Ben!" The phone gripped in her hand, she hurried to

the hall. He was already coming down the stairs. Reyna held up the phone. "This was under the sofa."

Ben took the phone and checked the screen. He nodded. "It's hers. I don't know her passcode, so I can't get past the lock screen."

The notifications had allowed Reyna to see there were missed calls from Ben, but now that those had cleared, they couldn't see anything else without the passcode.

But what was glaringly obvious was that Lucinda Kane had left her house without her car or her phone.

Cold slinking through her, Reyna dared to ask, "Did you find her handbag?"

"I didn't notice one sitting around in her room."

"Where does she enter the house most frequently? The front or the back?"

"The back."

Reyna led the way through the front hall and into the kitchen. The rack over the bench by the back door held a sweater, a raincoat and a taupe-colored handbag. Reyna's gut clenched.

"Do you want to check for her wallet? See if that's the handbag she's been carrying most recently?" Most women changed handbags fairly often. The essentials would be in the one she was currently using.

Ben opened the bag and withdrew her wallet. He looked to Reyna. "This can't be right. Whatever Sheriff Norwood believes, something is going on, and it involves my grandfather and my mother."

"You're right." Reyna glanced around the kitchen to give herself a moment to think before she spoke. "We should check the other widows' houses before we call the sheriff. If they're all three missing, that means something different from just your mom and your grandfather being MIA."

He tucked the wallet back into his mother's bag. "I'm locking up. I don't want to leave the house open like this."

"You have a key in case you need to get back in?"

He nodded. "Let's go."

Evans Residence
Blackberry Trail
11:00 a.m.

BEN PARKED NEXT to Harlowe Evans's car. It had been sitting in that same spot the last time he and Reyna had come over.

"We should try the door if she doesn't answer," Reyna suggested.

"Yeah."

They got out together and headed for the porch. It was too quiet. He already had this gut feeling that no one was home.

He knocked. "I hate to even say this out loud." Since no one answered the door and it remained quiet inside, he knocked again. "But if she's not here and then we go to Ms. Fuller's house and find the same situation…"

"That will be eerie, and let's not even go there until we have to. One step at a time."

After a third knock with no answer, Ben tried the door. It opened.

"You want me to go inside? I'm not from around here," Reyna offered. "The sheriff might cut me some slack for trespassing."

"We go together."

Again, inside there were no scents that suggested any sort of food or beverage prep had taken place that morning. The house was neat. And it was a clear shot from the front to the back considering the renovations that had been done. The wide-open first floor showed no sign of the owner's presence.

The drop zone for coats and shoes was next to the front door, and Ms. Evans's handbag hung next to a lightweight jacket. This time Ben preferred that Reyna did the honors. She unzipped the bag and spotted the woman's wallet.

"Try her cell number," Reyna suggested.

Ben withdrew his phone, scrolled his contacts until he found her name and tapped. Seconds later the muffled sound of the phone ringing came from the other side of the room. He followed the sound, found the phone on the island partially concealed by a tea towel.

The top notification visible was a missed called from a number not in the woman's contacts.

"You recognize this number?" Reyna asked, showing him the screen.

He entered the number into his screen, and Sheriff Norwood's name appeared. He ended the call.

Norwood had tried to reach all three of the Widows. The only reason her number hadn't been the top notification on Ben's mom's phone was because of his calls.

There was a passcode, so that was all they were getting from the phone. He placed it back on the counter.

"I'll take a walk-through upstairs," he said, heading for the staircase.

"I'll look around down here."

Being in his mother's house hadn't felt so strange because she was family. But this was different. If Ms. Evans walked in right now and caught them snooping around, she would likely not be happy. Not that Ben could blame her. And their only excuse would probably not make her feel any better.

While Ben had a look upstairs, Reyna explored downstairs. There were no photos or albums lying around. The entire downstairs was neat, everything in its place. Reyna thought about the note she'd gotten the other night, the one stuck on Ben's truck windshield. She checked through the cabinets in the island and near the sink until she found the one where the trash bin was tucked. Like the rest of the place, even the trash smelled clean. There was very little in the bin.

At the bottom, beneath a discarded potato chip bag and an empty cookie bag, were newspaper clippings. Reyna clawed them up from the bottom of the bin and spread them across the counter.

These weren't new clippings—these were from decades ago. Most were about the search for the missing men. But one was about the fundraiser being held at Our Lady of the Mountain Church. Reyna smoothed the crumpled article. A photo of the football team, the Three included, was front and center. Father Cullen was huddled close to one of the players, so close you could hardly see his face.

The difference between the article about the fundraiser at the church and the others was that Harlowe Evans had crumpled this one. Reyna read the article and found nothing that set off alarm bells. It was fairly cut-and-dried— the team had made the playoffs and extra funds were needed for travel, thus the fundraiser.

"You find anything?" Ben came up beside her.

"Just these clippings in the trash."

He surveyed the articles, then shook his head. "Whatever is going on, it doesn't feel like these women left voluntarily."

"We should check the Fuller home and call Sheriff Norwood."

If the women had been missing since yesterday…they could be running out of time.

Chapter Thirteen

Fuller Residence
Hawk's Way
11:45 a.m.

There was no answer at the Fuller house either, but the door was locked. A walk around the property showed the owner's car was not home. The detached garage had windows, so they could see inside. Ben had checked the one other larger building just in case the car was in there. It was not.

"So maybe we've overreacted," Reyna offered. "The three of them could have taken a trip somewhere. A shopping spree or a spa getaway." She shrugged. "Girl trip."

"Except," he countered, "why would my mom and Ms. Evans leave their phones at home? Leave their houses unlocked?"

Reyna put her hands up. "You got me there."

Ben thought for a moment about what he wanted to do. It might not have been the smartest step, but his curiosity was getting the better of him. He really needed to see if Ms. Fuller was inside the house—car or no car. And whether her phone was in there.

"I think I'll check a few windows. If there's one unlocked I'm going inside to check things out. You let me know if company arrives."

"I'm sure there are things I should say to you right now," Reyna pointed out. "Like the fact that breaking and entering is a crime."

"I promise I won't break anything." He shot her a grin, and she just shook her head. "Keeping watch."

She sat down in the glider on the porch and gestured for him to carry on.

Ben started with the windows on the porch. The home's windows were double hung with sliding screens that made the task far easier. All four front windows on the first level were locked. He moved all the way around the house until, next to the back door, he found the one he needed. The screen slid up out of the way, and the window sash followed. Not a very big window, but he felt confident he could work his way through.

He pulled his upper body into the opening and reached for the floor. Once he'd braced his hands there, he pulled his lower torso and legs through. He closed the window and locked it just to make sure no one else did the same.

The laundry room, where he'd entered, led into the kitchen. He checked around the room, remembered to look in the garbage can before moving on. Reyna had found newspaper clippings in Ms. Evans's trash.

The entire first floor was in order, and there was no sign of the owner, her cell phone or a handbag. He called her cell to ensure it was not in the house. If it was, it had either been silenced or the battery had died and it no longer rang. He moved on to the upstairs, where he found the same. No Deidre Fuller.

As he approached the front door to join Reyna on the porch, it occurred to him that none of the security systems in the houses had been armed. He stared at the keypad next to the front door.

He was surprised this one hadn't been.

He couldn't exit via the front door since the dead bolt was the kind that needed a key to engage or disengage. The back door, on the other hand, had no dead bolt. When he had exited via that back door, locking it behind him, and reached the front of the house, Reyna looked to him for an update.

He sat down next to her. "No handbag. No cell phone. No sign of the owner."

"Time to call the sheriff," she suggested.

Ben nodded and reached for his phone. He put through the call and relayed all the details they'd discovered—except for the part about him going into Ms. Fuller's locked house. He left it at *no answer and no car.*

When he'd hung up, he passed along the sheriff's response. "She's sending deputies to check the Kane and Evans homes for any signs of forced entry or a struggle— which we know she won't find. That's about all she can do at this point."

"What do you think we should do now?" Reyna asked. "We can't just sit around and wait to see who disappears next."

She was right about that. They had to do something.

"We can go back to see the priest." Ben shrugged. "Maybe he's home now. If so, we tell him what's going on. Maybe if he knows anything at all he'll toss us a bone. Anything to give us a direction to go."

"Unless he's the one hiding the most secrets."

Ben considered the probability that many priests knew plenty of secrets about their parishioners. Secrets they could never share with anyone.

"Then I guess we've kind of hit a brick wall." Where

on earth were his mother and his grandfather? This was all kinds of crazy.

"Back when I was writing fiction," she said, "I developed a number of sources in areas where I might need to do research. One of them was a retired FBI agent. I emailed him about Father Cullen. I know it might seem a reach, but the fact that when I did some digging on the net I couldn't find anything about him feels off. Scrubbing your history from cyberspace is not an easy feat. I didn't mention this before because maybe it's nothing, but I don't want to ignore even the most unlikely possibility. In any event, I hope to hear back from him later today."

Ben shook his head and laughed out loud. "This is just a small town in Tennessee—how can we have all these unsolved mysteries?"

And missing people?

"Let's go see the priest." Reyna stood, grabbed him by the hand and pulled him to his feet. "Who knows—maybe we'll hear from the sheriff or my FBI contact by the time we've interviewed the priest again, assuming he's home."

He had a feeling that was wishful thinking.

Our Lady of the Mountain
Kings Lane
1:00 p.m.

LIKE EVERY DOOR they'd knocked on so far today, there was no answer at the rectory.

Reyna wasn't one to easily admit defeat, but this was getting ridiculous. Where the hell was everyone?

"Maybe he's in the church," she suggested. "If not, the current priest might know where he is."

"Could be out for a walk," Ben said as they took the

cobblestone path that led back to the parking area. "It's a nice day. I've seen him out walking before."

"Or maybe at lunch." Reyna's stomach had already reminded her that they hadn't stopped long enough to grab a bite.

Ben grinned. "We should do that before our next stop."

"You won't get any argument from me."

Father Garrett Jordan had just exited the church and was coming down the steps when they reached the front of the building. He sucked on a cigarette and released a puff of smoke.

"Afternoon, Father," Ben said, announcing their presence since the man hadn't spotted them.

"Good afternoon to you." The priest smiled and waved the smoke in his hand. "A bad habit I've never been able to kick."

Reyna returned his smile. "We all have one kind or the other." She offered her hand as he reached the bottom step. "Reyna Hart. Father Cullen may have told you I'm here researching the Three."

He gave a nod. "Several dedicated parishioners have reported your activities, Ms. Hart—Father Cullen included."

She laughed. "It's a small town," she agreed. "The news of a stranger picking through the past travels quickly."

"Indeed." He looked from Reyna to Ben and back. "How can I help you today?"

"We don't want to hold you up," Ben said, "if you were on your way out."

"Off to lunch at the diner. Nothing that can't wait."

Garrett Jordan wasn't much older than Ben, Reyna decided. Fortyish, maybe.

"We hoped to speak with Father Cullen again," she said. "But he's out. Do you know when he might return?"

Jordan's brows drew together. "I haven't seen him today. Yesterday either, for that matter. When last we spoke he seemed distressed over the stir about the past." He smiled at Reyna. "He's never talked about it very much. My impression is that he feels he failed those three young men. As we get older we tend to reflect on the mistakes—or those things we perceive as mistakes—we've made. Father Cullen is looking back a great deal lately."

"When you see him, Father," Ben said, "can you let him know we'd like to speak with him again? It's very important."

Jordan gave a slow nod and appeared to struggle a bit with himself before responding. "I feel I should share something with you that will perhaps give you some insight into Father Cullen's current situation. He's not been himself for a bit. You see, he has a brain tumor. Sadly, it's inoperable, and it's only a matter of time before he will be leaving us. It's not common knowledge, but I hope you might be able to make your judgments a bit more accurately knowing this."

"I'm so sorry to hear that." Reyna looked to Ben, uncertain what else to say. Good grief, they'd found the prescription in his grandfather's room, and now this. It was true that all those who might've known details about the Three and their disappearance were going fast.

"Thanks for letting us know, Father," Ben said. "It's a shame. He's an institution in this town."

"A hard act to follow, for sure," Jordan said. "As for catching him, generally if he's out for a walk or lunch, he comes back fairly quickly. Feel free to wait for him. He never locks his door."

"We'll do that," Ben said. "Enjoy your lunch. We'll be heading that way next."

Father Jordan gave another nod and hurried to his car. He tucked his half-smoked cigarette into his mouth and climbed in and drove away.

"Wow." Reyna turned to Ben. "Eudora and your grandfather are right. We're running out of time."

"That's what worries me," he admitted. He hitched his head toward the cobblestone path that led to the rectory. "The father said we could wait."

"He did," she agreed.

As Father Jordan had said, the door to the rectory was unlocked.

"Father Cullen?" Reyna called out as they entered.

No answer, of course.

Rather than have a seat and wait, they wandered around the space. Looking but not touching. Ben checked the bedroom to ensure Cullen wasn't napping.

She perused the few framed photos and the notes lying around for anything related to the Three.

Her cell vibrated, and Reyna dug it free of her pocket. It was Jimmy Corbin. She accepted the call from her FBI research source and said, "Hey."

"Hey, Reyna. Got your email last night, and I was intrigued. You're right. It's not easy removing your history so thoroughly. So I checked into your priest, Cullen."

Reyna stilled, waited for the news that might very well point them in the right direction. He wouldn't have responded by phone if he'd found nothing.

"There's not a lot I can tell you because it's classified."

Classified? There was an answer she hadn't seen coming. "Okay."

"What I can say is that if there's trouble with this guy… it might be more than a little dangerous, so I'd steer clear if possible. And," he said, "if something is going on, we probably need to know about it. So keep me posted but give this man a wide berth. You got it?"

"Got it. Thanks, Jimmy. I'll let you know if this gets hairy."

"Good, and if you get back up to New York," he said, "let me know. We can do lunch and catch up."

"That would be nice," she agreed. "Maybe one day soon."

When the call ended, Ben looked at her expectantly.

"He couldn't tell me a lot about Cullen." She glanced around the room. "But it sounds like this man is not who we think he is, and...we should be careful because his past... It could be dangerous to anyone poking around."

Ben made a face. "Are you serious?"

"Yeah." Reyna glanced around the room. "I'm not sure how this helps us in what we're looking for."

"Unless whatever trouble revolving around him struck thirty years ago."

"I guess that's possible," she admitted.

Ben shook his head. "I'm sure your source knows what he's talking about, but honestly I can't see Father Cullen making anyone disappear."

The wiliest killers were the ones you didn't see coming. Besides, based on what Jimmy had said, this priest could be in witness protection. Maybe he'd ratted out a mob boss or something.

"We hanging around here for a while longer?" She didn't really see the point. If he reappeared, he wasn't going to tell them anything they didn't already know, particularly if it implicated him and his past somehow.

Ben showed her a photo he'd taken with his phone. "This is hanging on the lamp next to his bed. It looks familiar, but I can't place it."

It was a cross on a silver chain. The cross was small and rustic. Not your typical polished-with-smooth-edges silver cross. It looked handmade, primitive. Like ancient nails or little daggers held together by small lengths of barbed wire.

"I don't recognize it, but I'm glad you snapped a pic in case we figure it out later."

Reyna took one more lingering look around. "I suppose there's nothing left to do except…" She turned to Ben. "Do you think we could go back to the cabin?"

"We'd have to get permission from Sheriff Norwood." He nodded. "But I'd like to see it again too."

"Let's give it a shot, then."

Trout Lake
2:00 p.m.

THEY'D GRABBED BURGERS, fries and drinks from the diner on the way to the Fuller lake property. Reyna hadn't realized how hungry she'd been until she'd smelled those fries. She also hadn't eaten so fast since she'd been a kid.

By the time they were parked, she was ready to walk off those couple thousand or so calories. Norwood had said that her head forensic guy, Sergeant David Snelling, might still be there wrapping things up, and as long as they didn't get in his way, they could look around. They'd been there before, so it wasn't like they were new to the scene. Their prints would already be there. Maybe hairs or other clothing fibers too.

Snelling was gone when they reached the cabin. Crime scene tape was still draped around the place. They walked around to the back and checked out the holes left from digging up the area where the three wooden crosses had been.

The smell of freshly turned earth hung in the air. The three crosses were gone—taken in as evidence, she supposed. They walked around the entire exterior before ducking under the tape and going to the door.

A warning that the cabin was a crime scene had been posted on the door.

"She didn't say we couldn't go in," Ben pointed out.

"She did not," Reyna agreed.

He opened the door, and they walked inside. The gloom had them pulling out their cell phones and turning on the flashlight apps. Reyna walked around the room slowly, surveying every photo on the wall again, examining each closely for anything she might have missed before. When she reached another photo that showed Duke Fuller standing apart from the others and looking distant or upset, she turned to Ben. He was examining the jerseys hanging on the wall as closely as she had been the photos. She wondered if the idea that his father had worn that jersey was tearing at him inside.

"Hey." When he glanced her way, she went on. "This is another example of the Duke thing I was telling you about."

He walked over to join her.

"See how he's standing back and he looks upset or distracted?"

"I do," he said. "There was something going on with him, don't you think?"

"But unless he shared whatever it was with someone besides his two best friends, we may never know what it was."

Ben leaned closer to the photo. "Is he wearing a chain?" He touched his own throat.

Reyna peered at the photo. "He is. Can't tell what kind it is, but he's definitely wearing something."

As if mutual understanding that it could be the cross found in Father Cullen's room hit them both at the same time, they moved from photo to photo that included Duke, looking for a better view of whatever sort of chain he wore.

"Got it," Ben said.

Reyna hurried over to see. "That's it." She nodded. "I mean, it could just be one like it, but it's definitely the same sort of cross."

Their gazes met, and they both understood that was not the case. Neither of them had ever seen one anything like it.

"If that isn't Duke Fuller's cross and chain hanging in the priest's room, then it's one just like it."

"Maybe the priest gave it to him," Reyna offered. "He may have had one like it."

"Do priests usually give teenage guys chains with crosses?"

She shrugged. "I don't know. I guess we'll have to ask him."

"We should take this one with us." Ben snagged the photo. "I'll give it to Norwood when I see her again and tell her about the cross in Cullen's room."

"We should just find out where she is and go there now before something happens to the cross."

Ben considered the idea, then nodded. "You're right. If Cullen figures out we've been there, it could disappear."

"After that," Reyna said, "I think we should pay another visit to Coach Landon. Just to make sure he hasn't disappeared too. Everybody else appears to have vanished."

"Good idea."

As they drove back to town, Ben was just about to call Norwood when his cell sounded off. "Hey, Sheriff. I was just about to call you." He glanced at Reyna before turning his attention back to the highway.

Reyna hoped this was good news, but she had a bad, bad feeling it was not.

Her own cell started to vibrate in her pocket, and she tugged it out and answered. "This is Reyna."

"Reyna, it's Birdie. I'm so sorry to bother you, but I really need your help. Would you mind coming to the Jewel and helping me out?"

"Of course I will. Are you okay?"

"Well, it's a little embarrassing, but I was working in the yard all day, trying to get ahead of the weeds. I got all sweaty and dirty, so I decided to shower and, good Lord, I fell getting out. I'm so embarrassed. I'm as naked as the day I was born, and I can't even crawl to my room."

"Don't try to move. I'm on my way." Reyna ended the call and turned to Ben, who was just ending his own. "Everything okay?"

"I don't know. They found my grandfather's truck."

Dread slid through her veins as she waited for him to go on.

"He wasn't there. No sign of foul play."

Relief gushed along the same path the dread had taken. "That's good, right?"

"Hopefully." The worry etched in his profile warned he was far from sure about that. "I need to get over there." He glanced at her. "You were saying you'd be right there to someone."

Oh, no. "I'm sorry. Birdie needs me." Reyna felt torn about leaving Ben, but she certainly couldn't ignore the elderly woman. She may have broken something. "Do you mind just dropping me off there?"

"No problem. You take care of Birdie. I can handle this. I'll catch up with you as soon as I can."

"Okay."

She really hated that Ben had to do this alone. But Birdie needed help. How could Reyna say no?

Chapter Fourteen

Reyna watched Ben drive away, and worry that she should have gone with him settled on her shoulders. The sheriff would be there, maybe other deputies with whom he was acquainted. He would be okay. She repeated this twice more.

Deep breath. Reyna started forward. Birdie needed her. She was alone, and she was elderly. She could be seriously injured.

Her cell vibrated in her pocket, and she pulled it free to check the screen. The Light Memory Care Center. Her heart sped up. Had Eudora taken another turn for the worse?

Barely able to get the word out, she said, "Hello."

"Reyna Hart?"

"Yes, this is she."

"Ms. Hart, I'm calling to see if you've heard from Ms. Davenport—she seems to have disappeared."

"What do you mean?" More worry joined the mix of fear already twisting in Reyna's belly.

"After lunch, when the therapist went to her room for her session, Eudora was gone. When we didn't find her anywhere on the first floor of the center, we checked the security footage. She was seen leaving the facility with an unidentified woman around one thirty."

"Was this woman not someone who works at the facility? I mean, I'm assuming you're saying she wasn't a registered visitor. So was she an employee?"

"We can't be sure. She was wearing a hoodie."

Oh dear God. "Have you called the authorities?" Who would take Eudora out of the facility? This was beyond inexplicable.

"We have. They're here now reviewing the security footage and questioning employees and patients. We hoped you might have heard from her since you visited her so often over the past few months. One of her nurses remembered you and we found your number in Eudora's bedside table. We hated to call but we haven't been able to reach her emergency contact, Birdie Jewel. Frankly, we're a little desperate."

A frown tugged at Reyna's brow. "I'm sorry, no. I haven't heard from her since we visited yesterday. But I'm at Ms. Jewel's home now. Unfortunately, she's had a fall." Reyna walked faster toward the entrance. "I'll check with her to see if there is anyone else we can call."

"If you hear from Eudora or learn any new information," the woman said, "please let us know."

"I will, of course. I can check with her friends here in Whispering Winds. If I learn anything, I will let you know that as well," Reyna assured her.

When the call ended, she reached for the door of the Jewel. It was locked. Oh, no. Sheriff Norwood had urged Birdie to keep the door locked. How was Reyna going to get inside?

Reyna called Birdie's phone.

"Are you here?" she asked without a hello.

"I am but the door is locked. Should I call 911?"

The call abruptly ended.

Reyna stared at the screen. "What the...?"

The sound of the locks releasing had Reyna shifting her attention to the door.

The door opened and Birdie stood there—fully clothed. She put her hand to her chest. "Thank goodness you're here."

Before Reyna could demand to know what was going on or consider telling her about Eudora, Birdie grabbed her by the arm and pulled her inside. Just as quickly, she closed and secured the door once more.

"What's going on?" The notion that Birdie had obviously lied to her had frustration bubbling over. The possibility that she could have taken Eudora from the facility suddenly seemed far too possible. No, Reyna decided. Not possible. Probable. "Birdie, have you—"

"Come with me," she interrupted. She grabbed Reyna and ushered her along with surprising strength and swiftness.

The elderly woman didn't stop until she'd reached a back room, a former rear parlor that she'd transformed into a library complete with hundreds, if not thousands, of books.

For a moment Reyna could only stare, certain she wasn't seeing what...she was obviously seeing. People were seated around the room on sofas and chairs. *Eudora.* Birdie had taken her from the center! Holy cow! Before she could demand to know what the meaning of all this was, Reyna's attention settled on the others present. Ward Kane! He was sitting right there as if his grandson and the sheriff weren't out looking for him.

The sound of the pocket doors clacking shut jerked Reyna from the disbelief. She turned to Birdie. "What is this?"

"I think you know everyone," Birdie said.

The Widows were here. The three of them sat together on a sofa. All three glanced at Reyna and smiled. Father Cullen sat in a chair on the far side of the room as if he had been speaking to or directing the group meeting.

Reyna lost her breath when her gaze landed on yet another person in the room—one in a wheelchair. Coach Wade Landon.

"You should call Sheriff Norwood."

Reyna recognized the voice of the man who had spoken. Not the coach or the priest…or Ward. Her head swiveled around, sending her attention beyond where the Widows sat, and then she spotted Gordon Walls. She started in his direction, stalling just shy of reaching him. He was handcuffed to a chair.

She stared back at Birdie. "What is going on here? Why is he in handcuffs?"

The fact that he'd had a motive to get rid of at least one of the Three wasn't lost on Reyna. For that matter, it seemed everyone in the room had a motive.

"Please, Reyna," Birdie said. "We've been waiting for your time to arrive. Your seat is at the desk. You'll find the pens and pencils and the notepad you need to assist in what we have to do."

"What is it you have to do?" She had a very bad feeling about where this was going.

"We're conducting a trial," Birdie explained. "We need you to be our official recorder."

"Stenographer," Eudora corrected.

Frustration pumped through Reyna. "Eudora, the center believes you've been kidnapped. They have called in the authorities."

She made a face that said *so what?* "That place needed a little excitement."

Reyna wheeled on Birdie. "How did you get her out?"

Birdie shrugged. "I used yesterday's pass. No one seemed to notice, and they didn't make me sign in since I had one."

Reyna's jaw dropped. "That's why you called me to your bedside yesterday. You weren't ailing more than usual. You just needed Birdie to get a visitor's pass."

Eudora smiled patiently. "We do what we must."

Okay. Reyna was sure now. These people—every single one of them, except maybe Deputy Walls—was on something. Alcohol, drugs…something.

"Reyna," the priest said, "humor us. Take your seat and prepare to take notes. You don't have to record everything verbatim, just the important parts."

No way. She moved her head side to side. "I'm not doing anything until you tell me what's going on here." Her attention landed on Ward. "Your grandson is frantic to find you. What in the world are you doing?"

"Sit down, Reyna," he said in the voice that she imagined he had used to scold his son and his grandson when necessary. "You'll know what you need to very shortly."

If his gaze hadn't held hers so steadily…so urgently… she would have walked out and promptly called the sheriff. He needed her to do this. She looked from one person to the next. They all needed her to cooperate. Whatever their reasons, how could she say no?

She turned lastly to Eudora, who gave her a reassuring and somehow hopeful look.

"If I'm staying," Reyna countered, "you have to let me call Ben. He should be here."

Heads started to shake. When Reyna would have argued, Ward spoke up again. "His being here would make him culpable. We can't allow that."

"But I can be culpable?" she asked, mostly to buy time to think of another reason to call Ben.

"We brought you here under false pretense," Birdie explained. "You are not here of your own volition."

There was no point arguing with these people. "Okay." She walked to the desk and sat down, grabbed a pen and readied the notepad. Besides, Ben would come back looking for her.

Birdie suggested, "You might want to list all those present, yourself included." She stepped forward and addressed the group. "Ward, Eudora." She shifted her attention to the Widows. "Lucinda, Deidre, Harlowe. The five of you are the jury."

For the love of God. They really were having a trial. Reyna looked from the coach to the priest and then to Walls. But who was the defendant?

"Deputy Walls, you are a special witness."

"Ms. Birdie," he shot back, "if you take these cuffs off now, I won't tell a soul about you luring me here with that story about a break-in and then feeding me those brownies that put me out for—"

"Order in the courtroom," Father Cullen demanded.

His harsh tone yanked Reyna's attention in his direction.

Noting her focus on the man, Birdie said, "Father Cullen is our judge."

So it was Coach Landon. Reyna's gaze landed on him

next. He stared back, fear in his eyes, sweat beading on his forehead.

Walls was right—they needed to call the sheriff. She reached into her bag for her cell. It was suddenly yanked from her reach.

Reyna glared at Birdie. "What are you doing?"

Birdie glared right back. "We all gathered here late yesterday to determine how best to move forward. The decision was unanimous. It took some doing to get prepared to proceed but we're ready now. There is no going back, Reyna. Believe that if you believe nothing else. We have run out of time."

Reyna surveyed those present. Her gaze settled on Ben's mother. "He's worried sick about you."

"You'll understand soon," Lucinda assured her. "We've all seen to our final arrangements and we are now doing what we have to do."

Horror pounded Reyna in the chest. Was this going to be some sort of mass suicide?

"We're wasting time," Cullen announced. "We should begin and we will conduct ourselves appropriately as we proceed." He looked directly at Reyna. "And no one is leaving until this is done."

"Thirty years ago," Birdie began but hesitated. She turned to Reyna. "I'm sorry—I forgot to tell you that I'm the prosecutor."

Reyna drew in a deep breath and looked around the room. Okay, if this was the way it was going to be, there was one thing missing. "He needs an attorney."

Birdie flashed her a look of annoyance. "He waived the right to an attorney." She pointed her attention at Coach Landon. "Isn't that right, Landon?"

He nodded, his eyes wide and bulging with unadulterated fear.

Birdie smiled at Reyna. "There you go."

"Thirty years ago," she said again before Reyna could protest more, "Ward Kane Junior, Duke Fuller and Judson Evans disappeared, and as far as the authorities are concerned, their case remains unsolved." She looked from one of those present to the next. "But we all know differently."

Heads nodded, and agreements rumbled through those gathered.

"You're all going to be arrested," Walls warned.

"Shut up, Gordon," Ward snapped.

Reyna opted not to write that down. All she could hope to do was be patient and be ready to stop any harm from happening.

"Coach Landon," Birdie said, "can you tell us about your relationship with the three missing men who came to be known as the Three?"

He heaved out a breath. "Everyone here knows I was their coach from middle school through high school."

"When would you say the trouble began between you and these men?" Birdie asked.

Landon shrugged. "At that ten-year reunion. Duke got jealous—"

"Liar!"

Reyna jumped at the word Deidre Fuller had hurled at the man.

"Tell them when it began," she roared like a mama bear protecting its cub.

"Let me remind you," the priest said to Landon, "I know the whole truth. I will know if you lie."

Reyna stared at the man of God, the keeper of the secrets. Dear God, it was him. He knew the truth. Why had he never told anyone? Had any of the Widows told him within the sanctity of the vow of confession? Was this his way of helping see that justice was finally done? He was dying—Father Jordan had said as much.

Understanding settled on Reyna like a load of bricks. He was dying, and he wanted to make this right before he died. Her gaze swung to Ward Kane. He figured his days were numbered as well... He wanted the truth. Her gaze swept across the room. They all wanted something more than just the truth... They wanted justice.

Landon shook his head frantically. "I can't. I can't talk about it."

"Deputy Walls." Birdie turned toward the man hand-cuffed to his chair. "We'd like you to tell us the relevant events you saw and heard the day the Three went missing."

The deputy glared at Birdie, shook his head. "I was at the diner. I overheard a tense conversation where JR told Duke 'it was the only way.' Duke didn't seem to agree, but Judson was ready to go with whatever plan JR had."

"Did they mention where they were going?" Birdie asked.

He stared at the floor for a moment.

"Answer the question," Cullen demanded.

"They were meeting Coach Landon to confront him."

Reyna's breath exited her lungs so sharply it hurt. "Have you known this all along?" she demanded.

"You don't get to ask questions," Cullen warned.

Reyna stood. "This has gone far enough," she snapped. She walked toward Walls. "You knew they were meeting with Coach Landon, and you never told anyone." It wasn't a question. His own words had just confirmed as much because she hadn't found a single statement he'd given thirty years ago that said where the Three had been going the day they had disappeared.

"He had his reasons," Birdie said, "but we're correcting that slip now. It's going on the record." She nodded to Reyna. "Write it down."

Reluctantly, Reyna went back to the desk and wrote the statement on the notepad hard enough to indent every page beneath it.

"You were saying," Birdie said, her voice hard.

Walls said nothing.

"Finish your statement," Cullen ordered, "or I will answer it for you."

Walls sneered at him. "You can't. You took a vow."

Cullen laughed, a dry sound. "What do I care about what man can do to me? My fate will lie with the Heavenly Father, and I'm good with whatever He decides."

"I knew why they wanted to confront him," Walls admitted reluctantly. "I knew it was the reason Duke went off at the reunion when the scumbag talked about little Jesse Carson."

"Will you please identify the scumbag you mean?" Birdie directed.

"Landon." He looked anywhere but at the man in the wheelchair.

"He's lying," Landon cried. "He killed them to get back at Lucinda for choosing someone else besides him."

"This," Walls roared, "was never about Lucinda. It was about Landon and the monster he kept hidden all those years."

"We know what you did," Lucinda charged.

"We're no longer satisfied with what you've lost," Harlowe snarled. "We want you to pay the price you should have all those years ago, even if we have to pay for the mistake we made trusting you."

"We should have known you wouldn't stand by your word," Deidre said with utter disdain. "You're a coward."

"You can't prove any of it," Landon argued. "You never had any evidence, and you never will." He laughed. "Have your fun. The worst you can do is try finishing what you started thirty years ago." He swung his attention to Reyna.

She flinched at his ugly stare.

"Are you going to be a witness to them killing me, or are you going to save me?" he asked. "The way I see it, you're the only chance I've got of surviving this."

All eyes rested on Reyna then. Heart pounding, she moistened her lips and said the only thing she could think to say. "Tell me what you did, and I'll tell you what I can do." Sounded fair enough. She was here for answers, after all. At the moment she just needed to buy time. Ben would be coming back at some point. She prayed it was sooner rather than later.

"You had a choice, Landon," Cullen said, drawing the room's attention back to him. "You made the wrong one."

Landon shot him a look. "I think I'll just wait until you're in hell. I hear you're headed that way real soon."

The jury started shouting again.

"Order!" When the shouting continued, Cullen stood. "I said shut up and listen! We're likely short on time here." He glanced at Reyna. "Ben will probably show up anytime. We can't be sure how long he and Sheriff Norwood will be distracted."

Reyna felt her jaw drop again. These people had set this up—all of it.

The arguing and shouting ceased instantly.

"When we found out what he'd done," Deidre said, clearly speaking to Reyna, "we gave him a choice."

"Deidre," Cullen warned.

"If we expect her cooperation," she argued, "we need to explain. Otherwise we will run out of time."

"Just get this over with," Walls whined. "Kidnapping is a serious crime."

Reyna looked from one to the next. She had so many questions, but she didn't want to stop their conversation, afraid it would disrupt the truth from coming out.

Lucinda stood next to Deidre. She pointed to Landon. "He chose Duke Fuller when he was just ten years old."

Deidre wilted back onto the sofa and put her face in her hands.

"For the next six years," Lucinda went on, "he used Duke to make videos, which he sold to the highest bidder. When Duke tried to make him stop, Landon threatened to tell his friends and his parents. To take him off the team."

Deidre was crying now.

Reyna felt sick. Harlowe hugged her friend close and swiped at her own tears. Eudora and Birdie held each other, and they cried too.

"Walls," Cullen said, "do you have anything to say?"

He glared at Cullen. "He did the same thing to me."

"Why didn't you tell anyone?" Reyna demanded.

Cullen lifted his eyebrows at her, but she ignored him.

"Why?" she demanded.

"Who was going to believe me over the town's be-loved coach?" Walls snarled. "Even now, the school is planning to give him a lifetime achievement award. He hasn't coached in nearly thirty years, and still his coach-ing record rises above all else."

Ward stood. "That is our fault," he snapped. "If we'd

told the world the truth when we discovered it, everyone would have known and the bastard would be rotting in prison now. Instead, we did what we thought was right to protect the reputation of the boys."

"No," Cullen said. "He wouldn't be in prison. We had no real evidence. And even if we had been able to convince anyone, the most he would have gotten was ten years."

"For murder?" Ward howled.

The anguish in his words ripped at Reyna's heart.

"You know we couldn't prove the murders," Cullen argued. "The best we could have hoped for was child pornography. He never touched the boys, as far as we know—it was only the videos."

Reyna stood again. "You all believe that Coach Landon killed those men?"

"We know he did," Ward said. "We just can't prove it."

"He was seen coming from the funeral home that night," Walls said. "The night they disappeared."

"We believe," Harlowe said, "that he drugged them or poisoned them when they went to confront him and then cremated their bodies. He worked summers and on occasions throughout the year at Addison Funeral Home. That's why we never found them." She dropped back to the sofa, and the Widows held each other and struggled with their composure.

Reyna's heart was in her throat. "How do you know they went to confront him?"

If these women knew all this thirty years ago, why the hell hadn't they told someone?

"They didn't know until I told them," Cullen said. "After the incident at the reunion, Duke came to me and told me everything. He said he'd finally told his best friends, and they had insisted on going with him to confront Landon. He asked me to pray for them, and he gave me his cross to pray over until it was finished."

"Why the hell didn't you tell anyone?" Reyna demanded. The explanation certainly clarified why the cross was in the rectory. But it didn't explain what her FBI friend had told her. "Were you afraid the police would connect you to your own secret?"

All eyes were on Reyna again.

Cullen's gaze remained locked with hers as he answered the accusation. "My secret is only that I witnessed something I could not unsee. For that, my former life had to be left behind. And that, Ms. Hart; is for another time. Not today."

He was in witness protection. She nodded. "You're right. Forgive me."

"They're going to kill me," Landon cried. "They already tried once. You can't let them do this."

"Shut up, you bastard," Walls snarled. "You should have died in that fire, and maybe the rest of us would have had some peace the last three decades." He jerked at his restraints. "Take off these cuffs," he commanded, "and I'll end this now."

"And here you thought," Cullen said, "we secured you to keep you from escaping."

Walls glared at him. "This is not going to end the way you hope." He shifted his glower to Reyna. "Not now."

"Tell the truth, Landon," Eudora said, standing with the help of Birdie, "and this will be over. You can be arrested, and we can go on with what's left of our lives."

Landon shook his head. "You have no evidence, and I'm not saying anything." He swung his attention to Reyna. "They tried to kill me—are you aware of that? This so-called priest got me drunk and left me passed out on the floor of my bedroom. Then he left, and they—" he pointed to the Widows "—set my house on fire. It's a miracle I woke up and was able to jump out the window." He glared at the women. "You're lucky I never said a word. I kept your secret."

Ward jabbed a finger in the man's direction. "You murdered my son and his friends. Nothing you have suffered mitigates murder."

"Prove it," Landon challenged.

Reyna surveyed the crowd… No one said a word.

Because they didn't have the one thing they needed… *proof.*

Chapter Fifteen

"Telling you not to worry is pointless," Norwood said, "so I won't bother. But I can tell you that we will find your grandfather."

Ben shrugged. "Yeah, well, that's what they told my mother and my grandfather all those years ago about my father."

"I guess I deserved that one." Norwood stared at the ground a moment. "There's something going on, Ben. Something that your grandfather and the Widows are twisted up in. I don't know what exactly, but truth is it's got me worried." She eyed him skeptically. "You don't know what that might be, do you?"

Ben considered the idea that he probably shouldn't go on the record about anything, but he knew Tara Norwood and, more importantly, he trusted her. "Eudora Davenport contracted Reyna to come here and dig around in the disappearance. My grandfather agreed to be a part of it. My mom and Harlowe Evans talked to her, but Deidre Fuller refused. We've met with Father Cullen, Coach Landon and anyone else who would talk to her or to us both."

"All these strange things started to happen after Reyna came to town, right?"

"This is not her doing," Ben argued. "I'm not sharing this information with you to have you thinking Reyna is responsible for any of this, because that's not true at all. She has no idea who is behind all this. I think whoever it is, they're using her to…" He shrugged. "I don't know, call attention to the story, something."

"Obviously the retired priest didn't tell you anything."

Ben thought of the cross they'd found in his room. He decided it was best for now if he kept that to himself. "He did not."

"Have you learned anything," she asked, "that wasn't already a part of discovery in the original investigation?"

For a moment—a single moment—he considered again telling her all he knew. About the cross, the new suspicions he had about Coach Landon given the incident at the high school reunion. But he kicked the idea away.

"I can't say that we've learned anything you can grab on to and say here, this makes a difference. But there are pieces missing, and I think there are folks who have those pieces who haven't come forward."

She nodded. "So that's a yes."

He wasn't really surprised she understood he was being evasive. She was the sheriff. "Nothing I feel confident in sharing."

"You let me know if you change your mind. Meanwhile, I'll call you if we find anything or hear from anyone who's seen Ward."

"Thanks. I appreciate all you're doing, Sheriff Norwood."

"You just remember you said that if you find something you believe I need to know."

Now he felt guilty for not coming clean. "Yes, ma'am."

"One more thing," she said before letting him go. "That little cabin over on Trout Lake."

Maybe she'd been holding something back too. "Did you find anything?"

"Not really, but there was something odd about it." She set her hands on her hips and pinched her lips together for a moment. "The wood it was built from was old, but we determined that it had been put together out there just recently. There was no dust, no cobwebs, nothing to suggest it had been there long at all. We're thinking someone put it there, like, last week. Oddly enough, we found several items hidden behind photos and the jerseys that pointed to Wade Landon as having been the one who set the place up. There were notes in his handwriting about games and players. The sort of thing someone like him would keep in school files. There were Polaroid-type snapshots of him with the Three going back to their peewee football days. Just random stuff that appeared to have come from Landon. In fact, I sent a deputy to the school and checked on any files he might have had. All his files had been retired, as expected, but when the deputy and the administrator went to pull those files, they were missing. Any thoughts on how a man in a wheelchair could have made that happen?"

"Not offhand." He wasn't about to tell her that he had a sneaking suspicion his grandfather and maybe his mother and the other Widows might've been involved. Wow. How had they managed that—assuming they had—without him knowing?

Norwood nodded. "If you figure it out, you let me know."

"Yes, ma'am." Sounded like she'd already figured it out.

Ben headed back to his truck. Norwood had said that he could pick up his grandfather's truck when they'd finished processing it.

As he drove away, he deliberated on the idea of paying another visit to Landon. He and Reyna had talked about interviewing him again. Considering what he'd just learned from Norwood, a quick stop at the man's place wouldn't take long. Then he'd join Reyna at the Jewel. He figured everything must have been okay since she hadn't called to say otherwise.

The one thing on his mind right now was that if his grandfather and the Widows thought Landon had something to do with the disappearance, then he'd be a fool not to lean in that same direction.

Landon Residence
Harding Drive
5:30 p.m.

BEN WAS JUST about to knock on the door when he noticed that it was ajar. "Coach Landon!"

The house was silent inside. He glanced around the yard, up and down the street. No pedestrians. No vehicles coming or going.

Ben pushed the door open and stepped inside. "Mr. Landon? You home?"

No response.

He surveyed the living room. No sign of a struggle or any sort of foul play. Nothing out of place based on his one other visit here. He moved on to the kitchen. He opened the back door and checked the small yard that was more of a fenced-in patio-sized patch of grass. The gate on the back side of the fence was partially open. Four long strides later and he looked beyond the gate to find an alley. No cars, no one passing through on foot. He closed the gate and went back into the cottage. The place was small. Only one story and less than a thousand square feet. It took only a few seconds to poke his head through the doors of the two bedrooms and the one bathroom.

No Coach Landon. Like the rest of the place, the bedrooms showed no indication there had been trouble.

It was possible Landon had been picked up for a trip to the market. But why leave his front door ajar?

Ben knew he should call the sheriff…but first he needed a look. As illegal as it was, this might be his only chance.

He walked through the place again, more slowly this time. The second bedroom was a sort of office with a desk and computer. He touched the mouse and awakened the screen, which requested a passcode. A quick look through the drawers of the desk revealed only the usual—personal files, medical, insurance, tax returns. The closet was basically empty—a couple of heavy winter coats and a vacuum cleaner.

The bathroom fixtures, like everything else in the house, were handicap accessible. Beyond the prescription bottles of painkillers, there was little else of interest in the bathroom.

Moving on, he went back into the guy's bedroom. Though he should have felt guilty going through his stuff, he didn't. Ben had already crossed a line there was no going back from. He needed answers, and that was driving him.

His grandfather and his mother were missing. He was beyond reason at this point.

The latest information Norwood had passed along only made him more certain he and Reyna were getting close to the truth.

After picking through all the drawers and under the bed, he came up empty-handed. The only place left to look was the closet. Two rows of shirts more suited to twenty or thirty years ago hung one over the other. A handle enabled the top row to be pulled down to the same level as the lower rack.

On the wall behind the hanging shirts on the lower rack was something blue. Ben parted the shirts and found himself staring at a school football jersey. He considered that maybe it was the coach's, but then the number exploded in his brain.

18

Duke Fuller's number.

Ben reached out, took the jersey by the hanger and removed it from the clip where it hung. It was a little different from the one hanging in the cabin. Smaller, he decided. Maybe from sophomore or junior year. A small door—rustic and obviously homemade—on the wall, down closer to the floor behind where the jersey had hung, caught his eye. Ben crouched down and opened the door. Behind it was a niche built into the wall. Every square inch was covered with photos and newspaper clippings about the Three. Was this another shrine to the missing men? He doubted Landon could have built the one at Trout Lake in his condition. But this he could do. Or he could have hired someone to build it, for that matter.

Along the bottom of the built-in was a small wooden box shaped like the typical treasure chest. He opened it, and inside were three small velvet pull-string bags—the kind jewelers used. He tugged one open. It held dust or...

The air stalled in his lungs. *Ash.*

"Holy…"

His brain told him not to do it, but he wasn't operating with his brain right now. He grabbed the bags and hurried back to the front door. He had to get to Reyna…

If he was right…he'd found the Three.

The Jewel Bed & Breakfast
Main Street
6:15 p.m.

BEN SKIDDED TO a stop in the parking area. He considered again that he should have called Sheriff Norwood. He glanced at the velvet bags on the passenger seat. There was this thing called chain of custody. He'd already screwed that up, but he hadn't been able to leave the bags behind. If Coach Landon returned home before Ben could do whatever the hell it was he intended to do with this… He couldn't let that happen.

He reached behind to the back floorboard and grabbed the plastic bag from the hardware store that held those three-inch wood screws he'd picked up days ago for the Henry project. He dumped the screws and tucked the velvet bags inside. Bag in hand, he climbed out of the truck and rushed to the front entrance of the Jewel. Locked.

Dang it! He banged on the door. "Ms. Birdie! Reyna!"

He waited. No one came to the door. She had to be here. He'd left her here. If she'd had reason to go somewhere else, she would have called him. He checked his cell just in case he'd missed a call or text message. Nothing.

"Where are you?" He tapped her name in his contacts and waited for the phone to ring. No answer after the first ring. Another ring…

He drew the phone away from his ear and listened.

He could still hear the ringing…not from his phone but from somewhere beyond the front door.

Another bang on the door. "Reyna!"

If something had happened to her…

Still no answer.

"IF YOU DON'T allow me to let him in," Reyna argued, "he'll go to the sheriff." She glowered at Ward. "He's already worried sick about you." She glanced at Lucinda then. "And you."

Ward held her gaze for a moment, then said, "Let him be a part of this."

Reyna didn't wait for the responses of the others. She stepped around Birdie and hurried along the seemingly endless hall until she reached the door. She flipped the dead bolt and swung the door open. Ben had started down the steps.

"Ben."

He turned around.

She looked at the street beyond him, then motioned for him to come inside. Worry etched across his face, he joined her at the door.

"How's Birdie?" He searched her eyes, probably saw the confusion and worry there.

"Come with me." She grabbed him by the hand and ushered him inside. She closed and locked the door.

Holding on to his hand, she started down that long hall.

"Where are we going?"

Just before reaching the doors, she paused, turned to him. "I need you to brace yourself. Don't get angry or…" She shrugged. "Just stay calm and listen."

He nodded. "I'll do my best."

She opened the pocket doors and led him into the parlor where the others waited.

"Pops." His full attention settled on his grandfather. "Sheriff Norwood is looking for you. We've got folks all over town keeping an eye out for you."

"I'm sorry," Ward said. "I had to keep you in the dark, but it was necessary."

"We had no choice," his mother said, her voice and expression urging him to understand.

What the hell was going on here?

Ben scanned the room, noting the faces there. Confusion furrowed his brow, and he turned to Reyna. "Is Walls handcuffed to that chair?"

She nodded. "I'm afraid so."

"What the hell is going on here?" he demanded of no one in particular, all signs of uncertainty gone from his voice now.

"We need to proceed," Father Cullen said. "We're too close to let this opportunity be spoiled by the arrival of the sheriff's department."

Ben looked to Reyna again. "What's he talking about?"

"There is no time," Ward said. "We will catch you up when this is done."

"Mr. Landon," Cullen said, "we have motive, means, and we have opportunity. You had reason to want the Three to disappear. I am witness to that. Duke Fuller told me himself that he, Judson Evans and JR Kane would be meeting with you that evening." Cullen looked in Ben's direction. "The evening the Three left their homes for the last time and never returned." He turned back to Landon then. "There is an eyewitness who saw you leaving the funeral home, where you had access to a crematorium, late that night. Your employer at the funeral home stated that you had your own key but insisted that no one was working that night."

Landon shook his head. "You're wasting your time. You can talk about how I had motive and whatever else you want to drum up—you can keep spinning your fairy tales about how you think I did this or that. But none of it matters because you have no evidence."

The realization of what they were talking about slammed into Ben. He held up a hardware-store bag. Reyna looked from the bag to him and likely tried to imagine what was inside and how it could be important.

"You mean this?" he asked, his attention fixed on the coach.

Landon turned to Ben. He shook his head. "I have no idea what you have in that bag."

Ben reached into the bag and pulled out another smaller one. Black. With a gold string that pulled together to tighten the opening.

"There are three of these small sacks," Ben explained. "They were hidden in the little shrine you created in your closet, Coach Landon. I'm guessing what's inside are cremated remains—ashes." He shrugged. "Not all of them, obviously, but a portion. Maybe enough to keep close by, to remind you of what you'd done."

Landon's face paled, his jaw fell slack, but not a word came out of his mouth.

7:00 p.m.

BEFORE THE REAL fray started, Reyna called the center and reported that Eudora had been found and was safe. Reyna would get her back there in the morning.

Minutes later Sheriff Norwood and two of her deputies arrived, and that was when the frenzy exploded. Crime scene investigators were called. Paramedics were next, since Landon appeared to be on the verge of a heart attack. Walls had been uncuffed before Norwood had arrived. So far he hadn't told the sheriff that Ward Kane had kidnapped him. All involved had come of their own free will, except Walls and Landon. Both of whom Birdie and Ward had basically abducted.

Everyone involved, except Reyna and Ben, had been lined up in chairs in the long hall. A deputy stood guard, ensuring they didn't talk among themselves.

Norwood and the other deputy were interviewing the group one at a time. They had already interviewed Reyna and Ben, which was why they weren't seated in that line.

Once the other interviews were underway, Reyna had taken Ben to the kitchen and conveyed all that she had heard and seen before he'd arrived.

"You're saying Father Cullen had nothing to do with what happened. Duke gave him the cross and chain."

Reyna nodded. "That's correct."

"What about the other thing your FBI friend mentioned?"

"Cullen is in witness protection." Reyna shrugged. "He will report to his point of contact when this is done. Considering his health and if no one involved spills his secret, he may be able to stay here."

Ben braced his hands on either side of him on the kitchen counter. He'd been leaning there since she'd started talking. She understood completely. The entire story was difficult to believe... It was the sort of thing mystery movies were made of.

But it was true… It was real life.

Ben's life and the lives of all the other people lined up in that long hall.

Reyna had a feeling this was going to be a long night.

Chapter Sixteen

Kane Residence
Lula Lake Lane
Saturday, April 27, 2:20 p.m.

Eudora had decided not to return to the center. Birdie intended to temporarily close the Jewel so that she could take care of the woman she loved with all her heart until her time on this earth was done.

Reyna felt confident this was the right decision. Hospice would help when the time came. Until then, the two could enjoy Eudora's every lucid moment.

Reyna had packed her few things, only then realizing that she still had some of Birdie's clothes. She'd have to drop them off.

Reyna zipped the borrowed bag. She'd have to drop that off too. She laughed, looked around the room. She'd only slept in this room one night. She'd spent the rest of her time with Ben...in his room.

It wasn't going to be easy to go back to her life since he wasn't in it. But she couldn't put off going back forever.

"No use beating around the bush."

She walked out of the room and headed down the stairs. It was time to leave.

The whole story was out in the open now. No more secrets about the missing Three or the Widows. The players, the good ones and the bad ones, had been revealed.

Lucinda had explained that the note and the tire damage had been pulled off by the Widows. They hadn't meant
for Reyna to be hurt—the tire thing hadn't turned out the
way they'd expected. Birdie had started the fire in Reyna's
room at the bed-and-breakfast. All was a ruse designed
to support the idea that Reyna might be getting close to
the truth. Eudora had told them that Reyna was smart,
so they had to be prepared to draw her deeper into the
mystery. To keep her motivated to find the pieces of the
puzzle. The disappearance of Ward and the Widows had
been an attempt to keep Ben and Sheriff Norwood distracted. All had known Ben would start to worry if his
grandfather and mother suddenly weren't around for the
length of time expected to do what needed to be done
leading up to the mock trial.

The failing health of Ward and the priest had prompted
the two to consider whether they wanted to leave this earth
without finding a way for the truth to be revealed. But
when they had learned about the lifetime achievement
award that Landon would receive, the gloves had come
off and they had made a pact to do whatever necessary to
see that justice was done before that happened.

The Widows had been brought in on the plan first.
Together, they and Ward had erected that cabin shrine to
point to Landon. As for Eudora and Birdie, they were the
witnesses who'd seen Landon leaving the funeral home
that night. Later they'd realized he had likely been up to
no good, but they'd had no proof and the man had worked
at the funeral home part-time. Still, they had brought their

concerns to their priest, and that was how they had become a part of the group.

This group of savvy seniors had even planned for what came after their journey to deliver justice. Father Cullen had taken complete responsibility for the fire at the Landon home thirty years ago. He'd explained that the two of them, he and Landon, had been drinking and smoking cigars. At some point in the evening Landon had started to cry and asked if Cullen could perform the sacrament of confession, during which he admitted to pushing his wife down the stairs because she'd found out about his secret obsession. Since Landon had told Cullen this in confidence, he hadn't been able to bring it to the police. At least, until now. Now he was prepared to break his vows for the greater good.

Deputy Gordon Walls had given a statement as to what he'd overheard the Three discussing about confronting Landon on the day they'd disappeared. He said nothing of having been kidnapped and brought to the meeting at the Jewel. Birdie and Eudora gave their own statements about what they had witnessed that long-ago night when they saw Landon coming out of the funeral home.

With Ben's find of the ashes in the man's home, Landon had decided to confess. He'd blurted his confession before Sheriff Norwood could mention that there would likely be legal challenges regarding the find in his home. Considering he'd admitted to murdering the Three and cremating their bodies as well as pushing his wife to her death, Landon was going away for a very, very long time.

It was going to make an amazing story, and the whole group wanted Reyna to write it. She hoped she could do their incredible tale justice.

Downstairs, Ward, Ben and Lucinda waited for her. Her chest tightened at the idea of leaving.

Ward hugged her first. "Thank you, Reyna, for helping us get this done."

"Well, I don't know how much help I was, but I suppose my being here did move things along a bit."

Lucinda stepped forward and hugged her next. "Thank you." She drew back and glanced at her son. "For helping me give my son his father back. We're having a memorial week after next. I hope you'll come."

Reyna smiled, her lips quivering a little. "I wouldn't miss it for the world."

Ward cleared his throat. "Lucinda and I should check things out at the barn."

Ben's mother nodded. "That's right. We'll be a few minutes."

Ben laughed as the two left the room. "I have no idea what's in the barn that those two need to check, but I think that was code for giving us some privacy."

Reyna couldn't hold back her own smile. She was immensely grateful that his family was finally whole again. His father was still gone, but at least they had each other now with no more secrets between them. "I think you are probably right." She took a breath. "So I guess this is goodbye."

"Guess so."

"You walking me to my car?"

"Absolutely." He reached for her bag. "I'll take that."

He opened the door and followed her out onto the porch. It was such a nice day. The air was clean and crisp. Whispering Winds really was a nice town.

They descended the steps together and walked to her Land Rover. He stowed the bag in the back seat and joined her at the driver's-side door.

"I hope I see you again," he said, his eyes searching hers.

"We could make a date," she suggested. "Have dinner in the city."

He nodded. "Works for me."

Then he hugged her hard. She hugged him right back just as firmly. She never wanted to let go.

He drew back just far enough to kiss her gently on the lips. "I'm going to miss you, Reyna Hart."

"I'll miss you too."

Reyna blinked at the emotion burning her eyes as she climbed into her Land Rover. It wasn't like she wasn't going to see him again or that she was that far away, but her emotions apparently had a mind of their own.

He closed her door, and she started the engine. With one last wave, she backed up, pointed the vehicle toward town and drove away from him.

It had been a really long time since her heart had hurt so much. She wasn't sure if she could bear it. She had just reached the end of the long drive when she hit her brakes. She stared into the rearview mirror. He was still standing there watching her.

"No way am I driving away from this guy."

She shifted into Reverse, turned around and drove back up to the house. She shoved the gearshift into Park, opened the door and climbed out.

"Did you forget something?" he asked, looking confused and maybe a little hopeful.

She reached for the back door to retrieve her borrowed bag. "No. I just decided that if I'm going to do this story justice, I need to be here, in the setting." She paused and looked to him. "You okay with me staying with you for the next few months?"

A grin slid across his face. "I'm more than okay with

it." He grabbed her and kissed her on the lips. "Be careful, Ms. Hart—I might not ever let you get away."

She was more than okay with that.

* * * * *

Don't miss the stories in this mini series!

LOOKOUT MOUNTAIN MYSTERIES

Whispering Winds Widows
DEBRA WEBB
March 2024

Peril In Piney Woods
DEBRA WEBB
April 2024

MILLS & BOON

INTRIGUE

Seek thrills. Solve crimes. Justice served.

Available Next Month

Conard County: Murderous Intent Rachel Lee
Peril In Piney Woods Debra Webb

....

Smoky Mountains Graveyard Lena Diaz
K-9 Missing Person Cassie Miles

....

Innocent Witness Julie Anne Lindsey
Shadow Survivors Julie Miller

Larger Print

Keep reading for an excerpt of a new title
from the Romantic Suspense series,
A HIGH-STAKES REUNION by Tara Taylor Quinn

Chapter 1

He was stealing his newborn! Dr. Dorian Lowell ignored the pounding of her heart as she raced through the darkness toward the gray-hooded, hunched over man hurrying from the small stucco birthing center. Her frantic steps silenced by the grass, she ran full tilt toward the old red truck parked in a corner of the lot. The two-hour-old boy needed constant medical attention. He'd die within hours without it.

She'd seen Jeremy, the estranged father, pull in and head into the birthing center moments before. Had warned Security.

He was almost at his truck, not running like she was, but moving at a good clip, head down, shielding the newborn he held in both arms, upright against his chest.

If she screamed for help, it was unlikely anyone would hear her.

If she ran for help, he'd get away.

That baby's only hope lay with Dorian rescuing him before his father got to the truck.

Breath constricted by the panic tightening her chest, she crossed onto the pavement just steps away from the young, slim-framed man, hoping to reason with him. They'd all had a rough day, and he was overwrought.

As soon as he heard her steps, he jerked, straightening, and pinned her with a glare that was menacing in the moonlight. His eyes. She didn't recognize them. Two sharp pinpoints of warning…

It wasn't Jeremy! And in her peripheral vision, she noticed a second truck—Jeremy's truck—parked down a couple of spaces in the lot.

Too late to stop her forward motion, she upped her momentum toward the tiny baby boy the stranger held, her self-defense class of long ago taking over as she kneed the kidnapper, grabbing for the baby—not Jeremy's baby—at the same time.

Her blow was strong enough to make the hard-looking man loosen his grip for the split second she'd needed. With the blue bundle wrapped in one arm, she raised her other hand to the man's face, ramming her palm into the base of his nose. She felt a crack as he backhanded her upside the head, and, dizzy, stumbling briefly, she ran.

A shot rang out behind her.

Swerving in between cars, she just kept running.

FBI Agent Scott Michaels broke all speed limits as he raced across a desert highway to the small birthing center in Las Sendas, Arizona, forty miles southeast of Phoenix. Every second counted when it meant the kidnapper had another second to get away from him.

Six months of trying to track a series of newborn kidnappings, to find anything that linked them—other than the MO, a message board on the dark web and a hunch—and he might have just found his first real lead. The first kidnapping gone wrong.

A mistake made.

He had an eyewitness. A renowned physician who'd been leaving the facility late that night due to a complicated birth that had nearly killed both mother and child.

A heroic doctor, from what he'd heard. The woman had single-handedly saved another newborn male child.

There was already a BOLO out on the old red pickup she'd described with the California plate, and if there really was a God out there, someone would locate the vehicle.

It could crack the case that had been haunting him for months.

For a split second, just after Scott had turned onto the road that would lead him from the highway into the small town, he thought his non-prayer had been answered. At the first intersection, still on the outskirts of civilization, he saw a truck. Old. Beat up, just like the witness had described.

But as he drew closer, his heart accepted what he'd expected to see. The truck, while old, was black, not red. And not only was the guy behind the wheel not exhibiting any evidence of being in a hurry, he was wearing a white shirt, not the gray hoodie the witness had described. And a cowboy hat, which he tilted toward Scott, waving him to pass through the intersection without stopping.

Giving Scott a clear view of the Arizona plate. Not California like the doctor had reported.

Still, didn't mean someone else couldn't find the red truck. A few minutes later, with adrenaline pumping hard, he pulled into the birthing center parking lot, which was ablaze with red flashing lights. Showing his badge, he was inside within a minute, and being directed to the room where the doctor was waiting for him.

Each minute that passed was another opportunity for the kidnapper to get to another newborn.

Because there'd be another baby stolen that night.

The ring Scott's gut told him was behind the kidnappings had an order to fill and had just lost the merchandise. He'd seen the sale pop up on the dark web that morning…

Grim-faced and determined, he knocked on the door he'd been shown, and opened it before the feminine "Come in" had even been completed.

Opened it and stood there…staring.

"Dorian…" He couldn't remember her last name. It would have changed anyway.

But he remembered her. Far too vividly.

"Scott?" Open-mouthed, with a reddening bruise marking the left side of her face from the ear down the jaw, she stared at him. In wrinkled purple scrubs, with her red hair up in a bun, she didn't look like she'd aged at all in the fourteen years since he'd had her in class.

And…very briefly…in his arms.

"You aren't in the army," she said.

And she wasn't wearing a wedding ring.

"I was. Trained in law enforcement, made rank of sergeant, but wanted to fight crime on a broader scale." None of her business. Just as his plans in the past hadn't been. But that hadn't stopped him from sharing them with her. And then regretting having done so.

"You saved a baby's life tonight," she blurted, blushing. He remembered that about her, too. The way her fair skin turned red anytime she said anything that made her uncomfortable. "Or rather, your training did. I used what you taught me."

He'd been waiting to deploy, had been filling the time teaching a summer self-defense class at the community college. And she'd been…engaged.

To a guy who'd grown up with her, knowing her family.

By then, he'd already learned a hard lesson about him being on the outside looking into that kind of life. So he'd paid careful attention to avoid pursuing the instant attraction he'd had for her. One that had seemed to be returned, and on a level beyond the physical.

As if he really knew anything about living life on that level.

The younger version of the successful doctor had been impressively alert during his class, and he witnessed the exact same focus and attention to detail, the same ability to remember things, as she answered his questions about the thwarted kidnapping. She was able to describe her kidnapper, not only the size and build that closely matched the father she'd first taken him for, but the shape of his jaw, and the soullessly evil look in his eyes. She was certain she'd never seen him before. She'd already talked to the police, had sat with a local officer who'd responded to the scene and was also a sketch artist, but Scott needed other details. The kind you couldn't draw.

"Did he speak?" he asked. "Did he have an accent? Sound educated?"

"All I heard was a string of common swear words when I kneed him. No accent, but he slurred his *s*'s, like he had a tooth missing. And... I think he smokes. His voice had that raspy sound..."

If he could form a mental picture, he'd have more of an idea of where to look first.

"And he smelled like manure," she said. "And maybe hay. You know...like a farm..."

Bingo. Standing, he thanked her, looked her in the eye, and when he started to linger there, to smile his gratitude, he caught himself and immediately reached for his wallet, looking inside for one of his cards. Handing it to her, he told her to call him immediately if she thought of anything else, and, with a last directive to take care of herself, to follow police orders for her own protection, he turned to the door. He needed to get out of the small space.

Away from reminders of the things he wouldn't ever again let himself want.

But he looked back. Saw her watching him.

As if, for a second, she was remembering, too...

He refused to go back. Looked at her and said, "It looks like you might have a black eye by tomorrow." In a few more minutes it would already be tomorrow.

And he had an urgent job to do.

Find the kidnapper.

For three reasons now.

To save the babies yet to be taken. To find the ones who'd already been sold. And to make the fiend pay for that bruise filling up the side of Dorian's face.

What kind of weird fate brought Scott Michaels to investigate a thwarted kidnapping in Arizona? All the years Dorian and Sierra's Web—the firm of experts she and her friends had started—had been working with law enforcement, and he suddenly shows up at a crime scene?

It had to be some kind of warning sent by fate, issued to validate the choices she'd made so long ago. Reminding her why she'd made them.

With so many of the Sierra's Web partner experts finding love and settling down—with her own kidnapping the previous year still challenging her—maybe she'd been experiencing some weakening in her resolve to stay single.

Distracted by her initial reaction to seeing the man again, Dorian instinctively put on her professional face as Chief Ramsey came in to tell her that he would assign someone to escort her to wherever she was going as soon as she was ready.

"That's not necessary," she told him, emphatically certain of that fact. The bruise to her head, while painful when touched, and ugly looking, had been superficial as she'd had the advantage of being the aggressor in the second that the blow had been thrown. She'd been cut, right at the edge of her jaw, the result of the kidnapper's gloved hand jamming her earring into her skin, but overall, she was fine.

And she absolutely did not need one of Las Sendas' already overtasked police officers to follow her the two miles between the birthing center and the room that had been rented for her in the lovely old historic hotel downtown. All the Las Sendas law enforcers had been called in to work the attempted kidnapping, and they all needed to continue doing so.

She'd never forgive herself if they lost the guy because they'd pulled someone off the case to babysit her.

"This is the kind of thing Sierra's Web handles every day," she said, collecting the bag she'd dropped as she'd come out of the employee entrance at the side of the building and had seen the kidnapper leaving with the baby. "You've already seen how we work. Glen, our forensics and science guy, will probably be at the hotel by the time I get there. I'll be right back here in the morning, checking in on the patient I was here to assist with, and will be hanging around in Las Sendas as long as my partners think I can be of help to find the kidnapper."

"Still, this guy doesn't know you can't positively ID him," the chief said, but Dorian could tell the man was eager to keep his officers on the kidnapper's trail, as he should be. Major crime didn't happen in Las Sendas, which was one of the reasons the small town had been chosen to house the prototype birthing center.

"It's more likely he's going to be getting as far away

from here as he can, rather than hanging around for me," she reminded him, to assuage any guilt he might be harboring, as he walked her out to her car. After twelve years of being the medical expert on cases with her partners, many of them criminal cases, she knew the drill.

A thorough glance around the busy parking lot convinced them both that she was fine to walk to her vehicle. She saw him already heading to his squad car as she pulled out of the parking lot, shakier than she'd wanted the chief to know but eager to get to Glen.

Hudson Warner, Sierra's Web technical expert, was up and already working on the dark web site Scott Michaels had mentioned.

After giving Glen whatever he needed, Dorian was going to take a hot bath and put the night behind her. Or at least sit up with her newly-purchased-in-the-past-year handgun at her side for protection and watch old sitcoms until the sun rose.

She'd been abducted off a hiking trail sixteen months ago because she'd been unprepared. She was not going to let the fiend who'd taken her rob her of peace of mind.

Make her afraid to live her life.

When the idea of living life brought thoughts of Scott Michaels to mind as she drove, she allowed them to distract her. The self-defense instructor, former army sergeant turned FBI agent, had no idea that he'd brought a completely different moment to a horrible night. Seeing him again…she had no idea how she felt about that.

Had mixed emotions to the point of being slightly sick to her stomach.

She'd hurt a man she'd loved because of Scott. Had first started to lose her ability to trust herself because of him.

And yet…still got warm inside, just seeing his face again.

Her whole life, Dorian had been wise beyond her years, able to see clearly and make successful decisions, to remain practical in times of crisis, to be an asset to her family and those around her. She'd chosen her best friend, a man she'd known since she was born, to be her life's partner.

And then she'd met Scott, and, if not for the man's inner strength, she might actually have found herself in bed with him…

Turning the corner onto the road that led to Main Street, she saw an old pickup stopped at an adjacent corner ahead and for a second, her heart leaped to her throat, constricting her air. Then she got close enough to see that the truck was black, not red. And when she caught a glimpse of the cowboy hat the guy was wearing, she sat back in her seat, admonishing herself for being so jumpy, even as she gave herself some slack.

She'd been kidnapped and held for days. Not something she'd get over in a matter of months. Maybe not even years. And yet, when the baby had been at risk, she'd run straight into danger.

Still, she avoided looking at the driver as she passed the truck. Until her peripheral vision caught movement and she turned to see him staring right at her.

Her stomach jumped up to choke her.

She knew those eyes.

Gunning the gas, Dorian kept both hands glued to the wheel, her focus fully on the road in front of her. Reminding herself that if she didn't turn up at her hotel in the next ten minutes, her partners would have experts on the ground, looking for her.

The truck gained on her, coming up on her right, blocking her from making the turn onto Main Street.

Forcing her to continue straight on a deserted road that led toward the mountain.

Forcing her into darkness. Any second, it was going to run her off the road. No time for expert help.

She was going to die.

The thought was clear.

Suddenly it was as though she was in an operating room, looking at a patient who was coding. No panic. It was her job to stay calm. Aware. To make the best decision.

Letting go of the wheel with one hand, she reached into the pocket along the thigh of her scrubs, retrieving the card Scott Michaels had given her and, pushing her hands-free calling button on the steering wheel, rattled off the number on the card. Her partners would look for her, too late. But the next baby could still be saved. She had to let the agent know where his kidnapper was. She had to prevent other babies from being hurt.

"He's on my bumper," she blurted into the phone as soon as she heard the click that told her he'd picked up. "Black truck. Hampton Road." She pulled in a breath, maybe her last. "East." Another attempt to get air. "Past last turnoff…"

The truck's headlights reflected off her rearview mirror, blinding her, and then, with a jolt from behind, a crunch, her chin hit the steering wheel. She felt the sting, the split, felt a swoosh of air on an open wound. Moisture. Blood.

"What's going on?" Scott's urgent tone kept her gaze focused on the road. That was all. Blood. Pain. The road.

"Dorian! Talk to me."

"I'm…"

Another jolt. To the rear driver's side of her car.

Then, with a huge bump, the sharp explosion of the air bag against her upper body, she went careening off the road.